The White Scalper
A Story Of The Texan War

By

Gustave Aimard

Double 9
BOOKS

The White Scalper
A Story Of The Texan War
by Gustave Aimard

Copyright © 2024

All Rights reserved.

ISBN: 978-93-62205-15-5

Published by

DOUBLE 9 BOOKS

2/13-B, Ansari Road
Daryaganj, New Delhi – 110002
info@double9books.com
www.double9books.com
Tel. 011-40042856

This book is under public domain

ABOUT THE AUTHOR

Gustave Aimard wrote multiple volumes about Latin America and the American frontier. Oliver Aimard was born in Paris. As he previously stated, he was the offspring of two married individuals, "but not to each other". His father, François Sébastiani de la Porta (1775-1851), was a commander in Napoleon's army and a representative of the Louis Philippe government. Sebastiani was married to the Duchess of Coigny. In 1806, the couple had a daughter, Alatrice-Rosalba Fanny. The mother died shortly after she was born. Fanny was reared by her grandmother, Duchess of Coigny. Aimard was placed as a baby with a family that were paid to raise him. By the age of nine or twelve, he was sent off on a herring boat. Later, about 1838, he served briefly with the French Navy. After one more trip to America (when he claims he was adopted into a Comanche tribe), Aimard returned to Paris in 1847, the same year his half-sister, Duchess de Choiseul-Pralin, was cruelly killed by her noble husband. Reconciliation or acknowledgement by his biological family did not occur. After serving briefly in the Garde Mobil, Aimard returned to the Americas.

CONTENTS

CHAPTER I
A RECONNOISSANCE

Colonel Melendez, after leaving the Jaguar, galloped with his head afire, and panting chest, along the Galveston road, exciting with his spurs the ardour of his horse, which yet seemed to devour space, so rapid was its speed. But it is a long journey from the Salto del Frayle to the town. While galloping, the Colonel reflected; and the more he did so, the more impossible did it appear to him that the Jaguar had told him the truth. In fact, how could it be supposed that this partisan, brave and rash though he was, would have dared to attack, at the head of a handful of adventurers, a well-equipped corvette, manned by a numerous crew, and commanded by one of the best officers in the Mexican navy? The capture of the fort seemed even more improbable to the Colonel.

While reflecting thus, the Colonel had gradually slackened his horse's speed; the animal, feeling that it was no longer watched, had insensibly passed from a gallop into a canter, then a trot, and by a perfectly natural transition, fell into a walk, with drooping head, and snapping at the blades of grass within its reach.

Night had set in for some time past; a complete silence brooded over the country, only broken by the hollow moan of the sea as it rolled over the shingle. The Colonel was following a small track formed along the coast, which greatly shortened the distance separating him from Galveston. This path, much used by day, was at this early hour of night completely deserted; the ranchos that stood here and there were shut up, and no light gleamed through their narrow windows, for the fishermen, fatigued by the rude toil of the day, had retired to bed at an early hour.

The young officer's horse, which had more and more slackened its pace, emboldened by impunity, at length stopped near a scrubby bush, whose leaves it began nibbling. This immobility aroused the Colonel from his reverie, and he looked about him to see where he was. Although the obscurity was very dense, it was easy for him to perceive that he was still a long distance from his destination. About a musket-shot ahead was a rancho, whose hermetically-closed windows allowed a thin pencil of light to filter through the interstices of the shutters. The Colonel struck his repeater and found it was midnight. To go on would be madness; the more so, as it would be impossible for him to find a boat in which to cross to the island. Greatly annoyed at this obstacle, which, supposing the Jaguar's revelations to be true, might entail serious consequences, the young officer, while cursing this involuntary delay, resolved on pushing on to the rancho before him, and once there, try to obtain means to cross the bay.

After drawing his cloak tightly round him, to protect him as far as possible from the damp sea air, the Colonel caught up his reins again, and giving his horse the spur, trotted sharply towards the rancho. The traveller speedily reached it, but, when only a few paces from it, instead of riding straight up to the door, he dismounted, fastened his horse to a larch-tree, and, after placing his pistols in his belt, made a rather long circuit, and stealthily crept up to the window of the rancho.

In the present state of fermentation from which people were suffering in Texas, the olden confidence had entirely disappeared to make way for the greatest distrust. The times were past when the doors of houses remained open day and night, in order to enable strangers to reach the fireside with greater facility. Hospitality, which was traditional in these parts, had, temporarily at any rate, changed into a suspicious reserve, and it would have been an act of unjustifiable imprudence to ride up to a strange house, without first discovering whether it was that of a friend. The Colonel especially, being dressed in a Mexican uniform, was bound to act with extreme reserve.

This rancho was rather large; it had not that appearance of poverty and neglect which are found only too often in the houses of Spanish American Campesinos. It was a square house, with a roof in the Italian fashion, having in front an azotea-covered portillo. The white-washed walls were an agreeable contrast to the virgin vines, and other plants which ran over it. This rancho was not enclosed with walls: a thick hedge, broken through at several places, alone defended the approaches. The dependencies of the house were vast, and well kept up. All proved that the owner of this mansion carried on a large trade on his account.

The Colonel, as we have said, had softly approached one of the windows. The shutters were carefully closed, but not so carefully as not to let it be seen that someone was up inside. In vain did the Colonel, though, place his eye at the slit, for he could see nothing. If he could not see, however, he could hear, and the first words that reached his ear probably appeared to him very serious, for he redoubled his attention, in order to lose no portion of the conversation. Employing once again our privilege as romancers, we will enter the rancho, and allow the reader to witness the singular scene going on there, the most interesting part of which escaped the Colonel, greatly to his annoyance.

In a rather small room, dimly lighted by a smoky candle, four men, with gloomy faces and ferocious glances, dressed in the garb of Campesinos, were assembled. Three of them, seated on butacas and equipals, were listening, with their guns between their legs, to the fourth, who, with his arms behind his back, was walking rapidly up and down, while talking.

The broad brims of the vicuña hats which the three first wore, and the obscurity prevailing in the room, only allowed their faces to be dimly seen, and their expression judged. The fourth, on the contrary, was bare-headed; he was a man of about forty, tall, and well built; his muscular limbs denoted a far from common strength, and a forest of black and curly hair fell on his wide shoulders. He had a lofty forehead, aquiline nose, and black and piercing eyes; while the lower part of his face disappeared in a long and thick beard. There was in the appearance of this man something bold and haughty, which inspired respect, and almost fear.

At this moment, he seemed to be in a tremendous passion; his eyebrows were contracted, his cheeks livid, and, at times, when he yielded to the emotion he tried in vain to restrain, his eye flashed to fiercely, that it forced his three hearers to bow their heads humbly, and they seemed to be his inferiors. At the moment when we entered the room, the stranger appeared to be continuing a discussion that had been going on for some time.

"No," he said in a powerful voice, "things cannot go on thus any longer. You dishonour the holy cause we are defending by revolting acts of cruelty, which injure us in the opinion of the population, and authorise all the calumnies our enemies spread with reference to us. It is not by imitating our oppressors that we shall succeed in proving to the masses that we really wish their welfare. However sweet it may be to avenge an insult received, where men put themselves forward as defenders of a principle so sacred as that for which we have been shedding our blood the last ten years, every man must practise self-denial, and forget all his private animosities to absorb them in the great national vengeance. I tell you this frankly, plainly, and with no reserve. I, who was the first that dared to utter the cry of revolt, and inaugurate resistance: I, who, since I have reached man's estate, have sacrificed everything, fortune, friends, and relations, in the sole hope of seeing my country one day free, would retire from a struggle which is daily dishonoured by excesses such as the Redskins themselves would disavow."

The three men, who had been tolerably quiet up to this moment, then rose, protesting simultaneously that they were innocent of the crimes imputed to them.

"I do not believe you," he continued passionately; "I do not believe you, because I can prove the utter truth of the accusation I am now making. You deny it as I expected. Your part was ready traced, and you might be expected to act so: all other paths were closed to you. Only one of you, the youngest, the one who perhaps had the greatest right to employ reprisals, has always remained equal to his mission; and, though our enemies have tried several times to brand him, he has ever remained firm, as the Mexicans themselves allow. This Chief you know as well as I do: it is the Jaguar. Only yesterday, at the head of some of our men, he accomplished one of the most glorious and extraordinary exploits."

All pressed round the stranger, and eagerly questioned him.

"What need for me to tell you what has occurred? You will know it within a few hours. Suffice it for you to know for the present, that the consequence of the Jaguar's daring achievement is the immediate surrender of Galveston, which cannot hold out against us any longer."

"Then we triumph!" one of the Campesinos exclaimed.

"Yes; but all is not over yet: if we have succeeded in taking the town of Galveston from the Mexicans, they have fifty others left, in which they can shut themselves up. Hence, believe me, instead of giving way to immoderate joy, and imprudent confidence, redouble, on the contrary, your efforts and self-denial, if you wish to remain victors to the end."

"But what is to be done to obtain the result we desire as much as you do?" the one who had already spoken asked.

"Follow blindly the counsels I give you, and obey without hesitation or comment the orders I send you. Will you promise me this?"

"Yes," they exclaimed, enthusiastically; "you alone, Don Benito, can guide us safely and ensure our victory."

There was a moment's silence. The man who had just been addressed as Don Benito went to a corner of the room hidden behind a curtain of green serge. This curtain he drew back, and behind it was an alabaster statue of the Virgin Soledad, with a lamp burning in front of it, and then turned to the others.

"On your knees, and take off your hats," he said.

They obeyed.

"Now," he continued, "swear to keep faithfully the promise you have just made me of your own accord; swear to be merciful to the conquered in battle, and gentle to the prisoners after the victory. At this price I pledge myself to support you; if not, I retire immediately from a cause which is at least dishonoured, if not lost."

The three men, after piously crossing themselves, stretched out their right arms toward the statue, saying in a firm voice—

"We swear it, by the share we hope in Paradise."

"It is well," Don Benito replied, as he drew the curtain across again and made them a sign to rise; "I know you are too thoroughly Caballeros to break so solemn an oath."

The Colonel, confounded by this singular scene, which he did not at all comprehend, did not know what to do, when he fancied he heard an indistinct sound not far from him. Drawing himself up at once, he concealed himself behind the hedge, rather alarmed as to the cause of this noise, which was rapidly approaching. Almost immediately he noticed several men coming gently up; they were four in number, as he soon made out, and carrying a fifth in their arms. They walked straight to the door, at which they tapped in a peculiar way.

"Who's there?" was asked from inside.

One of the newcomers replied, but in so low a tone, that it was impossible for the Colonel to hear the word pronounced. The door was opened, and the strangers entered; it was then closed again, but not until the opener had cast a scrutinizing glance round him.

"What does this mean?" the Colonel muttered.

"It means," a rough voice said in his ear, "that you are listening to what does not concern you, Colonel Melendez, and that it may prove dangerous to you."

The Colonel, astounded at this unexpected answer, and especially at being so well known, quickly drew a pistol from his belt, cocked it, and turned to his strange speaker.

"On my word," he answered, "there is no worse danger to incur than that of an immediate death, which I should not at all object to, I swear to you."

The stranger began laughing, and emerged from the thicket in which he was hidden. He was a powerful-looking man, and, like the Colonel, held a pistol in his hand.

"You are aware that duelling is forbidden in the Mexican army," he said, "so take my advice, sir, and put up that pistol, which, if it exploded, might entail very disagreeable consequences for you."

"Lower your weapon first," the Colonel said, coldly, "and then I will see what I have to do."

"Very good," the other remarked, still smiling, as he thrust his pistol into his belt. The Colonel imitated him.

"And now," the stranger continued, "I have to converse with you; but, as you can see, this spot is badly chosen for a secret interview."

"That is true," the Colonel interrupted, frankly assuming the tone of the singular man with whom chance had so unexpectedly brought him together.

"I am delighted that you are of my opinion. Well, Colonel, as it is so, be kind enough to accompany me merely a few paces, and I will lead you to a spot I know, which is perfectly adapted for the conversation we must have together."

"I am at your orders, Caballero," the Colonel answered, with a bow.

"Come, then," the stranger added, as he made a start.

The Colonel followed him. The stranger led him to the spot where he had tied up his horse, by the side of which another was now standing. The stranger stopped.

"Let us mount," he said.

"What for?" the young officer asked.

"To be off, of course. Are you not returning to Galveston?"

"Certainly; still——"

"Still," the stranger interrupted, "you would have had no objection to prowl a little longer round the rancho, I presume?"

"I confess it."

"Well, on my honour, you are wrong, for two excellent reasons: the first is, that you will learn nothing more than you have surmised,—that is to say, that the rancho is the headquarters of the insurrection. You see that I am frank with you."

"I perceive it. And now, what is your second reason?"

"It is very simple: you run the risk, at any moment, of being saluted with a bullet, and you know that the Texans are decent marksmen."

"Certainly; but you know also that this reason possesses but slight value for me."

"I beg your pardon; courage does not consist, in my opinion, at least, in sacrificing one's life without reason; it consists, on the contrary, in being only killed for a good price,—that is to say, for a motive worth the trouble."

"Thanks for the lecture, Caballero."

"Shall we be off?"

"At once, if you will be good enough to tell me who you are and where we are going?"

"I am surprised that you did not recognise me long ago, for we have been for some time past on excellent, if not intimate terms."

"That may be; the sound of your voice is rather familiar to me, and I fancy I have heard it before, but it is impossible for me to recall either when or under what circumstances."

"By Heaven, Colonel! You will allow me to remark that you have a preciously short memory. But since our last meeting, so many events have occurred, that it is not surprising you should have forgotten me. With one word I will recall everything to your mind—I am John Davis, the ex-slave dealer."

"You!" the Colonel exclaimed, with a start of surprise.

"Yes, I am that person."

"Ah! Ah!" the Colonel continued, as he crossed his arms haughtily and looked him in the face, "In that case we have an account to settle."

"I am not aware of the fact, Colonel."

"You forget, Master Davis, in what manner you abused my confidence in order to betray me."

"I? You are in error, Colonel. To do that I must have been a Mexican, which is not the case, thank Heaven! I served my country as you serve yours, that is all; each for himself in a revolution, you know."

"That proverb may suit you, Master Davis, I grant, but I only know one way of acting honourably, with uplifted head."

"Hum! There would be a good deal to say on that head, but it is not the question at this moment. The proof that you are mistaken and unjust toward me is, that a few minutes ago I held your life in my hands, and was unwilling to take it."

"You were wrong, for I swear to you that unless you defend yourself I shall take yours in a second," he said, as he cocked a pistol.

"You are in earnest, then?"

"Most earnest, he assured."

"You are mad," said Davis, with a shrug of his shoulders; "what strange idea is this of yours to insist on killing me?"

"Will you defend yourself; yes or no?"

"Wait a moment. What a man you are! There is no way of having an explanation with you."

"One word, then, but be brief."

"Well, as you are aware, I am not accustomed to make long speeches."

"I am listening to you."

"Why play with the butt of your pistol so? Vengeance is only real when complete. A shot fired would be the signal for your death, for you would be surrounded and attacked on all sides at once before you had even time to place a foot in the stirrup. You allow this, I suppose?"

"To the point, Master Davis, for I am in a hurry."

"You admit," the other said, with his old stoicism, "that I am seeking no unworthy subterfuge to avoid a meeting with you?"

"I know that you are a brave man."

"Thanks! I do not discuss the validity of the reason which makes you wish to exchange bullets with me: a pretext is nothing with men like ourselves. I pledge my word to be at your disposal on any day, and at any hour you please, with or without witnesses. Does that suit you?"

"Would it not be better to mount, gallop into the plain that stretches out before us, and settle the affair at once?"

"I should like to do so, but, unfortunately, I must, for the present, deprive myself of the pleasure. I repeat to you that we cannot fight, at least not at this moment."

"But the reason, the reason?" the young man exclaimed, with feverish impatience.

"The reason is this, as you absolutely insist on my telling it you: I am at this moment entrusted with very great interests; in a word, I am charged by the Chief of the Texan army with a mission of the utmost importance to General Rubio, Military Governor of Galveston. You are too much of a gentleman not to understand that this prohibits me risking a life which does not belong to me."

The Colonel bowed with exquisite politeness and uncocked the pistol, which he restored to his belt.

"I am confounded at what has taken place," he said. "You will excuse me, Señor, for having allowed my passion to carry me away thus; I recognise how worthy and delicate your conduct has been under the circumstances. May I venture to hope you will pardon me?"

"Not another word about the past, Colonel. So soon as I have terminated my mission, I shall have the honour of placing myself at your orders. Now, if nothing further keeps you here, we will proceed together to Galveston."

"I accept gladly the offer you make me. There is a truce between us: be good enough till further orders to consider and treat me as one of your friends."

"That is settled; I was certain we should end by understanding each other. To horse, then, and let us start."

"I ask nothing better; still, I would observe that the night is as yet only half spent."

"Which means?"

"That till sunrise, and perhaps later, it will be impossible for us to find a boat in which to cross over to the island."

"That need not trouble you, Colonel; I have a boat waiting for me, in which I shall be delighted to offer you a place."

"Hum! All the measures of you revolutionary gentlemen seem to be well taken; you want for nothing."

"The reason is very simple; would you like to know it?"

"I confess that I am curious in the matter."

"It is because, up to the present, we have appealed to the hearts, rather than the purses of our confidants. The hatred of the Mexican Government renders every intelligent man a devoted partisan; the hope of liberty gives us all we want; that is our whole secret. You are aware, Colonel, that the spirit of opposition is innate in the heart of every man; insurrection or opposition, whichever you like to call it, is only that spirit organised."

"That is true," said the Colonel, with a laugh.

The two enemies, temporarily friends, mounted and set out side by side.

"You have very singular ideas and opinions," the Colonel, whom the American's remarks amused, continued.

"Oh dear no!" the latter replied, carelessly; "Those ideas and opinions are nothing but the fruit of lengthened experience. I do not ask of a man more than his organisation allows him to give, and enacting these I am certain of never making a mistake. Hence, suppose that the Mexicans are expelled the country, and the government of Texas established and working regularly — — "

"Good," the Colonel said, with a smile; "what will happen then."

"This will inevitably happen," the American answered, imperturbably. "A hot-headed or ambitious man will emerge from the crowd and rebel against the Government. He will immediately have partisans, who will make a flag of truce, and the same men who today are ready to shed their blood for us with the most utter abnegation, will act in the same way for him; not because they have to complain of the Government they desire to overthrow, but merely on account of that spirit of opposition to which I have alluded."

"Come, that is a little too strong," the Colonel exclaimed, as he burst into a laugh.

"You do not believe me? Well, listen to this: I who am speaking to you once knew, no matter where, a man whose whole life was spent in conspiring. One day luck smiled on him, and chance enabled him, hardly knowing how or why, to occupy the highest post in the Republic — something like President. Do you know what he did, so soon as he obtained power?"

"Canarios! He tried to hold his ground, of course."

"You are quite out. On the contrary, he went on conspiring, and so famously that he overthrew himself and was condemned to perpetual imprisonment."

"So that — ?"

"So that, if the man who succeeded to power had not amnestied him, he would, in all probability, have died in prison."

The two men were still laughing at John Davis's last repartee, when the latter stopped, and made the Colonel a sign to follow his example.

"Have we arrived?" he asked.

"All but. Do you see that boat tossing about at the foot of the cliff?"

"Of course I see it."

"Well, it is the one which will convey us to Galveston."

"But our horses?"

"Don't be uneasy; the owner of that wretched rancho will take all proper care of them."

John Davis raised a whistle to his lip and blew it twice sharply. Almost immediately the door of the rancho opened and a man appeared; but, after taking one step forward, he took two backward, doubtless astonished at seeing two persons when he only expected one.

"Halloh! halloh, John!" Davis shouted, "don't go in again."

"Is it you, then?" he asked.

"Yes! Unless it be the demon who has assumed my face."

The fisherman shook his head with a dissatisfied air.

"Do not jest so, John Davis," he said; "the night is black and the sea rough; so the demon is about."

"Come, come, old porpoise," the American continued, "get your boat ready, for we have no time to lose. This Señor is a friend of mine. Have you any alfalfa for our horses in your cabin?"

"I should think so. Eh, Pedriello, come hither, muchacho. Take the horses from the Caballero, and lead them to the corral."

At this summons a tall young fellow came yawning from the rancho, and walked up to the two travellers. The latter had already dismounted; the peon took the horses by the bridle and went off with them, not saying a word.

"Shall we go?" John Davis asked.

"Whenever you please," the fisherman growled.

"I hope you have men enough?"

"My two sons and I are, I should think, enough to cross the bay."

"You must know better than I."

"Then, why ask?" the fisherman said with a shrug of his shoulders, as he proceeded toward the boat.

The two men followed him, and found that he had not deceived them. The sea was bad, being rough and lumpy, and it required all the old sailor's skill to successfully cross the bay. Still, after two hours of incessant toil, the boat came alongside Galveston jetty, and disembarked its passengers safe and sound; then, without waiting for a word of thanks, the sailor at once disappeared in the obscurity.

"We part here," said John Davis to the Colonel; "for we each follow a different road. Tomorrow morning, at nine o'clock, I shall have the honour of presenting, myself at the General's house. May I hope that you have spoken to him of me in sufficient favourable terms for him to grant me a kind reception?"

"I will do all that depends on myself."

"Thank you, and good night."

"One word, if you please, before parting."

"Speak, Colonel."

"I confess to you, that at this moment I am suffering from extreme curiosity."

"What about?"

"A moment before your arrival, I saw four men, carrying a fifth, enter the rancho to which accident had brought me."

"Well?"

"Who is that man?"

"I know no more about him than you do. All I can tell you is, that he was picked up dying on the beach, at eleven o'clock at night, by some of our men stationed as videttes to watch the bay. Now, who he is, or where he comes from, I do not know at all. He is covered with wounds; when picked up, he held an axe still clutched in his hand, which makes me suppose that he belonged to the crew of the *Libertad* corvette, which our friends so successfully boarded. That is all the information I am able to give you. Is it all you wish to know?"

"One word more. Who is the man I saw at the rancho, and to whom the persons with him gave the name of Don Benito?"

"As for that man, you will soon learn to know him. He is the supreme Chief of the Texan revolution; but I am not permitted to tell you more. Good bye, till we meet again at the General's."

"All right."

The two men, after bowing courteously, separated, and entered the town from opposite sides; the Colonel proceeding to his house, and John Davis, in all probability, to crave hospitality from one of the numerous conspirators Galveston contained.

CHAPTER II
A BARGAIN

There is in the rapidity with which all news spread, a mystery which has remained, up to the present, incomprehensible. It seems that an electric current bears them along at headlong speed, and takes a cruel pleasure in spreading them everywhere.

The most minute precautions had been taken by the Jaguar and El Alferez to keep their double expedition a secret, and hide their success until they had found time to make certain arrangements necessary to secure the results of their daring attempts. The means of communication were at that period, and still are, extremely rare and difficult. Only one man, Colonel Melendez, was at all cognizant of what had happened, and we have seen that it was impossible for him to have said anything. And yet, scarce two hours after the events we have described were accomplished, a vague rumour, which had come no one knew whence, already ran about the town.

This rumour, like a rising tide, swelled from instant to instant, and assumed gigantic proportions; for, as always happens under similar circumstances, the truth, buried in a mass of absurd and impossible details, disappeared almost entirely to make way for a monstrous collection of reports, each more absurd than the other, but which terrified the population, and plunged it into extreme anxiety.

Among other things, it was stated that the insurgents were advancing on the town with a formidable fleet of twenty-five ships, having on board ten thousand troops, amply provided with cannon and ammunition of every description. Nothing less was spoken of than the immediate bombardment of Galveston by the insurgents, large parties of whom, it was stated, were scouring the country to intercept all communication between the town and the mainland.

Terror never calculates or reasons. In spite of the material impossibility of the insurgents being able to collect so considerable a fleet and army, no one doubted the truth of the rumour, and the townspeople, with their eyes anxiously fixed on the sea, fancied in each gull whose wing flashed on the horizon, they saw the vanguard of the Texan fleet.

General Rubio was himself very much alarmed. If he did not place entire faith on these stupid rumours, still one of those secret forebodings, that never deceive, warned him that grave events were preparing, and would soon burst like a thundercloud over the town. The Colonel's prolonged absence, whose motive the General was ignorant of, added still further to his anxiety. Still the situation was too critical for the General not to try to escape from it by any means, or dispel the storm that was constantly menacing.

Unfortunately, through its position and commerce, Galveston is a thoroughly American town, and the Mexican element is found there in but very limited proportions. The General was perfectly aware that the North. Americans who represented the mercantile houses, sympathized with the revolution, and only waited for a favourable opportunity to raise the mask and declare themselves overtly. The Mexican population itself was not at all desirous of running the risk of a siege: it preferred to a contest, which is ever injurious to commercial interests, an arrangement, no matter its nature, which would protect them. Money has no country, and hence, politically regarded, the population of Galveston cared very little whether it was Texan or Mexican, provided that it was not ruined, which was the essential point.

In the midst of all this egotism and vexation, the General felt the more embarrassed, because he possessed but a very weak armed force, incapable of keeping the population in check, if they felt any desire to revolt. After vainly awaiting the Colonel's return till eleven o'clock, the General resolved to summon to his house the most influential merchants of the town, in order to consult with them on the means to protect individuals, and place the town in a posture of defence, were that possible. The merchants responded to the General's summons with an eagerness which, to any man less thoroughly acquainted with the American character, would have seemed a good omen, but which produced a diametrically opposite effect on the General. At about half-an hour after midnight, the General's saloon was crowded: some thirty merchants, the elite of Galveston, were collected there.

His Excellency, Don José Maria Rubio, was essentially a man of action, frank, loyal, and convinced that in all cases the best way of dealing is to go straight to the point. After the first compliments, he began speaking, and without any tergiversation or weakness, explained clearly and distinctly the state of their situation, and claimed the assistance of the notable inhabitants of the town to ward off the dangers that threatened it, promising, if that help were assured him, to hold out against the whole revolutionary army, and compel it to retire. The merchants were far from expecting such a requests which literally stunned them. For some minutes they knew not what answer to give; but at last, after consulting in whispers, the oldest and most influential of them undertook to reply in the names of all, and began speaking with that feigned frankness which forms the basis of the Anglo-American character—a frankness which conceals so much duplicity, and by which only those who are unacquainted with the inhabitants of the United States are at times entrapped.

This merchant, a native of Tennessee, had in his youth carried on nearly all those trades more or less acknowledgeable, by means of which men in the new world contrive in so short a time to raise the scaffoldings of a large fortune. Coming to Texas as a slave-dealer, he had gradually extended his trade; then he became a speculator, corn-dealer, and all sorts of things. In a word, he worked so well, that in less than ten years he was in possession of several millions. Morally, he was an old fox, without faith or law; a Greek by instinct, and a Jew by temperament. His name was Lionel Fisher; he was short and stout, and appeared scarce sixty years of age, although he was in reality close on seventy.

"Señor General," he said in an obsequious voice, after bowing with that haughty humility which distinguishes parvenus, "we are extremely pained by the sad news your excellency has thought it right to communicate to us, for none are more affected than ourselves by the calamities of our hapless country. We deplore in our hearts the situation into which Texas is suddenly cast, for we shall be the first assailed in our fortunes and affections. We should be glad to make the greatest sacrifices in order to prevent disasters and ward off the fearful catastrophe that menaces us. But, alas! What can we do?—nothing. In spite of our good will and warm desire to prove to your excellency that you possess all our sympathies, our hands are tied. Our assistance, far from helping the Mexican Government, would, on the contrary, injure it, because the populace and vagabonds who flock to all seaports, and who are in a majority at Galveston, delighted at having found a pretext for disorder, would immediately revolt, apparently to defend the insurrection, but in reality to plunder us. This consideration, therefore, compels us most reluctantly to remain neutral."

"Reflect, Señores," the General answered, "that the sacrifice I ask of you is but a trifle. Each of you will give me a thousand piastres; it is not too much, I suppose, to guarantee the security of your money and goods? For with the sum you collect, I pledge myself to preserve you from all harm by collecting a sufficient number of men to foil any expedition made against the town by the insurgents."

At this point-blank appeal the merchants made a frightful grimace, which the General did not appear to notice.

"The offering I claim from you at such a moment," he continued, "is not exorbitant; is it not just that in the hour of need you should come to the aid of a government under whose protection you have grown rich, and which, although it would have been perfectly justified in doing so, has, up to this day, demanded nothing from you?"

Caught in this dilemma, the merchants did not know what to answer. They were not all desirous to give their money in the defence of a cause which their secret efforts tended on the contrary to destroy, but when thus pressed by the General, their embarrassment was extreme; they did not dare openly to refuse, and wished still less to say yes. It is a singular fact, though perfectly true, that those men who have grown rich with the greatest facility, cling the most to their fortunes. Of all the natives of the New World, the North American is the one who most craves money. He professes a profound love for the precious metals; with him money is everything, and to gain it he would sacrifice relatives and friends without remorse and without pity. It is the North American who invented that egotistic and heartless proverb, which so thoroughly displays the character of the people, *time is money.* Ask what you will of a North American, and he will give it you, but do not try to burrow a dollar of him, for he will bluntly refuse, however great the obligations he owes you may be.

The great American bankruptcies which a few years back terrified the Old World by their cynical effrontery, edified us as to the commercial honesty of this country, which in its dealings never says, yes, and is so afraid of letting; its thoughts be penetrated, that even in the most frivolous conversations the people, through fear of compromising themselves by an affirmative, say at each sentence, "I suppose," "I believe," "I think."

General Rubio, who had been a long time in Texas, and accustomed to daily dealings with the Americans, was perfectly well aware in what way he should treat them, hence he was not at all disturbed by their embarrassed denials, their protestations of devotion, or their downcast faces. After leaving them a few moments for reflection, seeing that they could not make up their minds to answer him, he continued in his calmest voice and with his most pleasant air—

"I see, Señores, that the reasons I have had the honour of laying before you have not had the good fortune to convince you, and I am really vexed at it. Unfortunately, we are in one of those fatal crises where long deliberations are impossible. Ever since the President of the Republic appointed me Military Chief of this State, I have ever been anxious to satisfy you, and not make you feel too heavily the weight of the power entrusted to me, taking on myself on several occasions, to modify any harshness in the orders I received from high quarters with reference to you. I venture to believe that you will do me the justice of saying that you have always found me kind and complaisant toward you."

The merchants naturally burst into affirmations as the General continued.

"Unfortunately it can no longer be so. In the face of this obstinate and unpatriotic refusal you so peremptorily give me, I am, to my great regret, constrained to carry out literally the orders I have received,—orders that concern you, Señores, and whose tenor, I repeat, I find myself utterly unable to modify."

At this declaration, made in a sarcastic voice, the merchants began shivering; they understood that the General was about to take a brilliant revenge, although they did not know yet what was about to happen. For all that, they began to repent having accepted the invitation, and placed themselves so simply in the wolf's mouth. The General kept smiling, but the smile had something bitter and mocking in its expression, which was far from reassuring them. At this moment a clock, standing on a bracket, struck two.

"Caramba," said the General, "is it so late as that already? How quickly time passes in your agreeable company. Señores, we must wind up the business. I should be in despair if I kept you longer from your homes—the more so, as you must be desirous of rest."

"In truth," stammered the merchant who had hitherto spoken in the name of all, "whatever pleasure we feel at being here——"

"You would feel greater still at being elsewhere," the General interrupted, with a laugh; "I perfectly understand that, Don Lionel, hence I will not abuse your patience much longer. I only ask you for a few minutes more, and then I will set you at liberty, so be kind enough to sit down again."

The merchants obeyed, while exchanging a glance of despair on the sly. The General seemed on this night to be deaf and blind, for he saw and heard nothing. He struck a bell; at the summons a door opened, and an officer walked in.

"Captain Saldana," the General asked, "is all ready?"

"Yes, General," the Captain answered, with a respectful bow.

"Señores," the Governor continued, "I have received from the Mexican Government orders to lay on the rich merchants of this town a war tax of sixty thousand piastres in cash. As you are aware, Señores a soldier can only obey. Still, I had taken on myself to reduce this contribution by one-half, desiring, as far as in me lay, to prove to you up to the last moment, the interest I take in you. You would not understand me; I am vexed at it, but nothing is now left me save obedience. Here is the order," he added, as he took a paper from the table and unfolded it, "it is peremptory; still, I am ready to grant you five minutes to make up your minds; but when that period has elapsed, I shall be compelled to do my duty, and you are sufficiently well acquainted with me, Señores, to know that I shall do it at all hazards."

"But, General," the old merchant hazarded, "your Excellency will permit me to observe, that the sum is enormous."

"Nonsense, Señores; there are thirty of you—it only amounts to two thousand piastres per head, which is only a trifle to you. I made you an offer to knock off half, but you were not willing."

"Business has been very flat for some years, and money is becoming excessively scarce."

"To whom do you say that, Don Lionel? I fancy I am better aware of that fact than anybody else."

"Perhaps if you were to grant us a delay of a month or a fortnight, by collecting all our resources and making enormous sacrifices, we might manage to scrape together one-half the amount."

"Unfortunately, I cannot even grant you an hour."

"In that case, General, it is impossible."

"Nonsense! I feel certain that you have not reflected. Besides, that is no affair of mine: in asking you for this money, I carry out the orders I have received, it is for your to judge whether you will consent or not. I, personally, am completely out of the affair."

"Really, General," the old merchant continued, deceived, in spite of all his craft, by the Governor's tone, "really, it is impossible for us to pay the smallest amount."

All bowed in affirmation, supporting the remarks of their spokesman.

"Very good," the General continued, still in a coolly mocking tone, "that is clearly understood, then. Still, you will not, I trust, render me responsible for the consequences which this refusal may entail on you."

"Oh, General, you cannot suppose that!"

"Thanks. You heard, Captain?" he added, turning to the officer, who was standing motionless by the door; "order in the detachment."

"Yes, General."

And the officer quitted the room. The merchants gave a start of terror, for this mysterious order caused them to reflect seriously, and their anxiety became the greater, when they heard the clang of arms in the patios, and the heavy footfalls of approaching troops.

"What is the meaning of this, General?" they cried in terror, "Can we have fallen into a trap?"

"What do you mean?" the General said. "Oh, I beg your pardon, but I forgot to communicate to you the end of this order, which concerns you particularly, however, that will be soon done. I am instructed to have all persons shot, who refuse to subscribe to the loan demanded by the government, in order to get over the serious embarrassments the malcontents occasion it."

At the same instant, the doors were thrown wide open, and a detachment of fifty men silently surrounded the American merchants. The latter were more dead than alive—they fancied they were having a frightful dream, or suffering from a horrible nightmare. Certain that the General would not hesitate to execute the threat he had made them, the merchants did not know how to get out of the scrape. The Governor himself had made no change in his demeanour—his face was still gracious, and his voice gentle.

"Come, Señors," he said, "pray accept my heartfelt sympathy. Captain, lead away these gentlemen, and treat them with all the kindness their sad position claims."

He then bowed, and prepared to leave the room.

"One moment," the old merchant said, quite appalled by the approach of death; "are there no means of settling this business, General?"

"I only know one—paying."

"I am well aware of that," he said with a sigh; "but, alas! we are ruined."

"What can I do? You know, and yourselves allowed, that I am quite unconnected with this unhappy affair."

"Alas," the poor merchants exclaimed in chorus, "you will not kill us, surely, General; we are fathers of families, what will become of our wives and children?"

"I pity you, but, unfortunately, can do no more than that."

"General," they cried, falling at his knees, "in the name of what you hold dearest, have pity on us, we implore you."

"I am really in despair at what has occurred, and should like to come to your aid; unhappily I do not see my way, and then, again, you do nothing to help me."

"Alas!" they repeated, sobbing and clasping their hands desperately.

"I am well aware that you have not the money, and there is the insurmountable difficulty, believe me. However, let us see," he added, apparently reflecting.

The poor devils, who felt themselves so near death, looked at him with eyes sparkling with hope. There was a rather lengthened silence, during which you might have heard the heart throbs of these men, who knew that life and death depended on the man who held them panting under his eye.

"Listen," he continued, "this is all I can do for you, and believe me, that, in acting thus, I assume an enormous responsibility; there are thirty of you, I think?"

"Yes, Excellency," they exclaimed unanimously.

"Well, only ten of you shall be shot. You shall select them yourselves, and those you designate will be immediately led into the patio and executed. But now ask me for nothing further, as I shall be constrained to refuse you; and that you may have time to make your selection carefully, I grant you ten minutes."

This was a proof of incontestable cleverness on the part of the General. By breaking, through this decision, the agreement that had hitherto prevailed among the merchants, by opposing them to one another, he was certain of obtaining the result which, without, he would probably not have secured. For we prefer to suppose, for the honour of the General, whose career up to this day had been so free from excesses, and acts of this nature, that the threat of death was only a mode employed to cause these men, whom he knew to be opposed to the government he represented, into undoing their purse strings, and that he would not have been so cruel as to carry matters to extremities, and shoot in cold blood thirty of the most respectable townsmen.

Whatever General Rubio's intentions might have been, however, the Americans believed him, and acted accordingly. After two or three minutes' hesitation, the merchants came one after the other, to give their consent to the loan. But their tergiversation had cost them a thousand dollars a-piece. It was dear, hence we must allow that they consented with very ill grace. But the soldiers were there ready to obey the slightest sign from their chief;

the muskets were loaded, and the patio two paces off. There was no chance of getting out of it.

Still, the General did not let them off so cheaply. The Americans were led home one after the other by four soldiers and an officer, whose instructions were to shoot the prisoner at the slightest attempted escape, and it was not till the General had the two thousand piastres in his hands that a second prisoner was sent home in the same fashion. This went on until the whole sum was collected, and the only persons remaining in the saloon were the General and old Lionel.

"Oh, Excellency!" he said, reproachfully, "How is it possible that you, who have hitherto been so kind to us, could have had the thought of committing such an act of cruelty?"

The General burst out laughing.

"Do you imagine I would have done it?" he said, with a shrug of his shoulder.

The merchant struck his forehead with a gesture of despair.

"Ah!" he exclaimed, "We were idiots."

"Hang it, did you have such a bad opinion of me? Caramba, Señor, I do not commit such acts as that."

"Ah," the merchant said, with a laugh, "I have not paid yet."

"Which means?"

"That now I know what I have to expect. I shall not pay."

"Really, I believed you cleverer than that."

"Why so?"

"What? You do not understand that a man may hesitate to execute thirty persons, but when it comes to only one man, who, like yourself, has a great number of misdeeds on his conscience, his execution is considered an act of justice, and carried out without hesitation?"

"Then, you would shoot me?"

"Without the slightest remorse."

"Come, come, General, you are decidedly stronger than I am."

"You flatter me, Señor Lionel."

"No, I tell you what I think; it was cleverly played."

"You are a judge."

"Thanks," he answered, with a modest smile. "To spare you the trouble of having me executed, I will execute myself," he added, good temperedly, as he felt his coat pocket.

He drew out a pocketbook crammed with Bank of England notes, and made up the sum of two thousand piastres, which he laid on the table.

"I have now only to thank you," the General said, as he picked up the notes.

"And I you, Excellency," he answered.

"Why so?"

"Because you have given me a lesson by which I shall profit when the occasion offers."

"Take care, Señor Lionel," the General said, meaningly; "you will not, perhaps, come across a man so good-natured as myself."

The merchant restored the portfolio to his pocket, bowed to the General, and went out. It was three o'clock; all had been finished in less than an hour; it was quick work.

"Poor scamps, after all, those gringos," the General said, when he was alone; "oh, if we had not to deal with mountaineers and campesinos we should soon settle this population."

"General," said an aide-de-camp, as he opened the door, "Colonel Melendez asks whether you will deign to receive him, in spite of the late hour?"

"Is Colonel Melendez here?" the General asked in surprise.

"He has this instant arrived, General; can he come in?"

"Of course; show him in at once."

In a few minutes the Colonel appeared.

"Here you are at last," the General cried, as he went to meet him; "I fancied you were either dead or a prisoner."

"It was a tossup that one of the two events did not happen."

"Oh, oh! Then you have something serious to tell me."

"Most serious, General."

"Hang it, my friend, take a chair and let us talk."

"Before all, General," the Colonel remarked, "do you know our position?"

"What do you mean?"

"Only, General, that you may possibly be ignorant of certain events that have happened."

"I think I have heard grave events rumoured, though I do not exactly know what has happened."

"Listen, then! The *Libertad* corvette is in the hands of the insurgents."

"Impossible!" the General exclaimed, bounding in his chair.

"General," the young officer said, in a mournful voice, "I have to inform you of something more serious still."

"Pardon me, my friend, perhaps I am mistaken, but it seems to me highly improbable that you could have obtained such positive news during the pleasure trip you have been making."

"Not only, General, have the insurgents seized the *Libertad*, but they have also made themselves masters of the Fort of the Point."

"Oh!" the General shouted, as he rose passionately, "this time, Colonel, you are badly informed; the Fort of the Point is impregnable."

"It was taken in an hour by thirty Freebooters, commanded by the Jaguar."

The General hid his face in his hands, with an expression of despair impossible to render.

"Oh! It is too much at once," he exclaimed.

"That is not all," the Colonel continued, sharply.

"What have you to tell me more terrible than what you have just said?"

"A thing that will make you leap with rage and blush with shame, General."

The old soldier laid his hand on his heart, as if wishful to arrest its hurried beating, and then said to the Colonel, in a tone of supreme resignation—

"Speak, my friend; I am ready to hear all."

The Colonel remained silent for some minutes; the despair of the brave old soldier made him shiver.

"General," he said, "perhaps it would be better to defer till tomorrow what I have to say to you; you appear fatigued, and a few hours, more or less, are not of much consequence."

"Colonel Melendez," the General said, giving the young officer a searching glance, "under present circumstances a minute is worth an age. I order you to speak."

"The insurgents request a parley," the Colonel said, distinctly.

"To parley with me?" the General answered, with an almost imperceptible tinge of irony in his voice. "These Caballeros do me a great honour. And what about, pray?"

"As they think themselves capable of seizing Galveston, they wish to avoid bloodshed by treating with you."

The General rose, and walked sharply up and down the room for some minutes. At length he stopped before the Colonel.

"And what would you do in my place?"

"I should treat," the young officer replied, unhesitatingly.

CHAPTER III
THE RETREAT

After this frankly expressed opinion there was a rather lengthened silence, and the Colonel was the first to resume the conversation.

"General," he went on, "you evidently know nothing of the events that have occurred during the last four and twenty hours."

"How could I know anything? These demons of insurgents have organised Guerillas, who hold the country and so thoroughly intercept the communications, that out of twenty spies I have sent out, not one has returned."

"And not one will return, be assured."

"What is to be done, then?"

"Do you really wish for my advice, General?"

"On my honour, I desire to know your real opinion; for you are the only one among us, I fancy, who really knows what is going on."

"I am aware of it. Listen to me, then, and do not feel astonished at anything you may hear, for all is positively true. The information I am about to have the honour of communicating to you was given me, by the Jaguar himself, scarce three hours back, at the Salto del Frayle, whither he invited me to come to converse about some matters in no way connected with politics."

"Very good," the General remarked, with a slight smile. "Go on, I am listening to you with the deepest attention."

The Colonel felt himself blush under his chief's slightly ironical smile; still he recovered himself, and continued—

"In two words, this is our position: while a few bold men, aided by a privateer brig under the American flag, carried by surprise the *Libertad*—"

"One of the finest ships in our navy!" the General interrupted, with a sigh.

"Yes, General, but unhappily it is now an accomplished fact. While this was taking place, other insurgents, commanded by the Jaguar in person, got into the Fort of the Point, and carried it almost without a blow."

"But what you tell me is impossible!" the old soldier interrupted with a burst of passion.

"I tell you nothing that is not rigorously true, General."

"The vague rumours that have reached me, led me to suppose that the insurgents had dealt us a fresh blow but I was far from suspecting such a frightful catastrophe."

"I swear to you, on my honour, as, a soldier, General, that I only tell you the most rigid truth:"

"I believe you, my friend, for I know how brave and worthy of confidence you are. Still, the news you give me is so frightful, that, in spite of myself, I should like to be able to doubt it."

"Unhappily, that is impossible."

The General, suffering from a fury which was the more terrible as it was concentrated, walked up and down the room, clenching his fists, and muttering broken sentences. The Colonel looked after him sadly, not dreaming of offering him any of those conventional consolations which, far from offering any relief to pain, only render it sharper and more poignant. At the end of some minutes, the General succeeded so far in mastering his emotion as to draw back to his heart the annoyance he felt. He sat down again by the Colonel's side, and took his hand kindly.

"You have not yet given me your advice," he said with a ghost of a smile.

"If you really insist on my speaking, I will do so, General," the young man answered, "though I am convinced beforehand that our ideas are absolutely similar on this question."

"That is probable. Still, my dear Colonel, the opinion of a man of your merits is always precious, and I should be curious to know if I really agree with you."

"Be it so, General. This is what I think: we have but insufficient forces to sustain an assault effectively. The town is very badly disposed toward us: I am convinced that it only wants an opportunity to rise and make common cause with the insurgents. On the other hand, it would be a signal act of folly to shut ourselves up in a town with an issue, where we should be forced to surrender—an indelible stain for the Mexican army. For the present, we have no succour to expect from the government of Mexico, which is too much engaged in defending itself against the ambitious men of every description who hold it continually in check, to dream of coming effectively to our assistance, either by sending us reinforcements, or carrying out a diversion in our favour."

"What you say is unfortunately only too true; we are reduced to reckon on ourselves alone."

"Now, if we obstinately shut ourselves up in the town, it is evident to me that we shall be compelled eventually to surrender. As the insurgents are masters of the sea, it is a mere question of time. On the other hand, if we quit it of our free will, the position will be singularly simplified."

"But, in that case, we shall be compelled to treat with these scoundrels?"

"I thought so for an instant; but I believe we can easily avoid that misfortune."

"In what way? speak, speak, my friend."

"The flag of truce the insurgents send you, will not arrive at the cabildo till nine in the morning; what prevents you, General, evacuating the town, ere he makes his appearance?"

"Hum!" said the General, growing more and more attentive to the young man's remarks. "Then you propose flight to me?"

"Not at all," the Colonel retorted; "remember, General, that the position is admitted, that in war, recoiling is not flying. If we render ourselves masters of the country by leaving the town to the insurgents, by this skilful retreat we place them in the difficult position in which we are today. In the open plains, and through our discipline, we shall be enabled to hold our own against a force four times our strength, which would not be possible here; then, when we have obtained those reinforcements Santa Anna will probably himself bring us ere long, we will re-enter Galveston, which the insurgents will not attempt to defend against us. Such is my opinion, General, and the plan I should adopt, had I the honour to be Governor of this State."

"Yes," the General answered, "the advice you offer would have some chance of success, were it possible to follow it. Unluckily, it would be madness to reckon on Santa Anna's support: he would allow us to be crushed, not perhaps of his own will, but compelled by circumstances, and impeded by the constant obstacles the Senate creates for him."

"I cannot share your opinion on that point, General; be well assured that the Senate, ill-disposed though it may be to the President of the Republic, is no more desirous to lose Texas than he is. Besides, under the present circumstances, we must make a virtue of necessity; it would be great madness for us to await here the enemy's attack."

The General seemed to hesitate for some minutes, then, suddenly forming a determination, he rang a bell. An aide-de-camp appeared.

"Let all the general officers assemble here within half an hour," he said. "Begone."

The aide-de-camp bowed, and left the room.

"You wish it," the General continued, turning to the Colonel; "well, be it so. I consent to follow your advice. Besides, it is, perhaps, the only chance of safety left us at this moment."

In Europe, where we are accustomed to see great masses of men come in contact on the field of battle, it would cause a smile to hear the name of army given to what, among us, would not even be a regiment. But we must bear in mind that the new world, excepting North America, is very sparely populated; the inhabitants are scattered over immense districts, and the most imposing regular forces rarely attain the number of five or six thousand men. An army is usually composed of fifteen to eighteen hundred troops, all told, infantry, cavalry, and artillery. And what soldiers! ignorant, badly paid, badly armed, only half obeying their Chiefs, whom they know to be as ignorant as themselves, and in whom they naturally have not the slightest confidence.

In Mexico, the military profession, far from being honoured as it is in Europe, is, on the contrary, despised, so that the officers and soldiers are generally blemished men to whom every other career would be closed. The officers, with a few honourable exceptions, are men ruined by debt and in reputation, whose ignorance of their profession is so great, that one of our sergeants could give them lessons. As for the soldiers, they are only recruited among the leperos, thieves, and assassins. Hence the army is a real scourge for the country. It is the army that makes and unmakes the Governments, which succeed each other with perfectly headlong rapidity in Mexico; for, since its pretended emancipation, this unhappy country has witnessed nearly three hundred pronunciamentos, all organised in the army, and carried through for the benefit of the officers, whose only object is to be promoted.

Still, what we say is not absolute. We have known several Mexican officers, highly educated and honourable men; unluckily their number is so limited, that they are impotent to remedy the evil, and are constrained to put up with what they cannot prevent. General Rubio was undeniably one of the most honourable officers in the Mexican army. Still, we have seen that he did not hesitate to plunder the very persons whom his duty obliged him to protect against all annoyance. My readers can judge by this example, selected from a thousand, what tricks the other Generals play.

The corps d'armée placed under the command of General Rubio, and shut up with him in Galveston, only amounted to nine hundred and fifty officers and men, to whom might be found at a given signal some three hundred lanceros scattered in little posts of observation along the coast. Though incapable of effectually defending the town, this force, well directed, might hold in check for a long time the worse armed, and certainly worse disciplined insurgents.

The General had rapidly seen the value of the Colonel's advice. The plan the latter proposed was, in truth, the only practicable one, and hence he accepted it at once. Still, it was necessary to act with vigour; the sun was rising, and the coming day was Sunday; hence it was important that the army should have evacuated the town before the end of mass, that is to say, eleven in the morning, for the following reason:

In all the slave states, and especially in Texas, a strange custom exists, reminding us distantly of the Lupercalia of ancient Rome. On a Sunday masters grant their slaves entire liberty; one day in seven is certainly not much; but it is a great deal for the Southern States, where slavery is so sternly and strictly established. These poor slaves, who seek compensation for six days of hard servitude, enjoy with childish delight their few holiday hours: not caring a whit for the torrid heat that transforms the streets into perfect ovens, they spread over the town singing, dancing, or galloping at full speed in carts belonging to their masters which they have appropriated. On this day the town belongs to them, they behave almost as they please, no one interfering or trying to check their frolic.

General Rubio rightly feared lest the merchants of Galveston, whom he had so cleverly compelled to disgorge, might try to take their revenge by exciting the slaves to mutiny against the Mexicans, and they would probably be ready enough to do so, delighted at finding a pretext for disorder, without troubling themselves further as to the more or less grave results of their mutiny. Hence, while his aide-de-camp performed the commission he had entrusted to him, General Rubio ordered Colonel Melendez to take with him all the soldiers on duty at the Cabildo, place himself at their head, and seize the requisite number of boats for the transport of the troops to the main land.

This order was not difficult to execute. The Colonel, without losing a moment, went to the port, and not experiencing the slightest opposition from the captains and masters of the vessels, who were well aware, besides, that a refusal would not be listened to, assembled a flotilla of fifteen light vessels, amply sufficient for the transport of the garrison. In the meanwhile, the aide-de-camp had performed his duties with intelligence and celerity, so that within twenty minutes all the Mexican officers were collected at the General's house.

The latter, without losing a moment, explained to them in a voice that admitted of no reply, the position in which the capture of the fort placed the garrison, the necessity of not letting the communication with the mainland be cut off, and his intention of evacuating the town with the least possible delay. The officers, as the General expected, were unanimous in applauding his resolution, for in their hearts they were not at all anxious to sustain a siege in which only hard blows could be received. Taking the field pleased them, on the contrary, for many reasons: in the first place, the pillage of the estancias and the haciendas offered them great profits, and then they had a hope of taking a brilliant revenge on the insurgents for the numerous defeats the latter had inflicted on them since they had been immured in the town.

Orders were therefore immediately given by the General to march the troops down to the quay with arms and baggage; still, in order to avoid any cause for disorder, the movement was executed very slowly, and the Colonel, who presided over the embarkation, was careful to establish numerous posts at the entrance of each street leading to the port, so that the populace were kept away from the soldiers, and no disputes were possible between them. So soon as one boat had its complement of troops on board it pushed off, though it did not start, as the General wished the entire flotilla to leave the town together.

It was a magnificent day, the sun dazzled, and the bay sparkled like a burning-glass. The people, kept at a distance by the bayonets of the soldiers, watched in gloomy silence the embarkation of the troops. Alarmed by this movement, which they did not at all understand, and were so far from suspecting the departure of the Mexican garrison, that they supposed, on the contrary, that the General was proceeding with a portion of his troops to make an expedition against the insurgents.

When all the soldiers, with the exception of those intended to protect the retreat of their comrades, had embarked, the General sent for the alcade mayor, the Juez de letras, and the corregidor. These magistrates came to the General, concealing, but poorly, under a feigned eagerness, the secret alarm caused them by the order they had just received. In spite of the rapidity with which the troops effected their embarkation, it was by this time nearly nine o'clock. At the moment when the General was preparing to address the magistrates whom he had so unexpectedly convened, Colonel Melendez entered the cabildo, and after bowing respectfully to the Governor, said—

"General, the person to whom I had the honour of referring last night is awaiting your good pleasure."

"Ah! Ah!" the General replied, biting his moustache with an ironical air, "Is he there, then?"

"Yes, General; I have promised to act as his introducer to your Excellency."

"Very good. Request the person to enter."

"What!" the Colonel exclaimed, in surprise, "Does your Excellency intend to confer with him in the presence of witnesses?"

"Certainly, and I regret there are not more here. Bring in the person, my dear Colonel."

"Has your Excellency carefully reflected on the order you have done me the honour to give me?"

"Hang it! I should think so. I am sure you will be satisfied with what I am about to do."

"As you insist, General," the Colonel said with marked hesitation, "I can only obey."

"Yes, yes, my friend, obey; do not be uneasy, I tell you."

The Colonel withdrew without any further remark, and in a few moments returned, bringing John Davis with him. The American had changed his dress for one more appropriate to the circumstances. His demeanour was grave, and step haughty, though not arrogant. On entering the room he bowed to the General courteously, and prepared to address him. General Rubio returned his bow with equal courtesy, but stopped him by a sign.

"Pardon me, sir," he said to him, "be kind enough to excuse me for a few moments. Perhaps, after listening to what I shall have the honour of saying to these Caballeros, you will consider your mission to me as finished."

The American made no further reply than a bow, and waited.

"Señores," the General then said, addressing the magistrates, "orders I have this moment received compel me to leave the town at once with the troops I have the honour to command. During my absence I entrust the direction of affairs to you, feeling convinced that you will act in all things prudently and for the common welfare. Still, you must be cautious not to let yourselves be influenced by evil counsels, or led by certain passions to which I will not allude now, particularly here. On my return, which will not be long delayed, I shall ask of you a strict account of your acts during my absence. Weigh my words carefully, and be assured that nothing you may do will be concealed from me."

"Then, General," the Alcade said, "that is the motive of the movement of the troops we have witnessed this morning. Do you really intend to depart?"

"You have heard me, Señor."

"Yes, I have heard you, General; but in my turn, in my capacity as magistrate, I will ask you by what right you, the military governor of the state, leave one of its principal ports to its own resources in the present critical state of affairs, when the revolution is before our gates, and make not the slightest attempt to defend us? Is it really acting as defenders of this hapless town thus to withdraw, leaving it, after your departure, a prey to that anarchy which, as you are aware, only the presence of your forces has hitherto prevented breaking out? The burden you wish to lay upon us, General, we decline to accept; we will not assume the responsibility of so heavy a task; we cannot bear the penalty of another person's faults. The last Mexican soldier will scarcely have left the town, ere we shall have handed in our resignations, not being at all desirous to sacrifice ourselves for a government whose conduct toward us is stamped with egotism and cold-blooded cruelty. That is what I have to say to you in my name and in that of my colleagues. Now, in your turn, you will act as you think proper, but you are warned that you can in no way reckon upon us."

"Ah, ah, Señores!" the General exclaimed, with an angry frown, "Is that the way you venture to act? Take care, I have not gone yet; I am still master of Galveston, and can institute a severe example before my departure."

"Do so, General, we will undergo without a murmur any punishment you may please to inflict on us, even were it death."

"Very good," the General replied, in a voice quivering with passion; "as it is so, I leave you free to act, according to circumstances. But you will have a severe account to render to me, and that perhaps shortly."

"Not we, Excellency, for your departure will be the signal of our resignation."

"Then you have made up your mind to plunge the country into anarchy?"

"What can we do? What means have we to prevent it? No, no, General, we are not the persons who deserve reproach."

General Rubio in his heart felt the logic of this reasoning; he saw perfectly well how egotistic and cruel his conduct was toward the townsmen, whom he thus surrendered, without any means of defence, to the fury of the popular passion. Unfortunately, the position was no longer tenable—

the town could not be defended, hence he must depart, without answering the decade; for what reply could he have made him? The General gave his aides-de-camp a sign to follow him, and prepared to leave the cabildo.

"Pardon me for detaining you for a moment, General," John Davis said: "but I should have liked to have a short conversation with your Excellency, prior to your departure."

"For what good object, sir?" the General answered, sharply; "did you not hear what was said in this room? Return to those who sent you, and report to them what you have seen, that will be sufficient."

"Still, General," he urged, "I should have desired—"

"What?" the General interrupted, and then added, ironically, "To make me proposals, I presume, on the part of the insurgents. Know, sir, that whatever may happen, I will never consent to treat with rebels. Thank Colonel Melendez, who was kind enough to introduce you to my presence. Had it not been for his intervention I should have had you hung as a traitor to your country. Begone!—or stay!" he added, on reflection; "I will not leave you here after I am gone. Seize this man!"

"General, take care," the American replied. "I am intrusted with a mission; arresting me is a violation of the law of nations."

"Nonsense, sir," the General continued, with a shrug of his shoulders, "why, you must be mad? Do I recognize the right of the persons from whom you come to send me a flag of truce? Do I know who you are? Viva Dios! In what age are we living, then, that rebels dare to treat on equal terms with the government against which they have revolted? You are my prisoner, sir! But be at your ease I have no intention of ill-treating you, or retaining you any length of time. You will accompany us to the mainland, that is all. When we have arrived there you will be free to go wherever you please; so you see, sir, that those Mexicans, whom you like to represent in such dark colours, are not quite so ferocious as you would have them supposed."

"We have always rendered justice to your heart and loyalty, General."

"I care very little for the opinion you and yours have of me. Come on, sir."

"I protest, General, against this illegal arrest."

"Protest as much as you please, sir, but follow me!"

As resistance would have been madness, Davis obeyed.

"Well," he said, with a laugh, "I follow you, General. After all, I have not much cause to complain, for everything is fair in war."

They went out. In spite of the dazzling brilliancy of the sun, whose beams spread a tropical heat through the town, the entire population encumbered the streets and squares. The multitude was silent, however; it witnessed with calm stoicism the departure of the Mexican army; not an effort was attempted by the people to break the cordon of sentries drawn up on the fort. When the General appeared, the crowd made way respectfully to let him pass, and many persons saluted him.

The inhabitants of Galveston detested the Mexican Government; but they did justice to the Governor, whose honest and moderate administration had effectually protected them during the whole time he remained among them, instead of taking advantage of his authority to plunder and tyrannize over them. They saw with pleasure the departure of the troops, with sorrow that of the General. The old soldier advanced with a calm step, talking loudly with his officers, and courteously returning the bows he received, with smiling face and assured demeanour. He reached the port in a few minutes, and at his order the last soldiers embarked. The General, with no other weapon but his sword, remained for some minutes almost alone in the midst of the crowd that followed him to the quay. Two aides-de-camp alone accompanied him. John Davis had already entered a boat, which took him on board the schooner, in which the General himself intended to cross.

"General," one of the aides-de-camp said, "all the troops have embarked, and we are now only waiting your Excellency's pleasure."

"Very good, Captain," he answered. He then turned to the magistrates, who had walked by his side from the cabildo. "Farewell, señores," he said, taking off his hat, whose white plumes swept the ground, "farewell, till we meet again. I pray Heaven, from my heart, that, during my short absence, you will be enabled to avoid the scenes of disorder and anarchy which the effervescence of parties too often occasions. We shall meet again sooner than you may possibly suppose. Long live Mexico!"

"Long live Mexico!" the two officers shouted.

The crowd remained dumb; not a man took up the General's shout. He shook his head sadly, bowed for the last time, and went down into the boat waiting for him. Two minutes later the Mexican flotilla had left Galveston.

"When shall we return?" the General muttered, sadly, with eyes fixed on the town, whose buildings were slowly disappearing from sight.

"Never!" John Davis whispered in his ear; and this prophetic voice affected the old soldier to the depth of his heart, and filled it with bitterness.

CHAPTER IV
JOHN DAVIS

The Mexican flotilla, impelled by a favourable breeze, accomplished the passage from the island to the mainland in a comparatively very brief period. The brig and corvette, anchored under the battery of the fort, made no move to disturb the General; and it was evident that the Texans did not suspect the events taking place at this moment, but awaited the return of their Envoy ere making any demonstration.

Colonel Melendez had seized the few boats capable of standing out to sea in Galveston harbour, so that the magistrates could not, had they wished it, have sent a boat to the Texans to inform them of the precipitate departure of the Mexican garrison. The General's resolution had been formed so suddenly, and executed with such rapidity, that the partisans of the revolution in the town, and who were ignorant of the cause of that retreat, felt singularly embarrassed by the liberty so singularly granted them, and did not know what arrangements to make, or how to enter into communication with their friends, whose position they were ignorant of. Only one man could have enlightened them, and he was John Davis. But General Rubio, foreseeing what would have inevitably happened had he left the ex-slave dealer behind him, had been very careful to carry him off with him.

The landing of the troops was effected under the most favourable conditions. The point they steered for was in the hands of the Mexicans, who had a strong detachment there, so that the army got ashore without arousing the slightest suspicion, or any attempt to prevent the landing. The General's first care, so soon as he reached the mainland, was to send off spies in every direction, in order to discover, were it possible, the enemy's plans, and whether they were preparing to make a forward movement.

The boats which had been used to convey the troops were, till further orders, drawn up on the beach, through fear lest the insurgents might make use of them. Two schooners, however, on each of which two guns were put, received orders to cruise in the bay, and pick up all boats the inhabitants of Galveston might attempt to send off to the Chief of the Texan army.

The banks of the Rio Trinidad are charming and deliciously diversified, bordered by rushes and reeds, and covered with mangroves, amid which sport thousands of flamingoes, cranes, herons, and wild ducks, which cackle noisily as they swim about in tranquil and transparent waters. About four miles from the sea, the banks rise gradually with insensible undulations, and form meadows covered with a tall and tufted grass, on which grow gigantic mahogany trees with their oblong leaves, and Peru trees with their red fruit, and magnolias, whose large white flowers shed an intoxicating perfume. All these trees, fastened together by lianas which envelop them in their inextricable network, serve as a retreat for a population of red and grey squirrels, that may be seen perpetually leaping from branch to branch, and of cardinal and mocking birds. The centzontle, the exquisite Mexican nightingale, so soon as night arrives, causes this picturesque solitude to re-echo with its gentle strains.

On the side of a hill that descends in a gentle slope to the river, glisten the white walls of some twenty cottages, with their flat roofs and green shutters, hanging in clusters from the scarped side of the hill, and hidden like timorous birds amid the foliage. These few cottages, built so far from the noise of the world, constitute the rancho of San Isidro.

Unfortunately for the inhabitants of this obscure nook, General Rubio, who felt the necessity of choosing for the site of his camp a strong strategic position, came suddenly to trouble their peace, and recall them rather roughly to the affairs of this world. In fact, from this species of eagles' nests, nothing was easier than for the General to send his columns in all directions. The Mexican army, therefore, marched straight on the rancho of San Isidro, where it arrived about midday. At the unexpected appearance of the troops, the inhabitants were so terrified that, hastily loading themselves with their most valuable articles, they left their houses and fled to hide themselves in the woods.

Whatever efforts the General might make to prevent them, or bring them back to their houses, the poor Indians offered a deaf ear to all, and were resolved not to remain in the vicinity of the troops. The Mexicans therefore remained sole possessors of the rancho, and at once installed themselves in their peaceful conquest, whose appearance was completely changed within a few hours. Tall trees, flowers, and lianas, nothing was respected. Enormous masses of wood lay that same evening on the ground, which they had so long protected with their beneficent shadow. The very birds were constrained to quit their pleasant retreat, to seek a shelter in the neighbouring forest.

When all the approaches to the forest had been cleared for a radius of about twelve hundred yards, the General had the place surrounded by powerful barricades, which transformed the peaceful village into a fortress almost impregnable, with the weak resources the insurgents possessed. The trees on the interior of the rancho were alone left standing, not for the purpose of affording, but to conceal from the enemy the strength of the corps encamped at this spot.

The house of the Indian Alcade, somewhat larger and more comfortably built than the rest, was selected by the General as headquarters. This house stood in the centre of the pueblo; from its azotea the country could be surveyed for a great distance, and no movement in Galveston roads escaped notice. The Texans could not stir without being immediately discovered and signaled by the sentry, whom the General was careful to place in this improvised observatory.

At sunset all the preliminary preparations were finished, and the rancho rendered safe against a coup de main. About seven in the evening the General, after listening to the report of the spies, was sitting in front of the house in the shadow of a magnificent magnolia, whose graceful branches crossed above his head. He was smoking a papillo, while conversing with several of his officers, when an aide-de-camp came up and told him that the person who had come to him that morning from the rebels, earnestly requested the favour of a few minutes' conversation. The General gave an angry start, and was about to refuse, when Colonel Melendez interposed, representing to the General that he could not do so without breaking his word, which he had himself pledged in the morning.

"As it is so," the General said, "let him come."

"Why," the Colonel continued, "refuse to listen to the propositions this man is authorized to offer you?"

"What good is it at this moment? There is always a time to do so if circumstances compel it. Now our situation is excellent; we have not to accept proposals, but, on the contrary, are in a position to impose those that may suit us."

These words were uttered in a tone that compelled the Colonel to silence; he bowed respectfully, and withdrew softly from the circle of officers. At the same moment John Davis arrived, led by the aide-de-camp. The American's face was gloomy and frowning; he saluted the General by raising his hand to his hat, but did not remove it; then he drew himself up haughtily and crossed his hands on his chest. The General regarded him for a moment with repressed curiosity.

"What do you want?" he asked him.

"The fulfilment of your promise," Davis replied drily.

"I do not understand you."

"What do you say? When you made me a prisoner this morning, in contempt of the military code and the laws of nations, did you not tell me that so soon as we reached the mainland, the liberty you had deprived me of by an unworthy abuse of strength, would be immediately restored to me?"

"I did say so," the General answered meekly.

"Well, I demand the fulfilment of that promise; I ought to have left your camp long ago."

"Did you not tell me that you were deputed to me by the rebel army, in order to submit certain propositions?"

"Yes, but you refused to hear me."

"Because the moment was not favourable for such a communication. Imperious duties prevented me then giving your words all the attention that they doubtless deserve."

"Well, and now?"

"Now I am ready to listen to you."

The American looked at the officers that surrounded him.

"Before all these persons?" he asked.

"Why not? These Caballeros belong to the staff of my army, they are as interested as I am in this interview."

"Perhaps so: still, I would observe, General, that it would be better for our discussion to be private."

"I am the sole judge, Señor, of the propriety of my actions. If it please you to be silent, be so; if not, speak, I am listening."

"There is one thing I wish to settle first."

"What is it?"

"Do you regard me as an envoy, or merely as your prisoner?"

"Why this question, whose purport I do not understand?"

"Pardon me, General," he said with an ironical smile, "but you understand me perfectly well, and so do these Caballeros—if a prisoner, you have the right to force silence upon me; as a deputy, on the other hand, I enjoy certain immunities, under, the protection of which I can speak frankly and clearly, and no one can bid me be silent, so long as I do not go beyond the limits of my mission. That is the reason why I wish first to settle my position with you."

"Your position has not changed to my knowledge. You are an envoy of rebels."

"Oh, you recognise it now?"

"I always did so."

"Why did you make me a prisoner, then?"

"You are shifting the question. I explained to you a moment ago, for what reason I was, to my great regret, compelled to defer our interview till a more favourable moment, that is all."

"Very good, I am willing to admit it. Be kind enough, General, to read this letter," he added, as he drew from his pocket a large envelope, which, at a sign from the General, he handed to him.

Night had fallen some time before, and two soldiers brought up torches of acote-wood, which one of the aides-de-camp lit. The General opened the letter and read it attentively, by the ruddy light of the torches. When he had finished reading, he folded up the letter again pensively, and thrust it into the breast of his uniform. There was a moment's silence, which the General at last broke.

"Who is the man who gave you this letter?"

"Did you not read his signature?"

"He may have employed a go-between."

"With me, that is not necessary."

"Then, he is here?"

"I have not to tell you who sent me, but merely discuss with you the proposals contained in the letter."

The General gave a passionate start.

"Reply, Señor, to the questions I do you the honour of asking you," he said, "if you do not wish to have reasons for repenting."

"What is the use of threatening me, General? You will learn nothing from me," he answered firmly.

"As it is so, listen to me attentively, and carefully weigh your answer, before opening your mouth to give it."

"Speak, General."

"This moment,—you understand, this moment, Señor, you will confess to me, where the man is who gave you this letter, if not—"

"Well?" the American nominally interrupted.

"Within ten minutes you will be hanging from a branch of that tree, close to you."

Davis gave him a disdainful glance.

"On my soul," he said ironically, "you Mexicans have a strange way of treating envoys."

"I do not recognise the right of a scoundrel, who is outlawed for his crimes, and whose head is justly forfeited, to send me envoys, and treat with me on an equal footing."

"The man whom you seek in vain to brand, General, is a man of heart, as you know better than anybody else. But gratitude is as offensive to you as it is to all haughty minds, and you cannot forgive the person to whom we allude, for having saved, not only your life, but also your honour."

John Davis might have gone on speaking much longer, for the General, who was as pale as a corpse, and whose features were contracted by a terrible emotion he sought in vain to master, seemed incapable of uttering a syllable. Colonel Melendez had quietly approached the circle. For some minutes he had listened to the words the speakers interchanged, with gradually augmenting passion; judging it necessary, therefore, to interpose ere matters had reached such a point as rendered any hope of conciliation impossible, he said to John Davis, as he laid his hand on his shoulder:

"Silence! You are under the lion's claw, take care that it does not rend you."

"Under the tiger's claw you mean, Colonel Melendez," he exclaimed, with much animation. "What! Shall I listen calmly to an insult offered the noblest heart, the greatest man, the most devoted and sincere patriot, and not attempt to defend him and confound his calumniator? Come, Colonel, that would be cowardice, and you know me well enough to feel assured that no consideration of personal safety would force me to do so."

"Enough," the General interrupted him, in a loud voice, "that man is right; under the influence of painful reminiscences I uttered words that I sincerely regret. I should wish them forgotten."

John Davis bowed courteously.

"General," he said, respectfully, "I thank you for this retraction; I expected nothing less from your sense of honour."

The General made no answer; he walked rapidly up and down, suffering from a violent agitation.

The officers, astonished at this strange scene, which they did not at all understand, looked restlessly at each other, though not venturing to express their surprise otherwise. The General walked up to John Davis and stopped in front of him.

"Master Davis," he said to him, in a harsh and snapping voice, "you are a stout-hearted and rough-spoken man. Enough of this; return to the man who sent you, and tell him this: 'General Don José Maria Rubio will not consent to enter into any relations with you; he hates you personally, and only wishes to meet you sword in hand. No political question will be discussed between you and him until you have consented to give him the satisfaction he demands.' Engrave these words well in your memory, Señor, in order to repeat them exactly to the said person."

"I will repeat them exactly."

"Very good. Now, begone, we have nothing more to say to each other. Colonel Melendez, be good enough to give this Caballero a horse, and accompany him to the outposts."

"One word more, General."

"Speak."

"In what way shall I bring you the person's answer?"

"Bring it yourself, if you are not afraid to enter my camp a second time."

"You are well aware that I fear nothing, General. I will bring you the answer."

"I wish it; good-bye."

"Farewell," the American answered.

And bowing to the company, he withdrew, accompanied by the Colonel.

"You played a dangerous game," the latter said, when they had gone a few steps; "the General might very easily have had you hung."

The American shrugged his shoulders.

"He would not have dared," he said, disdainfully.

"Oh, oh! and why not, if you please?"

"How does that concern you, Colonel; am I not free?"

"You are."

"That must be sufficient for you, and prove to you that I am not mistaken."

The Colonel led the American to his quarters, and asked him to walk in for a moment, while a horse was being got ready.

"Master Davis," he said to him, "be good enough to select from those weapons, whose excellence I guarantee, such as best suit you."

"Why so?" he remarked.

"Confound it! you are going to travel by night; you do not know whom you may meet. I fancy that under such circumstances it is prudent to take certain precautions."

The two men exchanged a glance; they understood each other.

"That is true," the American said, carelessly; "now that I come to think of it, the roads are not safe. As you permit me, I will take these pistols, this rifle, machete, and knife."

"As you please, but pray take some ammunition as well; without that your firearms would be of no service."

"By Jove! Colonel, you think of everything, you are really an excellent fellow," he added, while carelessly loading his rifle and pistols, and fastening to his belt a powder flask and bullet pouch.

"You overwhelm me, Master Davis; I am only doing now what you would do in my place."

"Agreed. But you display a graciousness which confuses me."

"A truce, if you please, to further compliments. Here is your horse, which my assistant is bringing up."

"But he is leading a second; do you intend to accompany me beyond the advanced posts?"

"Oh, only for a few yards, if my company does not seem to you too wearisome."

"Oh, Colonel, I shall always be delighted to have you for a companion."

All these remarks were made with an accent Of excessive courtesy, in which, however, could be traced an almost imperceptible tinge of fun and biting raillery. The two men left the house and mounted their horses. The night was limpid and clear; millions of stars sparkled in the sky, which seemed studded with diamonds; the moon spread afar its white and fantastic light; the mysterious night breeze bowed the tufted crests of the trees, and softly rippled the silvery waters of the Rio Trinidad, as they died away amorously on the bank.

The two men walked side by side, passing without being challenged by the sentinels, who, at a signal from the Colonel, respectfully stepped back. They soon descended the hill, passed the main guard, and found themselves in the open country. Each of them yielded to the voluptuous calmness of nature, and seemed no longer to be thinking of his comrade. They proceeded thus for more than an hour, and reached a spot where two paths, in crossing, formed a species of fork, in the centre of which stood a cross of evil omen, probably erected in memory of a murder formerly committed at this solitary spot.

As if by common accord, the two horses stopped and thrust out their heads, while laying back their ears and snorting loudly. Suddenly aroused from their reveries and recalled to actual life, the two riders drew themselves up in the saddle, and bent a scrutinising glance around. No human sound disturbed the silence; all around was calm and deserted as in the first days of creation.

"Do you intend, my dear Colonel," the American asked, "to honour me with your charming society any longer?"

"No," the young man answered, bluntly; "I shall stop here."

"Ah!" John Davis continued, with feigned disappointment, "shall we part already?"

"Oh no," the Colonel answered, "not yet."

"In spite of the extreme pleasure I should feel in remaining longer in your company, I am obliged to continue my journey."

"Oh, you will surely grant me a few moments, Master Davis?" the other said, with an emphasis on each syllable.

"Well, a few moments, but no more; for I have a long distance to go, and whatever pleasure I feel in conversing with you—"

"You alone," the Colonel interrupted him, "shall decide the time we shall remain together."

"It is impossible to display greater courtesy."

"Master Davis," the Colonel said, raising his voice, "have you forgotten the last conversation we had together?"

"My dear Colonel, you must know me well enough to be sure that I only forget those things which I ought not to remember."

"Which means?"

"That I perfectly well remember the conversation to which you allude."

"All the better. In that case your excellent memory spares me half the trouble, and we shall soon come to an understanding."

"I believe so."

"Do you not find the spot where we are admirably adapted for what we have to do?"

"I consider it delicious, my dear Colonel."

"Then, with your consent, we will dismount?"

"At your orders; there is nothing I detest so much as a lengthened conversation on horseback."

They leaped to the ground and tied up their horses.

"Do you take your rifle?" the American inquired.

"Yes, if you have no objection."

"Not at all. Then we are going to see some sport?"

"Oh yes, but on this occasion the game will be human."

"Which will add greatly to the interest of the sport."

"Come, you are a delightful comrade, Master Davis."

"What would you, Colonel? I never was able to refuse my friends anything."

"Where shall we place ourselves?"

"I trust to you entirely for that."

"Look! On each side the road are bushes, which seem to have grown for the express purpose."

"That is really singular. Well, we will each hide behind one of the bushes, count ten, and then fire."

"First-rate; but suppose we miss? I am perfectly well aware that we are both first-rate marksmen, and that is almost impossible; but it might happen."

"In that case nothing is more simple: we will draw our machetes and charge each other."

"Agreed. Stay, one word more; one of us must remain on the ground, I suppose?"

"I should think so. If not, what would be the use of fighting?"

"That is true; so promise me one thing."

"What is it?"

"The survivor will throw the body into the river."

"Hum! Then you are very desirous that I should not come to life again?"

"Well, you can understand—"

"All right, that is agreed."

"Thank you."

The two men bowed, and then went off in opposite directions, to take up their stations. The distance between them was about seventy yards; in a few seconds a double detonation burst forth like a clap of thunder, and woke up the echoes. The two adversaries then rushed on each other, machete in hand. They met nearly half way, and not uttering a word, attacked each other furiously.

The combat lasted a long time, and threatened to continue longer, without any marked advantage for either of the champions, for they were nearly of equal strength, when all at once several men appeared, and, aiming at the two adversaries, ordered them to lay down their arms immediately. Each fell back a step, and waited.

"Stop!" the man shouted, who seemed to be the Chief of the newcomers; "do you, John Davis, mount your horse and be off!"

"By what right do you give me that order?" the American asked, savagely.

"By the right of the stronger," the leader replied. "Be off, if you do not wish a misfortune to happen to you!"

John Davis looked around him. Any resistance was impossible— for what could he have done alone, merely armed with a sabre, against twenty individuals? The American stifled an oath, and mounted again, but suddenly reflecting, he asked, "And who may you be, who thus pretend to dictate to me?"

"You wish to know?"

"Yes."

"Well, I am a man to whom you and Colonel Melendez offered an atrocious insult. I am the Monk Antonio!"

At this name the two adversaries felt a thrill of terror run through their veins; without doubt the monk was about to avenge himself, now that in his turn he had them in his power.

CHAPTER V
BEFORE THE BATTLE

John Davis recovered almost immediately.

"Ah, ah!" he said, "Then it is you, my master?"

"It astonishes you to meet me here."

"On my honour, no. Your place, in my opinion, is wherever a snare is laid; hence nothing is more natural than your presence."

"It is wrong, John Davis, for a man to take advantage of his weakness to insult people, especially when he is ignorant of their intentions."

"Ah, they appear to me tolerably clear at this moment."

"You might be mistaken."

"I do not believe it. However, I shall soon be certain."

"What are you doing?"

"As you see, I am dismounting."

In fact, the American leapt from his horse, drew his pistols from the holsters, and walked toward the monk with a most quiet step and thoroughly natural air.

"Why do you not go, as I advised you to do?" Fray Antonio continued.

"For two reasons, my dear Señor. The first is, that I have no orders or advice to receive from you; the second, because I shall not be sorry to be present at the pretty little act of scoundrelism you are of course meditating."

"Then your intention is—"

"To defend my friend, by Heaven!" the American exclaimed, warmly.

"What! your friend?" the monk said, in amazement: "why, only a minute ago you were trying to take his life."

"My dear Señor," Davis remarked, ironically, "there are certain remarks whose sense you unhappily never catch. Understand me clearly: I am ready to kill this gentleman, but I will not consent to see him assassinated. That is clear enough, hang it all!"

Fray Antonio burst into a laugh.

"Singular man!" he said.

"Am I not?" Then turning to his adversary, who still stood perfectly quiet, he continued: "My dear Colonel, we will resume, at a later date, the interesting interview which this worthy Padre so untowardly interrupted. For the present, permit me to restore you one of the pistols you so generously lent me; it is undoubted that these scamps will kill us; but, at any rate, we shall have the pleasure of settling three or four of them first."

"Thank you, Davis," the Colonel answered, "I expected nothing less from you. I accept your proposition as frankly as you make it."

And he took the pistol, and cocked it. The American took his place by his side, and bowed to the stranger with mocking courtesy.

"Señores," he said, "you can charge us whenever you think proper, for we are prepared to sustain your charge bravely."

"Ah, ah!" said Fray Antonio, "Then you really mean it?"

"What!—mean it? The question seems to me somewhat simple; I suppose you think the hour and place well chosen for a joke?"

The monk shrugged his shoulders, and turned to the men who accompanied him.

"Be off!" he said. "In an hour I will join you again, you know where."

The strangers gave a nod of assent, and disappeared almost instantaneously among the trees and shrubs. The monk then threw his weapons on the ground, and drew so near to the men as almost to touch them.

"Are you still afraid?" he said; "It is I now who am in your power."

"Halloh!" Davis said, as he uncocked his pistol, "why, what is the meaning of this?"

"If, instead of taking me as a bandit, as you did, you had taken the trouble to reflect, you would have understood that I had but one object, and that was, to prevent the resumption of the obstinate fight which my presence so fortunately interrupted."

"But how did you arrive here so opportunely?"

"Accident did it all. Ordered by our Commander-in-chief to watch the enemy's movements, I posted myself on the two roads, in order to take prisoner all the scouts who came in this direction."

"Then you do not owe either the Colonel or myself any grudge?"

"Perhaps," he said, with hesitation, "I have not quite forgotten the unworthy treatment you inflicted on me; but, at any rate, I have given up all thoughts of vengeance."

John Davis reflected for a moment, and then said, as he offered him his hand, "You are a worthy monk. I see that you are faithful to the pledge of amendment you made. I am sorry for what I did."

"I will say the same, Señor," the Colonel remarked; "I was far from expecting such generosity on your part."

"One word, now, Señores."

"Speak," they said, "we are listening."

"Promise me not to renew that impious duel, and follow my example by forgetting your hatred."

The two men stretched out their hand with a simultaneous movement.

"That is well," he continued, "I am happy to see you act thus. Now let us separate. You, Colonel, will mount and return to camp—the road is free, and no one will try to oppose your passing. As for you, John Davis, please to follow me. Your long absence has caused a degree of alarm which your presence will doubtless dissipate. I had orders to try and obtain news of you."

"Good-bye for the present," the Colonel said; "forget, Señor Davis, what passed between us at the outset of our meeting, and merely remember the manner in which we separate."

"May we, Colonel, meet again under happier auspices, when I may be permitted to express to you all the sympathy with which your frank and loyal character inspires me."

After exchanging a few words more, and cordially shaking hands, the three men separated. Colonel Melendez set off at a gallop in the direction of the rancho, while the monk and Davis started at an equal pace in exactly the opposite direction. It was about midnight when the Colonel reached the main guard, where an aide-de-camp of the General was waiting for him. A certain degree of animation appeared to prevail in the rancho. Instead of sleeping, as they might be expected to be doing at so late an hour, the soldiers were traversing the streets in large numbers; in short, an extreme agitation was visible everywhere.

"What is the matter?" the Colonel asked the aide-de-camp.

"The General will tell you himself," the officer answered, "for he is impatiently expecting you, and has already asked several times for you."

"Oh, then, there is something new."

"I believe so."

The Colonel pushed on ahead, and in a few minutes found himself before the house occupied by the General. The house was full of noise and light; but so soon as the General perceived the young man, he left the officers with whom he was talking, and walked quickly toward him.

"Here you are at last," he said; "I was impatiently expecting you."

"What is the matter then?" the Colonel asked, astounded at this reception, which he was far from expecting, for he had left the camp so quiet, and found it on his return so noisy.

"You shall know, Señores," the General added addressing the officers in the room: "be kind enough not to go away. I shall be with you in an instant. Follow me, Colonel."

Don Juan bowed, and passed into an adjoining room, the door of which the General shut after him. Hardly were they alone, ere the General took the young man affectionately by one of his coat buttons, and fixed on him a glance that seemed trying to read the depths of his heart.

"Since your departure," he said, "we have had a visit from a friend of yours."

"A friend of mine?" the young man repeated.

"Or, at any rate, of a man who gives himself out as such."

"I only know one man in this country," the Colonel replied distinctly, "who, despite the opinions that divide us, can justly assume that title."

"And that man is?"

"The Jaguar."

"Do you feel a friendship for him?"

"Yes."

"But he is a bandit."

"Possibly he is so to you, General; from your point of sight, it is possible that you are right. I neither descry his character, nor condemn him; I am attached to him, for he saved my life."

"But you fight against him, for all that."

"Certainly; for being hurled into two opponent camps, each of us serves the cause that appears to him the better. But, for all that, we are not the less attached to each other in our hearts."

"I am not at all disposed to blame you, my friend, for our inclinations should be independent of our political opinions. But let us return to the subject which at this moment is the most interesting to us. A man, I say, presented himself during your absence at the outposts as being a friend of yours."

"That is strange," the Colonel muttered, searching his memory; "and did he mention his name?"

"Of course; do you think I would have received him else? However, he is in this very house, for I begged him to await your return."

"But his name, my dear General?"

"He calls himself Don Felix Paz."

"Oh," the Colonel exclaimed eagerly, "he spoke the truth, General, for he is really one of my dearest friends."

"Then we can place in him — —"

"Full and entire confidence; I answer for him on my head," the young officer interrupted warmly.

"I am the more pleased at what you tell me, because this man assured me that he held in his hands means that would enable us to give the rebels a tremendous thrashing."

"If he has promised it, General, he will do so without doubt. I presume you have had a serious conversation with him?"

"Not at all. You understand, my friend, that I was not willing, till I had previously conversed with you, to listen to this man, who after all might have been a spy of the enemy."

"Capital reasoning; and what do you propose doing now?"

"Hearing him; he told me enough for me, in the prevision of what is happening at this moment, to have everything prepared for action at a moment's notice; hence no time will have been lost."

"Very good! We will listen to him then."

The General clapped his hands, and an aide-de-camp came in.

"Request Don Felix to come hither, Captain."

Five minutes later, the ex-Major-domo of the Larch-tree hacienda entered the room where the two officers were.

"Forgive me, Caballero," the General said courteously as he advanced to meet him, "for the rather cold manner in which I received you; but unfortunately we live in a period when it is so difficult to distinguish friends from enemies, that a man involuntarily runs the risk of confounding one with the other, and making a mistake."

"You have no occasion to apologise to me, General," Don Felix answered; "when I presented myself at your outposts in the way I did, I anticipated what would happen to me."

The Colonel pressed his friend's hand warmly. A lengthened explanation was unnecessary for men of this stamp; at the first word they understood each other. They had a lengthened conversation, which did not terminate till a late hour of the night, or rather an early hour of the morning, for it struck four at the moment when the General opened the door of the room in which they were shut up, and accompanied them, conversing in whispers, to the *saguan* of the house.

What had occurred during this lengthened interview? No one knew; not a syllable transpired as to the arrangements made by the General with the two men who had remained so long with him. The officers and soldiers were suffering from the most lively curiosity, which was only increased by the General's orders to raise the camp.

Don Felix was conducted by the Colonel to the outermost post, where they separated after shaking hands and exchanging only one sentence—

"We shall meet again soon."

The Colonel then returned at a gallop to his quarters, while Don Felix buried himself in the forest as rapidly as his horse could carry him. On returning to camp, the Colonel at once ordered the boot and saddle to be sounded, and without waiting for further orders, put himself at the head of about five hundred cavalry, and left the rancho.

It was nearly five in the morning, the sun was rising in floods of purple and gold, and all seemed to promise a magnificent day. The General, who had mounted to his observatory, attentively followed with a telescope the movements of the Colonel, who, through the speed at which he went, not only got down the hill within a quarter of an hour, but had also crossed, without obstacle, a stream as wide as the Rio Trinidad itself. The General anxiously watched this operation, which is so awkward for an armed body of men; he saw the soldiers close up, and then, at a sign from the leader, this column stretched out like a serpent undoing its rings, went into the water, and cutting the rather strong current diagonally, reached the other bank in a few minutes, when, after a moment of inevitable tumult, the men formed their ranks again and entered a forest, where they were speedily lost from sight.

When the last lancero had disappeared, and the landscape had become quite desolate, the General shut up his glass, and went down again, apparently plunged in serious thought. We have said that the garrison of Galveston consisted of nine hundred men; but this strength had been raised to nearly fourteen hundred by calling in the numerous small posts scattered along the coast. Colonel Melendez had taken with him five hundred sabres the General left at the rancho, which he determined on retaining at all hazards as an important strategical point, two hundred and fifty men under the orders of a brave and experienced officer; and he had at his disposal about six hundred and fifty men, supported by a battery of four mountain howitzers.

This force, small as it may appear, in spite of the smile of contempt it will doubtless produce on the lips of Europeans accustomed to the shock of great masses, was more than sufficient for the country. It is true that the Texan army counted nearly four thousand combatants, but the majority of these men were badly-armed peasants, unskilled in the management of the warlike weapons which a movement of revolutionary fanaticism had caused them to take up, and incapable of sustaining in the open field the attack of skilled troops. Hence, in spite of his numerical inferiority, he reckoned greatly on the discipline and military education of his soldiers, to defeat this assemblage of men, who were more dangerous through their numbers than for any other reason.

The start from the rancho was effected with admirable regularity; the General had ordered that the baggage should be left behind, so that nothing might impede the march of the army. Each horseman, in accordance with the American fashion, which is too greatly despised in Europe, took up a foot soldier behind him, so that the speed of the army was doubled. Numerous spies and scouts sent out to reconnoitre in every direction, had announced that the Insurrectionary army, marching in two columns, was advancing to seize the mouth of the Trinidad and cover the approaches to Galveston, a movement which it was of the utmost importance to prevent; for, were it successful, the Insurgents would combine the movements of the vessels they had so advantageously seized with those of their army, and would be masters of a considerable extent of the seaboard, from which possibly the Mexican forces would not be strong enough to dislodge them. On the other hand, General Rubio had been advised that Santa Anna, President of the Republic, had left Mexico, and was coming with forced marches, at the head of twelve hundred men, to forcibly crush the Insurrection.

General Santa Anna has been very variously judged; some make him a profound politician and a thunderbolt of war; and he seems to have that opinion about himself, as he does not hesitate to say that he is the Napoleon of the New World; his enemies reproach him for his turbulence and his unbounded ambition; accuse him of too often keeping aloof from danger, and consider him an agitator without valour or morality. For our part, without attempting to form any judgment of this statesman, we will merely say in two words, that we are convinced he is the scourge of Mexico, whose ruin he accelerates, and one of the causes of the misfortunes which have for twenty years overwhelmed that ill-fated country.

General Rubio understood how important it was for him to deal a heavy blow before his junction with the President, who, while following his advice, would not fail, in the event of defeat, to attribute the reverses to him, while, if the Mexicans remained masters of the field, he would keep all the honour of victory to himself.

The Texan insurgents had not up to this moment dared to measure themselves with the Mexican troops in the open field, but the events that had succeeded each other during the last few days with lightning speed, had, by accelerating the catastrophe, completely changed the aspect of affairs. The Chiefs of the revolutionary army, rendered confident by their constant advantages, and masters without a blow of one of the principal Texan seaports, felt the necessity of giving up their hedge warfare, and consolidating their success by some brilliant exploit.

To attain this end, a battle must be gained; but the Texan Chiefs did not let themselves be deceived by the successes they had hitherto met with, successes obtained by rash strokes, surprises, and unexampled audacity; they feared with reason the moment when they would have to face the veteran Mexican troops with their inexperienced guerillas. Hence they sought by every means to retard the hour for this supreme and decisive contest, in which a few hours might eternally overthrow their dearest hopes, and the work of regeneration they had been pursuing for the last ten years with unparalleled courage and resignation. They desired, before definitively fighting the regulars, that their volunteers should have acquired that discipline and practice without which the largest and bravest army is only an heterogeneous compound of opposing elements, an agglomeration of men, possessing no consistency or real vitality.

After the capture of the fort a grand council had been held by the principal Texan Chiefs, in order to consult on the measures to be taken, so as not to lose, by any imprudence, results so miraculously obtained. It was then resolved that the army should occupy Galveston, which its position rendered perfectly secure against a surprise; that the freebooters should alone remain out to skirmish with the Mexicans and harass them; while the troops shut up in the town were being drilled, and receiving a regular and permanent organization.

The first care of the Chiefs, therefore, was to avoid any encounter with the enemy, and try to enter Galveston without fighting the Mexicans. The following was the respective position of the two armies; the Texans were trying to avoid a battle, which General Rubio was lodging, on the contrary, to fight. The terrain on which the adversaries would have to manoeuvre was extremely limited, for scarce four leagues separated the videttes of the two armies. From his observatory the General could clearly distinguish the camp fires of the rebels.

In the meanwhile Colonel Melendez had continued to advance; on reaching the cross where he and John Davis had fought so furiously on the previous evening, the Colonel himself examined the ground with the utmost care, then, feeling convinced that none of the enemy's flankers had remained ambushed at this spot, which was so favourable for a surprise, he gave his men orders to dismount. The horses were thrown down, secured, and their heads wrapped in thick blankets to prevent their neighing, and after all these precautions had been taken, the soldiers lay down on their stomachs among the shrubs, with instructions not to stir.

General Rubio had himself effected a flank march, which enabled him to avoid the crossways; immediately after descending the hill, he marched rapidly upon the river bank. We have said that the Rio Trinidad, which is rather confined at certain spots, is bordered by magnificent forests, whose branches form on the bank grand arcades of foliage overhanging the mangroves; it was among the latter, and on the branches of the forest trees, about two gunshots from the spot where he had landed, that the General ambuscaded about one-third of his infantry. The remainder, divided into two corps, were echeloned along either side of the road the Insurgents must follow, but it was done in the American fashion, that is to say, the men were so hidden in the tall grass that they were invisible.

The four mountain howitzers crowned a small hill which, through its position, completely commanded the road, while the cavalry was massed in the rear of the infantry. The silence momentarily disturbed was re-established, and the desert resumed its calm and solitary aspect. General Rubio had taken his measures so well that his army had suddenly become invisible.

When it was resolved in the council of the Texan Chiefs that the Insurrectionary army should proceed to Galveston, a rather sharp discussion took place as to the means to be adopted in reaching it. The Jaguar proposed to embark the troops aboard the corvette, the brig, and a few smaller vessels collected for the purpose. Unfortunately this advice, excellent though it was, could not be followed, owing to General Rubio's precaution of carrying off all the boats; collecting others would have occasioned an extreme loss of time; but as the boats the Mexicans had employed were now lying high and dry on the beach, and the guard at first put over them withdrawn a few hours later, the Texans thought it far more simple to set them afloat, and use them in their turn to effect the passage.

By a species of fatality the council would not put faith in the assertions of John Davis, who in vain assured them that General Rubio, entrenched in a strong position, would not allow this movement to be carried out without an attempt to prevent it; so that the abandonment of the boats by the Mexicans was only fictitious, and a trap adroitly laid to draw the Revolutionists to a spot where it would be easy to conquer them.

Unfortunately, the mysterious man to whom we have alluded had alone the right to give orders, and the reasons urged by Davis could not convince him. Deceived by his spies, he persuaded himself that General Rubio, far from having any intention of recapturing Galveston, wished to effect his junction with Santa Anna before attempting any fresh offensive movement, and that the halt at the rancho had been merely a feint to embarrass the rebels.

This incomprehensible error was the cause of incalculable disasters. The chiefs received orders to march forward, and were constrained to carry them out. Still, when this erroneous resolution had been once formed, the means of execution were selected with extreme prudence. The corvette and brig were ordered to get as near land as they could, in order to protect, by their cross fire, the embarkation of the troops, and sweep the Mexicans, if they offered any opposition. Flying columns were sent off in advance and on the flanks of the army, to clear the way, by making prisoners of any small outposts the enemy might have established.

Four principal chiefs commanded strong detachments of mounted freebooters. The four were the Jaguar, Fray Antonio, El Alferez, and Don Felix Paz, whom the reader assuredly did not expect to find under the flag of the rebels, and whom he saw only a few hours back enter the Mexican camp, and hold a secret conference with General Rubio and Colonel Melendez. These four chiefs were ordered by the Commander-in-Chief to prevent any surprise, by searching the forests and examining the tall grass. El Alferez was on the right of the army, Fray Antonio on the left, the Jaguar had the rear guard, while Don Felix, with six hundred sabres, formed the van. One word as to the guerillas of the ex-Mayor-domo of the Larch-tree hacienda. The men who composed his band, raised on lands dependent on the hacienda, had been enlisted by Don Felix. They were Indios *mansos*, vaqueros, and peons, mostly half savages, and rogues to a certain extent, who fought like lions at the order of their leader, to whom they were thoroughly devoted, but only recognising and obeying him, while caring nothing for the other leaders of the army. Don Felix Paz had joined the insurgents about two months previously, and rendered them eminent service with his guerillas. Hence, he had in a short time gained general confidence. We shall soon see whether he was worthy of it.

By a singular coincidence, the two armies left their camp at the same time, and marched one against the other, little suspecting that two hours later they would be face to face.

CHAPTER VI
THE BATTLE OF CERRO PARDO

The battle of Cerro Pardo was one of those sanguinary days, whose memory a nation retains for ages as an ill-omened date. In order to explain to the reader thoroughly how the events happened which we are about to narrate, we must give a detailed account of the ground on which they took place.

The spot selected by the Mexicans to effect their landing after leaving Galveston, had been very cleverly chosen by General Rubio. The stream, which, for some distance, is enclosed by high banks, runs at that spot through an extensive plain, covered with tall grass and clumps of trees, the last relics of a virgin forest, which the claims of trade have almost destroyed. This plain is closed by a species of *cañón*, or very narrow gorge, enclosed between two lofty Mils, whose scarped flanks are carpeted at all seasons with plants and flowers. These two hills are the Cerro Pardo and the Cerro Prieto, — that is to say, the Red Mountain and the Black Mountain.

At the canyon begins a road, or, to speak more correctly, a rather wide track, bordered by bogs and morasses, and running to the cross we have before visited. This road is the only one that can be followed in going from the interior to the seashore. A little in advance of the two hills, whose summit is covered with dense wood and scrub, extend marshes, which are the more dangerous, because their surface is perfidiously covered with close green grass, which completely conceals from the traveller the terrible danger to which he is exposed if he venture on to this moving abyss. The Cerro Pardo, which is much higher than the other hill, not only commands the latter, but also the surrounding country, as well as the sea.

After what we have said, the reader will easily perceive that the enterprise attempted by the Texans was only possible in the event of the coast being entirely undefended; but under the present circumstances, the inconceivable obstinacy of the Commander-in-Chief was the more incomprehensible, because he was not only thoroughly acquainted with the country, but at the moment when the army was about to begin its forward movements, several spies came in in succession, bringing news which entirely coincided with the positive reports already made by John Davis.

Whom the gods wish to destroy, they first blind. This wise and thoughtful man, who had ever acted with extreme prudence, and whose conceptions up to this day had been remarkable for their lucidity, was deaf to all remonstrances, and the order was given to march. The army at once set out; Don Felix Paz went on ahead with his guerillas, while the Jaguar's cuadrilla, on the contrary, remained in the rear. Tranquil, in spite of the wounds he had received, would not remain in the fort; he came along lying in a cart, having at his side Carmela and Quoniam, who paid him the utmost attention; while Lanzi, at the head of a dozen picked Freebooters given him by the Jaguar, escorted the cart, in the event of the army being disturbed during the march.

The Jaguar was sorrowful, a gloomy presentiment seemed to warn him of a misfortune. This daring man, who carried out as if in sport the maddest and most venturesome deeds, now advanced reluctantly, hesitating and constantly looking about him suspiciously, and almost timidly. Assuredly, he feared no personal danger; what did he care for an attack? What alarm did he feel about dying? Peril was his element; the heated atmosphere of battle, the odour of powder intoxicated him, and made him feel strange delight; but at this moment Carmela was near him; Carmela, whom he had so miraculously found again, and whom he feared to lose again. This strong man felt his heart soften at the thought, hence he insisted on taking the rear guard, in order to watch more closely over the maiden, and be in a position to help her if necessary.

The superior Commander had not dared to refuse the bold partisan this post, which he asked for as a favour. This condescension on the part of the Chief had terrible consequences, and was partly the cause of the events that happened a few hours later.

The Texan troops, in spite of the various element of which they were composed, advanced, however, with an order and discipline that would have done honour to regulars. Don Felix Paz had thrown out to the right and left of the road flankers ordered to investigate the chaparral, and guarantee the safety of the route; but in spite of these precautions, whether the Mexicans were really ambushed in inaccessible places, or for some other reason, the flankers did not discover them, and the vanguard advanced at a pace which heightened the security of the main body, and gradually induced the Chiefs to relax their previous watchfulness.

The vanguard reached the cross, and nothing had as yet happened in any way to trouble the march of the army. Don Felix, after allowing his cuadrilla to halt for twenty minutes, resolutely entered the road that led to the spot where the Mexicans had landed. From the cross to the Rio Trinidad was no great distance, and could be covered in less than two hours by troops marching at the ordinary pace. The road, however, after passing the cross, insensibly becomes narrower, and soon changes into a very confined track, in which three persons can scarce walk abreast.

We have said that trembling prairies extend on either side of this road. We will explain, in a few sentences, what these trembling prairies are, which are met with in several parts of America, but principally in Texas and Louisiana. These prairies, if we may trust to the frequently false theories of science, have a similar organ to that of Artesian springs, for the earth does in one case what water does in the other. Through the action of geological dynamics, the earthy matter which constitutes the trembling prairies ascends to the surface of lakes and ponds, while in Artesian wells the water rushes up from the depths through the pressure of the strata by which it was held down.

Nothing is more dangerous than those trembling prairies, covered with a perfidious vegetation that deceives the eye. The Rio Trinidad flows at a few hundred yards from the prairie we have just described, conveying into the Gulf of Mexico the sedimentary deposits which would consolidate this shifting soil. Nature has already traced canals intersecting the prairie, and which run between banks formed by mysterious forces. The wild beasts, whose admirable instinct never deceives them, have for ages past formed tracks across these dangerous zones, and the path followed by the Texan army was no other than one of those trails trodden by the wild beasts when they go down at night to water.

I know not whether, since Texas has gained its liberty and been incorporated with the United States, any attempt has been made to drain these prairies. And yet, I believe that it would require but a very slight effort to complete the work so intelligently sketched out by nature. It would be sufficient to dig a series of *colmates*, or aqueducts, which would introduce into the trembling prairie the turbid waters of the river, and convey to it the sedimentary matter; and, before all, the vegetation growing on the prairie should not be burnt, as is the unfortunate custom. With these two conditions, a firm, rich, and fertile soil would soon be attained in the line of these slimy and pestilential marshes that poison the air, produce contagious diseases, and cause the death of so many unfortunate travellers, deceived by the luxuriant appearance of these prairies, and who perish miserably, by being swallowed up in their fetid mud.

But in America it is not so much land that is wanting as men. Probably, the trembling prairies will remain for a long time what they are at the present day, for no one has a really personal interest in draining and getting rid of them.

We will now take up our story at the point where we broke it off, begging the reader to forgive us the long digression in which we indulged, but which has its value, we think, in a work intended to make known a country which is destined ere long to assume an important part in the trade of the world.

The Texan Vanguard passed the cross at about nine A.M. It had halted for about twenty minutes and then resumed its march. Still, without any apparent motive, after crossing without obstacle the defile of the Cerro Pardo, instead of advancing in the direction of the river, on the bank of which the stranded boats could already be seen, Don Felix ordered his cuadrilla to wheel at about two hundred yards from the defile, and formed a front of fifty horses by ten deep. After commanding a halt, he dug his spurs in and returned to the gorge, but on this occasion alone.

While galloping, the partisan looked searchingly around him. As far as the eye could see, the road was entirely deserted. Don Felix halted and bent over his horse's neck, as if wishing to arrange some buckle, but while patting his noble animal he twice repeated the croak of a rook. At once the harsh cry of the puffin rose from the bushes that bordered the right hand side of the road; the branches were then parted—a man appeared—it was Colonel Don Juan Melendez de Gongora. Don Felix did not appear at all surprised at seeing him; on the contrary, he advanced hurriedly towards him.

"Return to your ambush, Colonel," he said, "you know that there is an eye in every leaf. If I am seen alone on the road my presence will arouse no suspicions; but you, Cuerpo de Cristo! You must not be seen. We can converse equally well at a distance, as the ears able to overhear us are those of friends."

"You are always prudent, Don Felix."

"I, not at all; I merely wish to avenge myself on those bandits who have plundered so many magnificent haciendas, and hatred renders a man prudent."

"Whatever be the motive that impels you, it gives you good inspirations, that is the main point. But let us return to our business: what do you want with me?"

"Merely to know two things."

"What are they?"

"Whether General Rubio is really satisfied with the plan I submitted to him?"

"You have a proof of it before you; if he were not so, should I be here?"

"That is true."

"Now for the second."

"That is of an extremely delicate nature."

"Ah, ah! You pique my curiosity," the Colonel said, laughingly.

Don Felix frowned and lowered his voice, as it were involuntarily.

"It is very serious, Don Juan," he continued; "I wish, before the battle, to know if you have retained towards me that esteem and friendship with which you deigned to honour me at the Larch-tree hacienda?"

The Colonel turned away in embarrassment.

"Why ask that question at this moment?" he remarked.

Don Felix turned pale and fixed a flashing glance upon him.

"Answer me, I implore yon, Don Juan," he said, pressingly. "Whatever you may think, whatever opinion you may have of me, I wish to know it; it must be so."

"Do not press me, I beg, Don Felix. What can you care for any opinion I may have, which is isolated and unimportant?"

"What can I care, do you ask?" he exclaimed, hotly; "but it is, indeed, useless to press you farther, for I know all I wish to know. Thank you, Don Juan, I ask no more. When a man of so noble a character and such a loyal heart as yours condemns the conduct of another man, it is because that conduct is really blameable."

"Well, be it so; since you absolutely insist, I will explain my views, Don Felix. Yes, I blame but do not condemn you, for I cannot and will not be your judge. Don Felix, I am internally convinced in my soul and conscience that the man who makes himself, no matter the motive that impels him, the agent of treachery, commits worse than a crime, for he is guilty of an act of cowardice! Such a man I can pity, but no longer esteem."

The ex-Mayor-domo listened to these harsh words with a forehead dripping with perspiration, but with head erect and eye sparkling with a gloomy fire. When the officer stopped he bowed coldly and took the hand which Don Juan did not attempt to draw from his grasp.

"It is well," he said; "your words are rude, but they are true. I thank you for your frankness, Don Juan; I know now what remains for me to do."

The Colonel, who had involuntarily allowed his feelings of the moment to carry him away, fancied that he had gone too far, and was alarmed at the consequences of his imprudence.

"Don Felix," he added, "forgive me; I spoke to you like a madman."

"Come, come, Don Juan," he replied, with a bitter smile, "do not attempt to recall your words, you were but the echo of my conscience; what you have said aloud my heart has often whispered to me. Fear not that I shall let myself be overcome by a passing feeling of passion. No! I am one of those men who, when they have once entered a path, persevere in it at all hazards. But enough of this; I notice a dust, which probably announces our friends," he added, with a poignant irony. "Farewell, Don Juan, farewell."

And, not waiting for the answer Don Juan was preparing to give him, Don Felix spurred his horse, turned hastily round, and went off as rapidly as he had come. The Colonel looked after him for a moment thoughtfully.

"Alas!" he muttered, "that man is now more unhappy than culpable, or I am greatly mistaken; if he be not killed today it will not be for want of seeking death."

He then buried himself again in the chaparral with a melancholy shake of his head. In the meanwhile, the Texan army rapidly advanced; like the Mexicans, each mounted man had a foot soldier behind him. At about a gunshot from the cross roads, the Texans came upon the edge of the trembling prairie; they were consequently obliged to halt in order to call in their flankers, scattered on the right and left, which naturally produced a momentary disorder, promptly repaired, however, by the activity of the chief, then they started again.

The order of march was necessarily altered, the path grew narrower at every step, and the cavalry were unable to keep their ranks any longer. However, from the moment of the start, the vanguard had not announced any danger. The army, trusting in the experience of the officer detached to clear the way, marched in perfect security, which was augmented by the hope of speedily reaching the mouth of the Rio Trinidad, and at once embarking for Galveston.

The Jaguar alone did not share the general confidence: accustomed for a long period to a war of ambushes, the ground he now trod seemed to him so suitable in every way for a surprise, that he could not persuade himself that they would reach the seashore without an attack. In a word, the young Chief had an intuition of approaching danger. He guessed it, felt it, so to speak, though he could not tell from what quarter it would come, and suddenly burst on his comrades and himself.

There is nothing so terrible as such a situation, where a man is obliged to stand on his defence against space. The desert tranquilly surrounds him on all sides, in vain does he interrogate the air and earth, to find a clue which constantly escapes him, and yet he has in his heart a certainty for which he finds it impossible to account! He can only answer questions with the enigmatical, though strictly logical phrase, "I do not know, and yet I am sure of it."

The Jaguar resolved, whatever the consequences might be, to avoid personally a surprise, whose results would be disastrous to those he had vowed to protect and defend, that is to say, to Tranquil and Carmela. Gradually slackening the pace of his detachment, he succeeded in leaving a sufficiently wide distance between himself and the main body, to regain almost entirely his liberty of action. His first care was to collect round the cart the men in whom he placed most confidence. Then selecting those of his comrades whom he supposed most conversant with Indian tricks, he placed them under the command of John Davis, with orders to force their way, as well as they could, through the chaparral that skirted both sides of the track, and enclosed it so completely, that it was impossible to see anything beyond.

It could not enter the Jaguar's mind that the Mexicans would not profit by the opportunity offered them by the imprudence of the Texans, to try and take their revenge for the defeats they had suffered. In this view he was entirely supported by Davis, who, it will be remembered, had urgently, though vainly, begged the Commander-in-Chief to give up his plan. The two men, who had been so long acquainted, understood each other at the first word, and John Davis immediately spread out his men, as a forlorn hope, on either side of the road. The Jaguar proceeded to the cart after this, and addressed the hunter.

"Well, Tranquil," he said to him, "how do you find yourself?"

"Better," the other answered; "I hope within a few days to be sufficiently recovered to give up this wearisome position."

"And your strength?"

"Is rapidly returning."

"All the better. Would you be capable of firing in your own defence, without leaving the cart?"

"I think so. But do you fear any trap? The spot where we now are, appears most favourable for it."

"Does it not! Well, you have spoken the truth, I fear an ambuscade. Here is a rifle, and if needs must, make use of it."

"Trust to me. Thanks," he added, as he clutched the weapon with a delight he did not attempt to conceal.

The Jaguar then placed himself at the head of his troop, and gave orders to set out again. Long before this, the main body of the army had passed the cross, the heads of the columns were already entering the defile, a movement which, owing to the narrowness, produced some disorder the leaders were trying to repress, when suddenly a shower of canister burst from the Cerro Pardo, and made wide gaps in the crowded ranks of the Texans. At the same instant a terrible, shout was heard from the other end of the gorge, and Don Felix Paz' cuadrilla appeared galloping at full speed toward the main body.

At the first moment the Texans had to make way for these horsemen, whom they supposed to be closely pursued by a still invisible enemy; but their surprise changed into terror and stupor when they saw this vanguard dash at them and mercilessly sabre them with shouts of "Mejico! Mejico! Federación!"

The Texans were betrayed! Suffering from a terror that almost attained to madness, unable to form in this limited spot, decimated by the canister incessantly discharged at them, and sabred by Don Felix' cuadrilla, they had but one thought—that of flight. But at the moment when they tried to turn, the terrible cry of "Mejico! Mejico! mueran los rebeldes!" resounded like a funeral knell in their rear, and Colonel Melendez, at the head of his five hundred horses, dashed at the Texans, who were thus caught between two fires.

The medley then assumed the fearful proportions of one of those mediæval butcheries in which man, having attained the paroxysm of fury, intoxicated by the sharp smell of blood, the powder, smoke, and the din of battle, kills for the sake of killing with the pleasure of a wild beast, growing excited by the massacre of every victim that falls, and far from satiating his hatred, finds it increase in proportion to the corpses piled up on the blood-stained ground.

Flight was impossible, and resistance seemed the same. At this supreme hour, when all appeared lost and the cause of liberty was about to be eternally buried under the pile of corpses, an irresistible movement suddenly took place in the terrified crowd, which opened like a ripe fruit through the bloody track thus made by main force. The Jaguar now dashed forward, splendid in his wrath and despair, brandishing his machete above his head, and followed by his brave cuadrilla. A cry of delight saluted the arrival of the daring freebooter, who had been obliged to cut his way through Colonel Melendez' Mexicans, as they vainly strove to stop his passage.

"My lads!" the Jaguar shouted, in a voice that rose above the din of battle, "We are surrounded by the enemy, and have been betrayed and led into a trap by a coward. Let us show these Mexicans, who believe us already conquered, and are congratulating themselves on their easy victory, what men like ourselves are capable of. Follow me—forward! Forward!"

"Forward!" the Texans vociferated, electrified by these daring words.

The Jaguar made his horse bound, and dashed at the side of the mountain. His military instinct had not deserted him, for that was, in fact, the key of the battle. The Texans rushed after him, brandishing their weapons and uttering yells of fury. But at this moment the troops of General Rubio made their appearance, who had hitherto remained ambushed behind the trees and bushes; they crowned the heights, lined the sides of the road, and the fight began again more terrible and obstinate than before. The efforts were useless; the Texans returned eight times to the assault of the Cerro Pardo, and eight times were driven back in disorder to the foot of the mountain, which they were unable to scale.

In vain did the Jaguar, Davis, Fray Antonio, El Alferez, and the other Chiefs perform prodigies of valour; the Mexican bullets decimated their soldiers, who at length growing discouraged, refused any longer to continue an impossible contest. The Commander-in-Chief of the army, who by his imprudence had caused this grave disaster, resolved to make a final and supreme effort. Collecting around him all the willing men who still attempted resistance, he formed them into a column of attack, and dashed like a whirlwind at the Mexican guns, the artillerymen of which were cut down without yielding an inch. Surprised by this sudden and furious charge, the Mexicans broke and abandoned the battery; this audacious attempt might change the issue of the battle. Already the Texans, who were almost masters of the plateau, were preparing to take advantage of this fortuitous and unhoped-for success; but unfortunately, the revolutionary army, nearly entirely demoralized, did not support with the necessary vigour the heroic effort of these few chosen braves; the Mexicans had time to recover from their surprise and compare their strength with that of their foes. Ashamed at the check they had suffered, they rushed upon the enemy, and after a frightful hand-to-hand fight, they succeeded in driving the Texans from the plateau at the moment when the latter formed hopes of holding it.

Colonel Melendez and Don Felix Paz had at length effected their junction; the Texans had not even the possibility of flight left them, but the Jaguar did not yet despair; still, since he could no longer conquer, he would at least save Carmela. But between her and him stood a human wall, through which he must clear a road. The young man did not hesitate;

turning like a wounded lion, he bounded into the midst of the enemy's ranks, summoning his comrades, and waving round his head the terrible machete he had employed so well during the action. A man boldly rushed to meet him with uplifted sabre.

"Ah! the traitor Don Felix!" the Jaguar shouted, on recognising him, and split his skull open.

Then he rushed like an avalanche down the mountain side, overthrowing every one he came across; and followed by a few of his most devoted companions, the ranks of the Mexicans opened to let them pass.

"Thanks, brother," the Jaguar shouted with considerable emotion to Colonel Melendez, who had given his soldiers a sign to let him pass.

The Colonel turned away and made no answer. The carnage lasted a long time yet, as the Texans would not accept quarter. Six hundred Texans fell into the hands of the victors, while eight hundred found death on the field of battle.

The same evening General Rubio re-entered Galveston at the head of his victorious army; the insurrectionists fled in terror in all directions, without hope of ever again collecting. The cause of Texan liberty seemed lost for a long time, if not for ever.

The Jaguar, on reaching the cross roads, found the cart smashed, and most of its defenders lying dead on the ground. Singular to say, they had all been scalped. Tranquil, Quoniam, Carmela, and Lanzi had disappeared. What terrible drama could have been performed at this spot?

CHAPTER VII
THE ATEPETL

Texas is intersected by two lines of continuous forests, which run from the north, near the sources of the Rio Trinidad to the Arkansas river. These forests are called the "Cross Timbers;" behind them commence the immense prairies of Apacheria, on which countless herds of buffaloes and wild horses wander about at liberty.

In the centre of a narrow valley, enclosed on three sides by the denuded and serrated crests of the mountains—and on the banks of the Rio Sabina, a little above its confluence with the Vermejo, where it still flows wide and transparent between undulating banks, bordered by clumps of cotton-wood trees and dwarf palms—an Indian village was deliciously scattered among the trees. The latter formed a dense dome of foliage over the callis, which they sheltered from the hot beams of the southern sun, and protected from the cold gusts which at times descend from the mountains in the winter season. This village was a winter atepetl of the Comanche Indians, belonging to the Antelope tribe. We will describe in a few words this village, where several important scenes connected with our narrative will take place.

Although, built to the fancy of the Redskins, the callis affected a certain regularity of construction, as they all converged on a common point, which formed a species of grand square in the heart of the village. In the centre of this square could be seen a large unhooped barrel, deeply buried in the ground, and covered with lichens and stonecrop. It was the "ark of the first man." It was here that the war stake was planted before the great medicine lodge; and here, under grave circumstances, the Sachems lit the council fire, and smoked the sacred calumet ordinarily placed before the entrance of the calli of the chief Sachem, and supported on two forked sticks, as it must never touch the ground.

The Indian callis are generally constructed in a spherical shape, built on piles covered with mud, over which buffalo hides sewn together, and displaying numerous pictures of animals painted in vermilion, are thrown. On a scaffolding standing in front of the calli, Indian corn, forage for the horses, and the winter provisions of each inhabitant were stored. At intervals could be seen tall poles, from which waved, at the slightest breath of air, blankets, harness, and fragments of stuffs of every description, the homage raised by the superstitious Redskins to the Master of Life, a species of *ex voto* torn from them by their fears, and named the "Medicine of Hope."

The village, excepting on the side turned to the Sabina river, was surrounded by a strong palisade about fifteen feet high, made of enormous trunks of trees, fastened together with strips of bark and wooden cramp hooks. At about five or, six hundred yards from the atepetl was the cemetery, the exhalations from which, by disagreeably affecting the traveller's sense of smell, advised him that he was approaching an Indian tribe. The natives of America, like most of those in Polynesia, have a very singular mode of burial. As a general rule, they do not inter their dead, but suspend them between earth and sky. After wrapping them carefully in blankets and buffalo robes, they place them on platforms supported on four poles some fifty feet high, and leave them exposed to the rain and sun to decompose gradually. The birds of prey incessantly hover over these strange tombs, uttering shrill and discordant cries, while making a disgusting meal on the putrefying flesh.

Two months after the battle of the Cerro Pardo, on the day when we resume our narrative, and about an hour before sunset, on a delicious afternoon of September,—which the Indians call the Moon of the Wild Oats—several riders, mounted on fiery mustangs, harnessed in the desert fashion, that is to say, painted of several colours, and adorned with plumes and bells, were following, while conversing together rather eagerly, a winding path, which runs for several leagues along the winding course of the Rio Sabina, and terminates at the winter atepetl of the Antelope Comanches, which we described at the beginning of this chapter.

These horsemen, five in number, were armed with rifles, tomahawks, and machetes. They wore the cotton hunting shirt of the wood rangers fastened round the waist, *mitasses*, or trousers, in two pieces tied at the ankles, fur caps, and Indian mocassins. Still, although this costume was almost identical with that worn by the majority of the Indian tribes, in whom constant contact with the Americans has produced a sort of bastard civilization, it was easy to recognise these riders as white men, not only through the ease of their manners, but also through the clearness of their complexion, which the hot sunbeams had been impotent to render so dusky as that of the aboriginals.

About two hundred yards behind the horsemen, came a sixth, mounted and dressed like them, but who was assuredly a Redskin. His head, instead of being covered by a fur cap, was bare; his hair, pulled up at the top of his head, and stained with red ochre, was fastened with strips of snakeskin; a falcon feather stuck in above his right ear, near his war-scalp lock, indicated his claim to high rank among his countrymen, while the numerous wolf tails fastened to his heels, proved that he was a renowned warrior; in his right hand he held a fan made of the entire wing of an eagle, and in his left he waved the short-handled and long-lashed whip, peculiar to the Comanche and Sioux Indians.

These riders employed none of the precautions usual on the prairie to avoid surprises, or foil the enemies generally ambushed in the track of hunters. From the way in which they conversed together, and the absent glances they at times took across the country, rather through habit than any prudential motive, it might easily be guessed that these men were reaching a spot perfectly well known to them, and where they felt certain of not falling into a trap. Still, had they not been absorbed in their conversation, and could their glances have pierced the dense curtain of verdure that formed a fragrant wall on their right, they would have seen amid the shrubs and lower branches of the trees an agitation not at all natural, and doubtless produced by the passage of a wild beast; at times, too, they might have noticed two eyes flashing among the leaves, which were fixed upon them with a savage expression of passion and hatred.

But, we repeat, these men, who, however, were wood rangers, renowned in these parts for their almost miraculous sagacity and skill, were so completely absorbed in their conversation; they felt so sure of having no snare to apprehend, their eyes and ears were so thoroughly closed, that they appeared blind and deaf, although ordinarily not the slightest noise, or the most futile object escaped their notice, but was analyzed with the searching and investigating spirit of individuals whose life may hang on a false step or a badly calculated movement.

On coming within pistol shot of the village, the horsemen stopped to give the Indian behind them time to rejoin them. So soon as the latter perceived this halt, he whipped his horse, and almost immediately ranged up alongside his comrades. He stopped his horse, and waited silently and calmly till he should be addressed.

"What are we to do now, Chief?" one of the travellers asked. "So soon as we have passed that projecting point we shall be at the valley."

"Our Pale brothers are brave; the Antelope Comanches will be happy to receive them and burn powder in their honour. A Chief will go alone to the village to announce their arrival to the Sachems."

"Go then, Chief, we will await you here."

"Wah! My brother has spoken well."

The Indian vigorously lashed his horse, which bounded ahead and speedily disappeared behind the peak to which the hunter had pointed. The horsemen drew up in line and waited motionless with their hands on their weapons. In a very few minutes a noise was heard resembling the rolling of thunder, and suddenly a crowd of mounted Indians appeared, coming up at full speed, brandishing their weapons, discharging their guns, howling and whistling in the long *iskochéttas* made of human thigh bones, which they wore hanging from their necks.

On their side, the hunters, at a sign from the man who appeared to be their leader, made their horses curvet, and discharged their weapons with repeated shouts and demonstrations of joy. For half an hour there was a deafening noise, augmented by the yells of the squaws and children who flocked up, blowing shells and rattling *chichikouès*, and the barking of the thousands of savage and half-tamed dogs which the Indians constantly take about with them. It was plain that the strangers to whom the Redskins, generally so haughty and retiring, offered so warm and friendly a reception, were great friends of the tribe; for, had it been otherwise, a deputation of Chiefs would have met them at the entrance of the village to do them the honours of the atepetl, but the brave and renowned warriors would not have thought it requisite to get under arms.

All at once the noise ceased as if by enchantment, and the Indian horsemen ranged themselves in a semicircle in front of the white hunters. A few paces before the line, four principal Chiefs, mounted on magnificent mustangs, formed a separate group. These warriors, completely armed and painted for war, wore the great cap of feathers which only renowned warriors who have raised many scalps are entitled to assume; their shoulders were decked with superb necklaces of grizzly bears' claws, five inches long and white at the tips; behind them floated the wide white buffalo robe, painted red inside, and on which their exploits were designed; in one hand they held their guns, in the other a fan made of the wing of a white-headed eagle. These Indian warriors, clothed in such a magnificent costume, had something majestic and imposing about them that inspired respect.

For some ten minutes the Indians and hunters stood thus, motionless and silent, in presence of each other, when suddenly a fresh horseman appeared, coming at full speed from the village. He was evidently a white man; he was dressed in the garb of a wood ranger, and two magnificent *rastreros*, or greyhounds, leaped up playfully on either side of his horse. At the appearance of the newcomer the Indians burst into yells of joy, and shouted—

"The great brave of the Antelope Comanches! Loyal Heart, Loyal Heart!"

The warrior was really the Mexican hunter, who has already made his appearance several times during the course of our narrative. He saluted the warriors by a wave of the hand, and took his place among the Chiefs, who respectfully made way for him.

"My brother Black-deer has informed me of the arrival of great friends of our nation," he said, "and I have hurried up in all haste to witness their reception and bid them welcome."

"Why has not the Black-deer accompanied our brother the great Brave of the tribe?" one of the Chiefs asked.

"The Sachem wished to remain in the village and watch the preparation of the medicine lodge."

The Chief bowed, but said nothing further. Loyal Heart then put his horse at a gallop and advanced toward the hunters, who, on their sides, made a move to meet him.

"You are welcome here, Tranquil," Loyal Heart said; "yourself and your comrades were impatiently expected."

"Thank you," Tranquil answered, pressing the hand the hunter offered him; "many events have happened since our separation, and it certainly did not depend on us that we did not arrive sooner."

The five white hunters were all old acquaintances—Tranquil, Lanzi, Quoniam, John Davis, and Fray Antonio. How was it that the American and the Monk had joined the three wood rangers! We shall explain that to the reader in the proper place. Loyal Heart took Tranquil's right hand, and both advanced at an amble towards the Chiefs.

"Sachems of the Antelope tribe," he said, "this Pale hunter is my brother; his heart is good, his arm strong, and his tongue is not forked; he loves the red men; he is renowned as a great brave in his nation, he is wise at the council fire; love him, for the Master of Life sustains him and has removed the skin from his heart, in order that his blood may be pure and the words he utters such as a wise warrior ought to pronounce."

"Wah!" one of the Sachems answered, with a graceful bow to the hunter; "the Comanches are great warriors; who can tell the extent of the hunting grounds the great spirit has given them? They are the masters of the red man because they are all great braves, whose heels are adorned with numerous wolf tails. My Pale brother and his warriors will enter the atepetl; they will receive callis, horses, and squaws to clean their arms and prepare their food, and the tribe of Antelope Comanches will count five braves more. I have spoken; have I said right, powerful Chiefs?"

"Chief," Tranquil replied, "I thank you for the hearty reception you are pleased to offer me. My brother, Loyal Heart, has told you the truth about my feelings towards your nation. I love the Red men, and especially the Comanches, who, of all the nations dwelling on the prairies, are the noblest and most courageous, and rightly call themselves the Queen Nation of the prairies, because their war horses and braves traverse it in all directions, and no one dares to oppose them. In my own name and that of my comrades I accept your frank and cordial hospitality, and we shall requite so great a favour by our wise and moderate conduct."

The principal Sachem then took off his buffalo robe, with a gesture full of dignity, and placed it on the shoulders of the hunter, while the other Chiefs did the same to his comrades.

"Warriors and braves of the powerful Antelope tribe," he said, turning to the Indians, who were still motionless and silent, "these Palefaces are henceforth our brothers. Woe to the man who insults them!"

At these words the shouts and yells recommenced with fresh vigour, and the Indians displayed signs of the liveliest joy. Possibly this joy was not so real as it appeared, and was not equally shared by all present. But those who might feel annoyed at the admission of the wood rangers into the tribe, carefully concealed their displeasure, and were, perhaps, the very men whose demonstrations of delight were the most vociferous.

Indian policy, very logical in this as in many other things, orders the natives to seek at any price an alliance with the whites, whose recognized skill in the management of arms, and profound knowledge of the manners of their countrymen, may at a given moment be of great service to the Indians, either in the interminable wars they wage against each other, or to defend them against the soldiers, *civicos*, and armed colonists, whom the civilized governments surrounding them frequently send to take vengeance for incursions on the territories of the White men, incursions in which the Indians indulge only too frequently, and during which they are guilty of deeds of unheard-of cruelty, and cause irreparable misfortunes.

After the final ceremony we have described, the Indian Sachems took the White hunters in their midst, and placing themselves at the head of their warriors, started at a gallop for the village, which they reached in less than a quarter of an hour. At the entrance Black-deer was waiting for them, surrounded by the most important and wisest Sachems of the tribe. Without uttering a syllable, he took the head of the column and led it to the centre of the village, near the Ark of the first man. On reaching it the Indians suddenly halted, as if the feet of their horses were imbedded in the ground. Black-deer then stationed himself at the doorway of the medicine lodge, between the hachesto, who held in his hand the totem of the tribe, and the pipe bearer, who supported the sacred calumet.

"Who are the Pale men who thus enter as friends the atepetl of the Antelope Comanches?" he asked, addressing Loyal Heart.

"They are brothers, who ask leave to sit by the hearth of the Red men," the latter answered.

"It is well," Black-deer continued; "these men are our brothers. The Council fire is lighted; they will enter with us the lodge of the Great Medicine, sit down by the fire and smoke *morichee* from the sacred calumet with the Sachems of the nation."

"Let it be as my brother has decided," Loyal Heart responded.

Black-deer gave a wave of the hand, upon which the hachesto raised the curtained door of the lodge, and the Chiefs entered, followed by the hunters. The medicine lodge, much larger than the other callis of the village, was also built with greater care. The buffalo skins that covered it entirely were painted red with a profusion of black designs, a species of sacred hieroglyphics, only understood by the medicine men and the most renowned Sachems of the tribe, who possessed the scent of the war trail. The interior of the lodge was perfectly empty. In the centre was a round hole dug in the earth to a depth of about two feet; in this hole the requisite wood and charcoal were prepared.

When all the Chiefs had entered the lodge, the hachesto let the curtain fall again that formed the entrance. A band of picked warriors immediately surrounded the lodge to keep off the curious, and insure the secrecy of the deliberations. The Indians are excessively strict about the laws of etiquette; with them everything is regulated with a minuteness we should be far from expecting among a semi-barbarous nation; and each is bound by the severest penalties to conform to the ceremonial. In order to make our readers thoroughly understand their strange manners, we thought it best to give them in their fullest detail.

Thus Black-deer was perfectly well aware who the Palefaces were that reached the village, since he had acted as their guide. But etiquette demanded that he should receive them as he had done, for otherwise the other Chiefs might have been scandalized by such a breach of custom, and the strangers would, in all probability, have questions to discuss. In the first place, it was proposed to organise a great expedition against the Buffalo

Apaches, a plundering tribe, who had several times stolen horses from the very villages of the Comanches, and on whom the Sachems desired to take exemplary revenge. Secondly, Tranquil, through the medium of Loyal Heart, whose influence was great with the tribe, requested that a band of picked braves, amounting to fifty, and placed under the command of Loyal Heart, should be entrusted to him for an expedition, the object of which he could not divulge at the moment, but its success would benefit his allies as much as himself.

The first question was, after several speeches, unanimously resolved in the affirmative. The council was proceeding to discuss the second, when a loud noise was heard outside, the curtain of the medicine lodge was raised, and the hachesto walked in. Let us shortly explain what the hachesto of an Indian village is, and the nature of his duties. The hachesto is a man who must be gifted with a loud and powerful voice. He represents among the Redskins the town crier, and his duty is to make news public, and convene the Chiefs to council. When he made his appearance in the lodge, Black-deer gave him an angry glance.

"When the Chiefs are assembled in the Medicine lodge, they must not be disturbed," he said to him.

"My father, Wah-Rush-a-Menec, speaks well," the Indian answered with a respectful bow; "his son knows it."

"Then, why has my son entered without the orders of the Sachems?"

"Because five warriors of the Buffalo Apaches have arrived at the village."

"Wah! And who is the brave that has made them prisoners? Why has he not taken their scalps? Does he prefer fastening them to the stake of torture?"

The hachesto shook his head.

"My father is mistaken," he said; "these warriors have not been made prisoners by any of our braves, they are free."

"Ooehst!" said Black-deer with a degree of surprise he could not entirely conceal; "How then did they enter the village?"

"Openly, in the sight of all; they call themselves ambassadors."

"Ambassadors! And who is the Chief that marches at their head?"

"Blue-fox."

"Blue-fox is a great brave. He is a terrible warrior in fight; his arm has raised many scalps belonging to my sons; his hand has robbed them of many horses. But his presence is disagreeable to the Comanches. What does he want?"

"To enter the Medicine lodge, and explain to the Sachems the mission with which he is entrusted."

"It is well," said Black-deer, giving an enquiring glance to the members of the council.

The latter replied by a nod of assent. Loyal Heart rose —

"My Pale brothers, I must not be present at the deliberation that is about to take place," he remarked; "will the Chief permit me to retire?"

"Loyal Heart is a son of the Comanches," Black-deer answered; "his place is among us, for, if he be young in years, his experience and wisdom are great. But he can do as he pleases — the Pale hunters can retire. If the Chiefs require Loyal Heart, they will request his return."

The young man bowed ceremoniously, and withdrew, followed by the hunters, who, we must confess, were delighted at getting away from the Medicine lodge, for they felt the need of rest after the fatigue they had undergone in making a long journey by almost impracticable roads.

CHAPTER VIII
HOSPITALITY

We have said that some callis had been got ready for the hunters. These callis, built like those of the Indians, were, however, comfortable enough for men who, accustomed to desert life, despise the superfluities of towns, and are contented with what is strictly necessary. On quitting the Medicine lodge, Loyal Heart led the travellers to two callis communicating with each other; then, making Tranquil a sign to follow him, he left the four hunters to make themselves as jolly as they could.

"As for you, my friend," he said to Tigrero, "I hope you will accept the hospitality my modest abode permits me to offer you."

"Why put yourself to trouble for me?" the Canadian replied, "the slightest thing suffices me. I assure you that I should be all right with my comrades."

"I do not put myself out at all; on the contrary, I feel a real pleasure in giving you a place at my fireside."

"As it is so, I no longer insist: do what you please with me."

"Thanks! Come on then."

Without further remark, they crossed the village square, which was almost deserted at this moment, for night had fallen some time previously, and most of the Indians had retired to their wigwams. Still, from the interior of the callis, songs and laughter could be heard, proving that if the inhabitants had shut themselves up, they were not the less awake for all that. We will remark in passing, that many travellers who have only seen Indians, and have not been in a position to study their character, represent them as gloomy, mournful men, speaking but little, and never laughing. This is a grave error; the Redskins, on the contrary, are generally very jovial when together, and are specially fond of telling stories. But with the strangers, whose language they do not understand, and who do not understand theirs, they maintain a reserve, and only speak when absolutely compelled, because, as they are extremely susceptible, they fear giving their listeners an opportunity of ridiculing them.

Loyal Heart, after walking for some minutes through the streets, stopped before a calli of sufficiently singular appearance to surprise Tranquil, although he was not easily astonished. This calli, which anywhere else would have been quite commonplace, justly appeared strange in an Indian village. It was a rather large rancho, built in the Mexican fashion, of planks painted of a dazzling whiteness. It formed a parallelogram, the roof was flat, and in front of the door was a porch formed of six enormous trees fastened together, and covered with an azotea. On either side the door, three windows were pierced in the frontage, and these windows had glass panes, a most singular thing at a spot so remote from all towns.

A man of about fifty years of age, tall and thin, and dressed in the Mexican garb, was smoking a cigarette as he sat on an equipal in the porch. This man, whose hair was turning grey, had the placid though resolute look of men who have suffered greatly. On seeing him, the rastreros, which hitherto had not left Loyal Heart a yard, rushed toward him with a joyous bark, and leaped up at him caressingly.

"Ah," the man said, as he rose and bowed respectfully to the hunter, "it is you, mi amo! You return home very late."

These words were uttered in that affectionate tone which is so pleasing in the mouth of an old and faithful servant.

"That is true, No Eusebio," the young man answered with a smile, as he squeezed the hand of the old man, whom those of our readers who have perused the "Trappers of Arkansas" have doubtless recognised, "I bring a friend."

"He is welcome," No Eusebio answered; "we will try to give him as hearty a welcome as he deserves, to the best of our ability."

"Oh, oh, gossip!" Tranquil remarked, gaily; "I am no troublesome guest, I shall not put you out of your way much."

"Come in, my friend," said Loyal Heart; "I should not like to keep my mother waiting any longer."

"The Señora is so restless when you are out late."

"Announce us; No Eusebio, we follow you."

The servant turned to obey, but the rastreros had long ago announced the hunter's return to his mother, by rushing madly into the house, hence the lady appeared in the doorway at the moment when the three men prepared to enter. At the moment when we meet Doña Garillas again, she was no longer the young and charming woman, with such pure and soft beauty, whom we saw in the prologue of the "Trappers;" eight years had pasted over her; eight long years of agony, alarm, and grief. She was still young and lovely, it is true, but this beauty had ripened beneath the burning blast of adversity. Her pale forehead and calm features won that expression of crushing resignation which the old sculptor succeeded in rendering on the admirable bust of Melancholy. When she saw her son her eyes sparkled, but that was all.

"Caballero," she said, in a gentle and melodious voice as she smiled on the Canadian, "enter this modest abode, where you have been impatiently expected for a long time. Although our hearth be small, we always keep a nook for a friend."

"Señora," the hunter replied with a bow, "your reception overcomes me with joy. I trust I shall prove deserving of the kindness you show me."

They entered the rancho, whose interior corresponded exactly with the exterior. A candil, suspended from a beam, illumined a rather large room, the furniture of which consisted merely of a few equipals, two butacas, and a chiffonier, all clumsily made with the hatchet. On the white-washed walls hung four of those coloured engravings with which Parisian commerce inundates both hemispheres. The first represented Napoleon at the St. Bernard; the second, Iturbide, that Mexican general who was for six months emperor, and died, like Murat, shot by his own subjects; the third, our Saviour on the cross between the two thieves; and the fourth, Nuestra-Señora-de-los-Dolores. Before the last two hung lamps that burned night and day.

During our lengthened wanderings we have been enabled to discover a singular fact; it is, that in Asia, America, Africa, and the heart of Polynesia, among the most savage tribes the name of Napoleon the First has not only penetrated, but is venerated like a god; and I even found his portrait among the Botocudos, that untameable horde hidden in the forests of Brazil. What is the magic influence exerted on humanity by this extraordinary man? It is vain to seek the solution of this problem, vain to try to discover by what remarkable concourse of events the name of the great Emperor penetrated beneath the grand domes of foliage, where all the rumours of civilization expire without an echo.

A European rarely visits an Indian tribe in which the Chiefs do not ask him news of Napoleon, and beg him to tell anecdotes about his reign; and strangely enough, their primitive natures will not allow that the great man is dead. When told so, the Chiefs content themselves with smiling cunningly. One day, after a lengthened hunt in Apacheria, I demanded hospitality of a party of Opata Indians. The Chief, on hearing that I was a Frenchman, did not fail to speak to me about the Emperor. After a long conversation,

I concluded by describing, in a way that the men who surrounded and listened to me with the most profound attention could understand, the death of the great man after long and painful sufferings. The Chief, an old man of venerable appearance, interrupted me, and laying his left hand on my arm to attract my attention, while with the right he pointed to the sun, whose fiery disc was sinking in the horizon in clouds of vapour, asked me with a most significant smile —

"Is the sun about to die?"

"Certainly not," I answered, not knowing what the Redskin was driving at.

"Wah!" he continued, "If the sun never dies, how can the great pale Chief be dead, who is the son of that planet?"

The Indians applauded this conclusion; I tried to alter their opinion in vain, and at length grew so tired, that I allowed them to be right. All my efforts had only produced the result of convincing them still more of the immortality of the hero whom they are accustomed to regard as a divinity. However, I believe that if a person would take the trouble to seek carefully, he would find in France peasants whose opinion is precisely similar. Asking the reader's pardon for this long digression, we will resume our narrative at the point where we interrupted it.

By the care of Doña Garillas and No Eusebio, a frugal meal was prepared for the travellers, who now sate down to table. Tranquil, especially, who had made a long journey, experienced that feeling of internal comfort which is produced after long fatigue, by finding, during a desert halt, a fugitive reflex of civilisation.

The meal was most simple; it consisted of pigoles with pimento, a lump of venison, and maize tortillas, the whole washed down with smilax water and a few mouthfuls of pulque, a wonderful luxury in these regions, and among the Comanches, the only Indians who never drink strong liquors. No Eusebio sate down with the hunter. The lady waited on them, and did the honours of her house with that kindly and graceful attention so rarely met with in our civilized countries, where everything is so expensive, even a kind reception. When the meal was ended, which was not long first, the three men rose from table and seated themselves round a copper brasero full of hot ashes, when they began smoking. The dogs, like vigilant sentries, had lain down across the door, with outstretched heads and pricked-up ears.

The greatest silence prevailed in the village; the songs and laughter had gradually died out; the Indians were asleep or appeared to be so. Doña Garillas had made in the corner of the room a bed of furs, which would seem delicious to a man accustomed, during the course of his adventurous life, to sleep most nights on the bare ground, and she was about to invite the hunter to rest his weary limbs, when the dogs raised their heads sharply and began growling; at the same instant, two slight taps were given on the door of the rancho.

"Tis a friend," Loyal Heart said; "open, no Eusebio."

The old servant obeyed, and an Indian stalked in; it was Black-deer. The Chiefs face was gloomy; he bowed slightly to the company, and, without saying a syllable, sat down on an equipal placed for him near the brasero. The hunters were too conversant with the Indian character to question the Chief, so long as he was pleased to keep silence. Tranquil, however, drew his pipe from his lips, and handed it to Black-deer, who began smoking, after thanking him with one of those emphatic gestures usual with the Redskins. There was a long silence, but at last the Chief raised his head.

"The Chiefs have left the Council lodge," he said.

"Ah!" Loyal Heart replied, for the sake of saying something.

"No determination was formed, no answer given the Envoy?"

"The Sachems are prudent, they wished to reflect."

The Sachem nodded in affirmation,

"Does my brother Loyal Heart wish to learn what happened at the Council after his departure?" he asked.

"My brother is thoughtful, his heart is sad; let him speak, the ears of a friend are open."

"The Chief will eat first," Doña Garillas remarked, "he remained late at the Council; the squaws have not prepared his evening meal."

"My mother is good," he replied with a smile, "Black-deer will eat; he is here in the wigwam of the brother of his heart: the warriors have exchanged horses and weapons."

Who taught the Indians this affecting custom, which makes them select a friend, with whom they exchange arms and horses, and who, from that moment, is dearer to them than if blood ties attached them? Black-deer and Loyal Heart had really made the exchange referred to by the Sachem.

"My mother will retire to sleep," said Loyal Heart. "I will wait on my brother."

"Be it so," the Redskin answered; "my mother needs rest—the night is advanced."

Doña Garillas understood that the three men had to talk about secret affairs, so, after bidding her guests good-night, she withdrew without offering any objection. As for No Eusebio, considering his presence unnecessary, he went to bed after the Indian's arrival, that is to say, lay down on a hammock, suspended in the porch of the house, with the two rastreros at his feet, so that no one could enter or leave the house without awakening him. After hurriedly eating a few mouthfuls, rather through politeness than want, Black-deer spoke again.

"My brother Loyal Heart is young," he said, "but his wisdom is great; the Chiefs have confidence in him, and would not decide anything till they had heard his opinion."

"My brothers know that I am devoted to them. If my brother will explain, I will answer him."

"Blue Fox arrived at the village today."

"I saw him."

"Good; he came on the part of the Chiefs of his nation; Blue-fox has put on the skin of the timid asshatas, his words are gentle and his mouth distils honey; but the buffalo cannot leap like the elk, or the hawk imitate the dove. The Chiefs did not put faith in his words."

"Then they answered him in the negative?"

"No, they wished first to consult my brother."

"Wah! On what subject?"

"My brother will listen. The Palefaces on the other side of the Meche-chebe dug up the war hatchet against each other some moons ago, as my brother is aware."

"I know it, Chief and so do you. But how does it concern us? A quarrel among the whites cannot affect us in any way. So long as they do not invade our hunting grounds, do not steal our horses or burn our villages, we can only congratulate ourselves at seeing them destroy each other."

"My brother speaks like a wise man; the Sachems are of the same opinion."

"Good; I cannot understand, then, what reason can have determined the Chiefs to discuss such a subject."

"Wah! My brother can speedily understand if he will listen."

"Chief, you Redskins have an unhappy knack of wrapping up your thoughts in so many words, that it is impossible to guess the point you are aiming at."

Black-deer broke into that silent laugh peculiar to Indians.

"My brother knows how to discover a trail better than anyone," he said.

"Certainly; but to do so I must be shown a footstep or trace, however feeble it may be."

"And my brother has discovered the trail, which I merely indicated to him?"

"Yes."

"Oh! I should be curious to know my brother's thoughts."

"Then, listen to me in your turn, Black-deer—I shall be brief. Blue Fox was sent by the Buffalo Apaches to the Antelope Comanches to propose to them an offensive and defensive alliance against one of the two nations of the Palefaces which have dug up the hatchet against each other."

In spite of all the phlegm which nature and Indian training had endowed him with, the Chief could not conceal the amazement he experienced on hearing these words.

"It is well," he said; "my brother is not only a great, brave, and daring warrior, but is also a man inspired by the Wacondah. His medicine is irresistible, he knows everything. Blue Fox made this proposition to the Sachems."

"And have they accepted it?"

"No; I repeat to my brother that they would not give any answer till they heard his opinion."

"Very good, then. This is my opinion, and the Chiefs can follow it or not, as they please. The Comanches nation are the Queen of the Prairies; the most invincible warriors assemble beneath its totem; its hunting ground extends over the whole earth; the Comanches alone are indomitable. Why should they ally themselves with the Apache thieves? Are they desirous of exchanging their lances and guns for weavers' shuttles? Are they tired of being redoubtable warriors? Do they wish to put on women's petticoats? Why should they league with their most obstinate enemies against men who are fighting to obtain their liberty? Blue Fox is a renegade from the Snake-Pawnees; my brother knows him, since he is his personal enemy. Any peace proposed by such an ambassador must conceal a trap; sooner war than such an alliance."

There was a rather lengthened silence, during which the Chief reflected deeply on what he had just heard.

"My brother is right," he said at last; "wisdom resides in him, his tongue is not forked, the words he utters are inspired by the Wacondah! The Comanches will not treat with the plundering Apaches. The council has asked for three suns to reflect on this grave question; in three suns Blue Fox will return with a categorical refusal to those who sent him. The Comanches will dig up the war hatchet sooner than ally themselves with their enemies."

"My brothers, if they do that, will act like wise men."

"They will do it. I have now to speak to my brother on a matter that interests me personally."

"Good. Sleep does not yet weigh down my eyelids, so I will listen to my brother.

"Loyal Heart is a friend of Blackbird," the Chief continued, with some hesitation.

The hunter smiled knowingly.

"Blackbird is one of the most renowned braves of the tribe," he answered; "his daughter, Bounding Fawn, will count fourteen autumns at the fall of the leaves."

"Black-deer loves Bounding Fawn."

"I know it; my brother has already confessed to me that the virgin of the first love placed, during his sleep, a four-leaved shamrock under his head. But has the Chief assured himself as to Bounding Fawn's feelings?"

"The young virgin smiles when the Chief returns from an expedition with scalps hanging from his girdle; she trembles when he departs; she feeds his horse in secret, and her greatest pleasure is to clean his weapons. When the maidens of the tribe dance at night to the sound of the drum and chichikouè, Bounding Fawn gazes thoughtfully in the direction of Black-deer's calli, and forgets to dance with her companions."

"Good! And does the maiden recognise the sound of my brother's war whistle, and run joyfully to the meeting the Chief grants her? Tonight, for instance, were the Chief to call her, would she rise from her bed to obey his summons?"

"She would rise," the Chief answered, laconically.

"Good! Now, what does the Chief wish to ask of me? Blackbird is rich."

"Black-deer will give six mares which have never felt a bit, two guns, and four hides of the white she-buffalo; tomorrow the Chief's mother will give them to my brother."

"Good. And does my brother intend to carry off the woman he loves this night?"

"Black-deer suffers from being so long separated from her; since the death of his well-beloved wife, Singing-bird, the Chief's calli is solitary. Bounding Fawn will prepare the venison for the Chief; what does my brother think of it?"

"My horse is ready; if my brother say yes, I will accompany him, if it be that he desires, as I suppose."

"Loyal Heart knows everything; nothing escapes his discernment."

"Let us go without loss of time. Will you accompany us, Tranquil? Two witnesses are required, as you are aware."

"I wish for nothing better, if my presence be not disagreeable to the Chief."

"On the contrary; the Pale hunter is a great brave. I shall be pleased to know that he is by my side."

The three men rose and quitted the house. No Eusebio raised his head.

"We shall return in an hour," Loyal Heart said, as he passed.

The old servant made no objection, and fell back in his hammock. The Chief's horse was tied up near the rancho; he leaped into the saddle and waited for the two hunters, who had gone to fetch theirs from the corral. In a few minutes they arrived. The three men slowly traversed the village, whose streets were completely deserted at this late hour of the night. At times, however, dogs got up as they passed, and barked furiously after their horses' heels. Like all the winter villages, this one was carefully guarded. Numerous sentries, placed at different points, watched over the common safety; but, either that they recognised the three horsemen, or for some other motive, they did not challenge, but allowed them to pass apparently unnoticed.

After leaving the village, Black-deer, who rode in front, made a sharp turn to the right, and the horsemen almost immediately disappeared in a thick chaparral, where men and horses concealed themselves with the utmost care. The night was magnificent, the sky studded with a profusion of glistening stars; the moon shed a pale and soft light, which, owing to the purity of the atmosphere, allowed objects to be distinguished for a great distance. A solemn silence brooded over the forest, and a gentle breeze sighed through the treetops.

Black-deer advanced to the edge of the covert, and, raising his fingers to his lips, imitated the cry of the raven thrice with such perfection, that the two hunters concealed in the rear looked up mechanically to discover the bird that uttered the note. A few minutes after, the cry of the Blue-jay, borne on the breeze expressed like a plaintive sigh on the ears of the attentive hunters. Black-deer repeated his signal. This time the note of the sparrowhawk was mingled almost instantaneously with that of the jay. The Indian started, and looked in the direction where his friends were concealed.

"Is my brother ready?" he said.

"I am," Loyal Heart simply answered.

Almost immediately, four riders could be seen leaving the village at a gallop, and advancing rapidly toward the spot where the Chief stood motionless. The rider who galloped at the head of the band was a woman; she made her horse bound with feverish impatience, and compelled it to gallop in a straight line, clearing all the obstacles that were in its way. The three other riders were about a bow-shot behind her. This race had something fantastic about it in the night, amidst this grand scenery. Bounding Fawn, for it was she, fell panting into Black-deer's arms.

"Here I am! Here I am!" she cried in a joyous voice, choked, however, by emotion.

The Indian pressed her lovingly to his wide chest, and lifting her from the ground with that irresistible strength that passion produces, he leaped with her on to his horse, into whose flank he dug his spurs, and started at full speed in the direction of the desert. At the same moment, the horsemen arrived, uttering yells of anger, and brandishing their weapons; but they found before them the two hunters, who resolutely barred their passage.

"Stay, Blackbird," Loyal Heart shouted; "your daughter belongs to my brother. Black-deer is a great Chief, his calli is lined with scalps—he is rich in horses, arms, and furs; Bounding Fawn will be the *cihuatl* of a great brave, whose medicine is powerful."

"Does Black-deer mean, then, to carry off my daughter?" Blackbird asked.

"He does mean it, and we his friends will defend him. Your daughter pleases him, and he will have her. In defiance of you, and all who may attempt to oppose it, he will take her as his wife."

"Wah!" the Indian said, turning to the horsemen who accompanied him, "My brothers have heard: what do they say?"

"We have heard," the Redskins answered; "we say that Black-deer is truly a great Chief, and since he is powerful enough to seize the woman he loves in spite of her father and relatives, he ought to keep her."

"My brothers have spoken well," Loyal Heart remarked. "Tomorrow I will come to Blackbird's calli and pay him the purchase money for the maiden the Chief has robbed him of."

"Good! Tomorrow I shall expect Loyal Heart and his friend, the other Paleface warrior," Blackbird said with a bow.

After these remarks, the three Indian, warriors returned to the village, closely followed by the two hunters. As for Black-deer, he had buried himself with his booty in the thickest part of the forest, where no one attempted to disturb him. The preliminaries of a Comanche marriage had been strictly carried out on both sides.

A strange nation this Comanche, whose warriors love like wild beasts, and who think themselves obliged to carry off the woman they love, instead of obtaining her by the voluntary consent of her family! Is there not something grand and noble in their haughty and indomitable character?

As Loyal Heart told No Eusebio, he was hardly an hour absent.

CHAPTER IX
THE MARRIAGE

When the two hunters returned to the rancho, Tranquil looked at Loyal Heart.

"Well," he said to him, "and what are you going to do?"

"Well," the other replied with a smile, "the same as you are going to do yourself, I suppose, sleep—for it is close on two o'clock." But noticing the Canadian's anxious air, he hurriedly added—"Pardon me, friend, I forget that you have made a long journey to find me here, and that, probably, you have important matters to communicate to me. Well! if you do not feel too fatigued, I will rekindle the fire, we will sit down by the brasero, and I will listen to you; I do not feel at all disposed for sleep, and the present hour is admirably adapted for confidence."

Tranquil gently shook his head.

"I thank you for your kindness, my friend," he said; "but, on reflection, I prefer deferring the conversation till tomorrow; I have no serious motive that compels me to speak at this moment, and a few hours, more or less, will have no influence in the events I have cause to fear."

"You know better than I do the conduct best suited to you under the circumstances. I merely repeat that I am quite at your service whatever you may be pleased to do."

"Let us sleep," the Canadian answered, with a smile. "Tomorrow, after our visit to Blackbird, we will hold a palaver."

"Be it so, my friend, I will not press you; here is your bed," he added, pointing to the pile of furs.

"It is rare for me to have so good a one in the desert," said Tranquil.

The two men then lay down fraternally side by side, placed their weapons within reach, and ere long the calmness of their breathing indicated that they were asleep. Nothing disturbed the repose they enjoyed, and the night passed quietly. A few minutes before sunrise Loyal Heart awoke; a feeble light was beginning to penetrate into the rancho, through the windows, which had no sheltering or curtains. The hunter rose, and at the moment when he was going to awake his comrade, the latter opened his eyes.

"Ah, ah!" Loyal Heart said, "You are a very light sleeper, my friend."

"It is an old hunter's habit, which I think I should find it difficult to get rid of, unless I remained a long time with you."

"What prevents your doing so? Such a determination would cause great pleasure to my mother and myself."

"Do not form plans, my boy; you know that with us wood rangers we can hardly call the present moment our own, and it would be utter madness for us to enter on the future. We will revert to this subject; but now believe we have something more important to attend to."

"We have to perform the commission Black-deer entrusted to us; are you still of a mind to help me?"

"Certainly: the Chiefs of the tribe received me with too much courtesy for me not to eagerly take the first opportunity that offers to testify to them the lively sympathy I feel for them."

"Well, as it is so, go to your comrades, get ready to mount, and wait for me; I shall join them directly at their calli."

"All right," Tranquil answered.

The two men left the house; No Eusebio had deserted his hammock, and was probably attending to household duties. The Canadian went straight to the calli lent his comrades by the Indians.

Day had by this time entirely broken; the curtains of the callis were raised one after the other, and the Indian squaws were beginning to emerge to go in quest of the necessary wood and water for the preparation of breakfast. Small parties of warriors were going off in different directions, some to indulge in the pleasures of the chase, others to beat the forest and be certain that there was no enemy's trail in the vicinity of the village.

At the moment when the Canadian passed in front of the Medicine lodge, the sorcerer of the tribe came out of it. He held in his hand a calabash filled with water, in which a bunch of wormwood was dipped. The sorcerer ascended to the roof of the Medicine lodge, and turned to the rising sun. At the same instant the hachesto shouted three different times in a powerful voice, "The sun! The sun! The sun!"

A warrior then came out of each calli, holding in his hand, like the sorcerer, a calabash of water with a bunch of wormwood. The sorcerer began an incantation by murmuring mysterious words which he alone comprehended, and sprinkling the four cardinal points with the wormwood, an operation imitated exactly by the warriors. Then, at a signal given by the sorcerer, all the men threw the contents of the calabash towards the sun, shouting at the same time, "Oh, sun! Thou visible representative of the Invisible Master of Life! protect us on this commencing day! Give us water, air, and fire, for the earth belongs to us, and we can defend it!"

After this haughty prayer the warriors re-entered their callis, and the sorcerer descended from his elevated post. Tranquil, who was perfectly conversant with Indian customs, had stopped and waited, in a respectful attitude, the end of the ceremony. When the sorcerer had disappeared in the Medicine lodge, the hunter resumed his walk. The inhabitants of the village, already affected to regard him as one of themselves; they saluted him with a smile and a pleasant word as he passed, and the children ran up laughing to bid him good-day. When Tranquil entered the calli his comrades were still asleep, but he soon roused them.

"Hilloh!" John Davis said, good-humouredly, "You are very early, old hunter. Are we going to make any expedition?"

"Not that I know of, for the present, at any rate," the Canadian answered; "we are merely going to accompany Loyal Heart, while he accomplishes a ceremony."

"What is up, then?"

"The marriage of our friend Black-deer. I supposed it to be good policy not to refuse our aid, especially as you, Davis, have an interest in getting into the good graces of the Indians."

"I should think so. But tell me, old hunter, have you consulted with our friend on the matter that brings me here?"

"Not yet: various reasons urged me to wait for a favourable moment."

"As you please; but you know the matter is pressing."

"I know it, and you can trust to me."

"Oh! I leave you to act entirely as you please. What are we to do now?"

"Nothing but mount our horses, and wait till Loyal Heart comes to fetch us. He has undertaken the management of the ceremony."

"Well, that is not very difficult," the American said, with a laugh.

In an instant the hunters were up, performed their ablutions, and saddled their horses. They had scarce mounted, ere a great noise of shells, drums, and chichikouès, mingled with shouts of joy, shots, and the sharp barking of all the dogs in the village, announced the arrival of Loyal Heart.

The young Chief advanced at the head of a numerous procession of Indian warriors, dressed in their most magnificent costumes, armed and painted for war, and mounted on superb mustangs, which they caused to curvet with marks of the most lively delight. The procession halted before the calli.

"Well," Loyal Heart asked, "are you ready?"

"We are waiting for you," Tranquil answered.

"Come on, then."

The five hunters placed themselves by the side of their friend, and the procession started once more. The Indians saw with a lively feeling of pleasure the strange hunters join them; the part Loyal Heart and Tranquil took in the ceremony especially caused them great joy, and inspired them with considerable pride, by proving to them that their Paleface friends, far from despising their customs, or displaying an indifference towards them, took an interest in the ceremony, and evidenced their sympathy with the Comanches by accepting a place in the procession.

Loyal Heart proceeded straight to Blackbird's calli, in front of which a fire had been lighted, and the Chief's family were seated silent and motionless round it. Blackbird, dressed in his grand warpaint, and mounted on his battle charger, rode at the head of some twenty warriors of his family, whom it was easy to recognize as renowned warriors and great braves by the numerous wolf tails with which their heels were adorned. At the moment when the procession reached the great square, a solitary horseman, with a gloomy air and haughty demeanour, was crossing it, and proceeding toward the council lodge. It was Blue-fox. At the sight of the procession a smile of undefinable meaning played round his lips, and he halted to let the Comanche warriors defile before him. Tranquil whispered to Loyal Heart—

"Be on your guard against that man; if I am not greatly mistaken, his mission is only a trap, and he meditates some treachery."

"That is my notion too," the hunter replied; "that gloomy face forebodes nothing good; but the council are warned, and watch him closely."

"I have known him for a long time, he is a thorough-paced villain. I would not let him out of my sight, were I in your place. But we have reached our destination, so let us attend to our own business."

Loyal Heart raised his arm; at this signal the music, if such a name can be given to the abominable row made by all these instruments, which, held by unskilful hands, produced the most discordant sounds, was silent as if by enchantment. The warriors then seized their war whistles, and produced a shrill and prolonged note thrice. A similar whistle was immediately given by Blackbird's party. When the procession halted, a vacant space of about twenty yards was left between the two bands, and Loyal Heart and Tranquil advanced alone into this space, making their horses prance and brandishing their weapons, amid the joyous applause of the crowd, which admired their skill and good countenance. Blackbird and two of his comrades then left their party and rode to meet the hunters, and the five men halted at about halfway. Loyal Heart, after saluting the Chief respectfully, was the first to speak.

"I see that my father is a great Chief," he said; "his head is covered by the sacred feathered cap of the band of the old dogs; numerous exploits are painted on his broad chest; the wolf tails fastened to his heels make a hole in the ground, so many are they. My father must be one of the greatest braves of the Antelope Comanches: he will tell us his name, that I may remember it as that of a Chief of renown in the council, and brave and terrible in combat."

The Chief smiled proudly at this point-blank compliment; he bowed with dignity, and answered—

"My son is young, and yet wisdom dwells in him; his arm is strong in fight, and his tongue is not forked; his renown has reached me; my brothers call him Loyal Heart. Blackbird is happy to see him. What motive brings Loyal Heart to Blackbird with so large a party, when the heart of the Chief is sad, and a cloud has spread over his mind?"

"I know," Loyal Heart answered, "that the Chief is sad, and am aware of the motive of his grief. I have come with the braves who accompany me to restore tranquillity to the mind of the Chief, and change his sorrow into joy."

"My son Loyal Heart will then explain himself without further delay; he knows that a man of heart never plays with the grief of an aged man."

"I know it, and will explain myself without further delay. My father is rich, the Wacondah has always regarded him with a favourable eye; his family is numerous, his sons are already brave warriors, his daughters are virtuous and lovely; one of them, the fairest, perhaps, but certainly the one most beloved, was violently carried off last night by Black-deer."

"Yes," the Chief answered, "a Comanche warrior bore away my daughter Bounding Fawn, and fled with her into the forest."

"That warrior is Black-deer."

"Black-deer is one of the most celebrated warriors and wisest Chiefs of my nation. My heart leaped toward him. Why did he carry off my child?"

"Because Black-deer loves Bounding Fawn; a great brave has the right to take anywhere the wife who pleases him, if he is rich enough to pay her father for her. Blackbird cannot object to that."

"If such be Black-deer's intention, if he offer me a ransom such as a warrior like him ought to pay to a Chief like myself, I will allow that he has acted in an honourable way, and that his intentions were pure; if not, I shall be an implacable enemy to him, because he will have betrayed my confidence and deceived my hopes."

"Blackbird must not hastily judge his friend; I am ordered by Black-deer to pay for Bounding Fawn such a ransom as few Chiefs have ever before received."

"What is the ransom? Where is it?"

"The warriors who accompany me have brought it with them; but before delivering it to my father, I will remark, that he has not invited me to sit down by his fire, or offered me the calumet."

"My son will sit down by my fire, and I will share the calumet with him when the mission he is intrusted with is finished."

"Be it so; my father shall be immediately satisfied."

Loyal Heart, turning to the warriors, who during this conversation, which was sternly demanded by the laws of Indian etiquette, had stood silent and motionless, raised his hand. At once several horsemen left the procession and pranced up to him, brandishing their weapons.

"The ransom!" he merely said.

"One moment," Blackbird objected; "of what does this ransom consist?"

"You shall see," Loyal Heart replied.

"I know that, but should prefer being informed beforehand."

"For what reason?"

"Wah! That I may be in a position to refuse it if I find it unworthy of you."

"You ought not to have such a fear."

"That is possible, still I adhere to what I said."

"As you please," said Loyal Heart.

We must here disclose one of the bad sides of the Indian character. The Redskins are extraordinarily rapacious and avaricious. With them wealth is everything—not wealth as we understand it in our country, for they know not the value of gold: that metal, so precious to us, is as nothing in their eyes; but furs, arms, and horses constitute for these warriors veritable wealth, which they appreciate at its full value. Hence the transactions between the white men and natives become daily more difficult, from the fact that the Indians, seeing with what ardour the peltry dealers seek furs, have attached so high a value to that merchandise, that it is almost impossible for the traders to obtain it; hence arises, to a great extent, the hatred of the whites for the Redskins, who track, scalp, and kill the trappers whenever they meet with them, in order to destroy competition.

Blackbird was an Indian of the old school, gifted with a smart dose of avarice. The worthy Chief was not sorry, before pledging his word, to know what he had to depend on, and if he would make as good a bargain as was stated. This is why he had insisted on the objects comprising the ransom being shown him. Loyal Heart was perfectly acquainted with his man, and hence was not much affected by his demand; he merely ordered the bearers of the ransom to approach.

This ransom had been prepared for a long period by Black-deer, and was really magnificent; it consisted of four mares in foal, four others which had never bred, a three-year old charger, a mustang with slim legs and flashing eye, four muskets, each with twelve charges of powder; and four white female buffalo hides, a colour very rare, and greatly esteemed in this country. As the several articles were presented to the old Chief, his eye dilated under the influence of joy, and flashed with a wild lustre. He required to make extraordinary efforts to preserve the decorum necessary under such circumstances, and confine in his heart the pleasure he felt. When all the presents had been given and placed by him under the immediate guard of his relatives and friends, Loyal Heart spoke again.

"Is my father satisfied?" he asked him.

"Wah!" the old Chief shouted with delight. "My son, Black-deer, is a great brave; he did right to carry off Bounding Fawn, for she is really his."

"Will my father bear witness to that?" the hunter pressed him.

"This very moment," the Chief answered eagerly; "and before all the warriors here present."

"Let my father do so, then, that all may know that Black-deer is no false-tongued thief; and when he declares that Bounding Fawn is his squaw, no one will have the right to say that it is not true."

"I will do so," Blackbird answered.

"Good! my father will follow us."

"I will follow you."

Blackbird then placed himself at the right of Loyal Heart, the band of warriors who accompanied him joined the procession, and all proceeded toward the ark of the first man, at the foot of which the hachesto was standing, holding in his hand the totem of the tribe. The sorcerer was standing in front of the totem, having on either side of him two Sachems chosen from among the wisest of the nation.

"What do you want here?" the sorcerer asked loyal Heart, when the latter halted about two yards from him with the procession.

"We demand justice," the hunter replied.

"Speak! We will give you that justice, whatever the consequences may be," the sorcerer said. "Well reflect before speaking, lest you may presently regret your precipitation."

"We shall only have to repent of one thing, and that is not having appeared before you earlier."

"My ears are open."

"We wish that justice should be done to a warrior, whose reputation attempts have been made to tarnish."

"Who is the warrior?"

"Black-deer."

"Is his medicine good?"

"His medicine is good."

"Is he a brave?"

"He is a great brave."

"What has he done?"

"Last night he carried off Bounding Fawn, the daughter of Blackbird here present."

"Good! Has he paid a fine ransom?"

"Let Blackbird himself answer."

"Yes," the old Chief here said, "I will answer. Black-deer is a great warrior, he has paid a noble ransom."

"In that case," said the sorcerer, "my son is satisfied?"

"I am satisfied."

There was a momentary silence, during which the sorcerer consulted in a whisper with the Sachems who acted as assessors. At length he spoke again.

"Black-deer is a great warrior," he said in a loud voice. "I, the medicine man, standing beneath the totem of the tribe, declare, that he has employed the right all renowned warriors possess of seizing their property wherever they may find it. From this moment Bounding Fawn is the squaw of Black-deer, to prepare his food, clean his weapons, carry his burdens, and take care of his war-chargers, and whoever says the contrary speaks falsely! Black-deer has the right to convey Bounding Fawn to his calli, and no one can prevent it; he is empowered, if she deceive him, to cut off her nose and ears. Blackbird will give two female buffalo hides to be hung up in the great medicine lodge."

At this final clause, known beforehand, however, for everything is strictly regulated by the code of etiquette in the matter of marriage, Blackbird made a frightful grimace. It seemed to him hard to part with two of the hides he had received but a few moments previously. But Loyal Heart came to his assistance, and interposed in a way that brought the smile back to his lips.

"Black-deer," he said in a loud voice, "loves Bounding Fawn, and will only owe her to himself—he alone will pay the tribute to the Wacondah; not two, but four female buffalo hides will be given to the medicine lodge."

He made a sign, and a warrior advanced, bearing the hides across his horse's neck. Loyal Heart took them and offered them to the sorcerer.

"My father will receive these skins," he said; "he will make such use of them as will be most agreeable to the Master of Life."

At this unexpected generosity, the audience burst into shouts of frenzied joy. The shells, drums, and chichikouès recommenced their infernal noise, and the procession set out again for Blackbird's calli. The old chief knew too well what he owed to himself, and the son-in-law he had just accepted, not to behave with proper decorum in spite of his avarice. When the procession reached the calli, he therefore said, in a loud voice—

"My brothers and friends, deign to honour with your presence the marriage banquet, and I shall be happy to see you take part in it. My son Black-deer will come, I feel convinced, to give the feast that family appearance which it ought to have."

He had scarce uttered the words, when a great noise was heard. The crowd parted violently, and in the space left free a horseman appeared, galloping at full speed: he held a woman on his horse's neck with one hand, while with the other he led a filly. At the sight of the horseman, the shouts and applause were redoubled, for everybody recognised Black-deer. On reaching the calli he leapt to the ground without uttering a syllable; then he drew his scalping knife and buried it in the neck of the filly. The poor brute gave a plaintive whining, trembled violently, and sank to the ground. The chief then turned it on its back, ripped open its chest, and tearing out the still quivering heart, he touched Bounding Fawn's forehead with it, while shouting in a voice loud enough to be heard by all the spectators.

"This is my squaw; woe to the man who touches her."

"I am his," the young wife then said.

The official ceremony was over: Black-deer and Bounding Fawn were married according to the rites of Comanche law. All dismounted, and the marriage feast began. The white men, who were not very eager to eat their portion of this Indian meal, composed in great measure of dog, boiled milk, and horse's flesh, had drawn on one side and tried to escape unnoticed. Unfortunately Blackbird and Black-deer watched them, and cut off their retreat; hence they were compelled, whether they liked it or no, to sit down to the banquet.

Tranquil, Loyal Heart, and their comrades made up their minds to the worst, and ate, or pretended to eat, with as good an appetite as the rest of the guests. The repast was prolonged till late in the day; for, though the Comanches do not drink spirits, and have not to fear intoxication, still, like all Indians, they are extraordinarily voracious, and eat till they can swallow no more.

The whites had hard work in declining those provisions, of more or less suspicious appearance, which were constantly offered to do them honour. Still, thanks to their thorough knowledge of Indian habits, they managed to escape the greater part of the infliction and see out the truly Homeric banquet without much annoyance. At the moment when Loyal Heart and Tranquil rose to retire, Black-deer approached them.

"Where are my brothers going?" he asked.

"To my calli," Loyal Heart replied.

"Good! Black-deer will join them there soon; he has to speak with his brothers on serious matters."

"Let my brother remain with his friends, tomorrow will be time enough."

The Chief frowned.

"My brother Loyal Heart must be careful," he said; "I have to consult with him on matters of the utmost gravity."

The hunter, struck by the Chiefs anxious air, looked at him with alarm.

"What is the matter?" he asked him.

"My brother will know in an hour."

"Very good, Chief; I will await you in my calli."

"Black-deer will come there."

The Chief then withdrew, laying his finger on his lip, and the hunters went off deep in thought.

CHAPTER X
RETURN TO LIFE

We are now compelled to go a little way back, and return to one of the principal actors of our story, whom we have too long neglected; we allude to White Scalper. The reader of the "Freebooters" will, doubtless, remember that the terrible combat on the deck of the brig, between Tranquil and the Scalper, was continued in the sea, into which the ferocious old man had been hurled by the negro who followed him.

Quoniam had been in too great a hurry in telling the Canadian of the death of his enemy; it is true, though, that the negro acted in good faith, and really believed he had killed him. The last dagger stab dealt by Quoniam was buried deep in the old man's chest; the wound was so serious that the Scalper immediately left off further resistance; his eyes closed, his nerves relaxed like broken springs; he loosed hold of his enemy, to whom he had hitherto clung, and remained an inert mass, tossed at the mercy of the waves.

The Negro, exhausted with fatigue and half suffocated, hastened back to the deck of the vessel, persuaded that his enemy was dead; but it was not so. The Scalper had merely lost his senses, and his inanimate body was picked up by a Mexican boat. But, when this boat reached the shore, the crew, on seeing the horrible wounds which covered the stranger's body, his pallor and corpse-like immobility, had, in their turn, fancied him dead, and taking no further trouble about him, threw him back into the sea. Fortunately for the Scalper, at the moment when the crew formed this determination the boat was close to land, so that his body, supported by the waves, was gently deposited on the sand, the lower part remaining submerged, while the head and chest were left dry by the retirement of the waves.

Either through the fresh night air or the oscillating movement the sea imparted to the lower part of his body, within an hour the old man gave a slight start; a sigh heaved his powerful chest, and a few instinctive attempts to change his position clearly showed that this vigorous organisation was struggling energetically against death, and compelling it to retire. At length the wounded man opened his eyes, but profound gloom still enveloped him like a winding sheet. On the other hand, the fatigue produced by the gigantic struggle he had sustained, and the enormous quantity of blood which had escaped through his wounds, caused him a general weakness, so great, both morally and physically, that it was impossible for the Scalper, not merely to find out where he was, but to remember the circumstances that had brought him there.

It was in vain that he tried to restore order in his ideas, or bring back his fugitive thoughts; the shock had been too rude; the commotion too strong; in spite of all his efforts he could not succeed in refastening the broken thread of his thoughts. He saw himself, alone, wounded, and abandoned on the seashore; he understood instinctively all the horror and desperation of his position; but no gleam of intelligence flashed across his brain to guide him in this fearful chaos. He was angry with himself at the impotence to which he found himself reduced and the impossibility of attempting anything to get only a few yards away from the sea, at the edge of which, he was lying, and which would infallibly swallow him up, if his weakness overcame his will and betrayed his courage.

Then took place on that desolate shore a horrible drama, filled with moving and startling incidents—the wild struggles of a half-dead man striving to reconquer the existence which was ebbing from him, and struggling with savage energy against the death whose fatal hand already pressed heavily upon him. The slightest movement the Scalper attempted occasioned him unheard of sufferings, not only through the numerous wounds, whose lips were filled with sand and gravel, but also because he was compelled to confess to himself that all his efforts would lead to no result, and that, unless a miracle happened, he was infallibly lost.

That miracle, which the wretch did not hope for, the very thought of which could not occur to him, Providence, whose ways are impenetrable, and who often only appears to save a guilty man to inflict on him a more terrible chastisement, was preparing to perform at the moment when the wounded man, his strength and energy exhausted, was falling back conquered on the beach, resolved to await coldly that death which he could not avoid.

The Texans had scattered along the beach several parties of Freebooters, who were intended to watch the movements of the Mexican cruisers. These parties were all within hail of each other, and able to assemble at a given point with extreme rapidity. Chance willed it that when the Scalper's body was again thrown into the sea it touched shore not far from a rather large rancho standing close to the beach, and in which the most influential Chiefs of the Texan army were this night assembled, in prevision of the great events that were preparing. Naturally the approaches to the rancho were carefully guarded, and numerous patrols marched around it in order to ensure the safety of the Chiefs.

One of these patrols had seen the Mexican boats land, and hurried up to drive them off, which they easily effected, as the Mexicans were not at all desirous to begin a fresh fight with enemies whose number and strength they were not acquainted with, and whom they supposed, with some appearance of reason, to be in communication with those rebels with whom they had been fighting an hour previously. When the boats got out to sea again, the Texans began carefully examining the beach, in order to be certain that all their enemies had retired and left nobody behind them. The first to discover the Scalper's body summoned his comrades, and soon the wounded man had twenty individuals round him. At the first moment they fancied him dead; the Scalper heard all that was said around him, but was unable to make a move or utter a word. He felt terribly alarmed for a moment; it was when a Freebooter, after bending over and carefully examining him, rose again with the careless remark:

"The poor devil is dead, we have nothing to do but dig a hole in the sand and put him in it, so that the coyotes and vultures may not devour his corpse. Some of you go and fetch the largest stones you can find while we dig a hole here with our machetes; it will soon be over."

At this sentence, pronounced in a perfectly calm and careless voice, as if it were the simplest and most natural thing in the world, the Scalper felt a cold perspiration beading at the root of his hair, and a shudder of terror run over his body. He made a tremendous effort to speak or shriek, but it was in vain. He was in that almost cataleptic state in which, although the intellect retains all its lucidity, the body is an inert and insensible mass which no longer obeys.

"Stay," said another adventurer interposing, and checking by a sign those who were preparing to pick up the stones; "let us not be in such a hurry. This poor wretch is a creature made after God's own image; although his is in a pitiable state, a breath of life may still be left in him. We shall still be in a position to bury him if we find that he is really dead; but first let us assure ourselves that any assistance is in vain."

"Nonsense," the first speaker continued; "Fray Antonio is always like that; were we to listen to him, all the dead would only be wounded, and he would make us lose precious time in giving them useless care. However, as there is nothing to hurry us at this moment, I ask no better than to try and bring this man round, although he appears to me as dead as a fellow can well be."

"No matter," Fray Antonio answered, "let us try, at any rate."

"Very good," said the other with a shrug of the shoulders.

"And first let us remove him from here. When, he is perfectly dry, and runs no further risk of being carried off by the waves, we will see what we have to do."

The wounded man was immediately picked up by four Freebooters, and gently carried some twenty yards off to an entirely dry spot, where it was impossible for the sea to reach him. The worthy monk then produced a large case bottle of rum, which he uncorked, and after explaining his duty to each, that is to say, after ordering that the temples, wrists, and pit of the stomach should be vigorously rubbed with rum, he bent over him, and opening his jaws, which were tight as a vice, with the blade of his dagger, he poured into his mouth an honest quartern of rum. The effect of this double treatment was not long delayed. In a few seconds the wounded man gave a alight start, opened his eyes feebly, and, gave vent to a sigh of relief.

"Ah, ah," said Fray Antonio with a laugh: "what do you think of that, No Ruperto? I fancy your dead man is coming to life again, eh?"

"On my word, it is true," the other answered with a grin; "well, that is a man who can flatter himself with having his soul screwed into his body; by Bacchus! If he recover, which I did not yet assert, he can say that he has made a preciously long journey."

In the meantime, the friction was continued with the same vigour; the circulation of the blood was rapidly re-established; the Scalper's eyes became less haggard, his features were relaxed, and an expression of comfort spread over his countenance.

"Do you feel better?" the monk asked him kindly.

"Yes," he answered in a weak, though perfectly distinct voice.

"All the better. With the help of Heaven we will get you out of the scrape."

By a singular accident, the monk had not yet recognised the man to whom he had himself owed his life a few months previously. The wounds were carefully washed with rum and water, and cleared from the sand and gravel adhering to them; they were then poulticed with pounded oregano leaves, an extremely effective remedy for wounds, and then carefully tied up.

"There," the monk continued with an air of satisfaction, "that is finished. I will now have you carried to a spot where you will be much better able than here to enjoy that repose which is indispensable for you after so rude a shock."

"Do what you please with me," the wounded man answered with an effort; "I owe you too much to offer the slightest objection."

"The more so," Ruperto answered with a laugh, "because it would be perfectly useless; the reverend Father has undertaken your cure, and, whether you like it or no, you must follow his prescriptions."

At a sign from Fray Antonio, four powerful men raised the patient in their arms, and carried him into the rancho. It was he who Colonel Melendez had seen go in, when led by chance to the same rancho, he had for some minutes listened to, and surveyed what was going on inside. The rancho belonged to a rich Texan haciendero, a devoted partisan of the revolution, and who was delighted to place at the disposal of the Chiefs a retreat which he had built in happier times for a summer villa. This house, while agreeably situated, spacious, and well kept up, was abundantly provided, not only with everything indispensable for existence, but also with those thousand trifles and luxuries which are conventionally called comfort, and which rich persons, through lengthened habit, cannot do without.

The Chiefs were at first rather annoyed at the free and easy way in which Fray Antonio, without giving them notice, had encumbered them with a wounded stranger. But when they saw in what a pitiable state the poor fellow was, they made no further objection, but allowed the monk to instal him where he thought best. Fray Antonio did not allow the permission to be repeated. Aided by the master of the rancho, he transported the wounded man to a spacious and airy room, whose windows looked out on the sea, and in which the Scalper was placed in an admirably healthy condition.

So soon as the patient was laid in a bed expressly made for him—for in these torrid climates the inhabitants are accustomed to sleep on mats, or at the most in hammocks—the monk handed him a narcotic drink, which he requested him to swallow. The effect was almost immediate; a few minutes after he had drunk it, White Scalper fell into a calm and restorative sleep. The entire night passed without any incident; the wounded man slept for eight hours at a stretch, and when he awoke, he was no longer the same; he felt fresh, cheerful, and reposed.

Several days passed thus, during which Fray Antonio paid him the closest and most affectionate attention. If, at the first moment, the monk was unable to recognise the White Scalper, it was not long ere he did so by daylight; after carefully examining this man, whose appearance had really something strange and remarkable about it, his recollection returned, and he recognised the hunter so greatly feared on the prairie by the Redskins, and even by the whites, and to whom himself owed his life under such singular circumstances; hence, he was pleased at the opportunity chance afforded him of repaying his debt to this man. But as, on the other hand, the wounded man, either through obstinacy or defective memory, did not appear at all to remember him, the monk kept his discovery to himself, and continued his attentions to the wounded man without permitting himself the slightest allusion which might cause the other to suspect that he was recognised.

Things went on thus till the day of the battle of Cerro Pardo. In the morning, as usual, Fray Antonio entered his patient's room, whose cure was rapidly advancing, thanks to the efficacy of the oregano leaves. His wounds were almost cicatrized, and he felt his strength returning.

"My friend," said the monk to him, "I have done all for you I morally could; you will do me the justice of saying that I nursed you like a brother."

"I have only thanks to offer you," the wounded man said, stretching out his hand.

"Much obliged," said Fray Antonio, as he took this hand; "today I have bad news for you."

"Bad news?" the other repeated in surprise.

"After all," the monk continued, "the news may be good. Still, to deal frankly with you, I do not believe it; I augur no good from what we are going to do."

"I must confess that I do not at all understand you, so I should feel extremely obliged if you would explain yourself more clearly."

"That is true. Indeed, you cannot suspect anything. In two words, this is the affair: the army has received orders to march forward this very morning."

"So that— —?" the wounded man asked.

"I am, to my great regret," the monk said with a crafty smile, "compelled to leave you behind."

"Hum!" the White Scalper mattered in some alarm.

"Unless," Fray Antonio continued, "as I dare not hope, we beat the Mexicans, in which case you are certain to see me again."

The patient seemed to grow more and more restless about the position in which he ran a risk of being left.

"Did you come solely to tell me that?" he asked.

"No. I wished to make you a proposal."

"What is it?" the other eagerly asked.

"Listen. I picked you up in a most desperate state."

"That is true: I allow it."

"Although some people say," Fray Antonio continued, "that you received your wounds in fighting against us, and, indeed, some of our men declare themselves certain of the fact, I would not put faith in their words. I know not why, but since I have been nursing you, I have grown to take an interest in you; I should not like the cure I have carried on hitherto so successfully, to break down. This is what I propose: about one hundred miles from the spot where we now are, there is an encampment of white men and half-breeds, over whom I possessed considerable influence some time back. I believe that they have not yet quite forgotten me, and that anyone joining them as from me, would meet with a kindly reception. Will you go there? It is a risk to run."

"How could I perform this journey in my present state of weakness and prostration?"

"That need not trouble you. Four men, who are devoted to me, will conduct you to my old friends."

"Oh, if that be the case," the Scalper exclaimed eagerly, "I gladly accept. If I perished on the road, I would prefer that to remaining here alone."

"I trust that you will not perish, but reach your destination all right. So that is agreed. You will go?"

"With the greatest pleasure. When do we start?"

"At once, there is not a moment to lose."

"Good! Give the necessary orders, I am ready."

"I must warn you, however, that the men to whom I am sending you, are slightly of a scampish nature, and you must not assume any high moral tone with them."

"What does it concern me? if they were even pirates of the prairies, believe me, I should attach no importance to the fact."

"Bravo! I see that we understand each other, for I believe these worthy gentlemen dabble a little in all trades."

"Good, good!" the Scalper gaily answered; "Do not trouble yourself about that."

"In that case, get ready to start; I shall return in ten minutes at the latest."

With these words, the monk left the room. The old man, who had not many preparations to make, was soon in a position to take the road. As he had stated, within ten minutes the monk returned, followed by four men. Among them was Ruperto, who, it will be remembered, offered the advice to bury the wounded man in the sand. The Scalper was still very weak, and incapable of either walking or sitting a horse. The monk had remedied this inconvenience, as far as possible, by having a clumsy litter prepared for the wounded man, carried by two mules, and in which he could recline. This mode of transport was very slow, and extremely inconvenient, especially for the guides, in a country such as they had to cross; but it was the only one practicable at the moment, and so they must put up with it. The wounded man was carried to the litter, and laid on it as comfortably as was possible.

"And now," said the monk, "may Heaven direct you; do not feel at all alarmed, Ruperto has many instructions, and I know him well enough to be convinced that he will not depart from them, whatever may happen. So you can trust to him. Good bye!"

And, after giving the wounded man his hand, Fray Antonio made a movement to retire.

"One moment," said the old man, as he held the hand he had taken; "I wish to say but one word to you."

"Speak, but be brief. I have the weightiest reasons for desiring your immediate departure; in a few minutes some wounded men will arrive here, who have hitherto been kept in the fort, and whom you would probably not be at all pleased to meet."

"I fancy I can understand to whom you allude; but that is not the question. I wish, before parting with you, and not knowing whether I shall ever see you again, to express to you the gratitude I feel for your conduct toward me, a gratitude which is the greater because I am convinced you have recognised me."

"And suppose I have?"

"You needed only to say one word to surrender me to my most inveterate enemies; and yet you did not utter that word."

"Certainly not; for even supposing, as you seem to believe, that I have recognised you, I was only discharging a debt I had incurred with you."

The old man's face writhed; his eye became moist; he warmly squeezed the monk's hand, which he had till now held in his own, and it was with much emotion and tenderness that he added—

"Thanks. This kindness will not be lost; the events of the last few days have greatly modified my way of looking at certain things; you shall never regret having saved my life."

"I hope so; but be gone, and may Heaven guard you!"

"We shall meet again."

"Who knows?" the monk muttered, as he gave the guides a signal.

The latter flogged their mules, and the litter began moving. About an hour after the start, it met a covered cart, in which lay Tranquil, but they passed without seeing each other. The monk had only spoken the truth about Ruperto. The worthy adventurer was most attentive to the sick man, carefully watching over him, and trying to while away the tedium of the journey. Unluckily, the party had to cross an essentially primitive country, in which there were no roads, and where the guides were generally obliged to cut a path with their axes. The litter advanced but slowly, and with unheard of difficulty, along the abominable tracts, and, despite the most minute precautions, the wounded man suffered horribly from the jolting and shakes the mules gave the litter almost every moment.

Ruperto, to fatigue the patient as little as possible, only travelled by night, or very early in the morning, ere the sun had acquired its full strength. They marched thus for a fortnight, during which the country grew wilder, and the ground gradually ascended; the scenery became more abrupt and stern, the virgin forests closed in, and they could see that they were approaching the mountains.

One evening, when the little party had established their night bivouac on the banks of a rapid stream that flowed into the Arkansas, the Scalper, who, in spite of the privations and fatigue to which he had been constantly exposed since his departure from the rancho, felt his strength gradually returning, asked his guide how many days their journey would still last— which as yet he had been unwilling to do, through a feeling of delicacy. At this question, Ruperto smiled cunningly.

"Our journey has been finished for the last four days," he said.

"What do you mean?" the Scalper asked with a start of surprise.

"The people we are going to see," the adventurer went on, "do not like to receive visits without being previously advised; surprises do not agree with them. In order to avoid any misunderstanding, which is always to be regretted between old friends, I employed the only means in my power."

"And what is it?"

"Oh, it is very simple. Just look at our camp—do people guard themselves in this way on the desert? Instead of being at the top of a hill, we are at the watering place of the wild beasts; the smoke from our fire, instead of being concealed, is, on the contrary, visible for a great distance. Do all these acts of imprudence committed purposely teach you nothing?"

"Ah, ah," the old man said, "then you wish your friends to surprise us?"

"Quite right. In that way the recognition will be effected without striking a blow. And stay! If I am not mistaken, we are about to receive visitors."

At this moment the branches of a neighbouring thicket were roughly parted and several men rushed into the camp, with the machete in one hand, the rifle in the other.

CHAPTER XI
THE PIRATES OF THE PRAIRIES

The White Scalper gave an imperceptible start at the unexpected apparition of the strangers; but he had sufficient power over himself apparently to preserve that coolness and stoicism which the Redskins and wood rangers make a point of honour. He did not alter the careless attitude he was in, and though he appeared to look at the newcomers absently, he, however, examined them attentively.

They were at least twenty in number, for they had risen from all sides at once, and in a twinkling surrounded the travellers. These men, mostly clad in the trapper's hunting shirt and fox skin cap, had a vigorous appearance, and a ferocious look, not at all adapted to inspire confidence; moreover, they were armed to the teeth, not only having the rifle and machete, but also the scalping knife and tomahawk employed by the Indians.

The man who appeared to be their Chief was at the most thirty-five years of age, tall, well-built and proportioned; his wide forehead, black eyes, Grecian nose, and large mouth, made up a face pleasing at the first glance, though on examining it more closely, you soon perceived that his glance was false, and that a sardonic smile constantly played round his thin and pale lips. His face was framed in by thick black curls, which fell in disorder on his shoulders and mixed with a large beard, which the fatigues of a wandering and adventurous life were beginning to silver at places.

The four Texan adventurers had not made a move; the Chief of the strangers looked at them for a moment with his hands crossed on his rifle barrel, the butt of which rested on the ground. At length, by a movement that was familiar to him, he threw back his curls, and addressed Ruperto—

"Halloh, gossip," he said, "you here? What has brought you into our parts?"

"A wish to see you, gossip," the other answered, as he carelessly struck a light for the cigarette he had just finished rolling.

"Nonsense! Only that?" the stranger continued.

"What other motive could I have, Master Sandoval?"[1]

"Who knows?" the other said with a shake of his head; "Life has such strange changes."

"This time you are mistaken. Nothing disagreeable forces me to pay you a visit."

"That is more and more extraordinary. Then, you have come on your own accord, nothing compelling you to do so?"

"I do not say that, for my visit necessarily has a motive. Still, it is not at all of the nature you suppose."

"Canarios! I am glad to see that I am not so far from the truth as it appeared at first."

"All the better!"

"But why did not you come straight to our encampment, if you were seeking us, as you say?"

Ruperto burst into a laugh.

"That would have been a fine idea, to be welcomed with a shower of slugs! No, I think I acted more wisely as I have."

"We have been on your trail for three days."

"Why did you not show yourselves sooner?"

"I was not quite certain it was you."

"Well, that is possible. Will you not sit down?"

"What for? Now that we have met, I hope you will come to our camp?"

"I did not like to propose it; you see we are not alone, but have a stranger with us."

"What matter, if you answer for him?"

"With my life."

"Well, then, the friends of our friends are ours, and have a claim to our attention."

"I thank you, Caballero," the Scalper replied with a bow; "I trust you will have no cause to repent having offered me hospitality."

"The company in which I find you is an excellent guarantee to me, Señor," the adventurer continued with a courteous smile.

"Do you intend to lead us to your camp tonight?" Ruperto asked.

"Why not? We are not more than fifteen miles from it at the most."

"That is true; but this caballero is wounded, and so long a distance after a fatiguing day—"

"Oh, I feel very well, I assure you. My strength has almost entirely returned; I even believe that, were it absolutely necessary, I could sit a horse. Hence do not put yourself out of the way for me, I beg," the old man said.

"As it is so, we will start whenever you like."

"All right," said Sandoval; "however, I will undertake to lead you by a road which will shorten your distance one half."

All being thus arranged, the horses were saddled afresh, and they started. The strangers were on foot; the Scalper would not enter the litter, and even insisted on it being left behind, declaring that he did not want it, and cutting a rather long branch, he converted it into a staff. He then took his place by Sandoval's side, who, delighted by his manner, gave him a glance of satisfaction.

Sandoval, as we have said, was the Chief of the men who had so suddenly fallen on the bivouac of the adventurers. These men were pirates of the prairies. In a previous work, we have described what they are; but as it is probable that many of our readers do not know the book to which we allude, we will explain, in as few words as possible, what sort of persons these gentry are. In the United States, and most of the countries of the new world, men are encountered who, not being restrained by any species of moral obligation or family consideration, yield themselves without restraint to all the violence of their evil passions. These men, led in the first instance into debauchery by indolence, and almost certain of impunity in countries where the police are powerless to protect honest people and enforce the laws, at length grow to commit the most atrocious crimes in open daylight, though this is common enough in those countries where the strongest make the laws.

This goes on until the reprobation becomes general, and public indignation at last growing stronger than the terror inspired by these villains, they are compelled to fly from town to town in order to escape the exemplary punishment of Lynch-law. Everywhere pursued like wild beasts, abandoned by all, even by their accomplices, they draw nearer and nearer to the Indian border, which they eventually cross, and are henceforth condemned to live and die in the desert. But there, too, everything is hostile to them—white trappers, wood rangers, Indian warriors, and wild beasts— they are compelled to endure a daily and hourly struggle to defend their life, which is incessantly assailed. But they have before them space, the hiding places on the mountains and in the virgin forests, and hence can sustain the combat to a certain point. Still, if they remained isolated they would infallibly succumb to cold, hunger, and wretchedness, even supposing they were not surprised, scalped, and massacred by their implacable enemies.

These outlaws from society, whom every man thinks he has a right to hunt down, frankly accept their position. They feel proud of the hatred and repulsion they inspire, and collect in numerous bands to requite the anathema cast upon them. Taking as their rule the pitiless law of the prairies, eye for eye and tooth for tooth, they become formidable through their numbers, and repay their enemies the injuries they receive from them. Woe to the trappers or Indians who venture to traverse the prairies alone, for the pirates massacre them pitilessly. The emigrant trains are also attacked and pillaged by them with refined and atrocious barbarity. Some of these men who have retained a little shame, put off the dress of white men to assume that of Redskins, so as to make those they pillage suppose they have been attacked by Indians; hence their most inveterate enemies are the Indians, for whom they try to pass. Still, it frequently happens that the pirates, ally themselves with Redskins belonging to one nation to make war on another.

All is good for them when their object is plunder; but what they prefer is raising scalps, for which the Government of the United States, that patriarchal government which protects the natives, according to some heartless optimists, are not ashamed to pay fifty dollars a-piece. Hence, the pirates are as skilful as the Indians themselves in raising hair; but with them all scalps are good; and when they cannot come across Indians, they have no scruple about scalping white men; the more so, because the United States does not look into matters very closely, and pays without bargaining or entering into details, provided that the hair be long and black.

Captain Sandoval's band of pirates was one of the most numerous and best organised in Upper Arkansas; his comrades, all thorough food for the gallows, formed the most magnificent collection of bandits that could be imagined. For a long period, Fray Antonio, if not forming part of the band, had taken part in its operations, and derived certain though illegal profit by supplying the captain with information about the passage of caravans, their strength, and the road they intended to follow. Although the worthy monk had given up this hazardous traffic, his conversion had not been of so old a date for the pirates to have completely forgotten the services he had rendered them; hence, when he was compelled to abandon White Scalper he thought at once of his old friends. This idea occurred to him the more naturally, because White Scalper, owing to the mode of life he had hitherto led in the desert, had in his character some points of resemblance with the pirates, who, like him, were pitiless, and recognised no other law than their caprice.

In the band of Freebooters the monk had organised since his reformation were some men more beaten than the others by the tempest of an adventurous life. These men Fray Antonio had seen at work, and set their full value upon them; but he kept them near him, through a species of intuition, in order to have them under his hand if some day fate desired that he should be compelled to have recourse to an heroic remedy to get out of a scrape, which was easy to foresee when a man entered on the life of a partisan. Among these chosen comrades was naturally Ruperto; hence it was to him he entrusted the choice of three sure men to escort the wounded man to the camp of Captain Sandoval, in Upper Arkansas. We have seen that the monk was not mistaken, and in what way Ruperto performed the commission confided to him.

It has frequently been said that honest men always recognise each other at the first glance; but the statement is far truer when applied to rogues. The White Scalper and the Pirate Chief had not walked side by side for ten minutes ere the best possible understanding was arrived at between them. The Captain admired as an amateur, and especially as a connoisseur, the athletic stature of his new companion. His rigid features, which seemed carved in granite, for they were so firm and marked, his black and sparkling eyes, and even his blunt and sharp mode of speech, attracted and aroused his sympathy. Several times he proposed to have him carried on the shoulders of two of his most powerful comrades across awkward spots; but the old man, although his ill-closed wounds caused him extreme suffering, and fatigue overpowered him, constantly declined these kind offers, merely replying that physical pain was nothing, and that the man who could not conquer it by the strength of his will, ought to be despised as an old woman.

There could be no reply to such a peremptory mode of reasoning, so Sandoval merely contented himself with nodding an assent, and they continued their march in silence. Night had fallen for some time, but it was a bright and starry night, which allowed them to march in safety, and have no fear of losing their way. After three hours of a very difficult journey, the travellers at length reached the crest of a high hill.

"We have arrived," Sandoval then said, as he stopped under the pretext of resting a moment, but in reality to give his companion, whom he saw to be winded, though he made no complaint, an opportunity to draw breath.

"What, arrived?" the Scalper said in surprise, looking round him, but not perceiving the slightest sign of an encampment.

In fact, the adventurers found themselves on a species of platform about fifteen hundred yards long, entirely denuded of trees, save in the centre, where grew an immense aloe, more than sixty feet in circumference, which looked like the king of the desert, over which it soared. Sandoval allowed his comrade to look around him for a moment, and then said, as he stretched out his arm to the giant tree—-

"We shall be obliged to enter by the chimney. But once is not always, and you will not feel offended at it when I tell you that I only do this to shorten our journey."

"You know that I did not at all understand you," the Scalper answered.

"I suspected it," Sandoval said with a smile. "But come along, and you will soon decipher the enigma."

The old man bowed without replying, and both walked toward the tree, followed by their comrades, who were smiling at the stranger's amazement. On reaching the foot of the tree, Sandoval raised his head—

"Ohé!" he shouted, "Are you there, Orson?"

"Where should I be if I was not?" a rough voice answered, issuing from the top of the tree. "I was obliged to wait for you here, as you have taken it, into your head to wander about the whole night through."

The pirates burst into a laugh.

"Always amiable!" Sandoval continued; "it is astonishing how funny that animal of an Orson always is! Come, let down the ladder, you ugly brute!"

"Ugly brute, ugly brute!" the voice growled, although its owner still remained invisible; "That is the way in which he thanks me."

In the meanwhile, a long wooden ladder was let down through the branches. Sandoval caught hold of it, secured it, and then turned to the wounded man—

"I will go first to show you the way."

"Do so," the Scalper said resolutely; "but I swear that I will be the second."

"Halloh!" the Captain said, turning round, "Why you are a Yankee."

"What does it matter to you?" the other said roughly.

"Not at all. Still, I am not sorry to know the fact."

"Well, you know it. What next?"

"Next?" Sandoval answered with a laugh; "You will be among countrymen, that is all."

"It makes little difference to me."

"Canarios, and how do you suppose it concerns me?" the Captain said, still laughing, and ascended.

The wounded man followed him step for step. The ladder was resting against a platform about two yards in width, completely concealed in a mass of inextricable foliage. On this platform stood the giant to whom his Chief had given the name of Orson, a name which was exactly suitable, so rough and savage did he appear.

"Any news?" the Captain asked, as he stepped on the platform.

"None," the other answered laconically.

"Have all the detachments returned?"

"All except you."

"Are the Gazelle and the American girl in the grotto?"

"They are."

"That is well. When all the people have come up, you will remove the ladder and join us."

"All right, Caray, I suppose I know what I have to do."

Sandoval contented himself with shrugging his shoulders.

"Come," he said to the Scalper, who was a silent witness of this scene.

They crossed the platform. The centre of the tree was entirely hollow, but it had not been rendered so by human agency; old age alone had converted the heart of the tree into dust, while the bark remained green and vigorous. The pirates, who had for many years inhabited a very large cave that ran under the hill, had one day seen the earth give way at a certain spot, in consequence of a storm; this was the way in which the chimney, as they called it, had been discovered.

The pirates, like all plundering animals, are very fond of having several issues to their lairs; this new one, supplied to them by accident, caused them the greater pleasure, because by the same occasion they obtained an observatory, whence they could survey an immense extent of country, which enabled them to see any enemy who might attempt to take them by surprise. A platform was formed at a certain height to keep the bark intact; and by means of two ladders, fitted one inside and one out, a communication was established.

Sandoval, in his heart, enjoyed his guest's surprise. In fact, the pirate's ingenious arrangement seemed marvellous to White Scalper, who, forgetting his phlegm and stoicism, allowed his surprise to be seen.

"Now," he said to him, pointing to a second ladder, which descended a considerable depth into the ground, "we will go down."

"At your service, at your service," the stranger answered. "It is really admirable. Go on, I follow you."

They then began descending cautiously owing to the darkness, for the pirate placed as sentry on the *Mirador* had, either through forgetfulness or malice, neglected to bring torches, not supposing, as he said, that his comrades would return so late. White Scalper alone had followed the pirates by the strange road we have indicated. This road, very agreeable for foot passengers, was, of course, completely impracticable for horsemen; hence Ruperto and his three comrades quitted Sandoval at the foot of the hill, and making a rather long detour, sought the real entrance of the cave, with which all four had been long acquainted.

As the two men gradually descended, the light increased, and they seemed to be entering a furnace. On setting foot on the ground, the Scalper found himself in an immense cavern, lighted by a profusion of torches held by pirates, who, grouped at the foot of the ladder, seemed to find an honour in waiting the arrival of their Chief, and offering him a grand reception. The grotto was of an enormous size; the spot where White Scalper found himself was a vast hall, whence radiated several galleries of immense length, and running in diametrically opposite directions. The scene that offered itself to the Scalper in this hall, where he arrived so unexpectedly, would have been worthy of Callot's pencil. Here could be seen strange faces, extraordinary costumes, impossible attitudes, all of which gave a peculiar character to this multitude of bandits, who were hailing their Chief with shouts of joy, and howls like those of wild beasts.

Captain Sandoval knew too well the sort of people he had to deal with, to be affected in any way by the reception his bandits had improvised for him; instead of appearing touched by their enthusiasm, he frowned, drew up his head, and looked menacingly at the attentive crowd.

"What is this, Caballeros?" he said; "How comes it that you are all here waiting for me? *Viva Dios!* Some mistake must have occurred in the execution of my orders to make you collect so eagerly round me. Well, leave me, we will clear that up on another occasion, for the present I wish to be alone: begone!"

The bandits, without replying, bowed to the Chief, and immediately withdrew, dispersing so promptly in the side galleries, that in less than five minutes the hall was entirely deserted. At the same moment Ruperto appeared; he had left his companions with old comrades who had undertaken to do them the honours of the grotto, and now came to join the man who had been entrusted to his care. Sandoval offered his hand cordially to the adventurer, but it was the cordiality of a man who feels himself at home, which the Texan noticed.

"Halloh!" he said, "We are no longer on the prairie, it strikes me."

"No," the Captain answered, seriously, and he laid some stress on the words, "you are in my house, but," he added, with a pleasant smile, "that must not trouble you; you are my guests, and will be treated as you deserve to be."

"Good, good," Ruperto said, who would not let himself be imposed on by this cavalier manner, "I know where the shoe pinches, gossip. Well, I will find a remedy," and he turned to Orson, who at this moment came down the ladder with his rough and savage face; "beg White Gazelle to come hither; tell her particularly that Captain Sandoval wishes to see her."

The Chief of the pirates smiled and offered his hand to Ruperto.

"Forgive me, Ruperto," he said to him, "but you know how I love that girl. When I am a single day without seeing her, I fancy that I want something, and feel unhappy."

"Canarios! I am well aware of it," Ruperto answered, with a smile; "hence, you see, that to restore you to your right temper I did not hesitate to give Orson orders to fetch the only person you have ever loved."

The Captain sighed, but made no answer.

"Come," the adventurer continued, gaily, "she will come, so recover your spirits. Caramba! It would be a fine thing for you to feel any longer vexed about a child who probably forgot to kiss you on your return because she was at play. Remember, we are your guests, that we have the claims which hospitality gives us, and that you must not, under any pretext, look black at us."

"Alas, my friends," he answered, with a stifled sigh, "you know not, you cannot know, how sweet it is for a wretch like me, an outlaw, to be able to say to himself that there exists in the world a creature who loves him for himself, and without afterthought."

"Silence," Ruperto said quickly, as he laid his hand on his arm, "here she comes."

[1] See Trail-Hunter, same publishers.

CHAPTER XII
IN THE CAVERN

Ruperto was not mistaken: at this moment the most exquisite little creature imaginable came bounding up like a fawn. It was a girl of twelve years of age at the most, fresh, smiling, and beautifully formed. Her long black hair, her rosy-lipped mouth, with its pearly teeth, her magnificent black hair floating into immense curls down to her knee, her eccentric costume, rather masculine than feminine, all concurred to give an imprint of strangeness, and render her fantastic, extraordinary, almost angelic, so striking a contrast did her lovely head appear to the vulgar and hideous bandits who surrounded her. So soon as the girl perceived the Captain, a flash of delight shot from her eye, and with one bound she was in his arms, pressed to his large and powerful chest lovingly.

"Ah," he said, as he kissed her silken curls, and in a voice which he tried in vain to soften, "here you are at last, my darling Gazelle,[1] you have been long in coming."

"Father," she answered, as she repaid his caresses, and in a deliciously modulated voice, "I was not aware of your return. It was late, I did not hope to see you tonight, so I was about to sleep."

"Well, Niña," he said, as he put her on the ground again and gave her a final kiss, "you must not remain here any longer. I have seen you, I have kissed you, and my stock of happiness is laid in till tomorrow. Go and sleep. I am not egotistic, I do not wish you to lose your healthy cheeks."

"Oh," she said, with a little shake of her charming head, "I no longer feel inclined for sleep; I can remain a few minutes longer with you, father."

White Scalper gazed with growing astonishment on this admirable child, so gay, so laughing, so loving, and who appeared so beloved. He could not account for her presence among the pirates, or the affection their Captain testified for her.

"You love this child very dearly," he said, as he drew her gently towards him, and kissed her on the forehead.

She looked at him with widely opened eyes, but did not evince the slightest fear, or try to avoid his caresses.

"You ask if I love her," the pirate answered; "that child is the joy and happiness of our house. Do you think, then," he added, with some bitterness, "that because we are outlawed bandits we have stifled every generous feeling in our hearts? Undeceive yourself. The jaguar and panther love their cubs, the grizzly bear cherishes its whelps; should we be more ferocious than these animals, which are regarded as the most cruel in creation? Yes, yes, we love our White Gazelle! She is our good genius, our guardian angel; so long as she remains among us we shall succeed in everything, for good fortune accompanies her."

"Oh, in that case, father," she said eagerly, "you will always be fortunate, for I shall never leave you."

"Who can answer for the future?" he muttered in a choking voice, while a cloud of sorrow spread over his manly face.

"You are a happy father," the Scalper said, with a profound sigh.

"Yes, am I not? White Gazelle is not mine alone, she belongs to us all; she is our adopted daughter."

"Ah!" said the Scalper, without adding anything more, and letting his head drop sadly.

"Go, child," Sandoval exclaimed, "go and sleep, for night is drawing on."

The child withdrew, after saluting the three men with a soft glance, and soon disappeared in the depths of a side gallery. The Captain looked after her so long as he could perceive her, then turning to his guests, who, like himself, had remained under the spell of this touching scene, he said—

"Follow me, Señores; it is growing late, you must be hungry, and need rest. The hospitality I am enabled to offer you will be modest, but frank and cordial."

The two men bowed and followed him into a gallery, on each side of which were cells enclosed by large mats fastened to the walls in the shape of curtains; at regular distances torches of ocote wood, fixed in iron rings, spread a reddish and smoky light, sufficient, however to guide them. After walking for about ten minutes, and traversing several passages communicating with each other and forming a regular labyrinth, in which anyone else must inevitably have lost his way, the Captain stopped before a cell, and raising the curtains that formed the doorway, made his companions a sign to enter. Sandoval followed them, and let the mat fall again behind him.

The cell into which the Captain introduced his guests was vast; the walls were rather lofty, and allowed the air to penetrate through invisible fissures, which rendered it pleasant, while wooden partitions divided it into several chambers. A golden censer, probably stolen from a church, and hanging from the roof, contained a lamp of fragrant oil, which spread a brilliant light through the cavern. Unfortunately, the rest of the furniture did not at all harmonize with this princely specimen, but was, on the contrary, most modest. It was composed of a large table of black oak, clumsily shaped, six equipals, and two butacas, a sort of easy chair with sloping back, and which alone had any pretensions to comfort. The walls were decorated with antlers of elks and bighorns, buffalo horns, and grizzly bear claws, the spolia opima of animals killed by the pirates during their chase on the desert.

The only thing that attracted attention was a magnificent rack, containing all the weapons used in America, from the lance, arrow, and sagaie, up to the sword, the machete, the double-barrelled gun, and the holster pistol. It was evident that the pirate had given orders for the reception of his guests, for wooden plates, glasses, and silver dishes were arranged on the table among large pots of red clay containing, some water, and others mezcal and pulque, those two favourite beverages of the Mexicans. Orson, with his savage face and ordinary, sulky look, was ready to wait on the guests.

"To table, Señores," Sandoval said gravely, as he drew up an equipal and sat down on it.

The others followed his example, and each drawing his knife from his belt, began a general and vigorous attack on a magnificent venison pasty. The appetite of the guests, sharpened by a long day's fasting, needed such a comforter. However, we are bound to do the Chief of the pirates the justice of saying that his larder appeared amply supplied, and that he did the honours of the table admirably.

The first moments of the meal were passed in silence, as the Mexicans thought only of eating. But when the sharpest hunger was appeased, and, according to the Anglo-American fashion generally admitted on the prairies, the bottle circulated, the apparent coldness that had prevailed among the company suddenly disappeared, and each began conversing with his next neighbour; then the voices were gradually raised, and ere long everybody was talking at the same time.

During the repast which threatened to degenerate into an orgy, two men alone had moderately applied themselves to the bottle; they were Sandoval and White Scalper. The Chief of the pirates, while exciting his guests to drink, was very careful to retain his sobriety and coolness. He examined with some anxiety the singular man whom chance had given him as a guest; this gloomy face caused him a feeling of discomfort for which he could not account. Still he did not dare question him, for the law of the desert prohibits the slightest inquiry being made of a stranger, so long as he thinks proper to maintain his incognito.

Fortunately for Sandoval, whose impatience and curiosity momentarily increased, Ruperto had an equal desire to explain the object of his visit to the prairies. At the moment, therefore, when the private conversations, growing more and more animated, had become general, and each seemed to be trying which could shout the loudest, the Texan smote the table several times loudly with the pommel of his dagger to demand silence. The shouts stopped instantaneously, and all heads were turned towards him.

"What do you want, Ruperto?" Sandoval asked him.

"What do I want?" the other answered, whose tongue was growing dull under the influence of the numerous and copious draughts he had taken; "I want to speak."

"Silence!" the Captain shouted in a stentorian voice; "now, go on, Ruperto! No one will interrupt you, even if you spoke till sunrise."

"Demonios!" the Texan said, with a laugh, "I have no pretence to abuse your patience so long."

"Act as you please, gossip: you are my guest, and more than that, an old acquaintance, which gives you the right to do whatever you please here."

"Thanks for your gallantry, Captain; I must, in the first place, in my own name and in that of the persons who accompany me, offer you sincere thanks for your splendid hospitality."

"Go on, go on," the Captain said, carelessly:

"No, no; on the contrary, Caramba! A table so well served as yours is not to be found every day on the prairie. A man must be as ungrateful as a monk not to feel thankful."

"Halloh!" the Captain said, laughingly, "Did you not tell me, when I met you this evening, that you were sent to me by Fray Antonio?"

"I did, Captain."

"A worthy monk," Sandoval observed; "he reminds one of the Rev. John Zimmers, a protestant minister, who was hung about ten years back at Baton Rouge, for bigamy. He was a very holy man! I remember that at the foot of the gallows he made the crowd an edifying speech, which drew tears from most of his hearers. But let us return to Fray Antonio; I hope that no accident has happened to him, and that he still enjoys good health."

"When I left him his health was excellent. Still it is possible that he may be dangerously ill at this moment, or even dead."

"Rayo de Dios! You alarm me, gossip. Explain yourself."

"It is very simple: Texas, wearied with the incessantly renewed exactions of Mexico, has revolted to gain its liberty."

"Very good; I know it."

"You know too, of course, that all the men of talent have arrayed themselves beneath the flag of Independence. Naturally Fray Antonio raised a cuadrilla, and offered his services to the insurgents."

"That is very ingenious," the Captain said, with a smile.

"Is it not? Oh! Fray Antonio is a clever politician."

"Yes, yes, and proof of it is that at the beginning of the insurrection it often happened that he did not know himself to which party he belonged."

"What would you have?" Ruperto said, carelessly, "it is so difficult to find one's way in a general upset; but now it is no longer the case."

"Ah! It seems that he is fixed?"

"Completely; he forms part of the Army of Liberation. Now, on the very day of my departure the insurgents were marching towards the Mexican forces to offer them battle. That is why I said to you it was possible that Fray Antonio might be seriously indisposed, and perhaps even dead."

"I hope that misfortune has not happened."

"And so do I. A few minutes before setting out, Fray Antonio, who takes a great interest, as it seems, in the wounded Caballero who accompanies me, not wishing to abandon him alone and helpless in the power of the Mexicans, should the Liberating Army unfortunately be conquered, ordered me to lead him to you, for he felt certain you would take great care of his friend, and treat him well, in consideration of old friendship."

"He did right to count on me; I will not deceive his confidence. Caballero," he added, turning to the old man, who during the whole of this conversation had remained cold and apathetic, "you know us by this time, and are aware that we are pirates. We offer you the hospitality of the desert, a frank and unbounded hospitality, and offer it without either asking who you are or what you have done before setting foot on our territory."

"On what conditions do you offer me all these advantages?" the old man asked, as he bowed, with cold politeness, to the Chief of the bandits.

"On none, señor," he answered; "we ask nothing of you, not even your name; we are proscribed and banished men; hence, every proscript, whatever be the motives that bring him here, has a right to a place by our fire. And now," he added, as he seized a bottle and poured out a bumper, "here is to your fortunate arrival among us, señor! Pledge me!"

"One moment, señor. Before replying to your toast I have, if you will permit me, a few words to say to you."

"We are listening to you, señor."

The old man rose, drew himself up to his full height, and looked silently at the company. A deep silence prevailed; suffering from lively anxiety, all impatiently waited for the Scalper to speak. At length he did so, while his face, which had hitherto been cold and stern, was animated by an expression of gentleness of which it would not have been thought capable.

"Señores," he said, "your frankness challenges mine; the generosity and grandeur of your reception compels me to make myself known. When a man comes to claim the support of men like yourselves he must keep nothing hidden from them. Yes, I am proscribed! Yes, I am banished! But I am so by my own will. I could return tomorrow, if I pleased, to the bosom of society, which has never repelled me, I make here neither allusions nor applications. I remain in the desert to accomplish a duty I have imposed on myself; I pursue a vengeance, an implacable vengeance, which nothing can completely satiate, not even the death of the last of my enemies! A vengeance which is only a wild dream, a horrible nightmare, but which I pursue, and shall pursue, at all hazards, until the supreme hour when, on the point of giving my last sigh, I shall die with regret at not having sufficiently avenged myself. Such is the object of my life, the cause which made me abandon the life of civilized men to take up with that of wild beasts—VENGEANCE! Now you know what I am; when I have told you my name you will be well acquainted with me."

The old man's voice, at first calm and low, had gradually mounted to the diapason of the passions that agitated him, and had become sonorous and harsh. His hearers, involuntarily overpowered by his impassioned accents, listened with panting chests and, as it were hanging on his lips, to this strange man, who, by revealing the secret of his life, had stirred up their hearts, and caused the only sensitive fibre that still existed there to vibrate painfully. For they, too, had but one object left, a sole desire—vengeance on that society which had expelled them like impure scum. These men could comprehend such a powerful and vindictive nature, admire it, and even feel jealous of it, for it was more complete and more vigorously tempered than their own.

When the Scalper had ceased speaking, all rose as if by common accord, and, leaning their quivering hands on the table, bent over to him, awaiting, with feverish impatience, the revelation of his name. But, by a strange revolution, the wounded man seemed to have forgotten what was taking place around him, and no longer to remember either where he was or what he had said. His head was bowed on his chest; with his forehead resting on his right hand and his eyes fixed on the ground, he tried in vain to overcome the flood of bitter recollections, the ever-bleeding wound which in a moment of excitement he had so imprudently revived.

Sandoval regarded him for a moment with an expression of sadness and pity, and laid his hand on his shoulder. At this touch the old man, roughly recalled to a feeling of external things, drew himself up as if he had received an electric shock, and gazed wildly round him.

"What do you want with me?" he asked, in a hoarse voice.

"To tell you your name," the pirate answered, slowly.

"Ah!" he said, "Then you know it?"

"Ten minutes back I was ignorant of it."

"While now——?"

"Now I have guessed it."

An ironical smile curled the old man's pale lips.

"Do you think so?" he said.

"I am sure of it; there are not two men of your stamp in the desert; you are the genius of evil if you are not White Scalper."

At this name an electric quiver traversed the limbs of the hearers. The old man raised his head haughtily.

"Yes," he said, in a sharp voice, "I am White Scalper."

During this long conversation a number of pirates, brought up either by idleness or curiosity, had entered the dining room one after the other. On hearing this name uttered which they had been accustomed so long to admire, on seeing at length this man for whom they felt a secret terror, they burst into a formidable shout, which the resounding echoes repeated indefinitely, and which caused the roof to tremble as if agitated by an earthquake. The White Scalper made a signal to ask silence.

"Señores," he said, "I am very grateful for the friendly demonstrations of which I am the object. Up to the present I have refused every species of alliance; I obstinately resolved to live alone and accomplish, without help, the work of destruction to which I have devoted myself. But, after what has passed here, I must break the promise I made myself; he who receives is bound to give! Henceforth I am one of yourselves, if you deem me worthy to form part of your cuadrilla."

At this proposal the huzzas and shouts of joy were redoubled with extreme frenzy. Sandoval frowned; he understood that his precarious power was menaced. But, too skilful and crafty to let the secret fears that agitated him be guessed, he resolved to outflank the difficulty, and regain, by a masterstroke, the power which he felt instinctively was slipping from his grasp. Raising the glass he held in his hand, he shouted in a thundering voice:

"Muchachos! I drink to White Scalper!"

"To White Scalper," the bandits joined in enthusiastically.

Sandoval allowed the first effervescence time to calm down. Himself exciting this enthusiasm, he at length requested silence at the moment when this enthusiasm had attained its paroxysm. For a few minutes his efforts were in vain, for heads were beginning to grow hot under the influence of copious and incessant libations of mezcal, pulque, and Catalonian refino. By degrees, however, and like the sea after a storm, the cries died out, a calm was re-established, and nothing was audible save a dull and confused murmur of whispered words. Sandoval hastened to profit by this transient moment of silence to speak again.

"Señores," he said, "I have a proposal to make, which, I believe, will suit you."

"Speak, speak," the pirates shouted.

"Our association," Sandoval continued, "is founded on the most entire equality of its members, who freely elect the man they consider most worthy to command them."

"Yes, yes," they exclaimed.

"Long live Sandoval!" some said.

"Let him speak, do not interrupt him," the majority vociferated.

Sandoval, negligently leaning on the table, followed with an apparently indifferent glance these various manifestations, though he was suffering from lively anxiety, and his heart beat ready to burst his chest. He was playing for a heavy stake; he knew it, for he had, with the infallible glance of all ambitious men, calculated all the chances for and against. Hence, it was only by the strength of his will that he succeeded in giving his face a marble rigidity which did not permit the supreme agony he was suffering internally to be divined. When silence was nearly re-established, and he might hope to be heard, he continued, in a firm voice:

"You did me the honour to appoint me your Chief, and I believe that hitherto I have rendered myself worthy of that honour."

He paused as if to await a reply. A murmur of assent gently tickled his ear.

"What is he driving at?" Orson asked in a rough voice.

"You shall know," said Sandoval, who overheard him. And he continued: "In the common interest, I consider it my duty this night to hand you back the authority with which you entrusted me. You have at present among you a man more capable than myself of commanding you, a man whose mere name will inspire terror in the heart of your enemies. In a word, I offer you my resignation, proposing that you should elect on the spot White Scalper as your Chief!"

It was only then that Sandoval really knew the feeling of his comrades toward him. Of two hundred pirates assembled at this moment in the dining hall, two thirds pronounced immediately for him, energetically refusing the resignation he offered apparently with so much self-denial; one half the remaining third gave no sign of approval or disapproval. Thirty or forty of the bandits alone received the proposal with shouts of joy.

Still, as happens nearly always under similar circumstances, these thirty or forty individuals, by their shouts and yells, would soon have led away others, and would probably have become ere long an imposing majority, had not White Scalper himself thought it high time to interfere. The old adventurer did not at all desire the disgraceful honour of being elected the Chief of this band of ruffians, whom he despised in his heart, and whom the force of circumstances alone compelled him to accept as companions. He was, on the contrary, resolved to part with them so soon as his wounds were closed, and he felt capable of recommencing his wandering life. Hence, at the moment when the shouts and oaths crossed each other in the air with an intensity that grew more and more menacing, when already some of the pirates, their arguments being exhausted, were beginning to lay hands on their knives and pistols, and a frightful battle was about to begin between these men, among whom a moral feeling did not exist, and who were consequently restrained by no sentiment of honour or affection; he rose, and speaking amid the vociferations of these turbulent men, he protested energetically against the proposal made by Sandoval, not wishing, as he said, to accept anything but the honour of fighting by their side, and sharing their dangers, for he felt an incompetence to command.

In the face of such an energetic refusal, all opposition necessarily ceased. A reaction in the contrary sense set in, and the pirates implored Sandoval to retain the command, while protesting their devotion to him. Sandoval, after letting himself be a long time entreated, in order to convince them thoroughly of the frankness of his conduct, at length allowed himself to be persuaded, and consented to retain that power which he had felt for a moment such fear of losing.

Peace was thus restored as if by enchantment, and while the pirates drank floods of mezcal to celebrate the happy conclusion of this affair, the Captain led his guests to a compartment separate from the grotto, where they were at liberty at last to rest themselves. Still Sandoval, who, rightly or wrong, had for a moment found his power threatened by White Scalper, felt a malice for him in his heart, and promised to avenge himself on the first opportunity.

[1] See Pirates of the Prairies, same publishers.

CHAPTER XIII
A CONVERSATION

Tranquil and Loyal Heart, as we have seen, withdrew immediately the opportunity appeared favourable to them, and returned to the hunter's rancho, where No Eusebio had made all preparations to give them a hearty reception. Loyal Heart was too sad by nature, the Canadian too preoccupied by a fixed idea which he had hitherto; kept in his heart, for these two men to take the slightest interest in the coarse festivities of the Indians. All this noise and disturbance wearied them; they felt a desire to rest themselves.

Doña Garillas received them with that calm and radiant smile which seemed to pass over her pale and sad face like a sunbeam passing between two clouds. Attentive to satisfy their slightest desires, she seemed to be thankful to them for their return, and tried, by those thousand little attentions of which women alone possess the secret, to keep them as long as possible by her side.

The hunter's house, so peaceful and comfortable, although in the prejudiced sight of a European it would have seemed hardly above the most wretched labourer's cabin in this country, formed a contrast which was not without grandeur with the leather callis of the Redskins, those receptacles of vermin, where the most utter neglect and complete forgetfulness, not only of comfort, but of the most simple enjoyments of life, were visible.

Loyal Heart, after respectfully kissing his mother's forehead, shaking hands with No Eusebio, and patting his dogs, which leapt up at him with joyous whines, sat down to table, making Tranquil a sign to follow his example. Since the previous night a singular change had taken place in the manner, and even countenance of the old hunter. He whose movements were generally so frank and steady, seemed embarrassed; his eye had lost the fire which illumined it and gave it so noble an expression; his eyebrows continually met under the effect of some secret thought; his very speech was sharper than usual.

The young man watched pensively, and with a melancholy smile, the hunter's movements. When the meal was over, and the pipes were lit, after making his mother and No Eusebio a sign to withdraw, he turned to the Canadian—

"My guest," he said affectionately, "we are old friends, are we not? Although we have known each other but a short time."

"Certainly! Loyal Heart, in the desert friendships and hatreds grow rapidly, and we have been together under circumstances when two men, side by side, can appreciate each other in a few minutes."

"Will you let me ask you a question?"

"Of course," the hunter answered.

"Stay," the young man continued; "do we understand each other? Will you promise to answer me this question?"

"Why not?" Tranquil said quietly.

"Who knows—¿quién sabe? as we Spanish Americans say," the young man replied with a smile.

"Nonsense," the Canadian replied carelessly; "ask your question, mine host; I cannot foresee the possibility of my being unable to answer you."

"But, supposing it were so?"

"I do not suppose it; you are a man of too upright sense, and too great intelligence, to fall into that error. So speak without fear."

"I will do so, as you authorise me; for you do so, I think."

"Understood."

"In that ease, listen to me. I know you too well, or, at least, I fancy I know you too well to suppose that you have come here merely to pay me a visit, as you knew you could meet me any day on the prairie. You have, therefore, undertaken this journey with some definite object; a most serious motive impelled you to wish to see me."

Tranquil gave a silent nod of assent. Loyal Heart went on after a moment's silence, during which he seemed to be awaiting a reply, which did not come.

"You have been here now two days. You have already had several opportunities for a frank explanation, an explanation, by the way, which I desire with my whole heart, for I foresee that it will contain a service I can render you, and I shall be happy to prove to you the esteem I entertain for your character. Still, that explanation does not come; you seem, on the contrary, to fear it; your manner toward me has completely changed; since yesterday, in a word, you are no longer the man I knew, the man who never hesitates, and always utters his thoughts loudly and boldly, whatever might be the consequences at a later date. Am I mistaken? Answer, old hunter."

For some minutes the Canadian seemed considerably embarrassed; this point-blank question troubled him singularly. At length he boldly made up his mind, and raised his head—

"On my word," he answered, looking his questioner firmly in the face, "I cannot contradict it; Loyal Heart, you are right—all you have said is perfectly correct."

"Ah!" the young man said with a smile of satisfaction, "I was not mistaken, then; I am pleased to know what I have to depend on."

The Canadian shrugged his shoulders philosophically, like a man who does not at all understand, but who yet experiences a certain degree of pleasure at seeing his questioner satisfied, though he is completely ignorant why. Loyal Heart continued—

"Now, I demand in the name of that friendship that binds us—I demand, I say, that you should be frank with me, and without reservation or circumlocution, confess to me the motives which urged you to act as you have done."

"These motives are only honourable, be assured, Loyal Heart."

"I am convinced of it, my friend; but I repeat to you, I wish to know them."

"After all," the old hunter continued with the accent of a man who has formed a resolution, "why should I have secrets from you when I have come to claim your assistance? You shall know all. I am only a coarse adventurer, who received all the education he has on the desert; I adore God, and am mad for liberty; I have always tried to benefit my neighbour, and requite good for evil as far as lay in my power; such, in two words, is my profession of faith."

"It is rigorously true," Loyal Heart said, with an air of conviction.

"Thanks, and frankly I believe it. But, with the exception of that, I know nothing. Desert life has only developed in me the instincts of the brute, without giving me any of those refinements which the civilisation of towns causes to be developed in the most savage natures."

"I confess that I do not see at all what you are driving at."

"You will soon comprehend me. From the first moment I saw you, with the first word you uttered, by a species of intuition, by one of those sympathies what are independent of the will, I felt myself attracted towards you. You were my friend during the few days we lived together, sharing the same couch under the vault of Heaven, running the same dangers, experiencing the same joys and sorrows. I believed that I appreciated you at your true value, and my friendship only increased in consequence. Hence, when I needed a sure and devoted friend, I thought of you at once, and, without further reflection, started to go in quest of you."

"You did well."

"I know it," said Tranquil, with simple enthusiasm; "still, on entering this modest rancho, my ideas were completely modified; a doubt occurred to me—not about you, for that was impossible—but about your position, and the mysterious life you lead. I asked myself by what concourse of circumstances a man like you had confined himself to an Indian village and accepted all the wretchedness of a Redskin life, a wretchedness often so cruel and opposed to our manners. On seeing your mother so lovely and so kind, your old servant so devoted, and the way in which you behave within these walls, I thought, without prejudging anything, that a great misfortune had suddenly burst on you and forced you for a time into a hard exile. But I understood that I was not your equal, that between you and me there was a distinctly traced line of demarcation; then I felt oppressed in your company, for you are no longer the free hunter, having no other roof but the verdurous dome of our virgin forests, or other fortune than his rifle; in a word, you are no longer the comrade, the friend with whom I was so happy to share everything in the desert I no longer recognise the right to treat as an equal a man whom a passing misfortune has accidentally brought near me, and who would, doubtless, at a later date, regret this intimacy which has sprung from accident; while continuing to love and esteem you, I resume the place that belongs to me."

"All of which means?" Loyal Heart said, distinctly.

"That, being no longer able to be your comrade, and not wishing to be your servant, I shall retire."

"You are mad, Tranquil," the young man exclaimed, with an outburst of impatient grief. "What you say, I tell you, has not common sense, and the conclusions yon draw from it are absurd."

"Still——?" the Canadian hazarded.

"Oh!" the other continued, with considerable animation, "I have allowed you to speak, have I not? I listened to whatever you had to say without interruption, and it is now your turn. Without wishing it, you have caused me the greatest pain it is possible for me to suffer; you have caused an ever-living wound to bleed, by reminding me of things which I try in vain to forget, and which will cause the wretchedness of my whole life."

"I—I?" the hunter exclaimed, with a start of terror.

"Yes, you! But what matter? Besides, you were walking blindly, not knowing where you were going; hence, I have no right to be angry with you, and am not so. But there is one thing I value above all, which; I esteem more than life, and that is your friendship. I cannot consent to lose it. Confidence for confidence! You shall know who I am and what motive brought me to the desert, where I am condemned to live and die."

"No," Tranquil answered, clearly, "I have no claim to your confidence. You say that I have unintentionally caused you great suffering; that suffering would only be increased by the confession you wish to make me. I swear to you, Loyal Heart, that I will not listen to you."

"You must, my friend, both for your sake and my own, for in that way we shall learn to understand one another. Besides," he added, with a melancholy smile, "this secret which crushed me, and which I have hitherto kept in my own bosom, it will be a great consolation to me, be assured, to confide to a real friend. And then, you must know this: I have no one to complain of; the terrible misfortune which suddenly fell upon me, or chastisement, if you like that term better, was just, though perhaps severe; I have, therefore, no one to reproach but myself. My life is only one long expiation; unhappily I tremble lest the present and the future will not suffice to expiate the past."

"You forget God, my son," a voice said, with an accent of supreme majesty, "God, who cannot fail you and will judge you. When the expiation you have imposed on yourself is completed, that God will cause it to terminate."

And Doña Garillas, who had for some moments been listening to the conversation of the two men, crossed the room with a majestic step, and laid her white and delicate hand on the shoulder of her son, while giving him a glance full of that powerful love which mothers alone possess.

"Oh! I am a wretched ingrate!" the young man exclaimed, sorrowfully; "in my hideous egotism I for a moment forgot you, my mother, who gave up everything for me."

"Raphael, you are my first-born. What I did nine years ago I would do again today. But now, let what you are about to hear be a consolation to you. I am proud of you, my son; whatever pain you once caused me, the same amount of joy and pride you cause me today. All the Indian tribes that traverse the vast solitudes of the prairie have the greatest respect and deepest veneration for you; has not the name these primitive men have given you become the synonym of honour? Are you not, in a word, Loyal Heart, that is to say, the man whose decisions have the strength of law, whom all, friends and enemies, love and esteem? What more do you want?"

The young man shook his head sadly.

"Alas, mother," he said, in a hollow voice, "can I ever forget that I have been a gambler, assassin, and incendiary?"

Tranquil could not restrain a start of terror.

"Oh, it is impossible!" he muttered.

The young man heard him, and turning to him, said—?

"Yes, my friend, I have been a gambler, assassin, and incendiary. Well, now," he added, with an accent of sad and bitter raillery, "do you still fancy yourself unworthy of my friendship? Do you still consider you are not my equal?"

The Canadian rose while the young man bent on him a searching glance; he went up to Doña Garillas, and bowed to her with a respect mingled with admiration.

"Señora," he said, "whatever crimes a man may have committed in a moment of irresistible passion, that man must be absolved by all when, in spite of his fault, he inspires a devotion so glorious, so perfect, and so noble as yours. You are a holy woman, madam! Hope, as you said yourself a moment back, hope. GOD, who is omnipotent, will, when the moment arrives, dry your tears and make you forget your sorrow in immense joy. I am but a poor man, without talent or learning, but my instinct has never deceived me. I am convinced that if your son were ever guilty, he is now pardoned, even by the man who condemned him under the influence of an exaggerated feeling of honour, which he regretted at a later date."

"Thanks, my friend," Loyal Heart answered; "thanks for words which I feel convinced are the expression of your innermost thoughts; thanks in my mother's name and my own! Yours is a frank and upright nature. You have restored me the courage which at times abandons me, and have raised me in my own sight; but this expiation to which I condemned myself, would not be complete unless I told you, in their fullest details, all the events of my life. No refusal," he added, with a sign to the hunter, "it must be so! Believe me, Tranquil, this story bears its own instruction. Just as the traveller, after a long and painful journey, halts by the wayside, and looks with a certain degree of satisfaction at the distance he has covered, I shall feel a mournful pleasure in returning to the early and terrible events of my life."

"Yes," said his mother, "you are right, my son. A man must have courage to look back, in order to acquire the strength to walk worthily forward. It is only by reverting to the past that you can understand the present and have hope in the future. Speak, speak, my son, and if in the course of your narrative your memory or your courage fail you, your mother will be here at your side, as I have ever been, and what you dare not or cannot say, I will say."

Tranquil regarded with admiration this strange woman, whose gestures and words harmonized so well with her majestic bearing; this mother, whose sweet face reflected so well her noble sentiments; he felt himself very small and wretched in the presence of this chosen nature, who, of all the passions, knew only one, maternal love.

"Loyal Heart," he said, with an emotion he could not master, "since you insist, I will listen to the narrative of the events which brought you to the desert; but be assured of this, whatever I may hear, since you are willing still to give me the title of friend, here is my hand, take it, I will never fail you. Now, whether you speak or keep your secret, is of no consequence. Remember one thing, however, that I belong to you, body and soul, before and against all, today or tomorrow, tomorrow or ten years hence, and that," he added with a certain degree of solemnity, "I swear to you from my deepest soul, by the memory of my beloved mother, whose ashes now rest in Quebec cemetery. Now go on, I am ready to listen to you."

Loyal Heart warmly returned the pressure of the hunter's hand, and made him sit down on his right hand, while Doña Garillas took her place on his left.

"Now, listen to me," he said.

At this moment the door opened, and No Eusebio appeared.

"*Mi amo*," he said, "the Indian Chief, called Black-deer, wishes to speak to you."

"What, Black-deer?" the hunter said with surprise; "Impossible! He must be engaged with his marriage festivities."

"Pardon me," Tranquil observed; "you forget, Loyal Heart, that when we left the feast the Chief came up to us, saying in a low voice that he had a serious communication to make to us."

"That is true; in fact, I did forget it. Let him enter, No Eusebio. My friend," he added, addressing Tranquil, "it is impossible for me at this moment to begin a story which would be interrupted almost at the first sentence; but soon, I hope, you shall know it."

"I will leave you to settle your Indian affairs," Doña Garillas said with a smile, and rising, she quitted the room.

Tranquil, we are bound to confess, was in his heart delighted at an interruption which saved him from listening to the narrative of painful events. The worthy hunter possessed the precious quality of not being at all curious to know the history of men he liked, for his native integrity led him to fear seeing them break down in his esteem. Hence, he easily accepted the unexpected delay in Loyal Heart's confession, and was grateful to Black-deer for arriving so opportunely.

At the moment when Doña Garillas entered the room No Eusebio introduced the Indian Chief by another door. Forgetful of that assumed stoicism so habitual to Indians, Black-deer seemed suffering from a lively anxiety. The warrior's gloomy air, his frowns—nothing, in a word, recalled in him the man who had just contracted a union he had long desired, and which, fulfilled all his wishes; his countenance, on the contrary, was so grave and stern, that the two hunters noticed it at the first glance, and could not refrain from remarking on it to him.

"Wah!" Loyal Heart said good-humouredly, "You have a preciously sad face. Did you, on entering the village, perceive five crows on your right, or did your scalping knife stick in the ground thrice in succession, which, as everybody knows, is a very evil omen?"

The Chief, before replying, bent a piercing glance around.

"No," he at length said, in a low and suppressed voice, "Black-deer has not seen five crows on his right; he saw a fox on his left, and a flight of owls in the bushes."

"You know, Chief, that I do not at all understand you," Loyal Heart said, laughing.

"Nor do I, on my honour," Tranquil observed with a crafty smile.

The Chief bravely endured this double volley of sarcasm. Not a muscle of his face stirred; on the contrary, his features seemed to grow more gloomy.

"My brothers can laugh," he said, "they are Palefaces; they care little whether good or evil happens to the Indians."

"Pardon, Chief," Loyal Heart answered, suddenly becoming serious; "my friend and myself had no intention of insulting you."

"I am aware of it," the Chief replied, "my brothers cannot suppose that on a day like this I should be sad."

"That is true, but now our ears are open: my brother will speak, and we listen with all the attention his words deserve."

The Indian seemed to hesitate, but in a moment he walked up to Loyal Heart and Tranquil, seated by his side, and bent over them, so that his head touched theirs.

"The situation is grave," he said, "and I have only a few minutes to spare, so my brothers will listen seriously. I must return to the calli of Blackbird, where my friends and relatives await me. Are my brothers listening?"

"We are listening," the two men answered with one voice.

Ere going on, Black-deer walked round the room, inspecting the walls and opening the doors, as if fearing listeners. Then, probably re-assured by this inspection that no one could hear him, he returned to the two white men, who curiously followed these singular operations, and said to them in a low voice, as an additional precaution:

"A great danger menaces the Antelope Comanches."

"How so, Chief?"

"The Apaches are watching the neighbourhood of the village."

"How do you know that?"

The Chief looked around him, and then continued in the same low and suppressed voice:

"I have seen them."

"My brother has seen the Apaches?"

The Chief smiled proudly.

"Yes," he said, "Black-deer is a great brave, he has the fine scent of my brother's rastreros, he has smelt the enemy; smelling is seeing, with a warrior."

"Yes, but my brother must take care! Passion is an evil counsellor," Loyal Heart answered; "perhaps he is mistaken."

Black-deer shrugged his shoulders with disdain.

"This night there was not a breath of air in the forest, yet the leaves of the trees moved, and the tall grass was agitated."

"Wah! That is astonishing," said Loyal Heart; "An envoy of the Buffalo Apaches is in the village at this moment, we must be threatened by fearful trickery."

"Blue-fox is a traitor who has sold his people," the Indian continued with some animation; "what can be hoped from such a man? He has come here to count the braves, and send the warriors to sleep."

"Yes," said Loyal Heart thoughtfully, "that is possible. But what is to be done? Has my brother warned the Chiefs?"

"Yes, while Blue-fox requested the hachesto to assemble the council, Black-deer spoke with Bounding Panther, Lynx, and Blackbird."

"Very good, what have they resolved?"

"Blue-fox will be retained as a hostage, under various pretexts. At sunset two hundred picked warriors, under the orders of Loyal Heart, and guided by Black-deer, will go and surprise the enemy, who, knowing their emissary to be in the village, will have no suspicion, but fall into the trap they intended to set for us."

Loyal heart remained silent for a moment and reflected.

"Let my brother hear me," he said presently; "I am ready to obey the orders of the Sovereign Council of the Sachems of the tribe, but I will not let the warriors entrusted to me be massacred. The Buffalo Apaches are old chattering and crying squaws, without courage, to whom we will give petticoats, each time they find themselves face to face with us in the prairies. But here such is not the case; they are ambushed at a spot selected beforehand, and are acquainted with all its resources. However well my young men may be guided by my brothers, the Apaches will come on their trail, so that will not do."

"What does my brother propose?" Black-deer asked with some anxiety.

"The sun has run two-thirds of its course, Black-deer will warn the warriors to proceed each by himself, to the mountain of the Blackbear, one hour after sunset. In this way they will seem to be going hunting separately, and excite no suspicion. No one will see them depart, and if the enemy, as is probable, have spies in the camp, they cannot suppose that these hunters, starting one after the other, are sent off to surprise them. When the sun has disappeared on the horizon, in the sacred cavern of the Red Mountain, my brother the Pale hunter and myself will mount our horses and join the Redskins. Have I spoken well? Does what I have said please my brother?"

While Loyal Heart was thus explaining the plan he had instantaneously conceived, the Indian Chief gave marks of the greatest joy, and the most lively admiration.

"My brother has spoken well," he answered; "the Wacondah is with him; his medicine is very powerful, though his hair is black; the wisdom of the Master of Life resides in him. It shall be done as he desires; Black-deer will obey him; he will follow out exactly the wise instructions of his brother, Loyal Heart."

"Good; but my brother will take care: Blue-fox is very clever!"

"Blue-fox is an Apache dog, whose ears Black-deer will crop. My brother the hunter need not feel alarmed; all will happen as he desires."

After exchanging a few more sentences to come to a full understanding, and make their final arrangements, Black-deer withdrew.

"You will come with me, I suppose, Tranquil?" the young man asked the Canadian so soon as they were alone.

"Of course!" the other replied; "Did you doubt it? What the deuce should I do here during your absence? I prefer accompanying you, especially as, if I am not mistaken, there will be a jolly row."

"You are not mistaken. It is evident to me that the Apaches would not have ventured so near the village, unless they were in considerable force."

"Well, in that case, two hundred men are as nothing; you should have asked for more."

"Why so? In a surprise the man who attacks is always the stronger; we will try to get the first blow, that is all."

"That is true, by Jove! I am delighted at the affair; I have not smelt powder for some time, and feel myself beginning to rust; that will restore me."

At this outburst, Loyal Heart began laughing, Tranquil formed the chorus, and they spoke about something else.

CHAPTER XIV
TWO ENEMIES

In the high American latitudes, night comes on almost suddenly, and without sensible transition; there is no twilight, and when the sun has disappeared on the horizon, it is perfect night; now, at the period of the year when the events occurred which we have undertaken to describe, the sun set at seven o'clock. Half an hour later, Tranquil and Loyal Heart, mounted on excellent mustangs, left the rancho, followed by No Eusebio, who insisted on joining them, and whom no entreaties or exhortations could keep back. They had only gone a few yards across the square, however, when the Canadian laid his hand on the young man's bridle.

"What do you want?" the latter asked.

"Shall we not take our comrades with us?"

"Do you think it necessary?"

"Well, with the exception of the monk, who, I fear, is not worth much, they are stout fellows, whose rifles might prove very useful to us."

"That is true; warn them in a few words, and rejoin me here."

"Do you not think the departure of so large a party may arouse the suspicions of Blue-fox, who is doubtless prowling about the neighbourhood?"

"Not at all, they are white men; if he saw Indian warriors departing thus, I am sure his doubts would be aroused; but he will never suppose that hunters have discovered his treachery."

"You may be right, but in any case it is better to run the risk; wait for me, I shall be back in ten minutes."

"All right, go along."

Tranquil went off rapidly, while Loyal Heart and No Eusebio halted a few yards further on. The adventurers gleefully accepted the proposal Tranquil made them; for such men, a battle is a festival, especially when they have Indians to fight; ten minutes scarce elapsed, therefore, ere the Canadian rejoined the young man. The little band set out, and silently left the village.

Loyal Heart was mistaken in supposing that Blue-fox would not be alarmed on seeing the white hunters leave the atepetl. The Redskin, like all men who meditate treachery, had his eyes constantly open to the movements of the inhabitants of the village, and his watchful mind took umbrage at the most insignificant matters. Although the Comanche Chiefs had acted with the greatest prudence, the Apache Sachem speedily perceived that he was watched, and that, though honourably treated, and apparently free, he was in reality a prisoner. He pretended not to suspect what was going on, but redoubled his attention. During the past day, he had seen several warriors mount their horses one after the other, and set out in groups of two, three, and even four, to bury themselves in the forest.

Not one of these warriors having re-entered the atepetl by sunset, this circumstance caused the Redskin Chief deep thought, and he even came to the conclusion that his plans were discovered, and that the Comanches were attempting a countermine, that is to say, were trying to surprise the persons who desired to lay a trap for them, and the departure of the white hunters would have removed the Chief's final doubts, had any such remained. The situation was growing not only very critical, but most perilous for him; his scalp was extremely compromised; it was plain that the Comanche warriors on their return would perform the scalp dance, and the finest ornament of the feast would be the Apache Chief who had tried to lead them into a cleverly-prepared trap.

Blue-fox was a warrior renowned as much for his wisdom in council as for his bravery in fight; instances of extraordinary audacity and temerity, were narrated about him, but the courage with which the Chief was gifted was calm, reasoning, and ever subordinate to events; that is to say, Blue-fox, like a true Redskin, would never hesitate, when circumstances demanded it, to substitute craft and trickery for courage, considering it highly absurd, and very useless, to expose his life without any hope of profit.

Blue-fox was sitting in front of the entrance of the calli of honour the Comanches had given him during the period of his stay with them, calmly smoking his pipe, when the white hunters passed before him. He displayed neither surprise nor curiosity at the sight of them, but by an almost imperceptible movement of his head and shoulders, he looked after them with a flashing glance till they disappeared in the darkness. We have said that the night was dark, the village already appeared completely deserted, the Indians had withdrawn to the interior of their callis, while at lengthened intervals an isolated Redskin hastily crossed the square, hurrying homewards.

Blue-fox still sat before his calli smoking; gradually the arm that supported the calumet fell on his knees, his head bowed on his chest, and the Apache Sachem seemed, as so often happens to the Indians, to have yielded to the narcotic influence of the morichee; and a long time elapsed ere he made the slightest movement. Was the Chief really asleep? No one could have answered the question. His calm and regular breathing, and his careless attitude, led to the supposition that he had been overcome by sleep; but, if any sound suddenly smote his ear, an almost imperceptible tremor ran over his limbs, and his eyelash rose, probably through that instinct of personal prudence peculiar to the Indians, but more probably through a desire of investigation, as we think, and as anyone else would have thought who was in a position to see the piercing glances he at such moments darted into the obscurity. All at once the curtain of the calli was raised, and a hand was roughly laid on the sleeper's shoulder. The Chief started at this touch, which he did not at all expect, and sprang up as if a serpent had stung him.

"The nights are cold," said an ironical voice, which smote unpleasantly on the ear of Blue-fox; "the dew is profuse, and ices the blood; my brother is wrong to sleep thus in the open air, when he has a spacious and convenient calli."

Blue-fox, by a powerful effort, extinguished the fire of his glance, composed his features, and answered in the gentle voice of a man who is really waking—

"I thank my brother for his affectionate observation; in truth, the nights are very cold, and it is better to sleep in a calli than in the open air."

He rose without further discussion, and re-entered the hut with the calm step of a man delighted with the warning he has received. A great fire was kindled in the interior of the calli, which, besides, was illumined by a torch of ocote wood stuck in the ground, whose ruddy and vacillating glare imparted a blood-red hue to surrounding objects. The man whose charitable advice surprised Blue-fox, let the curtain fall behind him, and entered after the chief. This man was Black-deer, without uttering a syllable, he sat down before the fire, and began arranging the logs with a certain degree of symmetry. Blue-fox gazed on him for a moment with am undefinable expression, and then walked up and stood by his side.

"My brothers, the Antelope Comanches," he said, with an almost imperceptible tinge of irony in his voice, "are great warriors; they understand the laws of hospitality better than any other nation."

"The Antelope Comanches," Black-deer answered, peaceably, "know that Blue-fox is a renowned Chief, and one of the great braves of the Buffalo Apaches; they are anxious to do him honour."

The Chief bowed.

"Does this honour go so far as to compel so great a warrior as my brother to watch over my sleep?"

"My brother is the guest of the Antelopes, and in that quality has a claim to all possible attention."

Like two experienced duellists the Chiefs had crossed swords; having felt their blades, they perceived that they were of equal strength, and each fell back a step to continue the engagement on new ground.

"Then," Blue-fox continued, "my brother will remain in the calli with me."

The Chief gave a nod of assent.

"Wah! I know for what reason the Comanche Sachems treat me thus: they are aware that Black-deer and Blue-fox, though each adopted by a different tribe, are yet brothers of the great and powerful nation of the Snake Pawnees; hence they suppose that the two Chiefs would be pleased to converse together and recall their early years. My brother will thank the Sachems of his nation for Blue-fox; I was far from expecting so great a proof of courtesy on their part."

"My brother is rightly called the Fox," the Comanche replied, briefly, with a bitter accent; "his craft is great."

"What does my brother mean?" the Apache went on with the greatest air of surprise he could assume.

"I speak the truth, and my brother is well aware of it," Black-deer answered; "why should we thus try to deceive each other? We have been too long acquainted. Let my brother listen to me: the Antelope Comanches are not, as the Apaches suppose them, inexperienced children, they know for what purpose my brother has come to their winter atepetl."

"*Ohé!*" the Chief said, "I hear a mocking-bird singing in my ears, but I do not at all understand what it means."

"Perhaps so, but to remove my brother's doubt I will speak to him frankly."

"Can my brother do so?" the Apache continued, ironically.

"The Chief shall judge:—For some moons past the Buffalo Apaches have been trying to take a brilliant revenge on the Comanches for a defeat the warriors of my nation inflicted on them, but the Apaches are chattering old women who possess no craft; the Comanches will give them petticoats and send them to cut wood for them in the forests."

The Chief's eyebrows were almost meeting at this crushing insult; a flash of fury burst from his eyes, but still he managed to overpower his feelings. He drew himself up with supreme majesty and folded himself in his buffalo robe.

"My brother, Black-deer, forgets to whom he is speaking," he said; "Blue-fox is the envoy of his nation to the Comanches, he has sought shelter under the totem of the Antelopes and smoked their sacred calumet; his person must be respected."

"The Apache Chief is mistaken," Black-deer replied, with a disdainful smile; "he is not the envoy of a brave nation, but only the spy of a pack of savage dogs. While Blue-fox tries to deceive the Comanche Sachems, and lull them to sleep in a treacherous serenity, the Apache dogs are hidden like moles in the tall grass, awaiting the signal which will surrender their defenceless enemies into their hands."

Blue-fox looked round the calli, and bounding like a jaguar, rushed on his foeman, brandishing his knife.

"Die, dog!" he shouted.

Since the beginning of their singular conversation Black-deer had not stirred, he had remained tranquilly crouching over the fire, but his eyes had not lost one of the Apache's movements, and when the latter rushed madly at him he started aside, and springing up with extreme rapidity, seized the Chief in his nervous arms and both rolled on the ground, intertwined like serpents. In their fall they fell on the torch, which was extinguished; hence, the terrible and silent conflict went on between the two men by the uncertain gleam of the fire, each striving to stab his enemy. They were both of nearly the same age, their strength and skill were equal, and an implacable hatred animated them; in this horrible duel, which must evidently terminate in the death of one of them, they disdained the usual tricks employed in such fights, as they cared little about death so long as their enemy received the mortal blow simultaneously.

Still, Blue-fox had a great advantage over his adversary, who, blinded by fury, and not calculating any of his movements, could not long sustain this deadly contest without himself becoming a victim to the insensate rage which had urged him to attack the Comanche. The latter, on the contrary, completely master of himself, acted with the greatest prudence, and by the way he had seized his enemy had pinned his arms and rendered it impossible for him to employ his weapons; all the efforts of Black-deer tended to roll the Apache into the fire burning in the centre of the calli.

They had been wrestling thus for a long time, foot against foot, chest to chest, and it was as yet impossible to guess which would gain the upper hand, when suddenly the curtain of the hut was raised, and a brilliant light inundated the interior. Several men entered; they were Comanche warriors. They arrived later than they should have done, for all that took place at this moment had been arranged beforehand between them and Black-deer, but they had been delayed by circumstances beyond their control. Five minutes later their interference would have been useless, as they would probably have found one of the two combatants killed by the other, or perhaps raised two corpses, such fury and vindictiveness were displayed in this atrocious struggle.

When Blue-fox saw the help that arrived for his enemy he judged the position at a glance, and felt that he was lost; still, the cunning and coolness innate with Indians did not abandon him at this supreme moment; for Redskins, whatever may be the hatred they feel, do not kill an enemy who openly allows that he is conquered. The Apache Chief, so soon as he perceived the Comanches, ceased his efforts, and removed the arms which had hitherto held Black-deer as in a vice; then, throwing back his head and closing his eyes, he stood motionless.

Blue-fox was aware that he would be regarded as a prisoner and kept for the stake of torture; but until the hour marked for his punishment arrived he retained the hope of escaping, with whatever care he might be guarded. This chance was the last left him, so he did not wish to lose it.

Black-deer rose, greatly shaken by the rude embrace; but, instead of striking his enemy, who lay disarmed at his feet, he returned his knife to his belt. The Apache's calculations were correct: until the hour of punishment arrived he had nothing to fear from his enemy.

"Blue-fox is a great brave, he fought like a courageous warrior," said Black-deer; "as he must be fatigued he will rise, and the Comanche Chief will show him all the consideration he deserves."

And he offered his hand to help him in rising. The Apache made no movement to pick up his weapons, but frankly accepted the offered hand and rose.

"The Comanche dogs will see a warrior die," he said, with an ironical smile; "Blue-fox laughs at their tortures; they are not capable of making one of his muscles quiver."

"Good! My brother will see," and turning to the Sachems, who stood motionless and silent a few paces off, the Chief added; "when will this warrior die?"

"Tomorrow at sunset," the most aged of the Indians laconically answered.

"My brother has heard," Black-deer continued; "has he any remark to make?"

"Only one."

"My brother can speak, our ears are open."

"Blue-fox does not fear death, but ere he goes to hunt on the happy hunting grounds, beneath the powerful eye of the Wacondah, he has several important matters to settle on this earth."

The Comanches bowed in assent.

"Blue-fox," the Apache Chief continued, "has a necessity to return among the warriors of his nation."

"How long will the Chief remain absent?"

"One whole moon."

"Good! What will the Chief do to insure his word, and that the Comanche Sachems may put faith in what he says?"

"Blue-fox will leave a hostage."

"The Sachem of the Buffalo Apaches is a great brave; what warrior of his nation can die in his stead, if he forget to liberate his pledge?"

"I will give the flesh of my flesh, the blood of my blood, the bone of my bone. My son will take my place."

The Comanches exchanged a very meaning glance. There was a rather lengthened silence, during which the Apache, haughtily folded in his buffalo robe, stoically waited, and it was impossible to read in his motionless features one of the emotions that agitated him. At length Black-deer spoke again.

"My brother has recalled to my memory," he said, "the years of our youth, when we were both children of the Snake Pawnees, and hunted in company the elk and the asshata in the prairies of the Upper Missouri. The early years are the sweetest; the words of my brother made my heart tremble with joy. I will be kind to him; his son snail be my substitute, though he is still very young; but he knows how to crawl like the serpent and fly like the eagle, and his arm is strong in fight. But Blue-fox will reflect before pledging his word. If on the evening of the twenty-eighth sun my brother has not returned to take his place at the foot of the stake of torture, his son will die."

"I thank my brother," the Apache replied in a firm voice, "on the twenty-eighth sun I shall return: here is my open hand."

"And here is mine."

The two enemies clasped in cordial pressure the two hands which, a few minutes before, had been seeking so eagerly to take each other's life; then Blue-fox unfastened the cascabel skin that attached his long hair in the form of a cap on the top of his head, and removed the white eagle plume fixed above his right ear.

"My brother will lend me his knife," he said.

"My brother's knife is at his feet," the Comanche answered cautiously; "so great a warrior must not remain unarmed. He can pick it up."

The Chief stooped, picked up his knife, and thrust it in his girdle.

"Here is the plume of a Chief," he said as he gave it to Black-deer, cutting off a tress of the long hair, which, being no longer fastened, fell in disorder on his shoulders; he added, "My brother will keep this lock, it forms part of the scalp that belongs to him: the Chief will come to ask it back on the appointed day and hour."

"Good!" the Comanche answered, taking the hair and the plume, "My brother will follow me."

The Comanches, unmoved spectators of this scene, shook their torches to revive the flame, and all the Indians leaving the calli, proceeded in the direction of the Medicine Lodge, which stood, as we have seen, in the centre of the square between the ark of the first man and the stake of torture. It was toward the latter that the Chiefs proceeded with that slow and solemn step they employ in serious matters. As they passed in front of the callis, the curtains were raised, the inhabitants came out, holding torches, and followed the procession. When the Chiefs reached the stake, an immense crowd filled the square, but it was silent and reflecting.

There was something strange and striking in the scenes offered at this moment by the square, under the light of the torches, whose flame the wind blew in all directions. The Chiefs halted at the foot of the stake and formed a semicircle, in the centre of which Blue-fox stationed himself.

"Now that my brother has given his pledge, he can summon his son," said Black-deer; "the lad is not far off, I dare say."

The Apache smiled cunningly.

"The young of the eagle always follows the powerful flight of its parent," he replied; "the warriors will part to the right and left to grant him a passage."

At a silent sign from Black-deer there was a movement in the crowd, which fell back and left a passage through the centre; Blue-fox then thrust his fingers in his mouth, and imitated thrice the call of the hawk. In a few minutes a similar but very faint cry answered him. The Chief renewed his summons, and this time the answer was shriller and more distinct. For the third time the Apache repeated his signal, which was answered close at hand; the rapid gallop of a horse became audible, and almost immediately an Indian warrior dashed up at full speed. This warrior crossed the entire square without evidencing the slightest surprise. He stopped short at the foot of the stake, dismounted, and placed himself by the side of Blue-fox, to whom he merely said—

"Here I am."

This warrior was the son of the Apache Chief, a tall and nobly-built lad of sixteen to seventeen. His features were handsome, his glance was haughty, his demeanour simple, and noble without boasting.

"This boy is my son," Blue-fox said to the Comanche Chiefs.

"Good!" they replied, bowing courteously.

"Does my son consent to remain as a hostage in the place of his father?" Black-deer asked him.

The young man bowed his head in assent.

"My son knows that if his father does not come to liberate his pledge, he will die in his place?"

A smile of contempt played round the boy's lips.

"I know it," he said,

"And my son accepts?"

"I do."

"Good!" the Chief continued, "Let my son look."

He then went up to the stake and fastened to it the feather and lock of hair Blue-fox had given him.

"This feather and this hair will remain here until the man to whom they belong returns to claim them," he said.

The Apache Chief answered in his turn—

"I swear on my totem to come and redeem them at the appointed time."

"Wah! My brother is free," Black-deer continued; "here is the feather of a Chief; it will serve him as a recognition if the warriors of my nation were to meet him. Still, my brother will remember that he is forbidden communicating in any way with the braves of his nation ambushed round the village."

"Blue-fox will remember it."

After uttering these few words without even exchanging a look with his son, who stood motionless by his side, the Chief took the feather Black-deer offered him, leaped on the horse which had brought the young man, and started at a gallop, not looking back once. When he had disappeared in the darkness, the Chiefs went up to the boy, bound him securely, and confined him in the Medicine Lodge under the guardianship of several warriors.

"Now," said Black-deer, "for the others."

And mounting his horse in his turn, he left the village.

CHAPTER XV
THE AMBUSCADE

The European traveller, accustomed to the paltry landscapes which man has carved out corresponding with his own stature and the conventional nature he has, as it were, contrived to create, can in no way figure to himself the grand and sublime aspect presented by the great American forests, where all seems to sleep, and the ever open eye of God alone broods over the world. The unknown rumours, without any apparent cause, which incessantly rise from earth to sky like the powerful breathing of sleeping nature, and mingle with the monotonous murmur of the streams, as they rustle over the pebbles of their bed; and at intervals, the mysterious breeze which passes over the tufted tops of the trees, slowly bending them with a gentle rustling of leaves and branches—all this leads the mind to reverie, and fills it with a religious respect for the sublime works of the Creator.

We fancy we have given a sufficiently detailed account of the village of the Antelope Comanches, to be able to dispense with further reference to it; we will merely add that it was built in an amphitheatrical shape, and descended with a gentle incline to the river. This position prevented the enemy surrounding the village, whose approaches were guarded from surprise by the trees having been felled for some distance.

Loyal Heart and his comrades advanced slowly, with their rifles on their thigh, attentively watching the neighbourhood, and ready, at the slightest suspicious movement in the tall grass, to execute a vigorous charge. All, however, remained quiet round them; at times they heard a coyote baying at the moon, or the noise of an owl concealed by the foliage; but that was all, and a leaden silence fell again on the savannah. At times they saw in the bluish rays of the moon indistinct forms appear on the banks of the river; but these wandering shadows were evidently wild beasts which had left their lurking places to come down and drink.

The march continued thus without encumbrance or alarm of any description, until the adventurers had reached the covert, when a dense gloom suddenly enveloped them, and did not allow them to distinguish objects ten yards ahead. Loyal Heart did not consider it prudent to advance further in a neighbourhood he did not know, and where he saw the risk at each step of falling into an ambuscade; consequently the little band halted. The horses were made to lie down on their side, their legs were fastened, and their nostrils drawn in with a rope, so that they could neither stir nor make a sound, and the adventurers, concealing themselves, waited while watching with the most profound attention.

From time to time they saw horsemen crossing a clearing, and all going in different directions; some passed close enough to touch them without perceiving the hunters, owing to the precautions the latter had taken, and then disappeared in the forest. Several hours passed thus, the hunters being quite unable to comprehend the delay, the reason for which the reader, however, knows; the moon had disappeared, and the darkness become denser. Loyal Heart, not knowing to what he should attribute Black-deer's lengthened absence, and fearing some unforeseen misfortune had burst on the village, was about to give the order for returning, when Tranquil, who, by crawling on his hands and knees, had reached the open plain where he remained for some time as scout, suddenly returned to his comrades.

"What is the matter?" Loyal Heart whispered in his ear.

"I cannot say," the hunter answered, "I do not understand it myself. About an hour back, an Indian suddenly sprung up by my side as if emerging from the ground, and leaping on a horse of whose presence I was equally ignorant, started at full speed in the direction of the village."

"That is strange," Loyal Heart muttered; "and you do not know who the Indian is?"

"Apache."

"Apache, impossible!"

"That is just the point that staggers me; how could an Apache venture to the village alone?"

"There is something up we do not know; and then the signals we heard?"

"This man answered them."

"What is to be done?"

"Find out."

"But in what way?"

"Why, hang it, by rejoining our friends."

Loyal Heart shook his head.

"No," he said, "we must employ some other method, for I promised Black-deer to help him in this expedition, and I will not break my word."

"It is evident that important events have occurred among the tribe."

"That is my opinion too, but you know the prudence of the Indians, so we will not despair yet; stay," he added, as he tapped his forehead, "I have an idea, we shall soon know what is taking place; leave me to act."

"Do you require our help?"

"Not positively; I shall not go out of sight, but if you see me in danger, come up."

"All right,"

Loyal heart took a long rope of plaited leather, which served him as a picquet cord, and laying down his rifle, which might have impeded him in the execution of the daring plan he had formed, lay down on the ground and crawled away like a serpent. The plain was covered with dead trees and enormous stones, while there were wide trenches at certain spots. This open ground, so singularly broken up, offered, therefore, all the facilities desirable for forming an ambuscade or a post of observation.

Loyal Heart stopped behind an enormous block of red granite, whose height enabled him to stand up, in shelter on all sides save in the direction of the forest. But he had no great risk to run from any enemies concealed in the chaparral, for the night was so dark that it would have been necessary to have followed the hunter's every movement, to discover the spot where he now was.

Loyal Heart was a Mexican; like all his countrymen, whose skill is proverbial in the management of certain weapons, from his youth he had been familiarized with the lasso, that terrible arm which renders the Mexican horsemen so formidable. The lasso or reata, for this weapon has two names, is a strip of plaited leather, rendered supple by means of grease. It is ordinarily forty-five to fifty feet in length, one of the ends terminating in a running knot, the other being fastened to an iron ring riveted in the saddle; the rider whirls it round his head, sets his horse at a gallop, and on arriving within thirty or five-and-thirty yards of the man or animal he is pursuing, he lets the lasso fly, so that the running knot may fall on the shoulders of his victim. At the same time that he lets the lasso go, the rider makes his horse suddenly turn in the opposite direction, and the enemy he has lassoed is, in spite of the most strenuous resistance, hurled down and dragged after him. Such is the lasso and the way in which it is employed on horseback.

Afoot, matters are effected much in the same fashion, save that, as the lassoer has no longer his horse to aid him, he is obliged to display great muscular strength, and is often dragged along for a considerable distance. In Mexico, where this weapon is in general use, people naturally study the means to neutralize its effects, the most efficacious being to cut the lasso. This is why all horsemen carry in their boot, within arm's length, a long and sharp knife; still, as the horseman is nearly always unexpectedly lassoed, he is strangled ere he has had time to draw his knife. Of one hundred riders lassoed thus in a combat or chase, seventy-five are inevitably killed, and the others only escape by a miracle, so much skill, strength, and coolness are needed to cut the fatal knot.

Loyal Heart had the simple idea of forming a running knot at the end of his picquet rope, and lassoing the first rider who passed within reach. On getting behind the rock he unrolled the long cord he had fastened round his body; then, after making the slip knot with all the care it demands, he coiled the lasso in his hand and waited. Chance seemed to favour the project of the bold hunter, for, within ten minutes at the most, he heard the gallop of a horse going at full speed. Loyal Heart listened attentively; the sound approached with great rapidity, and soon the black outline of a horseman stood out in the night. The direction followed by the rider compelled him to pass within a short distance of the block of granite behind which Loyal Heart was concealed. The latter spread out his legs to have a firmer holdfast, bent his body slightly forward, and whirled the lasso round his head. At the moment when the horseman came opposite to him, Loyal Heart let the lasso fly, and it fell with a whiz on the shoulders of the rider, who was roughly hurled to the ground ere he knew what was happening to him. His horse, which was at full speed, went on some distance further, but then perceiving that its rider had left it, it slackened its pace, and presently halted.

In the meanwhile Loyal Heart bounded like a tiger on the man he had so suddenly unsaddled. The latter had not uttered a cry, but remained motionless at the spot where he had been hurled. Loyal Heart at first fancied him dead, but it was not so; his first care was to free the wounded man from the running knot, drawn so tightly round his neck, in order to enable him to breathe; then, without taking the trouble to look at his victim, he pinioned him securely, threw him over his shoulders, and returned to the spot where his comrades were awaiting him.

The latter had seen, or at least heard, what had happened; and far from dreaming of the means employed by the young man, although they were well acquainted with it, they knew not to what they should attribute the rough way in which the rider had been hurled from his horse.

"Oh, oh," Tranquil said, "I fancy you have made a fine capture."

"I think so too," Loyal Heart answered, as he deposited his burden on the ground.

"How on earth did you manage to unsaddle him so cleverly?"

"Oh! In the simplest way possible. I lassoed him."

"By Jove!" the hunter exclaimed, "I suspected it. But let us see the nature of the game. These confounded Indians are difficult to tame when they take it into their heads not to unlock their teeth. This fellow will not speak, in all probability."

"Who knows? At any rate we can question him."

"Yes—but let us first make sure of his identity, for it would not be pleasant to have captured one of our friends."

"May the Lord forbid!" Loyal Heart said.

The hunters bent over the prisoner, who was apparently motionless, and indifferent to what was said around.

"Oh," the Canadian suddenly said, "whom have we here? On my soul, compadre, I believe it is an old acquaintance."

"You are right," Loyal Heart answered, "it is Blue-fox."

"Blue-fox?" the hunters exclaimed, in surprise.

The adventurers were not mistaken; the Indian horseman, so skilfully lassoed by Loyal Heart, was really the Apache Chief. The shock he had received though very rude, had not been sufficiently so to make him entirely lose his senses; with open eyes and disdainful countenance, but with not a word of complaint at the treatment he had suffered, he waited calmly till it should please his captors to decide his fate, not considering it consistent with his dignity to be the first to speak. After examining him attentively for a moment, Loyal Heart unfastened the bonds that held him, and fell back a step.

"My brother can rise," he said: "only old women remain thus stretched on the ground for an insignificant fall."

Blue-fox reached his feet at a bound.

"The Chief is no old woman," he said, "his heart is large; he laughs at the anger of his enemies, and despises the fury which is impotent to affect him."

"We are not your enemies, Chief, we feel no hatred or anger towards you; it is you, on the contrary, who are our enemy. Are you disposed to answer our questions?"

"I could refrain from doing so, were it my good pleasure."

"I do not think so," John Davis remarked, with a grin, "for we have wonderful secrets to untie the tongue of those we cross-question."

"Try them on me," the Indian observed, haughtily.

"We shall see," said the American.

"Stop!" said Loyal Heart. "There is in all this something extraordinary, which I wish to discover, so leave it to me."

"As you please," said John Davis.

The adventurers collected round the Indian, and waited anxiously.

"How is it," Loyal Heart presently went on, "that you, who were sent by the Apaches to treat for peace with the Comanches, were thus leaving the village in the middle of the night, not as a friend, but as a robber flying after the commission of a theft?"

The Chief smiled contemptuously, and shrugged his shoulders.

"Why should I tell you what has passed? It would be uselessly losing precious time; suffice it for you to know that I left the village with the general consent of the Chiefs, and if I was galloping, it was probably because I was in a hurry to reach the spot I am bound for."

"Hum!" said the hunter; "You will permit me to remark, Chief, that your answer is very vague, and anything but satisfactory."

"It is the only one, however, I am enabled to give you."

"And do you fancy we shall be satisfied with it?"

"You must."

"Perhaps so, but listen; we are awaiting Black-deer at every moment, and he shall decide your fate."

"As it pleases the Pale hunter. When the Comanche Chief arrives, my brother will see that the Apache Sachem has spoken truly, that his tongue is not forked, and that the words that from his lips are sincere."

"I hope so."

At this moment the signal agreed on between Black-deer and the hunters was heard: the hunter said at once to his prisoner.

"Here is the Chief."

"Good," the latter simply answered.

Five minutes later, the Sachem indeed reached the spot where the adventurers were assembled. His first glance fell on the Apache, standing upright with folded arms in the circle formed by the hunters.

"What is Blue-fox doing here?" he asked in surprise.

"The Chief can ask the Pale warriors, they will answer," said the Apache.

Black-deer turned to Loyal Heart; the latter, not waiting till he was addressed, related in the fullest detail what had occurred; how he had captured the Chief, and the conversation he had had with him: Black-deer seemed to reflect for a moment—

"Why did not my brother show the sign of recognition I gave him?" he asked.

"For what good, as my brother was coming?"

The Comanche frowned.

"My brother will be careful to remember that he has passed his word, and the mere appearance of treachery will cost his son's life."

A shudder passed over the Indian's body, although his features lost none of their marble-like rigidity.

"Blue-fox has sworn on his totem," he replied; "that oath is sacred, and he will keep it."

"Ocht! My brother is free, he can start without farther delay."

"I must find my horse again which has escaped."

"Does my brother take us for children, that he says such things to us?" Black-deer replied angrily. "The horse of an Indian Chief never abandons its master; let him whistle, and it will come up."

Blue-fox made no reply; his black eye shot forth a flash of fury, but that was all; he bent forward, seemed to be listening for a few moments, and then gave a shrill whistle, almost immediately after which there was a rustling in the branches, and the Chief's horse laid its fine and intelligent head on its master's shoulder. The latter patted the noble animal, leaped on its back, and digging in his spurs, started at full speed without taking further leave of the hunters, who were quite startled by this hurried departure. John Davis, by an instinctive movement swift as thought, raised his rifle, with the evident intention of saluting the fugitive with a bullet, but Black-deer suddenly clutched his arm.

"My brother must not fire," he said; "the sound would betray our presence."

"That is true," the American said, as he took down his gun. "It is unlucky, for I should have been very glad to get rid of that ill-favoured scoundrel."

"My brother will find him again," said the Indian with an accent impossible to describe.

"I hope so, and if it should happen, I assure you that no one will be able to prevent me killing that reptile."

"No one will try to do so, my brother may rest assured."

"Nothing less than that certainly was needed to console me for the magnificent opportunity you make me lose today, Chief."

The Indian laughed, and continued—

"I will explain to yon at another moment how it happens that this man is free to retire in peace, when we are threatened by an ambuscade formed by him. For the present, let us not lose precious time in idle talk, for all is ready. My warriors are at their post, only awaiting the signal to begin the contest; do my Pale brothers still intend to accompany us?"

"Certainly, Chief, we are here for that purpose, you can count upon us."

"Good, still I must warn my brothers that they will run a great risk."

"Nonsense," Loyal Heart replied, "it will be welcome, for are we not accustomed to danger?"

"Then to horse, and let us start, as we have to deceive the deceivers."

"But are you not afraid," Loyal Heart observed, "lest Blue-fox has warned his comrades that their tricks are discovered?"

"No, he cannot do so, he has sworn it."

The hunters did not insist further, they knew with what religious exactness Indians keep oaths they make to each other, and the good faith and loyalty they display in the accomplishment of this duty. The Chiefs answer consequently convinced them that they had nothing to apprehend from the Apache Sachem, and, in truth, he had gone off in a direction diametrically opposite to that where his companions were hidden.

The horses were immediately lifted on their legs, the cords removed, and the party set out. They followed a narrow path running between two ravines covered with thick grass. This path, after running for a mile and a half, debouched on a species of cross roads, where the adventurers had halted for an instant. This spot, called by the Indians the Elk Pass, had been selected by Black-deer as the gathering place of some forty picked warriors, who were to join the white men and act with them. This junction was effected as the Sachem arranged. The hunters had hardly debouched at the crossroads, ere the Comanches emerged from behind the thicket which had hitherto concealed them, and flocked up to Black-deer.

The band was formed in close column, and flankers went ahead, preceding it but a few yards, and attentively examining the thickets. For many an hour they marched on, nothing attracting their attention, when suddenly a shot was fired in the rear of the band. Almost simultaneously, and as if at a given signal, the fusillade broke out on both sides of the war path, and a shower of bullets and arrows hurtled upon the Comanches and white men. Several men fell, and there was a momentary confusion, inseparable from an unforeseen attack.

By assent of Black-deer, Loyal Heart assumed the supreme command. By his orders, the warriors broke up into platoons, and vigorously returned the fire, while retreating to the crossroads, where the enemy could not attack them without discovering themselves; but they had committed the imprudence of marching too fast—the crossroads were still a long way off, and the fire of the Apaches extended along the whole line. The bullets and arrows rained on the Comanches, whose ranks were beginning to be thinned.

Loyal Heart ordered the ranks to be broken, and the men to scatter, a manoeuvre frequently employed in Europe during the Vendean war, and which the Chouans unconsciously obtained from the Indians. The cavalry at once tried to leap the ravines and ditches that bordered the path behind which the Apaches were hidden; but were repulsed by the musketry and the long barbed arrows, which the Indians fired with extreme dexterity. The Comanches and Whites leaped off their horses, being certain of recovering them when wanted, and retreated, sheltering themselves behind trees, only giving way inch by inch, and keeping up a sustained fire with their enemies, who, feeling certain of victory, displayed in their attack a perseverance far from common among savage nations, with whom success nearly always depends on the first effort.

Loyal Heart, so soon as his men reached the clearing, made them form a circle, and they offered an imposing front to the enemy on all sides. Up to this moment, the Apaches had maintained silence, not a single war yell had been uttered, not a rustling of the leaves had been heard. Suddenly the firing ceased, and silence once again brooded over the desert. The hunters and Comanches looked at each other with a surprise mingled with terror.

They had fallen into the trap their enemies had laid for them, while fancying they could spoil it.

There was a terrible moment of expectation, whose anxious expression no pen could depict. All at once the conches and chichikouès were heard sounding on the right and left, in the rear and front! At this signal, the Apaches rose on all sides, blowing their war whistles to excite their courage, and uttering fearful yells. The Comanches were surrounded, and nothing was left them but to die bravely at their posts! At this terrible sight, a shudder of fear involuntarily rose along those intrepid warriors, but it was almost instantaneously quelled, for they felt that their destruction was imminent and certain.

Loyal Heart and Black-deer, however, had lost none of their calmness; they hoped then, still, but what was it they expected?

CHAPTER XVI
THE SCALP DANCE

Far from us the thought of making humanitarian theories with reference to a fight in the heart of the desert between two savage tribes, for it has too long been a principle among civilized nations that the Indians are ferocious brutes, possessed of nothing human but the face, and who should be destroyed, like all other noxious animals, by all possible means, even by those which are too repugnant to humanity for us to attempt for a single moment to defend.

Still, much might be said in favour of these unhappy peoples, who have been oppressed ever since humanity decreed that a man of genius should find once more their country which had so long been lost. It would be easy for us to prove, if we thought proper, that these Peruvians and Mexicans, treated so haughtily and barbarously by the wretched adventurers who plundered them, enjoyed, at the period of the conquest, a civilization far more advanced than that of which their oppressors boasted, who had only one advantage over them in the knowledge of firearms, and who marched cased in steel from head to foot against men clothed in cotton and armed with inoffensive arrows. Placed beyond the pale of society by the unintelligent fanaticism and the inextinguishable thirst for gold which devoured the conquerors, the wretched Indians succumbed not only to the repeated assaults of their implacable conquerors, but were also destined to remain constantly beneath the oppression of a calumny which made them a stupid and ferocious race.

The conquest of the New World was one of the most odious monstrosities of the middle ages, fertile though they were in atrocities. Millions of men, whose blood was poured out like water, were coldly killed; empires crumbled away for ever, entire populations disappeared from the globe, and left no trace of their passage but their whitened bones. America, which had been so populous, was almost suddenly converted into an immense desert, and the proscribed relics of this unfortunate race, driven back into barbarism, buried themselves in the most remote countries, where they resumed the nomadic life of the old days, continually carrying on war against the whites, and striving to requite them in detail all the evils they had received at their hands for centuries.

It is only for a few years past that public opinion has been stirred up as to the fate of the Indians; and various means have been attempted — not to civilize them, though that wish has been put forward, but to put a stop to reprisals; consequently they have been placed in horrible deserts; which they have been forbidden to leave. A sanitary cordon has been formed round them, and as this method was not found sufficiently expeditious to get rid of them, they have been gorged with spirits. We will declare here the happy results obtained from these Anglo-American measures: ere a century has elapsed, not a single native will be left on the territory of the Union. The philanthropy of these worthy northern republicans is a very fine thing, but Heaven save us from it!

In every battle there are two terrible moments for the commander who has undertaken the great responsibility of victory: the one, when he gives the signal of attack and hurls his columns at the enemy; the other, when organizing the resistance, he calmly awaits the hour when the decisive blow must be dealt in accordance with his previous combinations. Loyal Heart was as calm and quiet as if witnessing an ordinary charge; with flashing eye and haughty lip he recommended his warriors to save their powder and arrows, to keep together, and sustain the charge of the Apaches, without yielding an inch of ground. The Comanches uttered their war yell twice, and then a deadly silence brooded over the clearing.

"Good!" the hunter said, "you are great braves; I am proud of commanding such intrepid warriors. Your squaws will greet you with dances and shouts of joy on your return to the village, and proudly count the scalps you bring back at your girdle."

After this brief address the hunter returned to the centre of the circle, and the Whites waited with their finger on the trigger, the Redskins with levelled bows. In the meanwhile, the Apaches had quitted their ambuscade, had formed their ranks, and were marching in excellent order on the Comanches. They had also dismounted, for a hand-to-hand fight was about to begin between these irreconcilable enemies.

The night had entirely slipped away; by the first beams of day, which tinged the tops of the trees, the black and moving circle could be seen drawing closer and closer round the weak group formed by the Comanches and the adventurers. It was a singular thing in prairie fashions that the Apaches advanced slowly without firing, as if wishing to destroy their enemies at one blow. Tranquil and Loyal Heart shook hands while exchanging a calm smile.

"We have five minutes left," said the hunter; "we shall settle a goodly number before falling ourselves," the Canadian answered.

Loyal Heart stretched out his hand toward the north-west.

"All is not over yet," he said.

"Do you hope to get us out of this scrape?"

"I intend," the young man answered, still calm and smiling, "to destroy this collection of brigands to the last man."

"May Heaven grant it!" the Canadian said, with a doubtful shake of the head.

The Apaches were now but a few yards off, and all the rifles were levelled as if by common agreement.

"Listen!" Loyal Heart muttered in Tranquil's ear.

At the same moment distant yells were heard, and the enemy stopped with alarmed hesitation.

"What is it?" Tranquil asked.

"Our men," the young man answered laconically.

A sound of horses and firearms was heard in the enemy's rear.

"The Comanches! the Comanches!" the Apaches shouted.

The line that surrounded the little band was suddenly rent asunder, and two hundred Comanche horsemen were seen cutting down and crushing every foeman within reach. On perceiving their brothers the horsemen uttered a shout of joy, to which the others enthusiastically responded, for they had fancied themselves lost.

Loyal Heart had calculated justly, he had not been a second wrong; the warriors ambuscaded by Black-deer to effect a diversion and complete the victory arrived at the decisive moment. This was the secret of the young Chief's calmness, although in his heart he was devoured by anxiety, for so many things might delay the arrival of the detachment. The Apaches, thus taken by surprise, attempted for a few minutes a desperate resistance; but being surrounded and overwhelmed by numbers, they soon began flying in all directions. But Black-deer's measures had been taken with great prudence, and a thorough knowledge of the military tactics of the prairies: the Apaches were literally caught between two fires.

Nearly two-thirds of the Apache warriors, placed under the command of Blue-fox to attempt the daring stroke he had conceived, fell, and the rest had great difficulty in escaping. The victory was decisive, and for a long long time the Apaches would not dare to measure themselves again with their redoubtable enemies. Eight hundred horses and nearly five hundred scalps were the trophies of the battle, without counting some thirty wounded. The Comanches had only lost a dozen warriors, and their enemies had been unable to scalp them, which was regarded as a great glory. The horses were collected, the dead and wounded placed on litters, and when all the scalps had been lifted from the Apaches who had succumbed during the fight, their bodies were left to the wild beasts, and the Comanche warriors, intoxicated with joy and pride, remounted their horses and returned to the village.

The return of the Expeditionary corps was a perfect triumphant march. Black-deer, to do honour to Loyal Heart and his comrades, whose help had been so useful during the battle, insisted on their marching at the head of the column, and on Loyal Heart keeping by his side, as having shared the command with him. The sun rose at the moment when the Comanches emerged from the forest, the day promised to be magnificent, and the birds perched on all the branches loudly saluted the advent of day. A large crowd, composed of women and children, could be seen running from the village and hurrying to meet the warriors.

A large band of horsemen soon appeared, armed and painted for war, at their head marching the greatest braves and most respected Sachems of the tribe. This band, formed in good order, came up to the sound of conches, drums, chichikouès, and war whistles, mingled with shouts of joy from the crowd. On coming within a certain distance of each other, the two bands halted, while the crowd fell back to the right and left. Then, at a signal given by Black-deer and the Chief commanding the second detachment, a fearful yell burst forth like a clap of thunder, the horsemen dug in their spurs, and the two parties rushed upon one another and began a series of evolutions, of which the Arab fantasias can alone convey an idea.

When this performance had lasted some time, and a considerable quantity of gunpowder had been expended, the two Chiefs gave a signal, and the bands, up to the present commingled, separated, as if by enchantment, and formed up about a pistol shot from each other. There was then a perfect rest, but in a few minutes, at a signal from Blackbird, who commanded the band that had come out of the village, the leaders of the two detachments advanced towards each other. The salutations and congratulations then began; for, as we have already made the observation, the Indians are excessively strict in matters of etiquette.

Black-deer was obliged to narrate in the fullest detail, to the assembled Chiefs, how the action had been fought, the number of the enemy killed, how many had been scalped—in short, all that had occurred. Black-deer performed this duty with the utmost nobility and modesty, giving to Loyal Heart, who in vain protested, all the merit of the victory, and only allowing himself credit for having punctually carried out the orders the Pale warrior had given him. This modesty in a warrior so renowned as Black-deer greatly pleased the Comanche Chiefs, and obtained him the most sincere praise.

When all these preliminary ceremonies had been performed, the wives of the Chiefs advanced, each leading by the bridle a magnificent steed, destined to take the place of their husband's chargers wearied in action. Black-deer's young and charming squaw led two. After bowing with a gentle smile to her husband, and handing him the bridle of one of the horses, she turned gracefully to Loyal Heart, and offered him the bridle of the second horse:

"My brother Loyal Heart is a great brave," she said, in a voice as melodious as a bird's song; "he will permit his sister to offer him this courser, which is intended to take the place of the one he has tired in fighting to save his brothers the Antelope Comanches."

All the Indians applauded this gift, so gracefully offered; Black-deer, in spite of his assumed stoicism, could not refrain from evidencing the pleasure which his young wife's charming attention caused her. Loyal Heart smiled sweetly, dismounted, and walked up to her.

"My sister is fair and kind," he said, as he kissed her on the forehead; "I accept the present she makes me; my brother Black-deer is happy in possessing so charming a squaw to clean his arms and take care of his horses."

The young wife withdrew, all confused and delighted, among her companions; the Chiefs then mounted the fresh horses brought them. Each returned to the head of his detachment, and the two bands advanced slowly towards the village, escorted by the crowd which incessantly filled the air with joyous shouts that mingled with the musical instruments, whose savage harmony deafened all ears.

The Apache prisoners, on foot and disarmed, marched at the head of the column, guarded by fifty picked warriors. These untameable Indians, although perfectly aware of the fate that awaited them and the refined tortures to which they were destined, walked with head erect and haughty demeanour, as if, instead of being interested actors in the scene that was preparing, they were only indifferent spectators.

However, this stoicism peculiar to the Red race surprised nobody. The Comanche warriors disdained to insult the misfortunes of the intrepid warriors, whose courage fortune had betrayed; the women alone, more cruel than the men, especially those whose husbands were killed in the battle, and whose bodies were now brought along in litters, rushed like furies on the unhappy prisoners, whom they overwhelmed with insults, casting stones and filth, and even at times trying to dig their sharp nails into their flesh. This was carried to such a point that the guards of the prisoners were compelled to interfere to prevent them being torn asunder alive, and get them away, at least for a while, from the fury of these Megeras, who grew more and more excited, and in whom wrath had gradually attained the proportions of indescribable fury.

As for the prisoners, perfectly calm and impassive, they endured the blows and insults without complaint; nothing moved them, and they continued their march as peaceably as if they had been complete strangers to what was going on. The procession, compelled to clear its way through a crowd which was momentarily augmented, only advanced slowly.

The day was far spent when it reached the palisade that formed the village defences. At about ten paces from the palisade the two bands stopped; two men were standing motionless at the entrance of the village—they were the master of the great medicine and the hachesto: as if by enchantment, at the sight of these men a profound silence fell on the crowd so noisy a moment previously. The hachesto held in his hand the totem of the tribe, and when the warriors halted the sorcerer took a step forward.

"Who are you, and what do you want?" he asked, in a loud voice.

"We are," Black-deer answered, "the great braves of the powerful nation of the Antelope Comanches; we ask leave to enter the village with our prisoners and the horses we have captured, in order to perform the scalp dance round the stake of torture."

"Good," the sorcerer answered, "I recognise you; you are, indeed, the great braves of my nation, your hands are red with the blood of our enemies; but," he added, taking a gloomy glance around, "all our warriors are not present; what has become of those who are missing?"

There was a moment of mournful silence at this question.

"Answer," the sorcerer continued imperiously; "have you abandoned your brothers?"

"No," Black-deer said, "they are dead, it is true, but we have brought back their bodies with us, and their scalps are untouched."

"Good," said the sorcerer; "how many warriors have fallen?"

"Only ten."

"How did they die?"

"Like brave men, with their face turned to their foe."

"Good, the Wacondah has received them into the happy hunting grounds; have their squaws bewailed them?"

"They are doing so."

The Seer frowned.

"Brave men only weep with tears of blood," he said.

Black-deer fell back a step to make room for the widows, who stood motionless and gloomy behind him; they then advanced.

"We are ready," they said, "if our father will permit us, we will bewail our husbands as they deserve."

"Do so," he answered; "the Master of Life sees it, and he will smile on your grief."

Then, a strange scene occurred, which only Indian stoicism could endure without shuddering with horror; these women, arming themselves with knives, cut off several joints of their fingers without uttering a complaint; then, not contented with this sacrifice, they began scarring their faces, arms, and bosoms, so that the blood soon ran down their whole bodies, and they became horrible to look upon. The seer excited and encouraged them by his remarks to give their husbands this proof of their regret, and their exaltation soon attained such a pitch of delirium, that they would eventually have killed themselves, had not the sorcerer checked them. Their companions then approached, took away their weapons, and dragged them off. When they had finally left the spot, the sorcerer addressed the warriors standing motionless and attentive before him—

"The blood shed by the Apache warriors has been ransomed by the Comanche squaws," he said; "the ground is saturated with it; grief can now give way to joy, and my brothers enter their village with heads erect, for the Master of Life is satisfied."

Then taking from the hands of the hachesto the totem which the latter had been waving round his head, he stationed himself on the right hand of Black-deer, and entered the village with the warriors, amid the deafening shouts of the crowd, and to the sound of the instruments which had recommenced their infernal charivari.

The procession marched straight to the great square where the scalp dance was to take place. Loyal Heart and his comrades desired most eagerly to escape this ceremony; but it would have been a great insult to the Indians to do so, and they were compelled to follow the warriors, whether they liked it or not. On passing before the hunter's rancho, they noticed that all the windows were hermetically closed. Doña Jesuita, not at all desirous to witness the cruel sight, had shut herself up; but No Eusebio, whose nerves were probably harder, was standing in the doorway, carelessly smoking his cigarette, and watching the procession defile, which, by Loyal Heart's orders, he had preceded by a few moments, in order to reassure Doña Jesuita as to the result of the engagement.

When the whole tribe had assembled on the square, the scalp dance commenced. In our previous works we have had occasion to describe this ceremony, so we will say nothing of it here, except that, contrary to the other dances, it is performed by the squaws, and that on this occasion it was Black-deer's newly-married wife who led the dance, in her quality of squaw of the Chief who had commanded the expedition.

The Apache prisoners had been fastened to stakes erected expressly; and for some hours they were exposed to the ridicule, jests, and insults of their enemies without displaying the slightest emotion. When the dance at length ended, the time for torture arrived.

We will not dwell on the frightful sufferings inflicted on the wretched men whom their evil destiny had delivered into the hands of their implacable foes, for we have no desire to describe horrible scenes; we have even felt a repugnance to allude to them, but are bound to be faithful historians. As we have undertaken the task of making known the manners of races hitherto almost unknown, and which are destined so shortly to disappear, we will not fail in our duty, and in order that our readers may thoroughly understand what Indian torture is, we will describe the punishment inflicted on one of the prisoners, a renowned Apache Chief.

This Chief was a young man of five-and-twenty at the most, of lofty and well-proportioned stature; his features were noble, and his glance stern, and though severely wounded in the action, it was only when literally overwhelmed by numbers, that he had fallen upon the pile of his warriors who had died bravely at his side.

The Comanches, who are judges of courage, had admired his heroic conduct, and treated him with a certain degree of respect by the express orders of Black-deer, who entertained a hope of making him renounce his nation, and consent to be adopted by the Comanches, for whom so brave a warrior would have been an excellent acquisition. My readers must not feel surprised at this idea of the Comanche Sachem; these adoptions are frequent among the Redskins, and it often happens that a warrior who has fallen into the power of his enemies, ransoms his life, and escapes torture by marrying the widow of the warrior he has killed, under the promise of bringing up the children of the defunct, and regarding them as his own.

The Apache Chief was called Running-elk. Instead of fastening him to the stake like the warriors of less value made prisoners at the same time as himself, he had been left at liberty. He was leaning his shoulder against the stake with folded arms, and watched calmly and disdainfully all the incidents of the scalp dance. When it was ended, Black-deer, who had previously consulted with the other Chiefs of the tribe, and communicated his idea, which they warmly approved of, walked up to him. The prisoner let him come up without seeming to notice him.

"My brother, Running-elk, is a renowned Chief and great brave," he said to him in a gentle voice; "what is he thinking of at this moment?"

"I am thinking," the Apache answered, "that I shall soon be on the happy hunting grounds, where I shall hunt by the side of the Master of Life."

"My brother is still very young, his life only counts spring seasons, does he not regret losing it?"

"Why should I regret it? A little sooner, or a little later, but a man must die after all."

"Certainly; but dying thus at the stake of torture, when you have a long future of joy and happiness before you, is hard."

The Chief shook his head mournfully, and interrupted the speaker.

"My brother need say no more," he replied; "I see his thoughts, he is indulging in a hope which will not be realised; Running-elk will not be a renegade to his nation to become a Comanche; I could not live among you, for the blood of your warriors I have shed would constantly cry out against me. Could I marry all the squaws whom my tomahawk has rendered widows, or give you back the numerous scalps I have raised? No, I could not. When an Apache and Comanche meet on the war trail, one must kill the other. Cease then making me proposals which are an insult to my character and courage; fasten me to the stake of torture, and do not kill me at once, but gradually, by tortures, in the Indian way. Invent the most atrocious torture, and I defy you to hear from me a complaint, or even a sigh." And growing more excited as he spoke, he said, "You are children who do not know how to make a man of courage suffer, you need the death of a brave to learn how to die. Try it on me, I despise you; you are cowardly dogs, you can only snarl, and the mere sight of my eagle feather has ever sufficed to put you to flight."

On hearing these haughty words, the Comanches uttered a yell of anger, and prepared to rush on the prisoner, but Black-deer checked them.

"Running-elk," he said, "is not a real brave, he talks too much; he is a mocking-bird, who chatters because he is afraid."

The Sachem shrugged his shoulders contemptuously.

"This is the last word you shall hear from me," he said; "you are dogs!"

And biting his tongue off, he spat it into Black-deer's face. The latter gave a leap of fury, and his rage no longer knew bounds. Running-elk was immediately fastened to the stake; the women then tore out the nails from his fingers and toes, and drove into the wounds little spiles of wood dipped in inflammable matter, which they fired. The Indian remained calm; no contraction of the muscles disturbed the harmony of his features. The punishment endured three hours; but though his body was one huge wound, the Sachem remained perfectly stoical. Blackbird approached in his turn.

"Wait," he said.

Room was made for him; rushing on the Apache, he plucked out his eyes, which he threw away with disgust, and filled the two burning cavities with live coals. This last agony was horrible; a nervous tremor ran for a second over the wretch's body, but that was all. The Comanche, exasperated by this stoicism, which he could not refrain from admiring, seized him by his long hair, and scalped him; then he lashed his face with the blood-dripping scalp. The prisoner was horrible to look on, but still remained erect and unmoved.

Loyal Heart could no longer endure this hideous spectacle; he dashed through the people in front of him, and, putting a pistol to the prisoner's forehead, blew out his brains. The Comanches, furious at seeing their vengeance slip from them, gave a start, as if about to rush on the White man, who had dared to rob them of their prey: but the latter drew himself up haughtily, folded his arms on his chest, and looked them full in the face.

"Well," he said, in a firm voice.

This one word was enough: the wild beasts were muzzled; they fell back cursing, but did not attempt to make him account for what he had done. The hunter then made a sign to the adventurers to follow him, and they left the square, where for some hours longer the Indians wreaked their fury on the hapless prisoners.

CHAPTER XVII
THE MEETING

We must now go back two months in our narrative, and leaving the deserts of Upper Arkansas for the banks of the Rio Trinidad, return to Cerro Pardo, in the vicinity of Galveston, on the very day of the battle so fatal to the Texans, in order to clear up certain points of our narrative, by telling the reader the fate of certain important personages, whom we have, perhaps, neglected too long.

We have said that the Jaguar, when he saw the battle irretrievably lost, rushed at full speed to the spot where he had left the cart, in which were Tranquil and Carmela; that, on reaching it, a frightful spectacle struck his sight; the cart, half broken, was lying on the ground, surrounded by the majority of his friends, who had bravely fallen in its defence; but it was empty, and the two persons to whose safety he attached such, importance had disappeared. The Jaguar, crushed by this horrible catastrophe, which he was so far from anticipating, after the precautions he had taken, fell senseless to the ground, uttering a loud cry of despair.

The young man remained unconscious for several hours; but his was a nature which a blow, however terrible it might be, could not destroy thus. At the moment when the sun was disappearing on the horizon in the ocean, and making way for night, the Jaguar opened his eyes. He looked round haggardly, not being yet able to comprehend the position in which he found himself, and the circumstances owing to which he had fallen in such a strange state of prostration. However strong a man may be, however great the energy with which nature has endowed him, when life has been suspended in him for several hours, the recollection of past facts completely fails him for a period, more or less long, and he requires some minutes to restore order in his ideas. This was what happened to the young man; he was alone, a sorrowful silence prevailed around him, gloom was gradually invading the landscape, and the objects by which he was surrounded became with each moment less distinct.

Still, the atmosphere was impregnated by a warm, sickly odour of carnage, and corpses covered the ground here and there. He saw the dark outline of the wild beasts, which darkness drew from their lairs, and which, guided by their sanguinary instinct, were already prowling about the battlefield, preparing to commence their horrible repast.

"Oh!" the young man suddenly exclaimed, leaping up, "I remember!"

We have said that the plain was deserted: nothing remained but corpses and wild beasts.

"What is to be done?" the Jaguar muttered;

"Whither shall I go? What has become of my brothers? In what direction have they fled? Where shall I find Carmela and Tranquil again?"

And the young man, crushed by the flood of desperate thoughts that rose from his heart to his brain, sank on a block of rock, and, paying no further attention to the wild beasts, whose roars increased at each second, and grew more menacing with the darkness, he buried his head in his hands, and violently pressing his temples as if to retain that reason which was ready to abandon him, he reflected.

Two hours passed thus—two hours, during which he was a prey to a desperation which was the more terrible, as it was silent. This man, who had set all his hopes on an idea, who had for several years fought, without truce or mercy, for the realization of his dream, whose life had been, so to speak, one long self-denial—at the moment when he was about at last to attain that object, pursued with such tenacity, had seen, by a sudden change of fortune, his projects annihilated for ever perhaps, in a few hours; he had lost everything, and found himself alone on a battlefield, seated amid corpses, and surrounded by wild beasts that watched him. For a moment he had thought of finishing with life, plunging his dagger into his heart, and not surviving the downfall of his hopes of love and ambition. But this cowardly thought did not endure longer than a flash of lightning; a sudden reaction took place in the young man's mind, and he rose again, stronger than before, for his soul, purified in the crucible of suffering, had resumed all its audacious energy.

"No," he said, casting a glance of defiance around, "I will not let myself be any longer crushed, God will not permit that a cause so sacred as that to which I have devoted myself should fail; it is a trial He has wished to impose on us, and I will endure it without complaint; though conquered today, tomorrow we will be victors. To work! Liberty is the daughter of Heaven: she is holy, and cannot die."

After uttering these words in a loud voice, with an accent of inspiration, as if desirous of giving those who had fallen a last and supreme consolation, the young man picked up his rifle, which had fallen by his side, and went off with the firm and assured step of a strong man, who has really faith in the cause he defends, and to whom obstacles, however great they may be, are incitements to persevere in the path he has traced. The Jaguar then crossed the battlefield, striding over the corpses, and putting to flight the wild beasts, which eagerly got out of his way.

The young man thus passed alone and in the darkness along the road he had traversed by the dazzling sunlight, in the midst of an enthusiastic army, which marched gaily into action, and believed itself sure of victory. His resolution did not break down for a moment, he no longer allowed the attacks of those sad thoughts which had so nearly crushed him: he had clutched his sorrow, struggled with it and conquered it; now, nothing more could overpower him.

On reaching the end of the plain where the battle had been fought, the Jaguar halted. The moon had risen, and its sickly rays sadly illumined the landscape, to which it imparted a sinister hue. The young man looked around him: in his utter ignorance of the road followed by the fugitives of his party, he hesitated about going along a path where he ran a risk of falling in with a party of Mexican scouts or plunderers, who must at this moment be scouring the plain in every direction, in pursuit of those Texans who had been so lucky as to escape from the battlefield.

It was a long and difficult journey to the Fort of the Point, and in all probability the victors, if they were not already masters of the fortress, would have invested it, so as to intercept all communications of the garrison with their friends outside, and force it to surrender. Nor could he dream of entering Galveston, for that would be delivering himself into the hands of his enemies. The Jaguar's perplexity was great; he remained thus for a long time hesitating as to what road he should follow. By a mechanical movement habitual enough to men when embarrassed, he looked vaguely around him, though not fixing his eyes more on one spot than another, when he gave a sudden start. He had seen, some distance off, a faint, almost imperceptible light gleaming among the trees. The young man tried in vain to determine the direction in which the light was; but at length, he felt certain that it came from the side where was the rancho, which, on the previous evening, had been the headquarters of the staff of the Texan army.

This rancho, situated on the sea shore, at a considerable distance from the battlefield, could not have been visited by the Mexicans, for their horses were too tired to carry them so far: the Jaguar therefore persuaded himself that the light he perceived was kindled by fugitives of his party; he believed it the more easily because he desired it, for night was advancing, and he had neither eaten nor drunk during the past day, in which he had been so actively occupied; he began to feel not only exhausted with fatigue, but his physical wants regaining the mastery over his moral apprehension, he felt a degree of hunger and thirst, that reminded him imperiously that he had been fasting for more than fourteen hours; hence he was anxious to find a place where it would be possible for him to rest and refresh himself.

It is only in romances that the heroes, more or less problematical, brought on the scene, cover great distances without suffering from any of the weaknesses incidental to poor humanity. Never stopping to eat or drink, they are always as fresh and well disposed as when they set out; but, unfortunately, in real life it is not, and men must, whether they like it or no, yield to the imperious claims inherent in their imperfect nature. The partisans and wood rangers, men in whom the physical instincts are extremely developed, whatever moral agony they may undergo, never forget the hours for their meals and rest. And the reason is very simple; as their life is one continual struggle to defend themselves against enemies of every description, their vigour must be equal to the obstacles they have to overcome.

The Jaguar, without further hesitation, marched resolutely in the direction of the light, which he continued to see gleaming among the trees like a beacon. The nearer he drew to the rancho, the firmer became his conviction that he had not deceived himself; after deep reflection it seemed to him impossible that the Mexicans could have pushed on so far; still, when he was but a short distance from the house, he judged it prudent to double his precautions, not to let himself be surprised, if, contrary to his expectations, he had to deal with an enemy.

On coming within five hundred paces of the rancho, he began to grow restless and have less confidence in the opinion he had formed. Several dead horses, two or three corpses lying pell-mell among pieces of weapons and broken carts, led to the evident supposition that a fight had taken place near the rancho. But with whom had the advantage remained? With the Mexicans or the Texans? Who were the persons at this moment in the house — were they friends or foes? These questions were very difficult to solve, and the Jaguar felt extremely embarrassed. Still he was not discouraged. The young man had too long carried on the profession of partisan and scout, not to be thoroughly acquainted with all the tricks of the wood ranger's difficult life. After reflecting for a few moments, his mind was made up.

Several times, while the rancho had served as headquarters of the Texan army, the Jaguar had gone there either to be present at councils of war, or to take the orders of the Commander-in-Chief. As the approach to the house was thus familiar to him, he resolved to slip up to a window, and assure himself with his own eyes of what was going on in the rancho. This enterprise was not so difficult as it appeared at the first glance; for we have already seen, in a previous chapter, another of our characters employing the same plan for a similar purpose. The young man was quick, sharp, and strong—three reasons for succeeding.

The light still gleamed, though no sound was heard from the interior, or troubled the deep silence of the night; the Jaguar, without quitting his rifle, which he supposed he might require at any moment, lay down on the ground, and crawling on his hands and knees, advanced towards the house, being careful to keep in the shadow thrown by the thick branches of the trees, in order not to reveal his presence, if, as it was probable, the inhabitants, whoever they might be, of the house had placed a sentry to watch over their safety. The reasoning of the young man, like all reasoning based on experience, was correct; he had scarce gone fifteen yards ere he saw, standing out from the white wall of the house, the shadow of a man leaning on a rifle, and motionless as a statue. This man was evidently a sentry placed there to watch the approaches to the rancho.

The situation was growing complicated for the Jaguar; the difficulties increased in such proportions, that they threatened soon to become insupportable; for in order to reach the window he wanted, he would be compelled to leave the shadow which had hitherto so fortunately protected him, and enter the white light cast by the moon with a profusion that did not at all please the young man. He mechanically raised his head, hoping, perhaps, that a cloud would pass over the face of the planet, and intercept its too brilliant light, were it but for a moment; but the sky was of a deep azure, without the smallest cloud, and studded with stars.

The Jaguar felt an enormous inclination to leap on the sentry and throttle him; but supposing it were a friend? It was a knotty point. The young man really did not know what to resolve on, and sought in vain how to get out of the scrape, when the sentry suddenly levelled his rifle in his direction, and aimed at him with the saucy remark:—

"Halloh! My friend, when you have crawled far enough like a snake, I suppose you will get up?"

At the sound of this voice, which he believed he recognised, the young man eagerly leapt to his feet.

"Caramba!" he answered with a laugh. "You are right, John Davis; I have had enough of that crawling."

"What!" the latter replied, in surprise; "Who are you that you know me so well?"

"A friend, *Cuerpo de Cristo!* So raise your rifle."

"A friend, a friend!" the American replied, without changing his position, "That is possible, and the sound of your voice is not unknown to me; but, no matter, whether friend or foe, tell me your name, for if you don't, I will keep you on the spot, as this is not the time for fishing."

"Viva Dios!" the young man said with a laugh, "That dear John is always prudent."

"I should hope so, but enough talking; your name, that I may know with whom I have to deal."

"What, do you not recognise the Jaguar?"

The American lowered his rifle, and the butt echoed on the ground.

"By Heaven!" he said joyously, "I suspected it was you, but did not dare believe it."

"Why not?" the young man asked as he approached.

"Hang it! Because I was assured that you were dead."

"I?"

"Yes, you."

"Who the deuce could have told you that nonsense?"

"It is not nonsense. Fray Antonio assured me that he leapt his horse over your body."

The Jaguar reflected for a moment.

"Well," he answered, "he told you the truth."

"What?" the American exclaimed as he gave a start of terror, "Are you dead?"

"Oh, oh! Make your mind easy," the young man answered with a laugh; "I am as good a living man as yourself."

"Are you quite sure of it?" the superstitious American said dubiously.

"*Rayo de Dios!* I am certain of it, though it is possible that Fray Antonio leaped his horse over my body, for I lay for several hours senseless on the battlefield."

"That is all right, then."

"Thanks; but what are you doing there?"

"As you see, I am on guard."

"Yes, but why are you so? Are there more of you inside?"

"There are about a dozen of us."

"All the better; and who are your comrades?"

The American looked at him for some moments fixedly, and then took his hand, which he squeezed.

"My friend," he said with emotion, "thank heaven, for it has shown you a great mercy this day."

"What do you mean?" the young man exclaimed, anxiously.

"I mean that those you confided to us are safe and sound, in spite of the dangers innumerable they incurred during the terrible day we have passed through."

"Can it be true?" he said, laying his hand on his chest, to check the beating of his heart.

"I assure you."

"Then, they are both here?"

"Yes."

"Oh! I must see them!" he exclaimed, as he prepared to rush into the rancho.

"Wait a moment."

"Why so?" he asked in alarm.

"For two reasons: the first being that before you enter, I must warn them of your arrival."

"That is true; go, my friend, I will await you here."

"I have not yet told you the second reason."

"What do I care?"

"More than you fancy; do you not wish me to tell you the name of the man who protected and eventually saved Doña Carmela?"

"I do not understand you, my friend. I entrusted the guardianship of Tranquil and Doña Carmela to you."

"You did so."

"Then, was it not you who saved them?"

The American shook his head in denial.

"No," he said, "it was not I, I could only have died with them."

"But who saved them, then? Whoever the man may be, I swear— —"

"This man," John Davis interrupted him, "is one of your dearest and most devoted friends."

"His name? My friend, tell me his name."

"Colonel Melendez."

"Oh! I could have sworn it," the young man said impetuously; "why cannot I thank him?"

"You will soon see him."

"How so?"

"At this moment he is busy seeking a safe retreat for the old hunter and his daughter. For the present we shall remain at this rancho, from which he will be able to keep the Mexican soldiers off; and so soon as he has found another shelter, he will himself come to tell us."

"Always kind and devoted! I shall never be able to pay my debt to him."

"Who knows?" the American said philosophically; "luck will, perhaps, turn for us, and then it will be our turn to protect our protectors of today."

"You are right, my friend; may Heaven grant that it is so; but how did it all happen?"

"The Colonel, who seemed, from what he said to me, to have foreboded the danger that Doña Carmela ran, arrived just at the moment, when attacked on all sides at once, and too weak to resist the enemies who overwhelmed us, we were preparing, as we had promised, to die at our post; you can guess the rest. By threats and entreaties, he drove back the soldiers who were attacking us: then, not satisfied with having freed us from our enemies, he desired to secure us against all danger, and accompanied us thus far, recommending us to wait for him here, which I believe we shall be wise in doing."

"Certainly, acting otherwise would be ungrateful. Go, now, my friend, I will wait for you."

John Davis, understanding the anxiety from which the young man was suffering, did not let the invitation be repeated, but entered the rancho. The Jaguar remained alone, and was not sorry for it, for he wished to restore some order in his ideas. He felt himself inundated with immense joy at finding again, safe and sound, those whom he had believed dead, and whom he so bitterly lamented; he could scarce dare believe in such happiness, and fancied he must be dreaming, so impossible did all this appear to him. In less than ten minutes John Davis returned.

"Well?" the young man asked.

"Come," he answered laconically.

The American led him forward through a room in which were about a dozen Texans, among them being Fray Antonio, Lanzi, and Quoniam, who were sleeping on trusses of straw laid on the boards. He then pushed open a door and the two men entered a second room not quite so large, and lighted by a smoky candle, standing on a table, which diffused but a dim light. Tranquil was lying on a bed of furs piled on each other, while Doña Carmela was sitting on an equipal by his side. On seeing the young man, she rose quickly and ran to meet him.

"Oh!" she cried, as she offered him her hand; "Heaven be praised, you have come at last!" And bending down, she offered him her pale forehead, on which the Jaguar imprinted a respectful kiss, the only answer he could find, as he was suffering from such emotion. Tranquil rose with an effort on his couch, and held out his hand to the young man, who hurried up to him.

"Now, whatever may happen," he said timorously, "I am assured as to the fate of my poor child, since you are near me. We have been terribly alarmed, my friend."

"Alas!" he answered, "I have suffered more than you."

"But what is the matter?" Carmela exclaimed; "you turn pale and totter: are you wounded?"

"No," he answered feebly; "it is the happiness, the emotion, the joy of seeing you again. It is nothing more, so reassure yourself."

And while saying this, he fell back into a butaca half fainting. Carmela, suffering from the most lively alarm, hurriedly attended to him, but John Davis, knowing better than the maiden what the sick man wanted, seized his gourd, and made him drink a long draught of its contents. The emotion the Jaguar was suffering from, combined with the want of food and the fatigue that oppressed him, had caused him this momentary weakness. Tranquil was not deceived; so soon as he saw the young man return to consciousness, he ordered his daughter to get him food, and, as she did not seem to understand, he said with a laugh to the Jaguar:

"I fancy, my friend, that a good meal is the only remedy you need."

The young man tried to smile as he confessed that, in truth, he was obliged to confess, in spite of the bad opinion Doña Carmela would form of him, that he was literally dying of hunger. The maiden, reassured by this prosaic confession, immediately began getting him a supper of some sort, for provisions were scanty in the rancho, and it was not an easy matter to procure them. However, in a few minutes, Carmela returned with some maize tortillas and a little roast meat, a more than sufficient meal, to which the young man did the greatest honour after apologising to his charming hostess, who now completely reassured, had resumed her petulant character, and did not fail to tease the young Chief, who bravely endured it.

The rest of the night was passed in pleasant conversation by these three persons, who had believed they would never meet again, and now felt so delighted at being together once more. The sun had risen but an hour when the sentry suddenly challenged, and several horsemen stopped at the gate of the rancho.

CHAPTER XVIII
A REACTION

After the sentry's challenge, loud shouts were raised outside the rancho, and, ere long, the noise and confusion since his return to honesty, the worthy monk had resumed his monastic habits of prolixity, we will take his place and narrate the facts as briefly as possible.

We have said that on entering the rancho the Jaguar, while passing through the first room, had perceived, among the sleepers upon straw, Lanzi, Quoniam, and Fray Antonio. All these men were really sleeping, but with that light sleep peculiar to hunters and wood rangers, and the sound of the young man's footsteps had aroused them; so soon as they saw the door of the second room close on the American they rose noiselessly, took up their weapons, and stealthily quitted the rancho. They had done this without exchanging a syllable, and were evidently carrying out a plan arranged beforehand, and which the presence of the sentry had alone impeded. Their horses were saddled in a twinkling, they leapt into their saddles, and when John Davis returned to his post they were far out of reach. The American, who immediately perceived their departure, gave a start of passion, and resumed his rounds, growling between his teeth:

"The deuce take them! I only hope they may get a dose of lead in their heads, provided they do not bring a cuadrilla of Mexican lancers down on us."

Still, the plan of these bold rangers was far from meriting such an imprecation, for they were about to accomplish a work of devotion. Ignorant of Colonel Melendez' promises, and having, moreover, no sort of confidence in the well-known Punic faith of the Mexicans, they proposed to beat up the country, and assembled all the fugitives of their party they came across, in order to defend Tranquil and Doña Carmela from any insult. In the meanwhile Lanzi would swim off to the brig, which would be cruising a cable's length from the beach, announce to Captain Johnson the result of the battle of Cerro Pardo, tell him the critical position in which the old hunter and his daughter were placed, and beg him to go to the rancho and remove the wounded man on board, if circumstances compelled it.

Fortune, which, according to a well-known proverb, always favours the brave, was far more favourable to the plans of this forlorn hope than they had any right to expect; they had hardly galloped ten miles across country in no settled direction, ere they perceived numerous bivouac fires sparkling through the night in front of a wretched fishing village, situated on the sea shore a little distance from the Fort of the Point. They stopped to hold a council; but at the moment they prepared to deliberate, they were suddenly surrounded by a dozen horsemen, and made prisoners, ere they had time to lay hands on their arms or make an effort at defence.

Only one of the three comrades succeeded in escaping, and that was Lanzi; the brave half-breed slipped off his horse, and passing like a serpent between the legs of the horses, he disappeared before his flight was noticed. Lanzi had reflected that by remaining with his comrades he let himself be captured without profit; while if he succeeded in escaping he might hope to accomplish the commission he had undertaken, so that he retained a chance of safety for Tranquil and his daughter. It was in consequence of this reasoning, made with the rapidity that characterised the half-breed, that he attempted and accomplished his bold flight, leaving his comrades to get as they best could out of the awkward scrape they had fallen into.

But a thing happened to the latter which they were far from anticipating, and which the half-breed would never have suspected. The capture of the two men was effected so rapidly; they had been so surprised that not a single word was exchanged on either side; but when they were secured the Chief of the detachment ordered them to follow him in a rough voice, and then a curious fact occurred: these men, who could not see each other for the darkness, became old friends again so soon as a sentence had been exchanged. Fray Antonio and his comrades had fallen into the hands of Texan fugitives from the battle, and were the prisoners of their own friends.

After numberless mutual congratulations, explanations came on the carpet, and these horsemen proved to belong to the Jaguar's cuadrilla. When their Chief left them to fly to the cart they continued to fight for some time while awaiting his return; but pressed on all sides, and not seeing him return, they broke and began flying in all directions. As they were perfectly acquainted with the country, it was easy for them to escape the pursuit of the Mexican cavalry; and each, with that instinct peculiar to partisans and guerillas, proceeded separately to one of the gathering places, whither the Jaguar was accustomed to summon them. Here they nearly all came together again, for the simple reason that as their cuadrilla formed the rearguard, it had been the last engaged, and suffered very slightly, as it was almost immediately broken up by the departure of its Chief.

During this flight a great number of other partisans had swelled their ranks, so that at this moment their band formed a corps of nearly six hundred resolute men, well mounted and armed, but who, unfortunately, had no leader. The capture of Fray Antonio, who found many of his soldiers among them, was, therefore, a piece of good luck for the partisans, who, though they had been left to their own resources for only a few hours, were already beginning to understand the difficulties of their position, and how dangerous it would become for them if fatality willed it that they should be discovered and attacked, by a Mexican corps.

Still, they had acted with great prudence up to this moment. Obliged to leave the retreat they had selected, and which offered them no resources, they had bivouacked a little distance from the Fort of the Point, in order to be protected both by the garrison of the fortress and the fire of their cruisers, which they knew to be close at hand.

When Fray Antonio had picked up this information, which was precious for him, and overwhelmed him with delight, by permitting him to dispose of numerous and determined corps, instead of a few demoralized fugitives of no value, he determined to requite the soldiers who had captured him for the pleasure they caused him by telling him that the Jaguar was not dead as they had falsely supposed—that he was not even wounded, but was in hiding at the rancho which had for a long time served as headquarters of the Texan army, and he would conduct them thither if they pleased. At this proposal of the worthy monk's the joy of the Freebooters became delirious, almost frenzied, for they adored their Chief, and longed to place themselves under his orders again. Consequently, the camp was immediately raised, the partisans formed in a column, Fray Antonio placing himself at its head, and the remains of the Texan army set out joyously for the rancho. The reader knows the rest.

The Jaguar warmly thanked Fray Antonio; he then stated that the rancho would temporarily be headquarters, and ordered his men to bivouac round the house. Still, there was one thing which greatly alarmed the young man: no news had been received, of Lanzi. What had become of him? Perhaps he had found death in accomplishing his rash enterprise, and trying to reach, by swimming, Captain Johnson's brig. The Jaguar knew the friendship that united Tranquil and the half-breed, and what deep root that friendship had taken in the heart of both, and he feared the effect on the Canadian of the announcement of a calamity which, unhappily, was only too probable. Hence, in spite of his promise of returning at once to the hunter, he walked anxiously up and down in front of the rancho, gazing at intervals out to sea, and not feeling the courage to be present when the Canadian asked after his old friend and was told of his death.

Presently, Carmela appeared in the doorway. The old hunter, not seeing the Jaguar return, and alarmed by the noisy demonstrations he heard outside, at length resolved to send the girl on a voyage of discovery, after warning her not to commit any act of imprudence, but return to his side at the slightest appearance of danger, Carmela ran off in delight to find the Jaguar; a few remarks she heard while passing through the house told her what was occurring, and she had no fear about venturing outside. On seeing her the young man checked his hurried walk and waited for her, while trying to give his features an expression agreeing with the lucky situation in which he was supposed to be.

"Well!" she said to him, with that little pouting air which she could assume if necessary, and which suited her so well; "What has become of you, deserter? We have been waiting for you with the most lively impatience, and there you are walking quietly up and down, instead of hurrying to bring us the good news you promised us."

"Forgive me, Carmela," he replied; "I was wrong to appear thus to forget you, and leave you in a state of anxiety; but so many extraordinary things have occurred, that I do not really yet know whether I am awake or dreaming."

"Everybody deserts us this morning, not excepting Lanzi and Quoniam, who have not yet made their appearance."

"You will pardon them, Señorita, for I am the sole cause of their absence. I found myself compelled to entrust them both with important duties, but I trust they will soon return, and directly they do so, I will send them to you."

"But are you not coming in, Jaguar? My father would be glad to talk with you."

"I should like to do so, Carmela, but at this moment it is impossible; remember that the army is utterly disorganized, at each moment fresh men who have escaped from the battle join us; only a few Chiefs have turned up as yet, the rest are missing. I alone must undertake to restore a little order in this chaos; but be assured that so soon as I have a second to myself, I will take advantage of it to join you. Alas! It is only by your side that I am happy."

The maiden blushed slightly at this insinuation, and answered at once with a degree of coldness in her accent, of which she immediately repented, in seeing the impression her words caused the young man, and the cloud they brought to his forehead.

"You are at liberty to remain here as long as you please, Caballero; in speaking to you as I did I merely carried a message my father gave me for you; the rest concerns me but little."

The young man bowed without replying, and turned away his head not to let the cruel girl see the sorrow she caused him by this harsh and so unmerited apostrophe. Carmela walked a few steps toward the house, but on reaching the threshold she ran back and offered her little hand to the young Chief with an exquisite smile.

"Forgive me, my friend," she said to him, "I am a madcap. You are not angry with me, I trust?"

"I angry with you?" he replied, sadly, "Why should I be so, by what right? What else am I to you than a stranger, an indifferent being, a stranger too happy to be endured without any great display of impatience on your part."

The maiden bit her lips angrily.

"Will you not take the hand I offer you?" she said with a slight tinge of impatience.

The Jaguar looked at her for a moment fixedly, and then seized her hand, on which he imprinted a burning kiss.

"Why should the head ever do injustice to the heart?" he said, with a sigh.

"Am I not a woman?" she replied with a smile that filled his heart with joy; "We are waiting for you, so come soon," she added, and shaking her finger at him, she ran back into the house like a startled fawn, and laughing like a madcap.

The Jaguar gazed after her until she at length disappeared in the interior of the rancho.

"She is but a coquettish child," he murmured in a low voice; "has she a heart?"

A stifled sigh was the sole answer he found for the difficult question he asked himself, and he bent his eyes again on the sea. Suddenly, he uttered a cry of joy; he had just seen, above the rocks which terminated on the right, the small bay on which the cuadrilla was encamped, the tall masts of the *Libertad* corvette, followed or rather convoyed by the brig. The two ships, impelled by a favourable breeze, soon doubled the point, and entered the bay; while the corvette made short tacks not to run ashore on the dangerous coast, the brig shortened sail and remained stationary. A boat was immediately let down, several persons seated themselves in it, and the sailors, letting their oars fall simultaneously into the water, pulled vigorously for the shore.

The distance they had to row was nearly half a mile, and hence the Jaguar was unable to recognise the persons who were arriving. Anxious to know, however, what he had to depend on, he mounted the first horse he came across, and galloped toward the boat, followed by some twenty Freebooters; who, seeing their Chief set out, formed him a guard of honour. The young man reached the coast at the precise moment when the bows of the boat ran up into the sand. There were three sailors in the boat: Captain Johnson and the person we have met before under the name of El Alferez, and lastly, Lanzi. On perceiving the latter, the young Chief could not restrain a shout of joy, and without thinking of even saluting the other two, he seized the half-breed's hand and pressed it cordially several times.

The Captain and his companion, far from being annoyed at this apparent want of politeness, seemed, on the contrary, to witness with pleasure, this frank and spontaneous manifestation of an honourable feeling.

"Bravo, Cabellero!" said the Captain; "By Heaven! You do right to press that man's hand, for he is a loyal and devoted fellow; ten times during the past night he risked his life in trying to reach my ship, which at length came aboard, half drowned and dead with fatigue."

"Nonsense," the half-breed said negligently; "it was nothing at all; the main point was to reach you, as my poor comrades had the ill-luck to be taken prisoners."

The Jaguar began laughing.

"Don't be alarmed, my brave fellow," he said to him; "your comrades are as free as yourself, and you will soon see them; there was a mistake in all this which they will have the pleasure of explaining to you."

Lanzi opened his eyes in amazement at this partial revelation, which he did not at all understand, but he made no answer, contenting himself with shrugging his shoulders several times. The Jaguar then offered the Captain and his two companions horses on which they could proceed to the rancho, and which they accepted. The partisans who had followed their Chief, on hearing this offer, hastened to dismount, and courteously presented their horses to the strangers. The latter, without stopping to make a choice, mounted the horses nearest to them, and started.

While galloping along, the three newcomers looked about them with surprise, not at all comprehending what they saw; for a time, the Jaguar paid no great attention to their manoeuvres, and continued to talk about indifferent topics; but their preoccupation soon became so marked that he perceived it, and could not refrain from asking them the cause of it.

"On my word, Caballeros," the Captain said, all at once taking the ball at the rebound; "if you had not asked me that question, I was on the point of asking you one, for I frankly confess that I understand nothing of what is happening to us."

"What is happening, pray?"

"Why, I learned last night from this worthy lad, the frightful defeat you experienced yesterday; the total loss and the utter dispersion of your army; I hurried up to offer you and yours, whom I supposed tracked like wild beasts and without shelter of any sort, an asylum aboard my vessel, and I have barely set foot on land, ere I find myself in the midst of this army which I supposed to be swept away like autumn leaves by a storm; and this army is as firm and well disciplined as before the battle. Explain to me, I beg, the meaning of this riddle, for I have really given it up, as impossible to guess."

"I am ready to satisfy your curiosity," the Jaguar answered with a smile; "but first of all I crave some valuable news from you."

"Very good; but answer me this first."

"Go on."

"Has the battle really taken place?"

"Certainly."

"And you have been whipped?"

"To our heart's content."

"That is strange, I understand leas than ever; well, speak, I am listening to you."

"Is the Fort of the Point still in the hands of our friends?"

"Yes; our ships have left it an hour at the most. Ever since you so daringly surprised it, the Mexicans have not come within gunshot."

"May Heaven be praised!" the young man exclaimed impetuously; "nothing is lost in that case, and all can be repaired. Yes, Captain, we have been beaten, we have suffered a frightful defeat; but, as you know, during the ten years we have been struggling against the Mexican power, our oppressors have often believed us crushed, and it is the same this time, thanks be to Heaven! Two of our best cuadrillas have escaped almost in safety the horrible massacre of the other corps, and they are those you see assembled here. At each moment straggling fugitives join us, so that within a week we shall probably be able to resume the offensive. GOD is on our side, for the cause we defend is sacred; we are the soldiers of an idea, and must conquer. The defeat of yesterday will be of use to us in the future."

"You are right, my friend," the Captain answered warmly. "This revolution in truth resembles no other; ever conquered, and ever up in arms, you are stronger today, after your numerous defeats, than when you began the struggle. The finger of Heaven is there, and a man must be mad not to perceive it. Hence your losses are limited to men and arms?"

"To men and arms solely; we have not lost an inch of ground. I seek in vain the reason that prevented the victorious Mexicans pursuing us, for we have kept all our positions, and are scarce ten miles from the battle field."

"Many of our Chiefs, I presume, have fallen, or are in the hands of the enemy?"

"I fear so; still, several have already come in, and others will probably still join us. There is one, unfortunately, about whom we have no news—you know to whom I refer; if the day pass without his making his appearance, I shall start in search of him."

The Jaguar had spoken the truth; each moment soldiers who had escaped from the battlefield arrived. During the short hour that had elapsed since he left the rancho, more than two hundred had joined the camp.

"You see," said the young Chief, looking around him proudly, "that, in spite of our defeat, nothing has really changed for us, as we have retained our head quarters, and the banner of Texan Independence still floats from its azotea."

The horsemen then dismounted, and entered the rancho.

CHAPTER XIX
A PAGE OF HISTORY

The Jaguar was mistaken, or rather flattered himself, when he said that the defeat of Cerro Pardo had caused but an insignificant loss to the revolutionary party; for Galveston, too weak to attempt resistance to the attack of the Mexican army, surrendered on the first summons, and did not even attempt a useless demonstration. Still, the young Chief was rightly astonished that General Rubio, an old experienced soldier, and one of the best officers in the Mexican army, had not attempted to complete his victory by definitively crushing his enemies, and pursuing them to the death. General Rubio really intended not to give those he had beaten breathing time, but his will was suddenly paralysed by another more powerful than his own.

The facts that then occurred are so strange, that they deserve to be described in their fullest details. Besides; they are intimately related to the facts we have undertaken to narrate, and throw a new light on certain events connected with the revolution of Texas, which are but little known.

We ask our reader's pardon; but we must go back once again, and return to General Rubio, at the moment when the Texans, broken by Colonel Melendez' charge, and understanding that victory was hopelessly slipping from their grasp, began flying in every direction, without trying to defend themselves longer, or keep the ground they held. The General had stationed himself on an eminence whence he surveyed the whole battlefield, and followed the movements of the various corps engaged. So soon as he saw the disorder produced in the enemy's ranks, he understood the advantage he could derive from this precipitate flight, by closely pursuing the fugitives up to the Fort of the Point, where he could certainly enter pell-mell without striking a blow. But haste was needed, not to give the enemy time to re-form a little further on, which the chiefs who commanded them would not fail to attempt, if but an hour's respite were granted them.

The General turned to an aide-de-camp by his side, and was just going to send Colonel Melendez orders to start all his cavalry in pursuit of the Texans, when a platoon of a dozen lancers suddenly appeared, commanded by an officer who galloped at full speed to the spot where the General was, making signs and waving his hat. The General looked in surprise at this officer, whom he knew did not belong to his army. A minute later he gave a start of surprise and disappointment, took, a sorrowful glance at the battlefield, and stood biting his moustache and muttering, in a low voice,

"Confound this saloon officer and sabre clunker! Why did he not remain in Mexico? What does the President mean by sending us this gold plumaged springald, to make us lose all the profits of the victory?"

At this moment the officer came up to the General, bowed respectfully, drew a large sealed envelope from his breast, and handed it to him. The General coldly returned the salutation, took the letter, opened it, and looked at it with a frown; but almost immediately he crumpled the letter up passionately, and addressed the officer, who was standing motionless and stiff before him.

"You are the aide-de-camp of the President General of the Republic?" he said, roughly.

"Yes, General," the officer answered, with a bow.

"Hum! Where is the President at this moment?"

"Four leagues off at the most, with two thousand troops."

"Where has he halted?"

"His Excellency has not halted, General, but, on the contrary, is advancing with forced marches to join you."

The General gave a start of anger.

"It is well," he continued, presently. "Return at full gallop to his Excellency, and announce to him my speedy arrival."

"Pardon me, General, but it seems to me that you have not read the despatch I had the honour of handing you," the officer said, respectfully, but firmly.

The General looked at him askance.

"I have not time at this moment to read the despatch," he said, drily.

At the period when our history takes place, General Don Antonio Lopez de Santa Anna was thirty-nine to forty years of age; he was tall and finely built; he had a lofty and projecting forehead, rounded chin, and slightly aquiline nose, large black eyes, full of expression, and a flexible mouth, which gave him an air of remarkable nobility, while his black and curly hair, which formed a contrast to the yellowish tinge of his complexion, covered his temples and his high-boned cheeks. Such, physically, was the man who, for thirty years, has been the evil genius of Mexico, and has led it to infallible ruin by making himself the cause or pretext of all the wars and revolutions which, since his first assumption of power, have incessantly overwhelmed this unhappy country.

We must now ask our reader's pardon, but we must talk a little politics, and describe cursorily the facts which preceded and led to the denouement of the too lengthy story we have undertaken to narrate.

If the Mexicans had gained an important advantage over the Texans, in another portion of the revolted territory they had experienced a check, whose consequences must prove immense for them. The Mexican General Cos was besieged in the town of Bejar by the Texans; the latter, with that want of foresight so natural to volunteers of all countries, believing that they had only a campaign of a few days, had laid in no provisions or winter clothing, though the rainy season was at hand, hence they were beginning to grow discouraged and talk about raising the siege; when El Alferez, that mysterious personage we have come across several times, went to the General in Chief and pledged himself to compel the Mexicans to capitulate, if three hundred men were given him.

The young partizan's reputation for intrepidity had long been famed among the Texans, and hence his offer was accepted with enthusiasm. El Alferez performed his promise. The town was captured after four terrible assaults; but the young Chief, struck by a bullet in the forehead, fell in the breach, with his triumph as his winding sheet. A fact was then ascertained which had hitherto been only vaguely suspected:—El Alferez, the daring and formidable partisan, was a woman. General Cos, his staff, and one thousand five hundred Mexicans laid down their arms, and all filed, in the presence of the handful of insurgents who had survived the assaults and the corpse of their intrepid Chieftain, which was clothed in feminine attire, and seated in a chair covered with the flags taken from the vanquished. The Mexicans left the territory of the New Republic, after pledging their word of honour not to oppose the recognition of independence.

Santa Anna received news of the defeat at Bejar while stationed at San Luis de Potosi. Furious at the affront the Mexican arms had received, the President, after flying into a furious passion with the generals who had hitherto directed the military operations, swore to avenge the honour of Mexico, which was so disgracefully compromised, and finally finish with these rebels whom no one had yet been able to conquer. The President organized an army of six thousand men, a truly formidable army, if we take into account the resources of the country in which these events occurred.

The preparations, urged on by that vigour produced by wounded pride and the hope of vengeance, were soon completed, and Santa Anna entered Texas, after dividing his army into three corps, under the orders of Filisola, Cos, Urrea, and Garrey. After effecting his junction with General Rubio, to whom he had sent an aide-de-camp with orders to remain in his quarters and not risk a battle before his arrival, an order which the General received too late, the President determined to deal a decisive blow by recapturing Bejar and seizing on Goliad.

Bejar and Goliad are two Spanish towns; roads run from them to a common centre, the heart of the Anglo-American settlements. The capture of these two towns, as the basis of operations, was, consequently, of the highest importance to the Mexicans. The Texans, weakened and demoralized by their last defeat, were unable to resist so formidable an invasion as the one with which they saw themselves menaced. The Mexican army carried on a true war of savages, passing like a flood over this hapless country, plundering and burning the towns. The two first months that followed Santa Anna's arrival in Texas were an uninterrupted series of successes for the Mexicans, and seemed to justify the new method inaugurated by the President, however barbarous and inhuman it might be in its results. The Texans found themselves in a moment reduced to so precarious a condition, that their ruin appeared to competent men inevitable, and merely a question of time.

Let us describe, in a few words, the operations of the Mexican army. Before resuming our narrative at the point where we left it, we have said already that the Mexican forces had been divided into three corps. Three thousand men, that is to say, one moiety of the Mexican army, commanded by Generals Santa Anna and Cos, and well supplied with artillery, proceeded to lay siege to Bejar. This town had only a feeble garrison of one hundred and eighty men, but this garrison was commanded by Colonel Travis, one of the greatest and purest heroes of the War of Independence. When completely invested, Travis withdrew to the citadel, not feeling at all alarmed by the numbers he had to fight. He was summoned to surrender.

"Nonsense!" he answered with a smile; "we will all die, but your victory will cost you so dearly that a defeat would be better for you."

And he loyally kept his word, resisting for a whole fortnight with unexampled bravery, and incessantly exhorting his comrades. Thirty-two Texans managed to throw themselves into the fort, after traversing the entire Mexican army.

"We have come to die with you," the chief of this heroic forlorn hope said to him.

"Thanks," was all the answer.

Santa Anna, whose strength had been more than doubled during the siege, summoned Colonel Travis for the last time, saying there would be madness in risking an assault with a practicable breach.

"We will fill it up with our dead bodies," the Colonel nobly answered.

The President ordered the assault, and the Texans were killed to the last man. The Mexicans then entered the citadel, not as conquerors, but with a secret apprehension, and as if ashamed of their triumph. They had lost fifteen hundred men.[1]

"Oh!" Santa Anna exclaimed bitterly, "another such victory and we are lost!"

So soon as Bejar was reduced, attention was turned to Goliad. But here one of those facts occurred which history is compelled to register, were it only to stigmatize and eternally brand the men who have been guilty. Goliad is an open town, without walls or citadel to arrest an enemy, and Colonel Fanni had abandoned it, as he had only five hundred Texan Volunteers with him. Compelled to leave his ammunition and baggage behind, in order to effect his retreat with greater speed, he was suddenly attacked on the prairie by General Urrea's Mexican division, nineteen hundred strong. Obeying their Colonel's orders, the Texans formed square, and for a whole day endured the attack of the foe without flinching. The Mexicans involuntarily admiring the desperate heroism of these men, who had no hope of salvation, implored them to surrender, while offering them good and honourable conditions. The Texans hesitated for a long time, for, as they did not dare trust the word of their enemies, they preferred to die. Still, when one hundred and forty Texans had fallen, the Colonel resolved to lay down his arms, on the condition that his soldiers and himself should be regarded as prisoners of war, treated as such, and that the American Volunteers should be embarked for the United States at the charges of the Mexican Government. These conditions having been accepted by General Urrea, the Texans surrendered.

Santa Anna, who was still at Bejar, refused to ratify the treaty; and by his *express orders*, in spite of the prayers and supplications of all his generals, he directed the massacre of the prisoners. The three hundred and fifty prisoners were murdered in cold blood, on a prairie situated between Goliad and the sea. General Urrea, whom this infamous treason dishonoured, broke his sword, weeping with rage. This horrible massacre was the signal for a general upheaval, and all ran to arms; despair restored the energy of the Insurgents, and a new army seemed to spring from the ground as if by enchantment. General Houston was appointed Commander-in-Chief, and on both sides preparations were made for the supreme and decisive struggle.

[1] It was at this marvellous siege, better known as that of the Alamo, that Colonels Crockett and Bowie were killed.— L.W.

CHAPTER XX
THE BIVOUAC

As we have already said, Texas had reached a decisive epoch: unfortunately, her future seemed as gloomy as that of the conquered: in spite of the heroic efforts attempted by the Insurgents, the rapid progress of the invasion was watched with terror, and no possible means of resistance could be seen. Still it was this moment, when all appeared desperate, which the Convention, calm and moved by a love of liberty more ardent than ever, selected to hurl a last and supreme defiance at the invaders. Not allowing itself to be intimidated by evil fortune, the convention replied to the menaces of the conquerors by a statement of rights, and the definitive declaration of the independence of a country which was almost entirely occupied by, and in the power of the Mexicans. It improvised a constitution, created a provisional executive authority, decreed all the measures of urgency which the gravity of circumstances demanded, and finally nominated General Sam Houston Commander-in-Chief, with the most widely extended powers.

Unhappily the Texan army no longer existed, for its previous defeats had completely annihilated it. But if military organization might be lacking, the enthusiasm was more ardent than ever. The Texans had sworn to bury themselves under the smoking ruins of their plundered towns and villages, sooner than return beneath the detested yoke of their oppressors. And this oath they were not only prepared to keep, but had already kept at Bejar and Goliad: however low a people may appear, and is really in the sight of its tyrants, when all its acting strength is concentrated in the firm and immutable will, to live free or die, it is certain to recover from its defeats, and to rise again one day a conqueror, and regenerated by the blood of the martyrs who have succumbed in the supreme struggle of liberty against slavery.

General Houston had scarce been appointed ere he prepared to obey, and he reached the banks of the Guadalupe three days after the capture of the Alamo. The Texan troops amounted to *three hundred* men, badly armed, badly clothed, almost dying of hunger, but burning to take their revenge. General Houston was a stern and sincere patriot; his name is revered in Texas, like that of Washington in the United States, or of Lafayette in France. Houston was a precursor, or one of those geniuses whom it pleases God to create when He desires to render a people free. At the sight of this army of three hundred men, Houston was not discouraged; on the contrary, he felt his enthusiasm redoubled, the heroic relics of the ten thousand victims who had succumbed since the beginning of the war had not despaired of the salvation of their country: like their predecessors, they were ready to die for her. It was a sacred phalanx with which he would achieve miracles.

Still, it was not with these three hundred men, however brave and resolute they might be, that General Houston could entertain a hope of defeating the Mexicans, who, rendered presumptuous by their past successes, eagerly sought the opportunity to finish once for all with the Insurgents, by crushing the last relics of their army. General Houston, before risking an action on which the fate of his new country would doubtless depend, resolved to form an army once more; for this purpose, instead of marching on the enemy, he fell back on the Colorado, and thence on the Brazos, burning and destroying everything in his passage, in order to starve the Mexicans out.

These clever tactics obtained all the success the General expected from them; for a very simple reason: as he fell back on the Mexican frontier, his army was daily augmented by fresh recruits, who, on the report of his approach, left their houses or farms to enlist under his banner; while the contrary happened to the Mexicans, who at each march they made in pursuit of the Insurgents, left a few laggards behind, who by so much diminished their strength.

The Texan General had a powerful motive for falling back on the American frontier; he hoped to obtain some help from General Gaines, who, by the order of President Jackson, had advanced on Texan territory as far as the town of Nagogdoches. Such was the state of affairs between Houston and Santa Anna, the one retreating, the other continually advancing; though ere long they must meet face to face, in a battle which would decide the great question of a nation's emancipation or servitude.

On the day when we resume our narrative it was about eight in the evening, the heat had been stifling throughout the day, and although night had fallen long before, this heat, far from diminishing, had but increased; there was not a breath of air, the atmosphere was oppressive, and low lightning-laden clouds rolled heavily athwart the sky; all, in fact, foreboded a storm.

On the banks of a rather wide stream, whose yellowish and turbid waters flowed mournfully between banks clothed with cotton-wood trees, the bivouac fires of a small detachment of cavalry might be seen glistening like stars in the darkness. This stream was a confluent of the Colorado, and the men encamped on its banks were Texans. They were but twenty-five in number, and composed the entire cavalry of the Army of Independence: they were commanded by the Jaguar.

While the horsemen were sadly crouching over the fires, not far from which their horses were hobbled, and conversing in a low voice; their Chief, who had retired to a jacal made of branches and lighted by a smoky candil, was sitting on an equipal with his back leant against a tree trunk, with his arms folded on his chest and gazing at vacancy. The Jaguar was no longer the young and ardent man we introduced to our readers; his face was pale, his features contracted, and eyes blood-shot with fever, and, though faith still dwelt in his heart, hope was dead.

The truth was that death had begun to make frightful gaps around him; his dearest friends, the most devoted supporters of the cause he defended, had fallen one after the other in this implacable struggle. El Alferez, Captain Johnson, Ramirez, Fray Antonio, were lying in their bloody graves; of others he received no news, nor knew what had become of them; he therefore stood alone, like an oak bowed by the wind and beaten by the storm, resisting intrepidly, but foreseeing his approaching fall.

General Houston, in his calculated retreat, had confided the command of the rear guard, that is to say, the most honourable and dangerous post, to the Jaguar; a post he had accepted with gloomy joy, as he felt sure that he would fall gloriously, while watching over the safety of all.

In the meantime the night became blacker and blacker, the horizon more menacing; a white and sharp rain began piercing the grey fog; the storm was rapidly approaching, and must soon burst forth. The soldiers watched with terror the progress of the storm, and instinctively sought shelter against this convulsion of nature, which was far more terrible than the other dangers which menaced them. For no one, who has not witnessed it, can form even a remote idea of an American hurricane, which twists trees like wisps of straw, fires forests, levels mountains, drives streams from their bed, and in a few hours convulses the surface of the soil.

Suddenly a dazzling flash furrowed the darkness, and a crashing burst of thunder broke the majestic silence that brooded over the landscape. At the same instant the sentry stationed a few paces in front of the bivouac challenged. The Jaguar sprang up as if he had received an electric shock, and bounding forward, as he mechanically seized the weapons lying within reach, listened. The dull sound of horses' hoofs could he heard on the soddened ground.

"Who's there?" the sentry challenged a second time.

"Friends," a voice replied.

"*¿Qué gente?*"

"Texas."

The Jaguar emerged from the jacal.

"To arms!" he shouted to his men, we must not let ourselves be surprised.

"Come, come," the voice continued, "I see that I have not diverged from the track, since I can hear the Jaguar."

"Halloh!" the latter said in surprise, "who are you, that you know me so well?"

"By Jove! A friend whose voice should be familiar to you, at any rate."

"John Davis!" the young man exclaimed with a joy he did not attempt to conceal.

"All right!" the American continued gaily. "I thought that we should understand one another presently."

"Come, come; let him pass, men, he is a friend."

Five or six horsemen entered the camp and dismounted.

At this moment the storm burst forth furiously, passing like a whirlwind over the plain, the twisted trees on which were in a second uprooted and borne away by the hurricane. The Texans had made their horses lie down, and were themselves lying down by their side on the Wet soil, in the hope of offering a smaller surface to the gusts that passed with a mournful howl above their heads. It was a spectacle full of wild grandeur, presented by this ravaged plain, incessantly crossed by flashes which illuminated the landscape with fantastic hues, while the thunder rolled hoarsely in the depths of the Heavens, and the clouds scudded along like a routed army, dashing against each other with electric collisions.

For nearly three hours the hurricane raged, levelling everything in its passage; at length, at about one in the morning, the rain became less dense, the wind gradually calmed, the thunder rolled at longer intervals, and the sky, swept clean by a final effort of the tempest, appeared again blue and star-spangled; the hurricane had gone away to vent its fury in other regions. The men and horses rose; all breathed again, and tried to restore a little order in the camp. This was no easy task, for the jacal had been carried away, the fires extinguished, and the logs dispersed in all directions; but the Texans were tried men, long accustomed to the dangers and fatigues of desert life. The tempest, instead of crushing them, had, on the contrary, restored their strength and patience, though not their courage, for that had never failed them.

They set gaily to work, and in two hours all the injury caused by the tempest was repaired as well as the precarious resources they had at their disposal permitted; the fires were lighted again, and the jacal reconstructed. Any stranger who had entered the camp at this moment would not have supposed that so short a time previously they had been assailed by so fearful a hurricane. The Jaguar was anxious to talk with John Davis, whom he had only seen since his arrival, and had found it impossible to exchange a syllable. When order was restored, therefore, he went up to him and begged him to enter the jacal.

"Permit me," the American said, "to bring with me three of my comrades whom I am convinced you will be delighted to meet."

"Do so," the Jaguar answered; "who are they?"

"I will not deprive you," Davis, said, with a smile, "of the pleasure of recognizing them yourself."

The young Chief did not press the matter, for he knew the ex-slave dealer too well not to place the most perfect confidence in him. A few minutes later, according to his promise, Davis entered the jacal with his comrades; the Jaguar gave a start of joy at seeing them, and quickly walked up to offer his hand. These three men were Lanzi, Quoniam, and Black-deer.

"Oh, oh!" he exclaimed, "Here you are, then. Heaven be praised! I did not dare hope for your return."

"Why not?" Lanzi asked; "As we are still alive, thanks to God! You ought to have expected us."

"So many things have happened since our parting, so many misfortunes have assailed us, so many of our friends have fallen not to rise again, that, on receiving no news of you, I trembled at the thought that you might also be dead."

"You know, my friend," the American said, "that we have been absent a very long time, and are consequently quite ignorant of what has happened since our departure."

"Well, I will tell you all. But first one word."

"Speak."

"Where is Tranquil?"

"Only a few leagues from here, and you will soon see him; he sent me forward, indeed, to warn you of his speedy arrival."

"Thanks," the young man replied, pensively.

"Is that all you desire to know?"

"Nearly so, for of course you have received no news of — —?"

"News of whom?" the American asked, seeing that the Jaguar hesitated.

"Of Carmela?" he at length said, with a tremendous effort.

"Of Carmela?" John Davis exclaimed, in surprise: "How could we have received any news? Tranquil, on the contrary, hopes to hear some from you."

"From me?"

"Hang it! You must know better than any of us how the dear child is."

"I do not understand you."

"And yet it is very clear. I will not remind you in what way we succeeded, after the capture of the Larch-tree, in saving the poor girl from that villain who carried her off; I will merely remind you that on the very day when Tranquil and I, by your express orders, started to join Loyal Heart, the maiden was confided in your presence to Captain Johnson, who would convey her to the house of a respectable lady at Galveston, who was willing to offer her a shelter."

"Well?"

"What do you mean by, well?"

"Yes, I knew all that, so it was useless to tell it me. What I ask you is, whether, since Carmela went to, Galveston, you have received any news of her?"

"Why, it is impossible, my friend; how could we have received any? Remember that we proceeded to the desert."

"That is true," the young man replied, disconsolately; "I am mad. Forgive me."

"What is the matter? Why this pallor, my friend, this restlessness I see in your eyes?"

"Ah!" he said, with a sigh, "It is because I have received news of Carmela, if you have not."

"You, my friend?"

"Yes, I."

"A long time ago, I presume?"

"No—yesterday evening," he said, with a bitter smile.

"I do not at all understand you."

"Well, listen to me. What I am going to tell you is not long, but it is important, I promise you."

"I am listening."

"We form, as you are doubtless aware, the extreme rear guard of the Army of Liberation."

"Yes, I know that, and it helped me in finding your trail."

"Very good; hence hardly a day passes in which we do not exchange musket shots and sabre cuts with the Mexicans."

"Go on."

"Yesterday—you see it is not stale—we were suddenly charged by forty Mexican Horse; it was about three in the afternoon, when General Houston was crossing the river with the main body. We had orders to offer a desperate resistance, in order to protect the retreat. This order was needless; at the sight of the Mexicans we rushed madly upon them, and the action at once commenced. After a few minutes' fighting the Mexicans gave way, and finally fled, leaving three or four dead on the battlefield. Too weak to pursue the enemy, I had given my soldiers orders to return, and was myself preparing to do the same, when two flying Mexicans, instead of continuing their flight, stopped, and fastening their handkerchiefs to their sabre blades, made me a signal that they desired to parley. I approached the two men, who bore a greater likeness to bandits than to soldiers; and one of them, a man of tall stature and furious looks, said to me at once, when I asked them what they wanted—

"'To do you a service, if you are, as I suppose, the Jaguar.'

"'Yes, I am he,' I answered, 'but what is your name? Who are you?'

"'It is of little consequence who I am, provided that my intentions are good.'

"'Still, I must know them.'

"'Hum!' he said, 'you are very distrustful, Comirado.'

"'Come, Sandoval,' the other horseman said, in a voice gentle as a woman's, as he suddenly joined in the conversation, 'do not beat about thus, but finish your business.'

"'I ask nothing better than to finish,' he replied, coarsely; 'it is this gentleman who compels me to swerve, when I wished to go straight ahead.'

"The second rider, shrugged his shoulders with a disdainful smile, and turned to me.

"'In a word, Caballero, here is a paper, which a person, in whom you take great interest, requested us to deliver to you.'"

"I eagerly seized the paper, and prepared to open it, for a secret foreboding warned me of misfortune.

"'No,' the Mexican continued eagerly arresting my hand, 'wait till you have joined your men again, to read that letter.'

"'I consent,' I said, 'but I presume you do not intend to do me a gratuitous service, whatever its nature may be?'

"'Why so?'

"'Because you do not know me, and the interest you take in me must be very slight.'

"'Perhaps so,' the rider answered; 'still, pledge yourself to nothing, I warn you, till you know the contents of that letter.'

"Then he made a signal to his comrade, and after bowing slightly, they started at a gallop, and left me considerably embarrassed at the way in which this singular interview had ended, and twisting in my fingers the letter I did not dare open."

"Well," the American muttered, "what did you, so soon as the men left you alone?"

"I looked after them a long time, and then, suddenly recalled to my duty by several carbine shots whose bullets whizzed past my ears, I bent down over my horse's neck and regained the bivouac at full gallop. On arriving, I opened the letter, for I was burning with impatience and curiosity."

"And it was?"

"From Carmela."

"By Heavens!" the American said, as he slapped his thigh; "I would have wagered it."

CHAPTER XXI
SANDOVAL

"Yes," the Jaguar continued presently in a broken voice; "this letter was entirely in Carmela's handwriting. Would you like to know the contents?"

The American looked around him.

"Well, what matter?" the Jaguar exclaimed with some violence; "Are not these brave lads our friends, faithful and devoted friends? Why keep secret from them a thing I should be forced to tell them, perhaps tomorrow?"

John Davis bowed.

"You did not understand my thought," he said. "I am not afraid about them, but of those who may be possibly listening outside."

The young man shook his head.

"No, no," he said, "fear nothing, John Davis, my old friend; no one is listening to us."

"Read the letter in that case, for I am anxious to know its contents."

Although the dawn was beginning to tinge the horizon with all the prismatic colours, the light was not sufficient yet for it to be possible to read by it. Lanzi, therefore, seized the candil, whose smoky wick smouldered without spreading any great light, snuffed it intrepidly with his fingers, and held it in a line with the Jaguar's face. The latter, after a moment's hesitation, drew from the pocket of his velvet jacket a dirty and crumpled piece of paper, unfolded it, and read:

"*To the Chief of the Texan Freebooters, surnamed the Jaguar.*"

"If you really take that interest in me you have so often offered to prove to me, save me, save the daughter of your friend! Having left Galveston to go in search of my father, I have fallen into the hands of my most cruel enemy. I have only hope in two men in this world, yourself and Colonel Melendez. My father is too far for me to be allowed to hope effectual assistance from him. And besides, his life is too precious to me for me to consent to him risking it. Whatever may happen, I trust in you as in God; will you fail me?"

"The disconsolate CARMELA."

"Hum!" the American muttered; "Is that all?"

"No," the young man answered, "there is a second note written below the first."

"Ah, ah! By Carmela?"

"No."

"By whom, then?"

"I do not know, for it is not signed."

"And do you suspect nobody?"

"Perhaps I do—but before telling you whom I suspect, I had better read you the second letter."

"For what reason?"

"In order to know whether you share in my suspicions, and if they corroborate mine."

"Good, I understand you. Read!"

The Jaguar took up the paper again and read:

"This letter, written in duplicate, is addressed by Doña Carmela to two persons, Señor El Jaguar and Colonel Melendez; but the second copy has not yet been delivered, as I am awaiting the Jaguar's answer ere doing so. It depends on him not only to save a young lady, interesting in every respect, but also, if he will, to secure the triumph of the cause for which he is combating so valiantly. For this purpose, he has only an easy thing to do: he will proceed, between eight and nine o'clock in the morning, to the Cueva del Venado; a man will issue from the grotto, and tell him on what conditions he consents to aid him in this double enterprise."

The Jaguar folded up the paper, and placed it in his jacket pocket.

"Is that all?" the American asked a second time.

"This time, yes, it is all," the young man answered; "now what do you think of this epistle?"

"Why, I think that the man who wrote it is the same who handed you the letter."

"We are agreed, for I think so too. And what, in your opinion, ought I to do?"

"Ah, that is a more difficult question than the first; the case is serious."

"Remember that it concerns Carmela."

"I am well aware of it. But reflect that this rendezvous may conceal a snare."

"For what object?"

"Why, to seize you."

"Well, and what then?"

"What do you mean?"

"Why, supposing that it is a trap, what will be the result of it?"

"In the first place that you will be a prisoner, and Texas be deprived of one of her most devoted defenders. In short, in your place I would not go, that is my brief and candid opinion. And," turning to his auditors, who had remained silent and motionless since their entrance, he asked them, "and you, Señores, what do you think of it?"

"It would be madness for the Jaguar to trust a man he does not know, and whose intentions may be bad," said Lanzi.

"He must remain here," Quoniam backed his friend up.

"The antelope is the wildest of animals, and yet its instinct makes it escape the hunters," the Comanche Chief said sententiously; "my brother will remain with his friends."

"The Jaguar walked up and down the jacal with visible annoyance and febrile impatience, while each thus gave his opinion.

"No," he said, with some violence, as he suddenly stopped; "no, I will not abandon Doña Carmela when she claims my assistance, for it would be an act of cowardice, which I will not commit, whatever the consequences may be: I will go to the Cueva del Venado."

"You will reflect, my friend," John Davis remarked.

"My reflections are all made; I will save Doña Carmela, even at the risk of my life."

"You will not do that, my friend," the American continued gently.

"Why shall I not?"

"Because honour forbids you; because, besides the heart, there is duty; besides private feelings, public interests. Stationed at the rear-guard, you are responsible for the safety of the army; and if you are killed or made prisoner, the army is perhaps lost, or, at any rate, in danger; that is why you will not do so, my friend."

The Jaguar let his head droop and sank quite crushed into an equipal.

"What is to be done; my God! What is to be done?" he murmured in despair.

"Hope!" John Davis answered. And, making a signal to his friends which the latter understood, for they immediately rose and left the hut, he continued:

"Jaguar, my friend, my brother, is it for me to restore your courage—you, a man with a lion's heart, and so strong in battle; whom adversity has never forced to bow his head? Do you dare to place your love for a woman and your devotion to the country on the same level? Do you dare to lament your lost love, Carmela, a prisoner, or even dead, when your native land is succumbing beneath the repeated blows of its oppressors? Do you forget that if you grow weak, or even hesitate to accomplish your glorious sacrifice, tomorrow, perhaps, that country, which is so dear to you for so many reasons—which has shed its best and most precious blood in a hopeless struggle, will be buried eternally, by your fault, beneath the corpses of the last of its children? Brother, brother, the hour is supreme; we must conquer or die for the salvation of all. The general welfare must put down all paltry or selfish passions. To hesitate is to act as a traitor. Up, brother, and do not dishonour yourself by a cowardly weakness!"

The young man started up as if a serpent had stung him on hearing these harsh words; but he suddenly subdued the wild flash of his eye, while a sad smile covered his handsome face like a winding sheet.

"Thanks, brother," he replied, as he seized John Davis's hand, and pressed it convulsively; "thanks for having reminded me of my duty. I will die at my post."

"Ah, I find you again at length," the American exclaimed joyfully. "I felt certain that your heart would not remain deaf to the call of duty, and that you would carry out your glorious sacrifice to the end."

The young man heaved a deep sigh; but he did not feel within him the strength to respond to the praise which in his heart he knew he did not deserve. At this moment the clang of arms and the sound of horses was audible without.

"What is the matter now?" the Jaguar asked.

"I do not know," the American answered; "but I fancy that we shall soon be informed."

In fact, the sentry had challenged; and, after an apparently satisfactory reply, a horseman entered the camp.

"A flag of truce!" Lanzi said, appearing in the doorway of the jacal.

"A flag of truce!" the Jaguar repeated, giving John Davis a glance of surprise.

"Perhaps it is the help you expect from heaven, and which has been sent you," the American answered.

The young man smiled incredulously, but turned to Lanzi and said,

"Let him enter."

"Come, señor," said the half-breed, addressing a person who was still invisible; "the Commandant is ready to receive you."

Lanzi fell back, and made room for an individual who at once entered. The Jaguar started on recognising him. It was Sandoval, who had delivered him the letter on the previous day. The Pirate Chief bowed politely to the two persons in whose presence he found himself.

"You are surprised to see me, I think, Caballeros," he said, with a smile to the Jaguar.

"I confess it," the latter said, with a bow no less polite than the one made to him.

"The matter is clear enough, however. I like a plain and distinct understanding. In the letter I delivered to you myself yesterday, I gave you the meeting at the Cueva del Venado, to discuss grave matters; as you will remember."

"I allow it."

"But," Sandoval continued, with the calmness and intrepid coolness that characterised him, "we had hardly separated ere I made a reflection."

"Ah! And would it be indiscreet to ask its nature?"

"Not at all. I reflected that, under the circumstances, regarding the position in which we stand to each other, and as I had not the honour of your acquaintance, it might possibly happen that you would place in me all the confidence I deserve, and that you might leave me to kick my heels in the grotto."

The two insurgents exchanged a smiling glance, which Sandoval intercepted.

"Ah, ah!" he said, with a laugh; "it appears that I guessed right. In short, as I repeat that we have serious matters to discuss, I resolved to come direct to you, and so cut this difficulty."

"You did well, and I thank you for it."

"It is not worth while, for I am working as much for myself as for you in this business."

"Be it so; but that does not render your conduct less honourable. Then you are not a flag of truce?"

"I; not a bit in the world. It was merely a title I thought it better to assume, in order to find my way to you more easily."

"No matter; so long as you remain with us you shall be treated as such, so do not feel alarmed."

"I alarmed! About what, pray? Am I not under the safeguard of your honour?"

"Thanks for the good opinion you are kind enough to have of me, and I will justify it. Now, if you think proper, we will come to the point."

"I ask nothing better," Sandoval answered with some hesitation, and looking dubiously at the American.

"This caballero is my intimate friend," the Jaguar said, understanding his meaning; "you can, speak frankly before him."

"Hum!" said Sandoval, with a toss of the head. "My mother, who was a holy woman, repeated to me frequently, that when two are enough to settle a matter, it is useless to call in a third."

"Your mother was right, my fine fellow," John Davis said, with a laugh; "and since you are so unwilling to have me as an auditor, I will retire."

"It is perfectly indifferent to me whether you hear me or not," Sandoval said, carelessly; "I only said so for the sake of the Señor, who may not wish a third party to hear what I have to say."

"If that be really your sole motive," the Jaguar continued, "you can speak, for I repeat to you I have no secrets from this Caballero."

"All right then," said Sandoval.

He seated himself on an equipal, rolled a husk cigarette, lit it by the candil, whose light had become quite unnecessary, owing to the daylight becoming each moment brighter, and then turned easily to his two hearers.

"Señores," he said, puffing out a large quantity of smoke from his mouth and his nostrils, "it is as well for you to know that I am the recognised Chief of a numerous and brave band of banished men, or proscripts, whichever you may call them, whom the so-called honest townsfolk fancied they branded by calling them skimmers of the Savannah, or pirates of the prairies, both of which titles are equally false."

At this strange revelation, made with such cool cynicism, the two men gave a start and regarded each other with considerable surprise. The pirate watched this double movement, and probably satisfied mentally by the effect he had produced, he continued:

"I have reasons that you should know my social position," he said, "for you to understand what is going to follow."

"Good," John Davis interrupted; "but what motive urged you to take the present step?"

"Two important reasons," Sandoval answered, distinctly; "the first is, that I wish to avenge myself; the second, the desire of gaining a large sum of money by selling you in the first battle, for the highest price I can obtain, the co-operation of the cuadrilla I have the honour to command, a cuadrilla composed of thirty well armed and famously mounted men."

"Now go on, but be brief, for time presses."

"Do not be frightened, I am not fond of chattering; how much do you offer me for my cuadrilla?"

"I cannot personally make a bargain with you," the Jaguar said; "I must refer the matter to the General in Chief."

"That is perfectly true."

"Still, you can tell me the price you ask; I will submit it to the General and he will decide."

"Very good; you will give me fifty thousand piastres,[1] half down, the rest after the battle is won. You see that I am not exorbitant in my demands."

"Your price is reasonable; but how can we communicate?"

"Nothing is easier; when you desire to speak to me you will fasten red pendants to the lances of your cavalry, and I will do the same when I have any important communication to make to you."

"That is settled; now for the other matter."

"It is this: one day a monk of the name of Fray Antonio sent me a wounded man."

"The White Scalper?" John Davis exclaimed.

"Do you know him?" the pirate asked.

"Yes, but go on."

"He is a pretty scamp, I think?"

"I am quite of your opinion."

"Well, I greeted him as a brother and gave him the best I had; do you know what he did?"

"On my word, I do not."

"He tried to debauch my comrades and supplant me."

"Oh, oh! That was rather strong."

"Was it not? Fortunately I was watching, and managed to parry the blow; about this time General Santa Anna offered to engage us as a Free Corps."

"Oh!" the Jaguar uttered, in disgust.

"It was not very tempting," the pirate continued, being mistaken in the young man's exclamation, "but I had an idea."

"What was it?"

"The one I had the honour of explaining to you a moment back."

"Ah! very good."

"Hence, I selected thirty resolute men from my band and started to join the Mexican army; of course, you understand, I was paid."

"Of course, nothing could be more fair."

"I was careful to bring this demon of a man with me, for you can understand that I did not care to leave him behind."

"I should think so."

"We went on very quietly till a day or two back, when, in beating up the country, I captured a girl, who, only escorted by three men, who fled like cowards at the first shot, was trying to join the Texan army."

"Poor Carmela!" the Jaguar murmured.

"Do not pity her, but rejoice, on the contrary, that she fell into my hands; who knows what might have happened with anyone else?"

"That is true, go on."

"I was willing enough to let the poor girl continue her journey, but the Scalper opposed it. It seemed that he knew her, for on seeing her he exclaimed—'Oh, oh! This time she shall not escape me;' is that clear, eh?"

The two men bowed their assent.

"However, the prisoner was mine, as I had captured her."

"Ah!" said the Jaguar, with a sigh of relief.

"Yes, and I would not consent to surrender her to the Scalper at any price."

"Good, very good! You are a worthy man."

The pirate smiled modestly.

"Yes," he said, "I am all right, but my comrade, seeing that I would not give up the girl to him, offered me a bargain."

"What was its nature?"

"To give me twenty-five gold onzas, on condition that I never restored my prisoner to liberty."

"And did you accept?" the Jaguar asked, eagerly.

"Hang it! Business is business, and twenty ounces are a tidy sum."

"Villain!" the young man exclaimed, as he rose furiously.

John Davis restrained him, and made him sit down again.

"Patience," he said.

"Hum!" Sandoval muttered, "You are deucedly quick; I allow that I promised not to set her at liberty, but not to prevent her flight; did I not tell you that I was a man of ideas?"

"That is true."

"The girl interested me, she wept. It is very foolish, but I do not like to see women cry since the day when— —but that is not the point,"—he caught himself up—"she told me her name and story; I was affected in spite of myself, and the more so, as I saw a prospect of taking my revenge."

"Then you propose to me to carry her off?"

"That's the very thing."

"How much do you want for that?"

"Nothing," the Pirate answered with a magnificent gesture of disinterestedness.

"How, nothing?"

"Dear me, no."

"That is impossible."

"It is so, however, though I will propose two conditions."

"Ah! Ah! There we have it."

The pirate smiled in reply.

"Let us hear them," the young man continued.

"In order not to compromise myself unnecessarily, you will carry off the girl during the first battle, when I come over to your side. Do not be frightened, it will not be long first, if I may believe certain forebodings."

"Good, that is granted. Now for the second."

"The second is, that you swear to free me from the White Scalper, and kill him, no matter in what way."

"Done again—I swear it. But now permit me one question."

"Out with it."

"How is it that as you hate this man so deeply, you have not killed him yourself, as there could have been no lack of opportunity?"

"Certainly not, I could have done it a hundred times."

"Well, why did you not do it?"

"Are you desirous of knowing?"

"Yes."

"Well, it was because the man has been my guest and slept under my roof by my side, eaten and drank at my table; but what it is not permitted me to do, others can do in my place. But now good bye, Señores, when will you give me a definite answer?"

"This very evening; I shall have seen the General in a few hours."

"This evening, then."

And bowing politely to the two men, he quietly left the jacal, mounted his horse, and set out at a gallop, leaving the two men terrified at his imperturbable effrontery and profound perversity.

[1] About £10,000.

CHAPTER XXII
LOYAL HEART'S HISTORY

After the scene of torture we described a few chapters back, Loyal Heart returned to his rancho with his friends, Tranquil, Lanzi, and the faithful Quoniam. Fray Antonio had left the village the same morning to convey to the Jaguar the news of the good reception given his companions by the Comanches. The Whites sat down sorrowfully on equipals, and remained silent for some minutes. The horrible tortures inflicted on Running-elk had affected them more than they liked to say. In fact, it was a frightful and repulsive spectacle for men accustomed to fight their enemies bravely, and, when the battle was over, help the wounded without distinction of victors or vanquished.

"Hum!" Quoniam muttered, "the Red race is a brutal race."

"All races are the same," Tranquil answered "when abandoned without restraint to the violence of their passions."

"The Whites are men more cruel than the Redskins," Loyal Heart observed, "because they act with discernment."

"That is true," John Davis struck in, "but that does not prevent the scene we have just witnessed being a horrible one."

"Yes," said Tranquil, "horrible is the word."

"Come," Loyal Heart remarked, for the purpose of changing the conversation, "did you not tell me, my friend, that you were entrusted with a message for me? I fancy the moment has arrived for an explanation."

"In truth, I have delayed too long in delivering it; besides, if my presentiments do not greatly deceive me, my return must be anxiously expected."

"Good! Speak, nobody will disturb you; we have all the time necessary before us."

"Oh, what I have to say to you will not take long; I only wish to ask you to lay a final hand to a work for which you have already striven?"

"What is it?"

"I wish to claim your help in the war of Texas against Mexico."

The young hunter frowned, and for some minutes remained silent.

"Will you refuse?" Tranquil asked, anxiously.

Loyal Heart shook his head.

"No," he said; "I merely feel a repugnance to mingle again with white men, and—shall I confess it? to fight against my countrymen."

"Your countrymen?"

"Yes, I am a Mexican, a native of Sonora."

"Oh!" the hunter said with an air of disappointment.

"Listen to me," Loyal Heart said, resolutely, "after all, it is better I should speak frankly to you; when you have heard me, you will judge and tell me what I ought to do."

"Good! Speak, my friend."

"You have, I think, been several times surprised at seeing a white man, like myself, dwelling with his mother and an old servant among an Indian tribe; you have asked yourself what reason could be powerful enough, or what crime was sufficiently great, to compel a man like myself, of gentle manners, gifted with a pleasant exterior, and possessing some degree of education, to seek a refuge among savages? This appeared to you extraordinary. Well, my friend, the cause of my exile to these remote regions was a crime I committed: on the self-same day I became an incendiary and an assassin."

"Oh!" Tranquil exclaimed, while the other hearers gave an incredulous glance; "you an incendiary and assassin, Loyal Heart! it is simply impossible."

"I was not Loyal Heart then," the hunter continued with a melancholy smile; "but it is true that I was only a lad, just fourteen years of age. My father was a Spaniard of the old race, with whom honour was a sacred inheritance, which he ever kept intact. He succeeded in saving me from the hands of the Juez de Letras, who had come to arrest me; and when the magistrate had left the house, my father assembled his tenants, formed a court, of which he constituted himself president, and tried me. My crime was evident, the proofs overwhelming, and my father himself uttered my sentence in a firm voice: I was condemned to death."

"To death?" his hearers exclaimed, with a start of horror.

"To death!" Loyal Heart repeated. "The sentence was a just one. Neither the supplications of his servants, nor the tears nor entreaties of my mother, succeeded in obtaining a commutation of my punishment. My father was inexorable, his resolution was formed, and he immediately proceeded to execute the sentence. The death my father reserved for me was not that vulgar death, whose sufferings endure a few seconds; no, he had said that he had determined to punish me, and designed a long and cruel agony for me. Tearing me from the arms of mother, who was half fainting with grief, he threw me across his saddle-bow, and started at a gallop in the direction of the desert.

"It was a long journey, for it lasted many hours ere my father checked the speed of his horse or uttered a syllable. I felt the trembling sinews of the wearied horse give way under me; but still it went on at the same rapid and dizzy speed. At length it stopped; my father dismounted, took me in his arms, and threw me on the ground. Within a moment, he removed the bandage that covered my eyes; I looked anxiously around me, but it was night, and so dark that I could see nothing. My father regarded me for a moment with an indefinable expression, and then spoke. Although many long years have elapsed since that terrible night, all the words of that address are still imprinted on my mind.

"'See,' he said to me in a quick voice, 'you are here more than twenty leagues from my hacienda, in which you will never set foot again, under penalty of death. From this moment you are alone—you have neither father, mother, nor family. As you are a wild beast, I condemn you to live with the wild beasts. My resolution is irrevocable, your entreaties cannot alter it, so spare me them.'

"Perhaps in the last sentence a hope was concealed; but I was no longer in a condition to see the road left open for me, for irritation and suffering had exasperated me.

"'I do not implore you,' I replied; 'we do not offer entreaties to a hangman.'

"At this insulting outrage, my father started; but almost immediately after every trace of emotion disappeared from his face, and he continued:

"'In this bag,' he said, to a rather large pouch thrown down by my side, 'are provisions for two days; I leave you this rifle, which in my hands never missed its mark; I give you also these pistols, this machete, knife, and axe, and gunpowder and bullets in these buffalo horns. You will find in the provision bag a flint and steel, and everything necessary for lighting a fire; I have also placed in it a Bible that belonged to your mother. You are dead to society, where you must never return; the desert is before, and it belongs to you: for my part, I have no longer a son—farewell! May the Lord have mercy on you! All is finished between us on this earth; you are left alone and without family; you have a second existence to begin, and to provide for your wants. Providence never abandons those who place their trust in it: henceforth it will watch over you.'

"After uttering these words coldly and distinctly, to which I listened with deep attention, my father cut with his knife the bonds that held my limbs captive, and leaping info the saddle, started at a gallop without once turning his head. I was alone, abandoned in the desert in the midst of the darkness, without hope or help from anywhere. A strange revolution then took place in me, and I felt the full extent of the crime I had committed; my heart broke at the thought of the solitude to which I was condemned; I got up on my knees, watching the fatal outline that was constantly getting further from me, and listening to the hurried gallop of the horse with feverish anxiety. And then, when I could hear no more, when all noise had died out in the distance, I felt a furious grief wither my heart; my courage all at once abandoned me, and I was afraid; then, clasping my hands with an effort, I exclaimed twice in a chocking voice:

"Oh, my mother—my mother!"

"Succumbing to terror and despair, I fell back on the sand and fainted."

There was a moment's silence. These men, though accustomed to the affecting incidents of their rough life, felt moved to pity at this simple and yet so striking recital. The hunter's mother and his old servant had silently joined the hearers, while the dogs, lying at his feet licked his hands. The young man had let his head sink on his chest, and hid his face in his hands, for he was suffering from terrible emotion. No one dared to risk a word of consolation, and a mournful silence prevailed in the rancho; at length Loyal Heart raised his head again.

"How long I thus remained unconscious," he continued in a broken voice, "I never knew; a feeling of coolness I suddenly experienced, made me open my eyes; the abundant morning dew, by inundating my face, had recalled me to life. As I was frozen, my first care was to collect some dry branches, and light a fire to warm me; then I began reflecting.

"When a great suffering does not kill on the spot, a reaction immediately takes place; courage and will resume their empire, and the heart is strengthened. In a few moments I regarded my position as less desperate. I was alone in the desert, it was true; but though still very young, as I was hardly fourteen, I was tall and strong, gifted with a firm character like my father, extremely tenacious in my ideas and will; I had weapons, ammunition, and provisions, and my position was, therefore, far from being desperate; frequently when I had been still living at my father's hacienda, I had gone hunting with the tigrero and vaqueros of the house, and during these hunts had slept under the open air in the woods; I was now about to begin a fresh hunt, though this time it would be much longer, and last for life. For a moment I had the thought of returning to the hacienda, and throwing myself at my father's knees; but I knew his inflexible character, and feared being ignominiously expelled a second time. My pride revolted, and I repulsed this thought, which was, perhaps, a divine inspiration.

"Still, being slightly comforted by the reflections I had just made, and crushed by the poignant emotions of the last few hours, I at length yielded to sleep, that imperious need of lads of my age, and fell off, after throwing wood on the fire to make it last as long as possible. The night passed without any incident, and at daybreak I awoke. It was the first time I saw the sun rise in the desert, and the majestic and grand spectacle I now had before me filled me with admiration.

"This desert, which seemed to me so gloomy and desolate in the darkness, assumed an enchanting aspect in the dazzling sunbeams: the night had taken with it all its gloomy fancies. The morning breeze, and the sharp odours exhaled from the ground inflated my chest, and made me feel wondrously comforted; I fell on my knees, and with eyes and hands raised to heaven, offered up an ardent prayer.

"This duty accomplished, I felt stronger, and rose with an infinite sense of confidence and hope in the future. I was young and strong; around me the birds twittered gaily, the deer and the antelopes bounded carelessly across the savannah: that God, who protected these innocent and weak creatures, would not abandon me, I felt, if by a sincere repentance I rendered myself worthy of His protection, whose goodness is infinite. After making a light meal, I put my weapons in my belt, threw my bag on one shoulder, my rifle on the other, and after looking back for the last time with a sigh of regret, I set out, murmuring the name of my mother—that name which would henceforth be my sole talisman, and serve me in good as in evil fortune.

"My first march was long; for I proceeded toward a forest which I saw glistening in the horizon, and wished to reach before sunset. Nothing hurried me, but I wished at once to discover my strength, and know of what I was capable. Two hours before nightfall I reached the spurs of the forest, and was soon lost in the ocean of the verdure. My father's tigrero, an old wood ranger, who had left his footmarks in every American desert, had told me during the long hunting nights we have spent together, many of his adventures on the prairies, thus giving me, though neither of us suspected it at the time, lessons which the moment had now arrived for me to profit by.

"I formed my bivouac on the top of a hill, lit a large fire, and after supping with good appetite, said my prayer, and fell asleep. All at once I woke up with a start: two rastreros were licking my hands with whines of joy, while my mother and my old Eusebio were bending over and carefully examining me, not knowing whether I were asleep or in a fainting fit.

"'Heaven be praised!' my mother exclaimed, 'he is not dead.'

"I could not express the happiness that suddenly flooded my soul at the sight of my mother, whom I never hoped to see again in this world, at my pressing to her heart, and hanging round her neck, as if afraid she would escape me again. I gave way to a feeling of immense joy; when our transports were somewhat calmed, my mother said to me—

"'And now, what do you intend doing? We shall return to the hacienda, shall we not? Oh! If you but knew how I suffered through your absence!'

"'Return to the hacienda?' I repeated.

"'Yes; your father, I am certain, will pardon you, if he has not done so already in his heart.' And while saying this, my mother looked at me anxiously, and redoubled her caresses.

"I remained silent.

"'Why do you not answer me, my child?' she said to me.

"I made a violent effort over myself. 'Mother,' I at length answered, 'the mere thought of a separation fills my heart with sorrow and bitterness. But before I inform you of my resolution, answer me frankly one thing.'

"'Speak, my child.'

"'Has my father sent you to me?'

"'No,' she answered, sorrowfully.

"'But, at any rate, you believe that he approves the step you are now taking?'

"'I do not believe—' she said, with even greater sorrow than before, for she foresaw what was about to happen.

"'Well, my mother,' I answered, 'God will judge me. My father has denied me, he has abandoned me in the desert. I no longer exist for him, as he himself told me—and I am dead to all the world. I will never set foot in the hacienda again, unless God and my father forgive my crime—and I am able to forgive myself. A new existence commences for me from today. Who can say whether the Deity, in permitting this great expiation, may not have secret designs with me? His will be done,—my resolution is immoveable.'

"My mother looked at me fixedly for a moment; she knew that once I had categorically expressed my will, I never recalled my words. Two tears silently coursed down her pale cheeks. 'The will of God be done,' she said; 'we will remain, then, in the desert.'

"'What!' I exclaimed, with joyous surprise, 'Do you consent to remain with me?'

"'Am I not thy mother?' she said, with an accent of ineffable kindness, as she pressed me madly to her heart."

CHAPTER XXIII
THE EXPIATION

Outside the rancho the yells of the Comanches still went on. After a momentary silence, Loyal Heart continued his narrative, which emotion had compelled him to interrupt.

"It was in vain," he said, "that I implored my mother to leave me to the care of Heaven, and return to the hacienda with No Eusebio. Her resolution was formed—she was inflexible.

"'Ever since I married your father,' she said to me, 'however unjust or extraordinary his demands might be, he found in me rather a submissive and devoted slave than a wife, whose rights were equal to his. A complaint has never passed my lips; I have never attempted to oppose one of his wishes. But today the measure is full; by exiling you as he has done coldly repulsing my prayers, and despising my tears, he has at length allowed me to read his heart, and the little egotism and cruel pride by which he allows himself to be governed. This man, who coldly and deliberately had the barbarity to do what he has done to the firstborn of his children, possesses not a spark of good feeling. The condemnation he pronounced against you I pronounce, in my turn, against him. It is the law of retaliation, the law of the desert in which we are going henceforth to live. Eye for eye, and tooth for tooth.'

"Like all timid natures, accustomed to bow their heads timidly beneath the yoke, my mother, when the spirit of revolt entered her heart, assumed an obstinacy at the least equal to her ordinary docility. The way in which she uttered those words proved to me that all my prayers would be useless, and that it was better to yield to her determination. I therefore turned to No Eusebio; but at the first word I addressed to him the worthy man laughed in my face, saying distinctly and peremptorily that he had seen me born, and meant to see me die.

"As there was nothing to be gained on this side, I gave up the contest. I merely observed to my mother that, so soon as my father noticed her departure, he would probably start, at the head of all his tenants, in pursuit of her, and that we should be inevitably discovered, if we did not start at once. My mother and No Eusebio had come on horseback, but unhappily one of the animals had foundered, and was incapable of following us; saddle and bridle were removed, and we left it to its fate; my mother mounted the other horse, No Eusebio and myself following on foot, while the rastreros cleared the way.

"We knew not whither we were going, and did not trouble ourselves at all about it; plains succeeded forests, streams rivers, and we continued our forward march, hunting to support life, and camping wherever night surprised us, without regret for the past or anxiety for the future. We advanced thus straight ahead for nearly a month, avoiding, as far as possible, any encounter with the wild beasts, or the savages, whom we believed to be as ferocious as them.

"One day—a Sunday—the march was interrupted, and we spent it in pious conversation, and my mother read the Bible and explained it to No Eusebio and myself. About three in the afternoon, when the great heat of the day was beginning to yield, I rose and took my gun, with the intention of killing a little game, as our provisions were nearly exhausted, and I was absolutely compelled to renew them. My mother made no objection, though, as I have stated, Sundays were generally consecrated to rest: and I went off with the two rastreros. I went on for a long distance without seeing anything deserving powder and shot, and was thinking of turning back, when my two dogs, which were running on ahead, according to their wont, came to halt, while evidencing unusual signs of terror and restlessness.

"Although I was still a novice in the wood ranger's art, I judged it necessary to act with prudence, as I did not know what enemy I might find before me. I therefore advanced step by step, watching the neighbourhood closely, and listening to the slightest noise. My uncertainty did not last long, for terrible cries soon reached my ear. My first impulse was flight, but my curiosity restrained me, and, cocking my rifle, so as to be ready for all events, I continued to advance in the direction whence the cries came, now louder and more desperate than before.

"Ere long all was revealed to me; I perceived through the trees, in a rather spacious clearing, five or six Indian warriors, fighting with the fury of despair, against a threefold number of enemies. These Indians had doubtless been surprised in their camp, for their horses were hobbled, their fire was just going out, and several corpses, already robbed of their scalps, lay on the ground. These warriors, in spite of the numerical superiority of their foes, fought with desperate courage, not yielding an inch, and boldly replying with their war yell to that of their opponents.

"The Indian who appeared the Chief of the weaker party, was a tall young man, of twenty, at the most, powerfully built, with a leonine face, and who, while dealing terrible blows, did not cease exciting his men to resist to the death. Neither of the parties had firearms, they were fighting with axes and long barbed lances. All at once, several men rushed simultaneously on the young Chief, and, despite his desperate efforts, succeeded in throwing him down, then a hand seized his long scalp lock, and I saw a knife raised above his head.

"I know not what I felt on seeing this, or what dizziness seized upon me, but, by a mechanical movement, I raised my rifle and fired; then, rushing into the clearing with loud cries, I discharged my pistols at the men nearest me. An extraordinary thing occurred, which I was far from expecting, and certainly had not foreseen. The Indians, terrified by my three shots, followed by my sudden apparition, believed that help was arriving to their adversaries, and without dreaming of resisting, they began flying with that intuitive rapidity peculiar to Indians, at the first repulse they meet with.

"I thus found myself alone with those I came to deliver. It was the first time I had been engaged in a fight, if such a name can be given to the share I took in the struggle, hence I felt that emotion inseparable from a first event of this nature; I neither saw nor heard anything. I was standing in the centre of the clearing, like a statue, not knowing whether to advance or retire, flanked by my two bloodhounds, which had not left me, but showed their teeth with hoarse growls of anger.

"I know not who was the first to say that ingratitude was a white vice, and gratitude an Indian virtue; but, whoever he was, he spoke the truth. The Chief I had so miraculously saved, and his comrades, pressed around me, and began overwhelming me with marks of respect and gratitude. I let them do so, mechanically replying as well as I could, in Spanish, to the compliments the Indians lavished on me in their sonorous language, of which I did not understand a syllable. When a little while had elapsed, and their joy was beginning to grow more sedate, the Chief, who had been slightly wounded in the fight, made me sit down by the fire; while his comrades conscientiously raised the scalps of their enemy who had fallen, and he began questioning me in Spanish, which language he spoke clearly.

"After warmly thanking me, and repeating several times that I was a great brave, he told me that his name was Nocobotha, that is to say, the Tempest; that he belonged to the great and powerful nation of the Comanches, surnamed the Queen of the Prairies, and was related to a renowned Sachem called Black-deer. Having set out with a few warriors to chase antelopes, he had been surprised by a detachment of Apaches, the sworn enemies of his nation, and if the Master of Life had not brought me to their help, he and his comrades would infallibly have succumbed, an opinion the justice of which I was compelled to recognise. The Chief then asked me who I was, saying to me that he should henceforth regard me as his brother, that he wished to conduct me to his tribe, and that he would never consent to separate from the man who had saved his life.

"Nocobotha's words suggested an idea to me; I was greatly alarmed about the existence I led, not for myself, for this free and unrestrained life charmed me to the highest degree, but for my poor mother, who, accustomed to all the comforts of civilization, would not, I feared, endure for long the fatigues she undertook through her affection for me. I immediately resolved to profit by the gratitude and goodwill of my new acquaintance, to obtain my mother an asylum, where, if she did not find the comfort she had lost, she would run no risk of dying of want. I therefore frankly told Nocobotha the situation I was placed in, and by what accident I had providentially arrived just in time to save his scalp. The Chief listened to me with the most earnest attention.

"'Good,' he said with a smile, when I had ended, and squeezed my hand. 'Nocobotha is the brother of Loyal Heart. (Such was the name he gave me, and I have retained ever since.) Loyal Heart's mother will have two sons.' "I thanked the Chief, as I was bound to do, and remarked to him that, as I had now left my mother for some time, I was afraid she might feel alarmed at my lengthened absence, and that, if he permitted me, I would return to her side to reassure her, and tell her all that had happened; but the Comanche shook his head.

"'Nocobotha will accompany his brother,' he said; 'he does not wish to leave him.'

"I accepted the proposition, and we at once started to return to my encampment. We did not take long in going, for we were mounted; but on seeing me arrive with six or seven Indians, my poor mother was terribly alarmed, for she fancied me a prisoner, and menaced with the most frightful punishment, I soon succeeded, however, in reassuring her, and her terror was converted into joy on hearing the good tidings I brought her. Moreover, Nocobotha, with that graceful politeness innate in Indians, soon entirely comforted, and managed to gain her good graces. Such, my dear Tranquil, is the manner in which I became a wood ranger, trapper, and hunter.

"On reaching the tribe, the Indians received me as a friend, a brother. These simple and kind men knew not how to prove their friendship. For my part, on growing to know them better, I began to love them as if they had been my brothers. I was adopted by the Sachems collected round the council fire, and from that moment regarded as a child of the nation. From this time I did not leave the Comanches again. All longed to instal me into the secrets of desert life. My progress was rapid, and I was soon renowned as one of the best and bravest hunters of the tribes. In several meetings with the enemy, I had opportunities to render them signal service. My influence increased; and now I am not only a warrior but a Sachem, respected and beloved by all. Nocobotha, that noble lad, whom his courage ever bore to the front, at length fell in an ambuscade formed by the Apaches. After an obstinate struggle, I managed to bear him home, though covered with wounds. I was myself dangerously wounded. On reaching the village, I fell senseless with my precious burden. In spite of the most devoted and assiduous care my mother lavished on my poor brother, she was unable to save him, and he died thanking me for not having left him in the hands of his foes, and having kept his scalp from being raised, which is the greatest disgrace for a Comanche warrior.

"In spite of the marks of friendship and sympathy the Sachems did not cease to bestow on me for the manner in which I had defended my brother. I was for a long time inconsolable at his loss; and even now, though so long a period has elapsed since that frightful catastrophe, I cannot speak of him without tears coming into my eyes. Poor Nocobotha! Kind and simple soul! Noble and devoted heart! Shall I ever find again a friend so certain and so devoted?"

"Now, my dear Tranquil, you know my life as well as I do myself. My kind and revered mother, honoured by the Indians, to whom she is a visible Providence, is happy, or at least seems to be so. I have completely forgotten my colour, to live the life of the Redskins, who, when my brethren spurned me, received me as a son, and their friendship has never failed me. I only remember my origin when I have to assist any unhappy man of my own complexion. The white trappers and hunters of these regions affect, I know not why, to regard me as their Chief, and eagerly seize the opportunity to show me their respect, whenever it offers. I am therefore in a position relatively enviable; and yet, the more years slip away, the more lively does the memory of the events that brought me to the desert recur to my mind, and the more I fear never to obtain the pardon of my crimes."

He was silent. The hunters looked at each other with a mingled feeling of admiration and respect for this man, who confessed so simply a crime which so many others would have regarded at the utmost as a pecadillo, and who repented of it so sincerely.

"By Jove!" Tranquil exclaimed all at once, "Heaven will be careful not to pardon you if it has not been done so long ago. Men like you are somewhat rare in the desert, comrade!"

Loyal Heart smiled gently at this simple outburst of the hunter.

"Come, my friend, now that you know me thoroughly, give me your advice frankly; whatever it may be, I promise you to follow it."

"Well, my advice is very simple; it is that you should come with us."

"But I tell you I am a Mexican."

The Canadian burst into a laugh.

"Eh, eh," he said; "I fancied you stronger than that, on my honour."

"What do you mean?"

"Hang it, it is as clear as day."

"I am convinced, my friend, that you can only offer me honourable advice, so I am listening to you with the most serious attention."

"Well, you shall judge; I shall not take long to convince you."

"I ask nothing better."

"Well, let us proceed regularly. What is Mexico?"

"What do you mean?"

"Well; is it a kingdom or an empire?"

"It is a Confederation."

"Very good; that is to say, Mexico is a republic, formed of several Confederated States."

"Yes," Loyal Heart said, with a smile.

"Better still; then Sonora and Texas, for instance, are free States, and able to separate from the Confederation, if they think proper?"

"Ah, ah," said Loyal Heart, "I did not expect that."

"I thought you did not. Well, you see, my friend, that the Mexico of today, which is neither that of Motecuhzoma nor that of the Spaniards, since the first merely comprised the plateau of Mexico, and the second, under the name of New Spain, a part of central America, is only indirectly your country, since you were born neither in Mexico nor Veracruz, but in Sonora. You said so yourself. Hence, if you, a Sonorian, assist the Texans, you only follow the general example, and are no traitor to your country. What have you to answer to that?"

"Nothing; save that your reasoning, though specious, is not without a certain amount of logic."

"Which means that you are convinced?"

"Not the least in the world. Still, I accept your proposition, and will do what you wish."

"That is a conclusion I was far from expecting, after the beginning of your sentence."

"Because, under the Texan idea, there is another, and it is that I wish to help you in carrying out."

"Ah!" the Canadian remarked, in surprise.

Loyal Heart bent over to him.

"Have you not a certain affair to settle with the White Scalper, or have you forgotten it?"

The hunter started, and warmly pressed the young man's hand.

"Thanks," he said.

At this moment Black-deer entered the rancho.

"I wish to speak with my brother," he said to Loyal Heart.

"Is my brother willing to speak before my friends the pale hunters?"

"The pale hunters are the guests of the Comanches; Black-deer will speak before them," the Chief answered.

CHAPTER XXIV
IN THE DESERT

The news Black-deer brought must be very important, for, in spite of that stoicism which the Indians regard as a law, the Chief's face was imprinted with the most lively anxiety. After sitting down at an equipal to which Loyal Heart pointed, instead of speaking, as he had been invited to do, he remained gloomy and silent The hunters looked at him curiously, waiting with impatience till he thought proper to explain. At length Loyal Heart, seeing that he obstinately remained silent, resolved to address him.

"What is the matter, Chief?" he asked him. "Whence comes the anxiety I see on your features? What new misfortune have you to announce?"

"An enormous misfortune," he answered, in a hollow voice; "the prisoner has escaped."

"What prisoner?"

"The son of Blue-fox."

The hunters gave a start of surprise.

"It is impossible," Loyal Heart said; "did he not surrender himself as a hostage? Did he not pledge his word? And an Indian warrior never breaks that; only white men do so," he added, bitterly.

Black-deer looked down in embarrassment.

"Come," Loyal Heart went on, "let us be frank, Chief; tell us clearly what things happened."

"The prisoner was bound and placed in the great medicine lodge."

"What!" Loyal Heart exclaimed, in indignation; "A hostage bound and imprisoned! You are mistaken, Chief, the Sachems have not done such a thing, or thus insulted a young man protected by the law of nations."

"I relate things exactly as they happened, Loyal Heart."

"And who gave the order?"

"I," the Chief muttered.

"The hatred you feel for Blue-fox led you astray, Black-deer; you committed a great fault in despising the word pledged by this young man; by treating him as a prisoner you gave him the right to escape; the opportunity offered itself, he profited by it, and acted rightly."

"My young men are on his trail," the Chief said, with a hateful smile.

"Your young men will not capture him, for he has fled with the feet of the gazelle."

"Is the misfortune irreparable, then?"

"Perhaps not. Listen to me: one way is left us of capturing our enemy again. The Pale hunters, my brothers, have asked my help in the war the Whites are carrying on at this moment against each other; ask of the council of the Chiefs one hundred picked warriors, whom I will command, and you can accompany me; tomorrow at sunset we will set out; the Apaches are burning to take their revenge for the defeat we inflicted on them, so be assured that ere we join our brothers the Palefaces, we shall see our road barred by Blue-fox and his warriors. This is the only chance left us to finish with this implacable enemy—do you accept it?"

"I do accept it, Loyal Heart; your medicine is good, it has never deceived you, the words your chest utters are inspired by the Wacondah!" the Chief said, eagerly, as he rose. "I am going to the council of the Chiefs, will you accompany me?"

"What to do? It is better that the proposition should come from you, Black-deer, for I am only an adopted son of the tribe."

"Good, I will do what my brother desires; I will return shortly."

"You see, my friend," Loyal Heart said to Tranquil, when the Chief had left, "that I have not delayed in fulfilling my promises; perhaps, of the hundred warriors we take with us one half will remain on the way, but the survivors will not be the less of great assistance to you."

"Thanks, my friend," Tranquil answered; "you know that I have faith in you."

As Loyal Heart had foreseen, the Indian warriors sent in pursuit of the prisoner returned to the village without him; they had beaten up the country in vain, the whole night through, without discovering any trace of his passage. The young man had disappeared from the medicine lodge, and it was impossible to find out what means he had employed to effect his escape. The only remark the Comanches made—but it had considerable importance—was that, at a spot in the forest exactly opposite to that where the battle with the Apaches had taken place, the soil was trampled and the bark of the trees nibbled, as if several horses had been standing there for some time, but there was no mark of human feet.

The warriors, consequently, returned completely disappointed, and thus augmented the anger of their countrymen. The moment was well selected for the request Black-deer wished to make of the Council of Sachems. He requested the expedition projected by Loyal Heart, not as an intervention in favour of the Whites, for that was only secondary, but as an experiment he desired to attempt, not merely to recapture the fugitive, but his father, who, doubtless, would be posted in ambush at a little distance from the village. As the question thus brought before them was acceptable, the Sachems authorised Black-deer to select one hundred of the most renowned warriors of the nation, who would make the expedition under his orders and those of Loyal Heart.

Black-deer spoke to the hachesto, who mounted on the roof of a calli and immediately convened the members of the tribe. When the braves knew that an expedition was meditated, under the command of two such renowned Chiefs, they eagerly offered to join the war party, so that the Chief really had a difficulty in selection. Shortly before sunset one hundred horsemen, armed with lances, guns, axes, and knives, wearing their war moccasins, from the heel of which hung numerous coyote tails, and having round their neck their long ilchochetas, or war whistles, made of a human thigh bone, formed one imposing squadron, drawn up in the finest order on the village square, in front of the ark of the first man. These savage warriors, with their symbolic paint and quaint dresses, offered a strange and terrific appearance.

When the white hunters ranged themselves by their side they were greeted with shouts of joy and unanimous applause. Loyal Heart and Black-deer placed themselves at the head of the band, the oldest Sachems advanced and saluted the departing warriors, and at a signal from Loyal Heart the troop defiled at a walking pace before the members of the council and quitted the village.

At the moment when they entered the plain the sun was setting in a mass of purple and golden clouds. Once on the war trail the detachment fell into Indian file, the deepest silence prevailed in the ranks, and they advanced rapidly in the direction of the forest. The Indians, when they start on a dangerous expedition, always throw out as flankers intelligent men, ordered to discover the enemy and protect the detachment from any surprise. These spies are changed every day, and, though afoot, they always keep a great distance ahead and on the flanks of the body they have undertaken to lead. Indian warfare in no way resembles ours; it is composed of a series of tricks and surprises, and Indians must be forced by imperious circumstances to fight in the open; attacking or resisting without a complete certainty of victory is considered by them an act of madness. War, in their sight, being only an opportunity for acquiring plunder, they see no dishonour in flight when they have only blows to gain by resisting, reserving to themselves the right of taking a brilliant revenge whenever the chance may offer.

During the first fortnight the march of the Comanches was in no way disquieted, and the scouts, since they left the village, had discovered no human trail. The only individuals they met were peaceful hunters, travelling with their squaws, dogs, and children, and returning to their village; all agreed with the statement that they had seen no suspicious trail. Two days after, the Comanches entered on Texan territory.

This apparent tranquillity greatly perturbed the two Chiefs of the detachment; they fancied themselves too well acquainted with the vindictive character of the Apaches to suppose that they would let them travel thus peacefully without attempting to check them. Tranquil, too, who had long known Blue-fox, completely shared their opinion. One evening the Comanches, after making a long day's march, bivouacked on the banks of a small stream upon the top of a wooded hill which commanded the course of the river and the surrounding country. As usual, the scouts had returned with the assertion that they had discovered no sign; when supper was over, Loyal Heart himself stationed the sentries, and each prepared to enjoy, during a few hours, a repose which the fatigues of the day rendered not only agreeable, but necessary.

Still, Tranquil, agitated by a secret presentiment, felt a feverish and apparently causeless anxiety which robbed him of sleep; in vain did he close his eyes with the firm intention of sleeping, they opened again in spite of his will; wearied with this sleeplessness, for which he could find no plausible reason, the hunter rose, resolved to keep awake and take a turn in the neighbourhood. The movement he made in picking up his rifle woke Loyal Heart.

"What is the matter?" he asked at once.

"Nothing, nothing," the hunter answered, "go to sleep."

"Then why do you get up?"

"Because I cannot sleep, that's all, and intend to profit by my wakefulness to take a walk round the camp."

These words completely aroused Loyal Heart, for Tranquil was not the man to do anything without powerful reasons.

"Come my friend," he said to him, "there is something, tell me.

"I know nothing," the hunter answered, "but I am sad and restless; in a word, I know not what I fancy, but I cannot help thinking an approaching danger menaces us; what it is I cannot say, but I noticed today two flocks of flamingoes flying against the wind, several antelopes, deers, and other animals running madly in the same direction; the whole day through I have not heard a single bird sing, and as all that is not natural, I am alarmed."

"Alarmed?" Loyal Heart said with a laugh.

"Alarmed of a snare, and that is why I wish to make a round; I suppose I shall discover nothing, I believe and hope it, but no matter, I shall at any rate be certain that we have nothing to fear."

Loyal Heart, without saying a word, wrapped himself in his zarapé and seized his rifle.

"Let us go," he said.

"What do you mean?" the hunter asked.

"I am going with you."

"What nonsense, my undertaking is only the fancy of a sick brain; do you remain here and rest yourself."

"No, no," Loyal Heart answered with a shake of his head, "I think exactly the same as you have just told me; I also feel anxious, I know not why, and wish to be certain."

"In that case come along; perhaps, after all, it will be the better course."

The two men quitted the bivouac. The night was fresh and light, the atmosphere extremely transparent, the sky studded with stars, the moon seemed floating in æther, and its light, combined with that of the stars, was so great, that objects were as visible as in open day. A profound calm brooded over the landscape, which the hunters could perfectly survey from the elevation on which they were standing; at times a mysterious breath passed over the leafy tops of the trees, which it bent with a hoarse murmur. Tranquil and Loyal Heart carefully examined the plain which stretched an enormous distance before them. Suddenly the Canadian seized his friend's arms, and by a sharp and irresistible movement, drew him behind the trunk of an enormous larch tree.

"What is it?" the hunter asked eagerly.

"Look!" his comrade answered laconically, as he stretched out his arm in the direction of the plain.

"Oh, oh, what does that mean?" the young man muttered a moment later.

"It means that I was not mistaken, and that we shall have a fight, but fortunately this time again it will be diamond cut diamond; warn John Davis, and let him take the villains in the rear, while we face them."

"There is not a moment to be lost," Loyal Heart muttered, and he bounded toward the camp.

The two experienced hunters had noticed a thing which would certainly have been passed over by the eyes of men less habituated to Indian customs. We have said that at intervals a capricious breeze passed over the tops of the trees; this breeze blew from the South West over the plain for a distance of some few hundred yards, and yet the same breeze ran along the tall grass, incessantly approaching the hill where the Comanches were encamped, but, extraordinary to say, it blew from the North East, or a direction diametrically opposed to the former. This was all the hunters had perceived, and yet it sufficed them to guess the stratagem of their foes, and foil it.

Five minutes later, sixty Comanches, commanded by Tranquil and Loyal Heart, crawled like serpents down the sides of the hill, and on reaching the plain stood motionless, as if converted into statues. John Davis, with the rest of the band, turned the hill. All at once a terrible cry was heard— the Comanches rose like a legion of demons, and rushed headlong on their enemies. The latter, once again surprised when they hoped to surprise, hesitated for a moment, and then, terrified by this sudden attack, they were seized by a panic terror, and turned to fly, but behind them rose suddenly the American's band.

They must fight, or surrender to the mercy of an implacable foe; hence the Apaches closed up shoulder to shoulder, and the butchery commenced. It was horrible, and lasted till day. These deadly enemies fought without uttering a cry, and fell without giving way to a sigh. As the Apaches fell, their comrades drew closer together, while the Comanches contracted the circle of steel in which they were enclosed.

The sun, on rising, illuminated a horrible scene of carnage; forty Comanches had fallen, while of the Apaches ten men, all more or less severely wounded, alone stood upright. Loyal Heart turned away in sorrow from this fearful sight, for it would have been useless for him to interfere to save the last victims. The Comanches, intoxicated by the smell of blood and powder, furious at the resistance their enemies had offered, did not listen to his orders, and the remaining Apaches were killed and scalped.

"Ah!" Black-deer exclaimed, pointing with a gesture of triumph to a mutilated and almost unrecognizable corpse, "the Sachems will be pleased, for Blue-fox is dead at last."

In truth, the formidable Chief lay on a pile of Comanche corpses; his body was literally covered with wounds, and his son, a poor lad scarce adolescent yet, was lying at his feet. Curiously enough, for the Indians only take the scalps of their enemies usually, a fresh cut-off head was fastened to the Chiefs girdle—it was that of Fray Antonio. The poor Monk, who had quitted the village a few days before Tranquil, had doubtless been surprised and massacred by the Apaches.

So soon as the carnage, for we cannot call it a battle, was over, the Indians prepared to pay the last rites to those of their friends who had found death in this sanguinary struggle. Deep graves were dug, and the bodies were thrown in without the usual funeral ceremonies, which circumstances prevented, still they were careful to bury their arms with them, and then stones were piled on the graves to defend them from wild beasts. As for the Apaches, they were left at the spot where they had fallen. After this, the war party, diminished by nearly one-half, started again sadly for Texas.

The victory of the Comanches was complete, it is true, but too dearly bought for the Indians to think of rejoicing at it. The massacre of the Apaches was far from compensating them for the death of forty Comanche warriors, without counting those who, in all probability, would perish on the journey from the wounds they had received.

CHAPTER XXV
THE LAST HALT

Now that we are approaching the last pages of our book, we cannot repress a feeling of regret on thinking of the scenes of blood and murder which, in order to be truthful, we were compelled to unfold before our readers. If this narrative had been a fable, and we had been able to arrange our subject at our pleasure, most assuredly many scenes would have been cut down and altered. Unhappily, we have been obliged to narrate facts just as they happened, although we have frequently been careful to tone down certain details whose naked truth would have scandalized the reader.

Were we to be reproached with the continual combats in which our heroes are engaged, we should reply; we describe the manners of a race which is daily diminishing in the convulsive grasp of the civilization against which it struggles in vain; this race is called upon by the fatal decree of fate to disappear ere long eternally from the face of the globe; its manners and customs will then pass into the condition of a legend and being preserved by tradition, will not fail to be falsified and become incomprehensible. It is therefore our duty, who have become the unworthy historian of this unhappy race, to make it known as it was, as it is still, for acting otherwise would have been a felonious deed on our part, of which our readers would have been justified in complaining.

Finishing this parenthesis, which is already too long, but which we believe to be not merely necessary but indispensable, we will resume our narrative at the point where we left it.

We will now lead the reader to the extreme outposts of the Mexican army. This army, six thousand strong on its entrance into Texas, now amounted to no more than fifteen hundred, including a reinforcement of five hundred men, which General Cos had just brought up. The successive victories gained by Santa Anna over the Texans had therefore cost him just five thousand men. This negative triumph caused the President of the Mexican Republic considerable reflection. He began to understand the extraordinary difficulties of this war against an exasperated people, and he speculated with terror on the terrible consequences a defeat would have for him, if those intractable enemies he had been pursuing so long resolved at last to wait for him and succeeded in defeating him. Unluckily, whatever Santa Anna's apprehensions might be, it was too late to withdraw, and he must try his fortune to the end.

A space of five leagues at the most separated the two belligerent armies, and that space was diminished nearly one-half by the position of their videttes. The vanguard of the Mexican army, composed of two hundred regulars, was commanded by Colonel Melendez, but a league further ahead was encamped a forlorn hope, which had to clear the way for the movements of the army. These were simply the pirates of the prairies, commanded by our old acquaintance Sandoval, whom we saw a short time back introduce himself to the Jaguar, and make so singular a bargain with him.

In spite of the extremely slight esteem in which the Mexican army held the honesty of the said Sandoval and his myrmidons, General Santa Anna found himself constrained to place a certain amount of confidence in these thorough-paced scoundrels, owing to their incontestable capability as guides, and above all, as flankers. The General, consequently, found himself obliged almost to close his eyes to the crimes they committed nearly daily, and to let them act as they pleased. Let us add, that the pirates conscientiously abused the liberty conceded them, and did not hesitate to indulge in the most extraordinary caprices, which we had better pass over in silence.

These worthy men, then, were bivouacked, as we have said, about a league in advance of the Mexican army, and as they liked to take their ease whenever the opportunity offered, they had found nothing better than quartering themselves in a pueblo, whose inhabitants had naturally fled at their approach, and the houses of which the pirates pulled down, in order to procure wood for their campfires. Still, either by accident or some other reason, one house, or rather hut, had escaped the general ruin, and alone remained standing. It was not only untouched, but shut up, and a sentry was stationed before the door. This sentry, however, did not appear to trouble himself much about the orders given him; for being probably annoyed by the sun, whose beams fell vertically on his head, he was lying cozily in the shade of a stall luckily standing opposite the house, and with his musket within reach, was smoking, sleeping, and dreaming, while waiting till his term of duty was over, and a comrade came to take his place.

As this house served at this moment as the abode of Doña Carmela, we will ask the reader to enter it with us. The maiden, sad and pensive, was reclining in a hammock suspended before a window, open, in spite of the heat of the day, and her eyes, red with weeping, were invariably fixed on the desolate plain, which the sun parched, and whose sand flashed like diamonds. Of what was the poor girl thinking, while the tears she did not dream of wiping away, coursed down her pallid cheeks, where they traced a furrow?

Perhaps at this age, when recollections do not go back beyond yesterday, she remembered in bitterness of spirit the happy days of the Venta del Potrero, where with Tranquil and Lanzi, those two devoted hearts to protect her, all smiled upon her, and the future appeared to her so gentle and calm. Perhaps, too, she thought of the Jaguar, for whom she felt such friendship, or of Colonel Melendez, whose respectful and profound love had made her so often dream involuntarily, in the way maidens dream.

But, alas! all this had now faded away; farewell to the exquisite dreams! Where were Tranquil and Lanzi, the Jaguar and Colonel Melendez? She was alone, unfriended, and defenceless, in the power of a man the mere sight of whom filled her with terror. And yet, let us add, the man whom we have represented under such gloomy colours, this White Scalper, seemed to have become completely metamorphosed. The tiger had become a lamb in the presence of the maiden, he offered her the most delicate attentions, and did everything she wished—not that she ever expressed a desire, for the poor girl would not have dared to have done so, but he strove to divine what might please her, and then did it with unexampled eagerness. At times he would stand for hours before her, leaning against a wall, with his eyes fixed on her with an undefinable expression, without uttering a word. Then he would withdraw with a shake of the head, stifle a sigh, and murmur—"Good God! If it were she!" There was something touching in the timid and humble grief of this terrible man, who made all tremble around him, and yet himself trembled before a girl; although Doña Carmela, unaffected by the egotism of suffering persons, did not seem to perceive the influence she exercised over this powerful and stern nature.

The door opened, and White Scalper entered. He was still dressed in the same garb, he was still as upright, but his face no longer wore that expression of haughty and implacable ferocity which we have seen on it. A cloud of sorrow was spread over his features, and his deep sunken eyes had lost that fire which had given his glance so strange and magnetic a fixity. The maiden did not turn at the sound of the Scalper's footsteps: the latter halted, and for a long time remained motionless, waiting, doubtless, till she would notice his presence. But the girl did not stir, and hence he resolved to speak.

"Doña Carmela!" he said in a voice whose roughness he tried to smooth.

She made no reply, but continued to gaze out on the plain. The Scalper sighed, and then said in a louder key:

"Doña Carmela!"

This time the maiden heard him, for a nervous tremor agitated her, and she turned quickly round.

"What do you want with me?" she asked.

"Oh!" he exclaimed, on perceiving her face bathed in tears, "you are weeping."

The maiden blushed and passed her handkerchief over her face with a feverish gesture.

"What matter?" she muttered, and then, striving to recover herself, she asked, "What do you want with me, señor? Heavens, since I am condemned to be your slave, could you not at any rate allow me the free enjoyment of this room?"

"I thought I should cause you pleasure," he said, "by announcing to you the visit of an acquaintance."

A bitter smile contracted the maiden's lips.

"Who cares for me?" she said with a sigh.

"Pardon me, Señorita, my intention was kind. Frequently, while you sit pensively as you are doing today, unconnected words and names have passed your lips."

"Ah! That is true," she answered; "not only is my person captive, but you will also like to enchain my thoughts."

This sentence was uttered with such an accent of concentrated anger and bitterness, that the old man started, and a livid pallor suddenly covered his face.

"It is well, Señor," the girl continued, "for the future I will be on my guard."

"I believed, I repeat," he replied with an accent of concentrated scorn, "that I should render you happy by bringing to you Colonel Melendez; but since I am mistaken, you shall not see him, Señorita."

"What!" she exclaimed, bounding up like a lioness; "What did you say, Señor? What name did you pronounce?"

"That of Colonel Melendez."

"Have you summoned him?"

"Yes."

"Is he here?"

"He is awaiting your permission to enter."

The maiden gazed at him for a moment with an indescribable expression of amazement.

"Why, you must love me!" she at length burst forth.

"She asks that question!" the old man murmured sadly. "Will you see the Colonel?"

"One moment, oh, one moment; I want to know you, to understand you, and learn what I ought to think of you."

"Alas, I repeat to you, señorita, that I love you, love you to adoration; oh! Do not feel alarmed; that love has nothing of an insulting nature: what I love in you is an extraordinary, supernatural likeness to a woman who died, alas! On the same day that when my daughter was torn from me by the Indians. The daughter I lost, whom I shall never see again, would be your age, señorita: such is the secret of my love for you, of my repeated attempts to seize your person. Oh, let me love you, and deceive myself; in looking at you I fancy I see my poor dear child, and that error renders me so happy. Oh señorita! If you only knew what I have suffered, what I still suffer, from this miserable wound which burns my heart—oh! You would have pity on me."

While the old man spoke with an impassioned accent, his face was almost transfigured; it had assumed such an expression of tenderness and sorrow, that the maiden felt affected, and by an involuntary impulse offered him her hand.

"Poor father!" she said to him in a gentle and pitiful voice.

"Thanks for that word," he replied in a voice choking with emotion, while his face was inundated with tears; "thanks, señorita, I feel less unhappy now."

Then, after a moment's silence, he wiped away his tears.

"Do you wish him to come in?" he asked softly.

She smiled: the old man rushed to the door and threw it wide open. The Colonel entered and ran up to the maiden. White Scalper went out and closed the door after him.

"At last," the Colonel exclaimed joyously, "I have found you again, dear Carmela!"

"Alas!" she said.

"Yes," he exclaimed with animation, "I understand you, but now you have nothing more to fear; I will free you from the odious yoke that oppresses you, and tear you from your ravisher."

The maiden softly laid her hand on his arm, and shook her head with an admirable expression of melancholy.

"I am not a prisoner," she said.

"What?" he exclaimed with the utmost surprise, "Did not this man carry you off?"

"I do not say that, my friend. I merely say that I am not a prisoner."

"I do not understand you," he remarked.

"Alas, I do not understand myself."

"Then, you think that if you wished to leave this house and follow me to the camp, this man would not attempt to prevent you?"

"I am convinced of it."

"Then we will start at once, Doña Carmela; I will manage to obtain you respectable shelter till your father is restored to you."

"No, my friend, I shall not go, I cannot follow you."

"Why, what prevents you?"

"Did I not tell you that I do not understand myself; an hour agone I would have followed you gladly, but now I cannot."

"What has happened, then, during that period?"

"Listen, Don Juan, I will be frank with you. I love you, as you know, and shall be happy to be your wife; but if my happiness depended on my leaving this room, I would not do it."

"Pardon what I am going to say, Doña Carmela, but this is madness."

"No it is not, I cannot explain it to you, as I do not understand it myself; but I feel that if I left this place against the wishes of the man who retains me here, I should commit a bad action."

The Colonel's amazement at these strange words attained such a height that he could not find a word to reply, but he looked wildly at the maiden. The man who loves is never mistaken as to the feelings of the woman he loves. The young man felt instinctively that Carmela was directed by her heart in the resolution she had formed. At this moment the door opened, and White Scalper appeared. His appearance was a great relief to the pair, for they were frightfully embarrassed, and the young man especially understood that this unexpected arrival would be of great help to him. There was in the demeanour and manner of the old man a dignity which Carmela had never before remarked.

"Pardon me disturbing you," he said, with a kindly accent, that made his hearers start.

"Oh," he continued, pretending to be mistaken as to the impression he produced; "excuse me, Colonel, for speaking in this way, but I love Doña Carmela so dearly that I love all she loves; though old men are egotistic, as you are aware, I have been busy on your behalf during my absence."

Carmela and the Colonel looked their amazement. The old man smiled.

"You shall judge for yourselves," he said. "I have just heard, from a scout who has come in, that a reinforcement of Indians has turned our lines, and joined the enemy, among them being a wood ranger, called Tranquil."

"My father!" Carmela exclaimed, in delight.

"Yes," the Scalper said, suppressing a sigh.

"Oh, pardon me!" the maiden said, as she offered him her hand.

"Poor child! How could I feel angry with you? Must not your heart fly straight to your father?"

The Colonel was utterly astounded.

"This is what I thought," the old man continued. "Señor Melendez will ask General Santa Anna's authority to go under a flag of truce to the enemy. He will see Doña Carmela's father, and, after reassuring him about her safety, if he desire that his daughter should be restored to him I will take her to him myself."

"But that is impossible!" the maiden quickly exclaimed.

"Why so?"

"Are you not my father's enemy?"

"I was the enemy of the hunter, dear child, but never your father's enemy."

"Señor," the Colonel said, walking a step toward the old man, "forgive me; up to the present I have misunderstood you, or rather, did not know you; you are a man of heart."

"No," he answered; "I am a father who has lost his daughter, and who consoles himself by a sweet error;" and he uttered a deep sigh, and added, "time presses; begone, Colonel, so that you may return all the sooner."

"You are right," the young man said. "Farewell, Carmela, for the present."

And, without waiting for the maiden's reply, he rushed out. But when the Colonel joined his men again, he learned that the order for the forward march had arrived. He was obliged to obey, and defer his visit to the General for the present.

CHAPTER XXVI
SAN JACINTO

The news told White Scalper by the scout was true; Tranquil and his comrades, after turning the Mexican lines with that craft characteristic of the Indians, had effected their junction with the Texan army; that is to say, with the vanguard, commanded by the Jaguar. Unfortunately, they only found John Davis, who told them that the Jaguar had gone to make an important communication to General Houston.

If the American had spoken to Tranquil about his daughter, and given him news of her, he would have been forced to reveal the bargain proposed by the Chief of the Pirates, and he did not feel justified in divulging a secret of that importance which was not his own. The Canadian consequently remained ignorant of what was going on, and was far from suspecting that his daughter was so near him; besides, the moment was a bad one for questioning; the march had begun again; and during a retreat the officers who command the rearguard have something else to do than talk.

At sunset the Jaguar rejoined his cuadrilla. He was delighted at the arrival of the Comanches, and warmly pressed Tranquil's hand; but as the order had been given to advance by forced marches, and the enemy was at hand, the young man had no time either to tell his old friend anything.

The General had combined his movement with great cleverness, in order to draw the enemy after him by constantly refusing to fight. The Mexicans, puffed up by their early successes, and burning with the desire to crush what they called a revolt, did not require to be excited to pursue their unseizable enemy.

The retreat and pursuit continued thus for three days, when the Texans suddenly wheeled, and advanced resolutely to meet the Mexicans. The latter, surprised by this sudden return, which they were far from expecting, halted with some hesitation, and formed their line of battle.

It was the twenty-first of August, 1836, a day ever memorable in the annals of Texas. The two armies were at length face to face on the plains of San Jacinto, and were commanded in person by the chiefs of their respective republics, Generals Santa Anna and Houston. The Mexicans numbered seventeen hundred well armed, veteran soldiers; the Texans amounted to only seven hundred and eighty-three, of whom sixty-one were cavalry.

General Houston had been compelled, on the previous evening, to detach the Jaguar's cuadrilla, which the Comanches and the hunters had joined; for, contrary to Sandoval's expectations, his men had refused to ratify the bargain he had made in their names with the Jaguar. Not that they were actuated by any patriotic feeling, we are bound to state, but merely because they had come across a hacienda, which seemed to offer them the prospect of splendid plunder. Hence, without caring for either party, they had shut themselves up in the hacienda, and refused to quit it, in spite of the entreaties and threats of the Chief, who, seeing that they had made up their minds, at length followed their example. The Jaguar was therefore detached by the General to dislodge these dangerous visitors, and the young man obeyed, though, unwillingly, for he foresaw that he should miss the battle.

General Houston gave Colonel Lamar, who was at a later date President of Texas, the command of the sixty horsemen left him, and resolutely prepared for action, in spite of the numerical disproportion of his forces. The two armies, whose struggle would decide the fate of a country, were hardly as numerous as a French regiment. At sunrise the battle commenced with extreme fury. The Texans, formed in square, advanced silently, within musket shot of the enemy.

"Boys!" General Houston suddenly shouted, as he drew his sword, "Boys! REMEMBER THE ALAMO!"

A terrible fire answered him, and the Texans rushed on the enemy, who were already wavering. The battle lasted eighteen minutes! At the expiration of that time, the Mexicans were broken, and in full flight; their flags, their camp, with arms, baggage, provisions, and equipage, fell into the hands of the victors. Considering the limited number of combatants, the carnage was immense, for six hundred Mexicans, including a General and four Colonels, were killed, two hundred and eighty-three wounded, and seven hundred made prisoners; only sixty men, among them being Santa Anna, succeeded in effecting their escape.

As for the Texans, owing to the impetuosity of their attack, they had only two men killed and twenty-three wounded, though six of these died afterwards — an insignificant loss, which proves once again, the superiority of resolution over hesitation, for most of the Mexicans were killed during the rout.

The Texans slept in the field of battle. General Houston, when sending off the Jaguar against the pirates, had said to him: —

"Finish with those villains speedily, and perhaps you will return in time for the battle."

These words were sufficient to give the Chief of the partisans wings; still, however great his speed might be, night surprised him, when still ten leagues from the hacienda, and he was compelled to halt, for both men and horses were utterly worn out. On the morrow, at the moment when he was about to start again, he received news of the battle of the previous day, in a very singular manner.

John Davis, while prowling among the chaparral according to his wont, discovered a man hidden in the tall grass, who was trembling all over. The American, taking him naturally enough for a Mexican spy, ordered him to get up. The man then fell on his knees, *kissed his hands*, and implored him to let him go, offering him all the gold and jewels he had about him. These supplications and intreaties produced no other effect on the American than converting his suspicions into certainty.

"Come, come," he said roughly to his prisoner, as he cocked a pistol, "enough of this folly; go on before me, or I will blow out your brains."

The sight of the weapon produced all the effect desired on the stranger, he bowed his head piteously, and followed his captor to the bivouac, with no further attempts to seduce him.

"Who the deuce have you brought us?" the Jaguar asked sharply.

"On my word," the American answered, "I do not know. He's a scamp I found in the tall grass, who looks to me precious like a spy."

"Ah, ah!" the Jaguar said with an ugly smile, "His business will soon be settled: have him shot."

The prisoner started, and his face assumed an earthy hue.

"One moment, Caballeros," he exclaimed, while struggling in the utmost terror with the men who had already seized him—"one moment; I am not what you suppose."

"Nonsense," the Jaguar said with a grin, "you are a Mexican, and that is sufficient."

"I am," the prisoner exclaimed, "Don Antonio Lopez de Santa Anna, President of the Mexican Republic."

"What?" the Jaguar exclaimed in amazement, "You are Santa Anna."

"Alas! Yes," the President answered, piteously, for it was really he.

"What were you doing concealed in the grass?"

"I was trying to fly."

"Then you have been defeated?"

"Oh, yes! My army is destroyed. Oh, your General is not born for common things, for he has had the glory of conquering the *Napoleon of the West*."[1]

At this absurd claim, especially in the mouth of such a man, his hearers, in spite of the respect due to misfortune, could not refrain from bursting into a loud and contemptuous laugh. To this manifestation the haughty Mexican was completely insensible; for, now that he was recognized, he felt sure of not being shot—he cared little for all else. The Jaguar wrote to General Houston, describing the facts, and sent off the prisoner to him, under the escort of twenty men, commanded by John Davis, to whom this honour belonged by right, as he had been the first to discover the prisoner.

"Well," the Jaguar muttered, as he looked after the escort along the winding road, "fortune does not favour me—I succeed in nothing."

"Ingrate that you are!" Loyal Heart said to him; "To complain when the most glorious trophy of the victory was reserved to you; through the capture of that prisoner, the war is over, and the Independence of Texas assured for ever."

"That is true," the Jaguar shouted, as he leapt with joy; "I did not think of that. Viva Dios! You are right, my friend, and I thank you for having put me on the track. By Jove! I should not have thought of that without you. Come, come," he gently exclaimed, "let us be off to the hacienda, comrades! We shall deal the last blow!"

The cuadrilla started under the guidance of its Chief; we will leave the adventurers to follow their road, and preceding them for a few moments, enter the hacienda.

The pirates, according to the custom of people of that stamp, had immediately made themselves at home in the hacienda, whose owner had fled on seeing the approach of war, and from which Sandoval and his men expelled the peons and servants. The pillage was immediately organized on a great scale, and they had naturally begun with the cellars, that is to say, with the French and Spanish wines and strong liquors, so that two hours after their arrival, all the villains were as full as butts, and yells and songs rose from all sides.

Naturally the White Scalper had been compelled to follow the pirates, and carry Carmela with him. In spite of the precautions taken by the old man, the maiden heard from the chambers in which she sought shelter the cries of these raging fellows which reached her, threatening and sinister as the rolling of thunder in a tempest. Sandoval had not renounced his plan of revenging himself on the man he regarded as his enemy, and the intoxication of his men seemed to him an excellent opportunity for getting rid of him.

White Scalper tried by all the means in his power to oppose this gigantic orgy, for he knew that these rough and rebellious men, very difficult to govern when sober, became utterly undisciplined so soon as intoxication got hold of them. But the pirates had already tasted the wines and spirits, and, excited by Sandoval, they only answered the Scalper's representations with murmurs and insults. The latter, despairing of making them listen to reason, and wishing to spare the maiden the odious and disgusting spectacle of an orgie, hastened to return to her, and after trying to calm her, he stationed himself before the door of the room that served as her refuge, resolved to smash the first pirate who attempted to approach her.

Several hours passed, and no one thought about disturbing the old man. He was beginning to hope that all would pass over quietly, when he suddenly heard a great noise, followed by yells and oaths, and a dozen pirates appeared at the entrance of the long corridor at the end of which he was standing sentry, brandishing their weapons and uttering threats. At the sight of these furious men, whom intoxication rendered deaf to all remonstrances, the old man understood that a terrible and deadly struggle was about to begin between them and him. He was alone against all, but yet he did not despair; a sinister light gleamed in his eye, his eyebrows met under the might of an implacable will; he drew himself up to his full height before the door he had sworn to defend, and in an instant became once more the ferocious and terrible demon who had so long been the terror of the Western countries.

However, the Scalper's position was not so desperate as it might appear. Foreseeing all that occurred at this moment, he had taken all the precautions in his power to save the maiden; the window of the room in which she was only a couple of feet from the ground, and opened on the yard of the hacienda, where a ready saddled horse was standing, in the event of flight becoming necessary. After giving Carmela, who was kneeling in the middle of the room and praying fervently, a final hint, the old man prepared to resist his aggressors.

The pirates, at the sight of this man who was awaiting them so menacingly, stopped involuntarily; the front men even took a timid glance back, as if to see whether a chance of retreat were left them; but the passage was interrupted by those who came behind them and thrust them on. Sandoval, who was well aware with what sort of a man his comrades would have to deal, had prudently abstained from showing himself, and remained with some of his friends in the banqueting hall, drinking and singing.

The delay in the pirates' advance had suggested to the Scalper the idea of setting the door ajar, so that he might escape with greater facility when the moment arrived. But the period of hesitation did not last a second; the yells burst forth again louder than before, and the bandits prepared to rush on the old man. The latter was still calm, and cold as a marble statue; he had placed his rifle against the wall, within reach, and stood with his pistols in his hands awaiting the opportunity to deal a decisive blow.

"Stop, or I fire!" he shouted, in a thundering voice.

The yells were doubled, and the bandits drew nearer. Two shots were fired, and two men fell; the Scalper discharged his rifle at the mob, then taking it by the barrel and using it like a club, he rushed on the bandits, who were startled by this sudden attack, and ere they could dream of resistance he drove them to the end of the corridor and down the stairs. Out of ten pirates six were killed, and four, dangerously wounded, fled with shrieks of terror.

The Scalper lost no time; bounding like a wild beast, he rushed into the room, the door of which he closed after him, took in his arms Carmela, who was lying senseless on the floor, leaped out of window, threw the girl across his saddle bow, and darting on the horse's back he started across country with headlong speed. All this took place in less time than we have required to describe it, and the pirates had not recovered from their terror ere the Scalper had disappeared.

"Viva Dios!" Sandoval shouted, striking the table with his fist; "Shall we let him escape? To horse, comrades, to horse!"

"To horse!" the bandits yelled, as they rushed to the corrals, where their horses were put up. Ten minutes later the pirates dashed off in pursuit of White Scalper, and the hacienda was thus freed of its unwelcome guests.

In the meanwhile White Scalper was flying at full speed, without following any settled direction; he had only one object, thought, or desire — to save Carmela. The maiden, revived by the fresh air, was setting up in the saddle, and, with her arms clasped round the old man's body, constantly repeated, in a voice choking with emotion, while looking with terror round her:

"Fly, fly! quicker, oh quicker!"

And the horse redoubled its speed, and thus ran with the rapidity of the stag pursued by a pack of hounds. All at once the old man perceived a band of horsemen debouching from a hollow way just ahead of him.

"Courage, Carmela!" he shouted; "We are saved."

"Go on, go on," the maiden replied.

This band was the Jaguar's; the young Chief in his impatience to reach the hacienda, was galloping a long distance ahead of his men. All at once he perceived the horseman coming towards him.

"Oh!" he exclaimed, with a feeling of deep hatred; "White Scalper."

He at once stopped his horse, so suddenly that the noble animal all but fell, and raised his rifle.

"Stop, stop, do not fire! In Heaven's name do not fire!" the Canadian shouted, who was spurring his horse and coming up at full speed, followed by Loyal Heart and the main body.

But, before the hunter could reach the Jaguar, the latter, who had not heard, or, probably, had not understood him, pulled the trigger. White Scalper, struck in the middle of the chest, rolled in the sand, dragging Carmela down with him in his fall.

"Ah!" Tranquil said, in despair, addressing Loyal Heart, "The unhappy man has killed his father!"

"Silence!" the latter exclaimed, placing his hand on his mouth; "Silence, in Heaven's name!"

The Scalper was not dead, however; the Jaguar approached him, probably to finish him, but Carmela, who was inspecting his wound, drew herself up like a lioness and repulsed him with horror.

"Back, assassin!" she shrieked.

In spite of himself the young man recoiled, astonished and confounded. Tranquil rushed toward the wounded man, while Loyal Heart took hold of the Jaguar, and speaking gently to him, led him from the spot where White Scalper was writhing in agony. The old man held the maiden's hands in his own, which were already bathed in a death sweat.

"Carmela, poor Carmela!" he said to her, in a broken voice; "Oh, Heaven, what will become of you now that I am dying."

"No, no, it is not possible, you will not die," the girl exclaimed, stifling her sobs.

The old man smiled sadly.

"Alas, poor child!" he had said, "I have but a few moments to live; who will protect you when I am gone?"

"I!" said the hunter, who had come up.

"You!" the wounded man replied; "you, her father?"

"No, her friend," the hunter remarked, with a melancholy accent, and drawing from his bosom the necklace Quoniam had torn from the Scalper during the fight in Galveston Bay, he said with supreme majesty, "James Watt,[2] embrace your daughter; Carmela, embrace your father."

"Oh!" the wounded man exclaimed, "My heart did not deceive me, then?"

"My father, my father, bless me!" the maiden murmured, falling on her knees.

White Scalper, or Major Watt, drew himself up as if he had received an electric shock, and laid his hands on the head of the kneeling girl.

"Bless you, my child!" he said; then after a moment of silence, he muttered in an almost indistinct voice, "I had a son too."

"He is dead," the hunter answered, as he looked sorrowfully at the Jaguar.

"May Heaven pardon him!" the old man muttered. And falling back, he breathed his last sigh.

"My friend," Carmela said to the hunter, "you, whom I no longer dare to call my father, what do you order me to do in the presence of this corpse?"

"Live!" the Canadian answered hoarsely, as he pointed to a horseman who was coming up at full speed, "for you love and are beloved; life is scarce beginning for you, and you may still be happy."

The rider was Colonel Melendez.

Carmela let her head fall in her hands, and burst into tears.

During my last visit to Texas, I had the honour of being presented to Doña Carmela, then married to Colonel Melendez, who retired from the service after the battle of San Jacinto.

Tranquil lived with them, but Loyal Heart had returned to the desert. The Jaguar, after the events we have described, resumed his adventurous life, and a year had scarce elapsed ere his death was heard of. Surprised by

Apache Indians, from whom he might easily have escaped, he insisted on fighting them, and was massacred by these pitiless enemies of the white race.

Did the Jaguar know that he had killed his father, or was it his despair at seeing his love despised by Carmela, that determined him to seek death?

That remained a mystery which no one was ever able to solve. Let us hope that a merciful and just God pardoned this son his involuntary parricide!

[1] The sentence is literally true, but was said by Santa Anna to Houston himself.

[2] See Border Rifles, same publishers.